Don't
STOP
Me
NOW

Don't STOP Me NOW

COLLEEN COLEMAN

Bookouture

Published by Bookouture
An imprint of StoryFire Ltd.
23 Sussex Road, Ickenham, UB10 8PN
United Kingdom
www.bookouture.com

ISBN: 978-1-78681-147-9
eBook ISBN: 978-1-78681-146-2

This book is a work of fiction. Names, characters, businesses,
organizations, places and events other than those clearly in the
public domain, are either the product of the author's imagination
or are used fictitiously. Any resemblance to actual persons, living or
dead, events or locales is entirely coincidental.

To Julian, Betty and Sadie,
for believing that this could be done.

Because there were times I wasn't so sure.

Thanks for ganging up on me with all that love, you guys.

CHAPTER ONE

'Poppy, have you got a moment?' Dr Burley taps me on the shoulder as I wait outside his office. You better believe I have. I've been waiting for this moment for... ooh, let me see. The last decade? Two decades even. Perhaps it's closer to forever. From my first spelling test in reception class to handing in my PhD thesis four weeks ago, this is the moment I've been waiting for; the moment I find out if I'm good enough, if it's been worth it, if I've been accepted into the highest echelons of academic life. It's a big moment. *The* moment.

'I'm ready, Doc.'

He invites me in and closes the heavy mahogany door behind us.

'It is with the greatest pleasure – and a healthy sprinkling of personal pride – that I inform you that you, Poppy Bloom...' he shakes his chubby fists up and down like meaty little maracas, 'are this year's doctoral valedictorian of the psychology faculty of Banbridge University!'

Omfg.

He grabs me by the shoulders with his cocktail-sausage fingers and laughs with delight. Valedictorian: even more than I'd hoped for. WAY more than I'd hoped for. I knew I'd put in the hours, grafted hard, but the competition at this level is fierce. Half of my class is addicted to uppers, the other half to downers. Even in my very small circle, the stress, the pressure and the sheer volume of work took its toll. At least twice a week my boyfriend Gregory would have to be talked out of quitting at the final hurdle. Sometimes it would take hours to talk him down, sometimes whole days. And with deadlines and exam dates looming, whole days spent pressed up against a locked door were hard won. There were times he'd threaten to set his thesis alight or pack everything in and flee to a remote lighthouse off the Scottish coast so he'd never have to face a research paper, a professor or an exam ever again.

But we've made it.

In the end, we have all made it.

Here I am, relatively unscathed. And more than that, proud. Really bloody proud. Valedictorian. Holy shit.

'I couldn't have done this without you, Doc. Thank you so, so much.' I give him a great big bear hug and see that he is beaming from ear to ear. Good ole Dr B, he really stuck with me. This achievement belongs to him as much as it does to me.

'Poppy dear, I have loved every moment of it. You know that for me your thesis is a thing of great beauty; a work of hope and ambition; a real force for good in the world.' He blinks back a little tear. 'Forgive me, I must compose myself! We've got a big day ahead and I have more to tell you.' He skips over to the small coffee table and whips off a tea cloth to reveal a bottle of port and a cheeseboard. 'But first, indulge me, one last toast.'

I laugh. This is so fitting. My entire thesis was fuelled by cheese – lengthy discussions, debates, questions posed and solved over chunks of Cheddar and gallons of port in Dr Burley's snug little book-lined den.

He pours us two fingers each and I pop a creamy yellow wedge in my mouth.

'A girl's Gouda do what a girl's Gouda do,' he chuckles.

'Oh Doc, I Camembert bad cheese puns,' I laugh back as we throw down our ports like they're Jägerbombs.

He pours us another. 'Now, this time a proper toast. *In vino veritas.*'

I bow my head in mock solemnity.

'As the great father of psychology Carl Jung said, let us be loved for who we are, not just what we do. And what you choose to do next, Poppy, well, that's the million-dollar question. Whatever it is, I hope it brings you not just what you want, but everything you need too.'

'In that case, what I *need* is the fellowship,' I tell him.

Dr Burley crosses his fingers. '*Obviously* there are no guarantees in this world, and the final decision lies with Dr Winters, as Dean, but let's just say…' he gives me a wry smile and drops his tone to a hush, 'I am quietly confident.'

Quietly confident? That'll do me.

We raise our glasses one last time as tutor and student and knock back our port.

Traditionally, the 'first among firsts' is offered a fellowship at the university –lodgings in Ivy Court, an office on the original grounds beside the Old Library and the chapel, not to mention the most amazing research, teaching and travel opportunities. A Banbridge fellowship; a prickle of heat travels up the back of my neck. Charlie Bucket, you know how I feel.

Dr Burley pours himself a third glass; I decline. Another would go to my head, and I'm a lightweight at the best of times. Burley holds his finger in front of his face.

'One final matter I need to discuss with you, Poppy.'

I lean on the edge of the solid oak desk to steady myself. I can tell by the twitch of his lips that it's something big. He leans in towards me. 'Ninety-six per cent, Poppy. Ninety… six… per cent: you know what that means?'

I shake my head.

'It's a new record! You have smashed Dr Winters' record.' His purple tongue glides over his hairy upper lip. 'Your mark is the highest we have ever awarded to a woman under thirty years old.' Meaty maracas pump at his sides again. 'Highest EVER.'

I pour myself that third port. It's not even midday yet, but as far as days go, this one is playing an absolute blinder.

'So the fellowship? You really think it's a possibility?' I ask.

'I know what it means to you, my little prodigy; I kid you not when I say that I'm confident. How could they pass you up with this result? I think they'd be crazy, even for a bunch of psychologists, and that's saying something.' Smiling, he nods to the heavy wooden door. 'If I was a gambling man, Poppy, I'd put my money on you calling the office across that corridor home, and slipping into a bright future as part of our Banbridge family.'

Home, family, Banbridge, bright, future. I hold my face; this is a like a haiku of everything I have ever wanted.

'I so look forward to working alongside you as a colleague and as a friend – may you have many, many happy years surrounded by the sweet scent of leather, mahogany, fresh coffee, stinky Danish Blue and the occasional whiff of an undergraduate.'

This is actually happening. I'm going to live in Ivy Court. I'm going to share my thesis with the world. *Dr Poppy Bloom* will be engraved into the small brass plaque on the door beside Dr Burley's. My mother will explode with pride. Frank will cry. My best friend Harriet will party and Gregory will be utterly blown away. My ex-dad may nod and turn up one corner of his mouth and claim that he knew best all along; that I belong tucked away in the safe, cosy enclave of academia and out of harm's way. I steady my velvet graduation cap squarely on my head and blow the red tassel away from my nose. I hear the bells of the chapel chime the hour. This is actually happening. And it's happening now.

The heavy old door creaks open and I look up to see Harriet draped in her black graduation gown, her finger on the face of her watch. 'Are you ready? It's time to go down. It's really time! I feel sick!'

We've dreamt of this, Harriet and I. Walking up the marble stairs into the ceremonial Old Hall, just as we walked in through its ancient doors nearly ten years ago. The two of us bound tight by a decade of library all-nighters, apocalyptic hangovers, streaky tan meltdowns and, of course, boys, then men, with lots of boy-men in between: fit ones, kind ones, clever ones. The search for a hybrid that possessed all these qualities; endless, rather emotional discourse on whether such a hybrid even exists.

We reach the stairs of the hall.

'Come on then, the quicker we get this done, the quicker we can start the celebrations.' She hooks my arm. 'I've already seen your parents – well, your mum and Frank; they're in their seats. Is your real dad coming?'

'Ex-dad. He is coming but not until the ceremony is over. He already had something booked at the recording studio – story of my life.'

Harriet shrugs. 'Well, it's not like you'll notice anyway, to be honest. It's absolutely thronged in there! Hundreds of people, hundreds and hundreds and hundreds…'

I feel a slight quake in my stomach. *Hundreds and hundreds* is hundreds and hundreds too many. Harriet squeezes my hand and I remind myself that I've rehearsed this scenario in my mind so often that I should be able to do it on autopilot by now: walk, bow, say thank you, turn, walk back to seat. If I lose my bottle, I'll find Frank's face in the crowd and everyone else will fade out.

I squeeze her back to signal that I'm ready. 'Right, let's do this,' I say, and together we step through the open doors.

'Poppy! Over here! It's me! IT'S MUM!'

Mum and my stepdad Frank are sitting amidst a solid crowd of over eight hundred people. I turn in the direction of her high-pitched voice and spot her pointing me out to a female vicar, who looks slightly bemused and embarrassed but also strangely familiar. Dark eyes and a long, slender Roman nose. Like Gregory. This must be Gregory's mother. The Reverend Stubbs talking to my mother. I squeeze my eyes shut.

'Poppy! Over here!' Mum's platinum bob is bouncing up and down.

O-kay. Just for the record, that dress is definitely not 'pale pink, classy and something Kate Middleton's mother would wear'. Mum is sporting some kind of zebra-print patchwork number with neon pink fringing and an asymmetric sleeve. A drag queen would find it garish. Even in San Francisco. During Gay Pride. On the Loud, Proud and Outlandish float.

I can guess what Gregory will think: that it came from the bargain bin at the big fat gypsy wedding shop. He's not met my parents before. That's supposed to happen today too. There is a flutter of panic in my stomach that not only will he meet my parents today for the first time, but I'll have to meet his. And our parents will have to meet each other *officially*. This has the potential to be a car-crash.

I squint vaguely into the distance, certain that my mother's dress is going to bring on a migraine or an epileptic seizure for someone in the Special Assistance row. I find poor Frank beside her and notice that he doesn't look quite right either. There is a lot of white tissue paper stuck to his face, as though a family of baby moths has landed on his mottled cheeks. I try a subtle wave, which causes Mum to jump even higher out of her seat and propel her arms above her head like an air traffic controller. I give her a discreet thumbs-up and she sends me a double thumbs-up back, looking like she will literally burst with pride – and she doesn't even know about the valedictorian bit yet. Or the ninety-six per cent. Or the Ivy Court lodgings with the original fireplace. Once she hears this, she will explode, a full-on biological combustion, and this ancient hall will look like a bloody scene from a zebra abattoir, shards of black and white satin with hot pink fringing splattered across the wood-panelled walls.

I lean in to Harriet's ear and whisper good luck.

Biological combustion and all, today is going to be the best day of our lives.

The ornate Vice Chancellor takes to the centre of the stage in front of us and strikes the gong. He calls order and a hush descends upon the audience. Running his hands down the sleeves of his gold and scarlet gown, he steps up to the podium, adjusts the stem of the microphone and begins the graduation in proper ceremonial style, turning to the two seated professors on the stage.

Dr Burley sits to the left of the infamous Dean, Dr Margaret Winters, both of them in throne-like brown leather chairs. They nod to the Vice Chancellor, giving their blessing for the proceedings to commence.

He clears his throat. 'We are here today to honour the exceptional achievements of our best and brightest, within not only Great Britain, but arguably the whole world. To be awarded a doctorate from Banbridge University is beyond the reach of the vast majority of human beings. It takes exceptional intellect, talent and discipline to reach such dizzying academic heights, and yet today we are honoured to be in the company of this elite. Please join me in applauding all our psychology graduates present.'

An encouraging ovation ensues. I can hear Mum whooping from her seat at the back.

'However, today's ceremony is a little different from those of previous years. Today we are here not only to congratulate this class as a collective, but also to celebrate and acknowledge the achievements of certain individuals within this class group.'

I place a hand on my stomach to settle the whirring butterflies.

'Three exceptional individuals. Three landmark achievements. Game-changers, if you will.'

There is a nervous titter from the crowd.

The Vice Chancellor's gaze settles on Harriet and me in the front row. 'Game-changer number one: three of you have achieved over ninety per cent in your final dissertation. This has never happened before. Poppy Bloom, Harriet Law and Gregory Stubbs, we offer you our heartfelt congratulations.'

Harriet's hands fly to her face in amazement, and I wrap my arms around her and give her an almighty hug. Go, Harriet!

Gregory is behind us. I turn to catch his eye, but he remains focused straight ahead, eyes on the stage. He looks fantastic. Black hair cut tight to show off his high cheekbones; deep, almost black eyes. He looks especially princely today in his robes. Ah, Gregory: fit, clever and mostly kind. The best hybrid I've come across. Today is a major game-changer for us too: from now on we'll no longer be students living in financial limbo; we will be free to do what we like, catch up with other, proper couples who are now at the stage of engagement parties and deposit-saving and caring about bins.

I breathe him in. We can so be like that. I'm going to get us Egyptian cotton sheets and cut-crystal glasses. I will learn to cook and bake and grow herbs, and he will bring me cups of tea while I pore over dusty tomes in my private little library. Ivy Court will be our hideaway home, sealing us safe from the outside world with all its madness. Just the two of us, cosied up together, safe and happy in our book-lined life. I can't wait; I honestly just cannot fucking wait.

The Vice Chancellor taps the microphone to restore order.

'Game-changer number two: the average age of a PhD graduate is thirty-seven. For the first time in our history, all three of our highest-achieving PhD graduates are under thirty years of age. So once more, huge congratulations to Poppy, Harriet and Gregory.'

Another round of applause; another shrill but gutsy whoop from my mum. I turn around in my seat to try and catch Gregory's eye again, but still the same steely stare ahead. What is up with him? Why is he being like this? I'm well aware that he is a moody bugger, and more than capable of marathon sulking, but really? Today of all days? I rang him last night numerous times but he didn't pick up; then this morning he texted me to say he was exhausted from travelling and would catch up with me after the graduation. He's probably just as nervous as Harriet and me. Still, he'll cheer up when I tell him about my plans for us at Ivy Court.

'And finally, game-changer number three: we have an astounding new precedent set by Dr Poppy Bloom.'

He motions for me to leave my seat in the front row and join him on the stage. This isn't something I had anticipated. I take a deep breath and Harriet gives me a wink as I smooth the lapels of my gown and walk towards the podium. *Just one foot in front of the other, then bow, say thanks and sit down.*

'Dr Bloom has achieved a staggering ninety-six per cent in her final doctoral thesis, thereby superseding the record previously held by our own esteemed Dean and world-famous author in the field of social psychology, Dr Margaret Winters.'

Skeletal and silver-haired, Dr Winters nods curtly behind dark-lensed reading glasses. The Vice Chancellor reaches out his hand to shake mine. 'Well done, Poppy.' The room erupts with applause and Dr Burley thumbs the armrest of his leather seat and shouts, 'Knew you could do it, Poppy!'

This is big. Beating *Dr Winters*? I still can't believe it. Dr Winters is a god.

I can't see Mum and Frank's faces in the crowd but I can see their outstretched hands holding up their phones, filming the whole thing. I spot Harriet in the front row clapping wildly, but Gregory is still staring ahead, his face unmoved.

The taste of port on my teeth is sweet and sickly. I can't say I'm a natural when it comes to being the centre of attention. Standing up and speaking in front of big groups of people fills me with bowel-emptying dread. When I was younger, I begged my mum NOT to throw a birthday party for me; all those people, swarming and expectant and impossible to predict. *Painfully shy* was written on every one of my reports through primary school. Painfully accurate, I'd say.

Dr Winters approaches the podium. Everyone returns to their seats and settles to hear her speak.

'Exceptional. This is our Vice Chancellor's choice of words. And it is quite fitting, as I am about to make an exception to a tradition we have respected in this faculty for a very long time.' She shifts her glasses to the top of her head.

'In the past, it has been traditional to award the highest-achieving doctoral graduate a place on our academic team as an esteemed fellow. They are appointed as a professor; they may live in the grounds of the university and undertake research and lecturing duties. It is a much-coveted and respected route into academic life.'

She turns from the crowd to look me straight in the eye. She is not smiling.

'However, this year we have the chance to cast off old traditions and create new ones. These new traditions reflect my vision for the future of this great institution. Therefore, I shall not be extending the invitation to become a Banbridge fellow to the highest academic achiever. Instead, I have decided to take a holistic approach, selecting not on academic ability alone but also with considerations of personality, social acumen and emotional intelligence.'

Sorry? Could you say that again in normal English?

'This may seem jarring initially, Poppy, but I'm sure in time you'll come to understand my rationale.'

At first I think I've misheard her, but the whispers and nudges from the crowd tell me that is not the case. Not extending an invitation? Not selecting on academic ability? I'll come to understand?

'This is a personal and professional judgement. Dr Bloom, your thesis has been the subject of tremendous debate amongst colleagues across the globe. Some believe that it is an example of academic genius, "a work of brilliance; full of hope, ambition and boundless possibility", to quote my colleague Dr Burley. But we are divided.' Dr Winters pauses a moment and then leans in to her microphone, as if unable to help herself.

'My selection has been based on a myriad of factors, not exclusively academic. To be a fellow at Banbridge, or indeed, a truly exceptional psychologist at any level, requires self-awareness, restraint. It requires maturity. It requires a deep appreciation of humanity that moves beyond the page, beyond the theory, beyond the university walls. This deep appreciation can only come when one is open to real life, real people, an understanding of the real world. Experience of life beyond the bookshelf.'

White noise, pins and needles in my face. I look to Dr Burley. His hands are cupped around his eyes, as if shielding himself from some horrible road accident. I find Frank's face in the crowd and try to focus on it. Frank knows best. He always knows best. I want to shout, scream, punch, run, rip that microphone from her hand and... and what? Tell her she's wrong? She's the dean of the university. She's got free rein to say what she likes, even if that does mean sabotaging my life's work, my future career and my reputation. I bite the inside of my cheek.

Frank holds my gaze from the crowd and gives me a gentle smile, as if to say, *Stay cool, stay calm. Do not react, just fade her out.*

But Dr Winters continues. 'However, whenever a door shuts, a window opens. Or in this case, two windows. Due to my recent promotion to Dean, and the expansion of the faculty as a whole, for the first time we are in a position to offer two fellowships.'

There is a shuffling in the seated crowd, nudges, whispers and sharp intakes of breath. Especially in the front rows. This could be anyone; this fellowship is now open game.

Dr Winters clears her throat. 'So without further ado, Dr Gregory Stubbs and Dr Harriet Law, it is my privilege and pleasure to invite you to join us as fellows of the University of Banbridge.'

The crowd erupts in applause. Everyone leaps to their feet. Gregory has deep colour in his cheeks now and is smiling broadly, bounding up the steps two at a time. Harriet's hands fly to her chest and she twirls around, bouncing in excitement as she sidles through our row of classmates to reach the stage.

I don't know what to do.

So I clap. I paint a smile on my face for Harriet and then I slope off the side of the stage. It's not that I'm not happy for her. Or Gregory. I'm just... sad and angry and confused. For Dr Burley and Mum and Frank and everyone I've let down. Including myself.

I push through the metal fire-exit doors. Nobody stops me. Nobody even notices. They clatter shut behind me and I stand in the car park, taking deep breaths of fresh air. I throw my cap to the gravel and strip out of my graduation gown; everything feels heavy and hot and tight. I jump as I feel a hand on my right elbow. It's Frank.

'It's okay, love, no need to be frightened. It's all behind you now.'

I press my palms into my eyes and slide down the wall onto the gravel. 'Did that just happen?'

Frank crouches down beside me and gently tucks a strand of hair behind my ear. 'We couldn't be more proud of you, Poppy love, okay? You've done better than we could ever have dreamed of. Amazing achievement. You should be proud of yourself and all.'

'Not so amazing, though, is it? I didn't get the fellowship.'

'Let's go home now, eh?' says Frank, his knees cracking as he gets up from the ground beside me.

'Home? I can't go home! It's my graduation!' I tell him. 'I can't just leave; I've waited for this for years.'

'It's up to you, love, you can stay if you like, of course you can. Stay here with all your friends, enjoy the night.'

All my friends: well, that's going to be awkward, seeing as I spend most of my time with either Harriet or Gregory. A night with the two people I love the most as they excitedly discuss their plans to do the job I wanted so badly in the place I never wanted to leave. Plans that do not involve me.

They will stay, but I will leave.

I hear a surge of applause coming from the other side of the metal doors. Mum's Ford Escort rolls up beside us. She keeps the engine running, either because she's afraid it won't restart or because she wants to make a very fast getaway.

A peal of laughter comes from inside; I can hear Gregory making his acceptance speech. Breathless and earnest and charming and utterly unscripted. An impromptu speech in front of hundreds of people wouldn't faze him at all. No need for Gregory to rehearse in front of the mirror; he can read a crowd of strangers, build a rapport, rise to the occasion without his tongue swelling thick in his mouth.

I don't want to go, but how can I stay? It's over. Just like that. I have no business being here now.

And suddenly I do want to get out of here. I can't face a night of pitying looks and booze-fuelled commiserations. I haven't the energy to pretend that it's no big deal that my entire life plan has caved in and that I have no plan B.

Home, family, Banbridge, bright, future – it's gone. It's not happening. Stop there Charlie Bucket, your ticket is invalid; no entry beyond this point, there'll be no factory tour for you today, or tomorrow, or ever. And waiting by the gates catching glimpses of the others won't do you any good. In fact it may make things a whole lot worse.

I nod my agreement. Frank helps me to my feet and we climb into the back seat.

We drive down the tree-lined avenue, past the redbrick dormitories and bespectacled cyclists. Past Ivy Court and the library and the chapel. Past the manicured gardens and neatly trimmed hedges. As we reach the junction, I spot my ex-dad's car speeding past us. Just as well really. I couldn't shoulder his disappointment along with everyone else's right now.

Once I lose the final view of Banbridge from the back window, I turn around in my seat and gaze at the long, grey motorway ahead. Mum turns the dial on the radio and taps her restless fingers on the steering wheel. She's not good with silence. Especially raw, stunned silences like this one. She's not sure what to say. Or how to say it. I should be cracking open the champagne with Harriet at the student bar. I should be kissing my gorgeous Gregory on his perfect bow lips and rebuffing his drunken attempts to carry me off to bed. I should be choosing curtains for my lodgings and ordering new bookshelves for my office.

I loop Frank's arm and feel his body clench tight and then soften to release a huge, trumpeting fart. I can feel it bubbling under my seat. At least he didn't do that mid-ceremony. Or in front of Gregory's parents. Oh my God, that would've been so awful. Despite myself, I half laugh. It's the only thing I can imagine right now that could actually make this situation even worse. Because one thing is for sure, today is nothing like I ever imagined.

I should not be in the back of the car enveloped in the thick fug of Frank's IBS. I should not feel as shit and ashamed and exhausted as I do. I hold my face. Something is going to crack.

Frank shuffles in his seat as he releases another massively loud fart. Mum darts us a confused look in the rear-view mirror.

'I'm sorry, love, I've just been holding it in for ages. It's not my fault; it's just the way my body works – when these things have got to come out, then they've just got to come out.'

As Mum tuts, turns up the radio and winds down the windows, I just give in. I stop fighting it and I start to laugh, right from the pit of my stomach. But then I realise I'm not laughing at all. I'm crying, great big breathless sobs. Mum tries to rub my knee from the front seat; Frank puts his arm around me and cuddles me.

'It's okay now, Poppy, just let it all out. Everything will make more sense once we get you back home. Onwards and upwards.'

Downwards and backwards, more like.

I slouch back in my seat and close my eyes. Resigned, defeated and absolutely bloody exhausted. And on my way back home. Because after all, I've got nowhere else to go.

CHAPTER TWO

This is officially my first day as a doctor. Yet I wake shivering in my vampire-themed teenage single bed. My mum's house is set at its customary erect-nipple temperature even though it is late October.

Objective reality: I am breathing. I am safe. I am warm… no, I'm not warm, they only ever heat this box room up for Christmas. Okay, anyway, I'm healthy…

Subjective reality: I AM FAILING AT EVERY CONCEIV-ABLE LEVEL.

The catastrophe of this whole thing has rendered me immobile. I can't move a muscle in my body, so I'm just going to lie here. Forever. Flat on my back, staring at the ceiling of my yesteryear bedroom, rubbing my eyes as I study the Destiny's Child Survivor Tour poster still suspended with Blu-Tack so old that it's turned green.

Beyoncé, can you handle this? Kelly, can you handle this? Michelle, can you handle this? Poppy… Oh no, not me, not today. I definitely don't think… in fact, no, I can't, it is my professional opinion that I cannot handle this.

Look away, Bey Knowles, look away, this isn't pretty or empowering in any way.

I turn my head into the corner of my pillow. My black gradu-ation gown is dumped in a crumpled heap at the base of the bed. I vaguely recall throwing it there last night before collapsing into a pit of codeine-induced oblivion. I don't remember much else of last night. There's a hazy memory of me lying on the couch in my pyjamas, flicking through TV channels and drinking hot chocolate while Mum talked on and on about fate and destiny and new paths and embracing change and curves in the road and stuff at the end of the rainbow and how nice it was going to be for us to spend time together and eventually something would come up and all sorts of irrational fluffy fluff that people tend to print on souvenir fridge magnets or cross-stitch on to cushions. Nice, well-meaning, but little more than frothy platitudes to keep the air moving between the rambling comforter and the person whose life is falling apart. Then the questions and helpful suggestions started, which were just as well-meaning but downright annoying.

Why didn't I give some old friends a call?

What did I want to eat?

What time should we eat?

Why didn't I join her at aqua aerobics?

Maybe I should take a bath? Or go for a walk?

Why was I being so quiet?

In the end I had no energy for anything, so I nodded, apologised – just generally, for anything and everything – dragged my duvet back up the stairs, nicked a sleeping tablet from Frank's emergency cabinet, shut my door and sank into the darkness, sobbing so hard that my jaw still aches.

And now it's morning. And I have not dreamt this. I am here, back in my parents' house, fighting the cold shafts of light that stream in through the gaps in my blinds and muttering curses at the people setting up their stalls on the street below, banging and clanging, hitching and hoisting and getting on with their lives. The south London dawn chorus of strident voices selling fish and fruit and flowers mixed with snatches of music and radio chat and cars and sirens and pneumatic drills. The musical of my life set to Beyoncé anthems would probably be called *Self-Destructilicious*. Or *Crazy in Debt* would also work. However, I already know that she won't be up for collaborating on this gig; nope, not her style. There are no redeeming features to this misery.

I survey the dusty shrine of my teenage self: plastic shelves lined with netball trophies and swimming medals; the small desk that Frank found in a churchyard skip littered with chewed pencils and stacks of outdated school books. Dr Poppy Bloom, eh? What a joke. How the hell have things turned out this way? Why am I back here? Winters, Harriet, Gregory… the applause, the laughter, the heat creeping up my neck, the blast of cold air once I snapped open those metal doors. I remember it all with razor-sharp clarity.

And I get it. I don't like it, but I get it. I was close, but ultimately, I didn't have what it takes. Not what they were looking for. Not up to scratch. I blow out my cheeks. I haven't anything left. I'm here now, and I'm going to have to make the best of it.

A dog barks fiercely outside, then a car alarm starts to sound. The room is too bright to fall back to sleep, so I sigh, kick off the duvet and think about facing the day.

I shuffle downstairs, relieved that I've at least got the house to myself; a few hours without intense worried looks, very unsubtle nudges and – mainly – *no* questions. Though I will have to face my ex-dad at some point, and he'll go in for the kill.

What do I mean, I haven't got the fellowship?

What did I do wrong?

What did I do to lose it?

Why haven't I applied anywhere else? Shouldn't I really have been applying all year?

Am I not aware of the competition? The demand? The race for jobs? For placements? For experience? For that crucial foot in the door?

Isn't it about time I stopped *thinking* and started *doing*?

I stop dead on the stairs and try to hold my brain together: calm down, Poppy, breathe, breathe, just concentrate on now.

I'll get some breakfast and a nice cup of coffee and think about whatever I need to think about later. But it won't be long. He'll be on the phone soon enough, and what will I tell him? What will he think?

My head starts swimming again. I scrunch my eyes shut as if it's a proper strategy to shut down stressful thoughts.

I know I've got at least six hours of peace, as both my parents are at work. Frank is the flower seller at the entrance to Brixton tube station, just around the corner, but my mum travels across London to work as a hairdresser in Holloway. The majority of her clients are well known to the women's prison there; Mum essentially just bleaches, shaves and spikes their hair in between sentences and when they are out on parole. She's worked there since I was a baby, so even when she met Frank and we moved into his house here in Brixton, she kept her job despite the hour-long tube commute.

I haven't actually set foot through the doors of the salon since I was a toddler, around the time my mum and my 'real' dad split up. It's weird to think that I'm edging thirty, the same age they were when everything went tits-up for them. I used to think that things could only go tits-up for grown-ups if you were incred-ibly reckless. Obviously I'm reassessing that viewpoint now as a twenty-nine-year-old standing in a onesie in my mum's kitchen, my only ambition for the day being not to see or speak to anyone.

I run my fingers through the knots in my hair, still full of kirby grips and sticky with the hairspray I used yesterday to secure my graduation hat against the wind. Twenty-four hours ago, that was my biggest concern. Oh, the naivety.

Even though my mum's a hairdresser, I've never even let her give me a shampoo and blow-dry, never mind a cut and restyle. I know that sounds bad, but her skill set very much reflects her clientele's tastes, and I've always worried about ending up with a crispy yellow bob or a badly shorn mullet.

Even though I tease her about the salon, she has never had a day off sick in her life, and when she effectively became a single parent with no money, it was that little salon that kept us afloat. She loves the other hairdressers in Holloway, loves the women who come in to pour their hearts out about fights they've been in and men they've threatened, and the way they tip her in SIM cards, semi-defrosted trays of meat and anything she wants from Superdrug. Maybe I should put an order in myself – is there such a thing as personality concealer? Mood contouring? I could totally reinvent myself and nobody would ever know it was me. I could return to Banbridge undetected, enrol as a new student and introduce myself as a more sociable, confident, charismatic version of myself. Dr Poppy Bloom take two.

Downstairs, I hear the landline ring from the hallway.

'Hello?'

It's my mum. 'Are you awake, love?'

'By virtue of me speaking to—'

'Yes, yes, yes; why is your mobile off?' She cuts me off. She hates it when I give smart answers. 'I've been trying to ring you on your mobile, but a weird tone comes up.'

'My mobile? I turned it off last night, remember, and took out the battery, because I didn't feel like dealing with anyone,' I remind her.

'Okay, well, fine. Actually, I think that was very wise. But turn it on again now, will you, so we can track you if you go out.'

'In what way do you want to track me?'

'You know perfectly well what I mean – so we know where you are, so you don't go and do anything silly.'

'Mum, I'm fine. I just want to relax and take a break from everything, be by myself for a bit.'

The phone goes quiet. It sounds like she's clapped her hand over the receiver and is whispering to someone; I can hear a deep, gravelly, hushed voice in the background.

Mum comes back on the line. 'Surround yourself with people,' she says.

'Huh?'

'Surround yourself with people. That's a good piece of advice, don't you think?'

'No, and no. No, I won't be doing that, and no, I don't think it's a good piece of advice. I think it's a patronising and ill-informed piece of advice. I don't want to see even one person, never mind throw myself into some kind of pseudo-social crowd surf because one of your clients watches *Oprah* and now thinks she can counsel me on what's best. What would really, really be best for me right now is some decent coffee, and some food, and some heating, and for you to stop discussing my prob... my *current status* with people who think feminism means shoplifting tampons.'

Silence. I feel a chill on the back of my neck. I know she means well, but I'm just not in the mood. Still silence, like the line has gone dead.

'Hello? Mum?' I say.

There is a very deep cough at the other end of the line. 'Poppy, Roberta here. I 'preciate you're having a hard time. You sound highly strung, but I have some news for you and I don't care if Angela is your mother. She's also my mate, has been for a very long time. So hear me when I say that if you dare speak to her like that again, I promise you I'll tear your legs off and stuff them in your ears so hard you'll need one of your brain doctor friends to get them out. Do you understand me?'

I squeeze out a very warbly, high-pitched sound that is understood as a yes. I hear shuffling, the receiver changing hands and the sound of heavy steps walking away.

My mum comes back on the line. 'Right, there's fifty pounds in my jewellery box. Go out and get some bits from the shop. I'll be back by four. And make sure you turn your phone on. Today is the first day of the rest of your life, sweetheart, so embrace it. Seize the day!'

'I will. I will definitely embrace it. Sorry for what I said earlier – just a bit out of sorts – but I'm seizing the day right now, okay? I promise!' I speak slowly and clearly and in the most upbeat singsong voice I can muster. Then I wait for my mum to hang up first. And then I wait for the tone to go dead. Absolutely dead. Then I wait some more just in case Roberta might still be around ready to pounce on me with some final violent words of encouragement.

I do exactly as Mum says straight away, as if there is a hidden camera planted and I'm being live-streamed into the salon and her tough-nut girl gang are watching me Big Brother style. I reassemble my phone, plug it in and make myself a strong cup of coffee. Mum is right about one thing: it was surprisingly wise of me to turn off my phone last night; uncharacteristically wise, since I have never, ever turned it off before. Actually, I hope it comes back on again; it is looking very dark and lifeless right now, so fingers crossed. It lights up, its little smartphone chest spluttering a hopeful screen breath, and then erupts machine-gun-like with beeps, firing notifications of new messages, missed calls and voicemails. I take a large gulp of coffee; it looks like I'm going to need something to get through this backlog.

Forty-two missed calls.

Eleven texts.

Three voicemails.

All the voicemails are from my ex-dad. There's one text from Gregory, and everything else is from Harriet. At least they love me. At least they care about what's happened to me. At least I've got a best friend and a boyfriend who give a shit about whether I've been sectioned or not.

Oh Gregory, maybe you've already realised that actually it doesn't matter that I haven't got the fellowship, because you have! We can still move into Ivy Court. We can still have the Egyptian cotton sheets and crystal glassware, and I can be the one who brings you cups of tea while you lose yourself in fascinating new research. I could pick up some teaching or casual administration; maybe I could even be your assistant!

I wait for my phone to charge and look fondly at Harriet's missed calls. Oh how I miss her already. She is my right-hand woman! And although I'm actually left-handed, I still use my right hand for all sorts of things, every single day. Life with no Harriet by my side… well, I'm already suffering from this amputation. I'll invite her here to stay. That'll count as surrounding myself with a person, which is close to what Mum wants, and I know I'll feel a trillion times better once she's here. Yes. Plans are hatching. I'd high-five myself if I could.

I delete all the voicemails from my ex-dad because I know what they are going to be about and I'm just not willing to go there right now. I open the first text, which was sent yesterday at around the time I bundled myself into my mum's car.

Harriet, 13.42: *'Are you okay? What's happening? Confused. Tell me where you are.'*

Harriet, 13.59: *'Where are you? Am looking everywhere but can't see you.'*

Harriet, 14.20: *'Am in the Fox and Hound. You are not here Poppy. Wtf?'*

Harriet, 15.00: *'This isn't funny. Why don't you pick up your phone?'*

Harriet, 16.10: *'Still trying to reach you. I have something to tell you…'*

Harriet, 16.30: *'Tried ringing again. No answer. I have been allocated Ivy Court. Wanted to tell you in person. Call me, Poppy. Worried about you.'*

Harriet, 17.47: '*Everyone is getting shitfaced. You should just come back. Honestly, nobody would care now. Jägerbomb time.*'

Harriet, 18.55: '*Gregory just asked me where you are. Come down here!*'

Gregory, 19.00: '*Dear Poppy, this is not the way I'd planned to do this, but I have been all over looking for you and it looks like you are not coming back. I think you know what's coming. Although I really enjoy your company and I think you're cheeky and funny in your own way, we both know that our time is up and I really want us to start new chapters after Banbridge with a clean break. I have wanted to have this discussion with you for a while, but with exams looming and living in such close proximity, I thought it best to wait until today; until we were ready to go our separate ways in every sense. Best regards, G.*'

Harriet, 21.56: '*Gregory actually very sweet, so funny.*'

Harriet, 04.12: '*House party at Gregory's.*'

Harriet, 10.30: '*Just woken up. Feel like shit. Don't know how to say this. Last night Gregory and I, well, you can prob guess. He told me you two were finished. My head is all over the place – I am so so sorry. Need to go. Sick as dog. Call me.*'

No more new messages. Oh my God. OH MY GOD. Gregory has finished with me and Harriet has slept with Gregory! Harriet has had actual naked, skin-to-skin sex with GREGORY. God, I cannot take it in. I feel sick. Do you hear that, Harriet, I'm the one who is as sick as a dog. Gregory wanted to break up with me for a while? The fucking cheek! I know things weren't perfect, but we were in the middle of exams! Nobody looks or acts their best when they've been squirrelled away in the library for six months, living off cheese and sugar and caffeine; no time to sleep or socialise or relax. What did he expect?

I smack my hand against the kitchen table. I honestly cannot believe that this is happening. The person I love the most with the other person I love the most and who doesn't love me back.

I grab my phone and go straight to my contacts. I then block and delete the number of every single person I met during my ten years at Banbridge. Except Dr Burley. He can stay. He, at least, tried to help me. Why? Because I'm livid at Harriet and Gregory for waiting until I was out of the picture to doubly betray me. Well done Harriet, nicely played. Congratu-fucking-lations on Gregory and Ivy Court and the fellowship and basically taking over everything that I've been living for. If this is friendship, then I'd rather go solo. Four numbers have survived my contact massacre. My mum, Frank, Burley and (by the skin of his teeth) my ex-dad. So that's it. I am as on my own as I've ever been.

My phone vibrates as if outraged. It's a text from Mum: '*Roberta suggests you go down and register at the job centre straight away. She says the paperwork can take forever so get down there PRONTO.*'

I answer straight away; such is my terror at Roberta's wrath: '*Will do it today! And be sure to thank her for all this great advice.*'

Day one of the rest of my life looks like this: no friends, no boyfriend, cold house, relentless torrent of invasive questions, deep dread of speaking with ex-dad and all other enquiring humans; and just in case that wasn't bad enough, now I've committed to a trip to the job centre.

And if day one of being a grown-up means stubbing your toe really badly when you kick the fridge barefoot and subsequently howl profanities through the double glazing at the neighbours' dog, then yeah, I'm all over it.

CHAPTER THREE

As I brush my teeth, I conjure up a three-step plan.

Step one: appeal the decision not to offer me the fellowship. Stalk Banbridge postgraduate vacancies and apply for anything that even sniffs of my qualification. Or just apply for everything: groundskeeper, librarian, landlady at the Fox and Hound, living specimen for medical students. Anything and everything. I need to get back there. I call Dr Burley but get no answer. I leave a message for him to call me back URGENTLY.

Step two: getting aforementioned job will enable me to move out and resume a life that merits getting dressed in the mornings.

Step three: regain dignity. Fall in love with someone gorgeous and rich and clever so I can montage my beautiful 'Best Thing I Never Had' life on social media for Harriet and Gregory to see. Get ripped and toned and serene and Zen-like. Be able to just let stuff go and not carry inwardly corrosive grudges; be all 'I wish you well, meagre hater'. I'm going to be the Xena: Warrior Princess of shit-togetherness.

This is good. This is going to work. It shouldn't even be that difficult, because if I manage to get a job back in Banbridge, then all the other stuff will just naturally follow.

I shower, pull on my jeans and jumper and do what most graduates do the day after they leave uni: go down to the job centre.

I sit in the waiting area with a ticker-tape number that makes me feel like I'm holding my own barcode. There's a very fat man wearing stained grey tracksuit bottoms, the dribble on his stubble looking weirdly like dew glistening on a black lawn. I smile at him when he makes eye contact, causing him to immediately dart his eyes away, like he's afraid I'm flirting with him. I take out my phone and play Candy Crush. It's a lesser hell.

The sign flashes *632* and shifty 'don't make eyes at me' man waddles forward. This means I'm up next, so it's time for me to start putting my career head on. I reread the application form I've filled in. I think it's pretty impressive, actually. I've got my CV up to date and the qualifications look great – first-class honours in my bachelor's degree, my MSc and my PhD. The second referee box is blank as I can't use Dr Winters any more and I'm not sure who to stick down in her place just yet. Employment history is also a teensy bit blank, but I can't do anything about that. I've been in education all my life and that's kind of the way I'd hoped to continue. I need to stay positive. Remember that this is only temporary. I'm just here until I can find my way back to Banbridge.

'A bend in the road is not the end of the road,' I mutter to myself. Oh lordy, what am I saying? I am channelling my mother in one of her more cringeworthy Mama Cliché moments. This fridge-magnet wisdom is infectious. As in, likely to gnaw away at your bruised intellect until you succumb to moistening your bleeding gums with ice-cold, numbing placebos. I run my tongue over my teeth. I've had an existential battering; I'm too weak to fight folly with conventional reason. Let's hope I make it to lunchtime without counting my chickens or crying over spilt milk.

A lady in a dark green headdress joins us, manoeuvring her pink double buggy in between the fixed plastic chairs. I want to congratulate her on having utterly silent kids until I catch a glimpse of four cats climbing in and over the padded seating. I decide just to leave it be and stare at my application form in my lap. I've got to make this work. When I get in there, I will make it crystal clear that I am open to *any* reasonable vacancy and that

I'll work anywhere, though nowhere cold or with a poor human rights record or on the Northern Line. Perfect. I smooth down my jeans, tighten my topknot and give my lips a quick lick of gloss. Number 633 is ready.

Number 632 must have left the building through some secret disposal chute, because within five minutes my number is flashing in red digits on the mounted screen. I turn the handle on the door labelled *Interview Room* to find a maze of grey partitioning. A very tall, very thin young man who looks no older than twelve years old leans over a desk stacked with handwritten forms that appear to be printed on recycled newspaper. His desk is a mess, the frames of his glasses are uneven, his tie is tugged to the side; even his teeth seem to be pulling in different directions. And he looks like he should be kicking a football in the car park with his school friends.

Stay positive, Poppy. This is only temporary.

I put on my best fake smile and this helps me relax enough to shake his hand and take the seat he has offered me.

'I'm Markus, your career facilitator and transition mentor. A pleasure to meet you…' he scans my application form, 'Poppy! Have I got that right?'

'Yes, Poppy Bloom, that's me. *Dr* Poppy Bloom, actually.'

He dips his chin and raises his eyebrows as if to say 'get you', then holds my application form close to his face, trying, I imagine, to read very quickly while hiding behind his computer screen.

'Right, the purpose of today is to establish your eligibility for full-time employment, identify your needs as a job seeker and try to answer any questions you may have regarding the process into permanent gainful employment. Sound okay with you?' he says, and I nod my co-operation.

'So, I'll just set you up on our database and that will kick-start the process of finding a suitable vacancy for your skill set.' He hasn't made wonky eye contact with me since our handshake, and I suspect this patter is so scripted that he doesn't even know what he's saying any more; he just rattles it off meaninglessly, a little like the Scout promise.

The computer bleeps its acceptance of my details. He shuffles in his seat and cracks his neck.

'And we are in! Welcome to your future, Poppy.' He taps the side of his monitor. 'In here is everything you could wish for in terms of your career. I like to call it the Job Genie. Get it?' He runs his hand up and down the monitor. 'Would you like to rub the Job Genie?'

I shuffle backwards into the seat of my chair, shaking my head.

'No? Not willing to move outside your comfort zone? Well, that's your call, Poppy. However, I have to admit it's not a good start. Maybe it's time to open your mind a little to possibilities you may not have previously considered? Do things you didn't think you could do?'

Markus closes his eyes and breathes deeply through his nose. I think he has watched *Matilda* too many times and is trying to control my mind. Finally I reach out, quickly air-swiping my hand down the side of his monitor. He joins his palms together and leers at me.

'Good. Very, very good. Okay, now that we are on the same page, the Genie needs to ask you a few questions. He can help make your wishes come true and grant you the job of your dreams.'

'Sounds great,' I tell him. 'Fire away.' This sounds easier than I thought.

Markus licks his dry, cracked lips and begins his line of questioning with all the solemnity of a *Mastermind* presenter.

'Do you drive?'

'No,' I tell him, and he types in my answer with one finger.

'Do you own a car?'

'Well, hardly… I don't drive.'

He flashes me a look.

'Sorry, the answer is no. No, I do not own a car.'

'Are you married?'

'No.'

He punches the same key again. No. No. No.

'Any children or dependants under the age of sixteen?'

'No.'

'Homeowner?'

'Nope.' Bloody hell, Markus, kick a girl while she's down, why don't you?

'Tenant?'

'Yes! Yes! The answer is yes. I am a tenant. Yes, I am.' Thank God, an affirmative answer.

Markus nods appreciatively. 'Okay, so how much is your weekly rent, excluding bills and council tax?'

'Oh, nothing. It's free,' I tell him. 'I'm living with my parents at the moment.'

Markus sighs and punches the NO button, deleting my previous affirmative answer.

'It's only temporary,' I say.

Markus winks at me. 'Yeah. Temporary. We hear that a lot.'

'But it *is* only temporary! I'm just here because I'm in between… opportunities at the moment. Make no mistake, Markus, I have no intention of sticking around at my parents' house with nothing to do and no one to do it with. I intend to implement my three-step plan as a matter of urgency and then I'll be on my way again very, very shortly.'

'Three-step plan? Isn't that for alcoholics?'

'No. That's the twelve-step plan. My plan has only THREE steps to get me back to where I belong, back home to the low lights and darkened corners of academic sanctuary. So when I say that this is only temporary, I really, really mean it, okay?'

Markus is studying the ragged cuticle of his thumbnail. 'National Insurance number?'

'I don't know.'

'Bank account number? Sort code?'

'I don't know. My mum usually deals with all this stuff. I haven't a clue.'

Markus looks over the rim of his glasses.

'Passport number?' He mouths, 'I don't know' along with me. 'Qualifications in…?'

Okay, I'm back in the game. I take a deep breath and resume *Mastermind* posture. 'Psychology – clinical research and analysis. Doctorate.'

He nods and punches in some more letters with his one stiffened typing finger. He looks at my application form, back to the screen, stabs the keyboard again, squinting back over to my application. I can't see the screen from where I'm sitting, but I can see the flummoxed look on his flat, asymmetrical face.

'Okay, I'm going to give it to you straight, Poppy. We haven't got a huge amount in your line.' He prints out two pages. 'We've got a vacancy here as a site manager, but minimum three years' experience is required, so we may put that to one side for now.' He balls it up and throws it into the bin beside my chair. 'Second and final vacancy that the Genie has presented us with today is… "Sign language interpreter. Freelance, competitive hourly rates." What do you think about that?'

Hmmmmm. I count to ten in my head and think about where the hell that came from.

'Markus, I think there's been an input error.' I grab a pen from his desk and scribble down the word PSYCHOLOGIST in capital letters. 'Ask the Genie to search with this spelling, please.'

He looks doubtful. 'Worth a try, I suppose. Let's see what he can do with this then.'

The computer bleeps compliance and Markus pouts with surprise and leans in to read the screen.

'Bingo! "Specialty doctor in adult psychiatry. South-east London. Immediate start. Excellent remuneration for the right candidate."' He passes the printout to me across the desk. 'Looks like the Job Genie has done it again.' He slaps his hands down onto one of his thighs and closes his eyes with such release and satisfaction that he looks like he's weeing himself.

Without needing to read the job description I know this is wrong, that Markus simply has no clue about psychology, or psychiatry, or spelling.

'Sorry, but I'm not qualified to do this,' I tell him.

'But you told me to search for it.' An angry Markus snaps back up in his chair.

'Yes, but I'm a *psychologist*, not a psychiatrist. You need to be a doctor to practise as a psychiatrist,' I try to explain.

'But you told me you were a doctor. Right at the start I said, "Are you Poppy?" and you said, "Actually I am *Dr* Poppy".' He wrinkles up his forehead and juts out his chin at me.

'I've got a PhD. A doctorate.'

He throws his hands in the air. 'Okay. Where are you a doctor at? At the hospital? At a surgery? You've got to help me out here, Poppy. I'm struggling to understand why you are throwing up so many obstacles. I'm beginning think you don't want a job at all. That you are purposely sabotaging the Genie's efforts to secure you gainful employment.' Judging by the vein in Markus's neck, which is kind of purple and protruding, I think he should get his blood pressure checked, but I refrain from telling him in case it confuses him further about the doctor business.

'Doctorate means…' I lose the will. 'Basically it means that I'm not a medical doctor, so not a real doctor in the sense that you mean.'

He takes a moment to stare at the desk, and then starts nodding, a smile breaking out on his lips.

'A-ha,' he says, rubbing his chin. 'So you are like Queen Latifah. Or Captain Birdseye.'

Markus is making me want to take heroin.

He cracks his knuckles and puts his hands behind his head. 'I get it. Very smooth, Poppy, very smooth indeed. I've got to say,

I did not see that one coming. But I see what you've done. It's like if Captain Birdseye came in here to the job centre, he might be embarrassed to tell us that he's just a fish-finger maker, so of course, like you, he's going to want to dress it up a little, add the Captain bit and make a bigger impact. He probably can't even drive a boat or whatever, but fair play, it's up to him at the end of the day. I expect he got the idea from Colonel Sanders at KFC; they looked around and saw that they were getting no respect so they militarised themselves and *boom!* World domination. Just like that. Professor Green. Dr Dre. *Dr Poppy.* Why not, right? I get it.'

I am speechless. This whole scene feels like a *You've Been Framed* set-up. Some toothy Saturday-night presenter is going to run in at any minute and reveal the whole hilarious prank. But it is not some sick wind-up. It's real. My new reality is that Markus is demented, yet Markus is the one with a job and I am not. And he's made me crave KFC.

I hate Markus.

'So, "Dr Poppy".' He has posed his fingers in inverted commas like twerking bunny ears. 'It appears that the Genie has been unable to grant you your wish of gainful employment at this current period of time, therefore you qualify for a weekly job seekers' allowance of £73.10. This is a state benefit that will ensure you have the means to transport yourself to interviews and buy any basics such as stationery, clean attire, etc. that will give you the best chance possible of entering the world of work. Personally, I suggest that you buy yourself some professional-looking clothes, get your hair fixed up; a bit of make-up always helps, paint your nails – all these things send the right message to employers, show effort.'

I nod, biting the inside of my mouth, and place my hands on either side of my chair to signal a close. I can't take Markus any more. The computer bleeps. I take this as my cue to gather my bag and go.

'Hold your horses there, Poppy, something just in. And I think this one has your name written all over it.' He presses print and hands me the details.

'"Psychic, clairvoyant. Work from home",' I read flatly. 'Not something I can see myself doing.'

He shakes his head and tuts at me. 'Do you really think that's a sensible idea in your position? Is it wise to turn down a perfectly decent income without a second thought?' He points to the paper in my hand. 'Especially if everything is just *temporary*.'

I tighten my jaw and smile my murderous gratitude.

'Indeed. Thank you, Markus, I'll give it a shot. Who knows, clairvoyance might be the future.'

He looks satisfied. 'Check your inbox regularly. We'll send you opportunities as and when they become available.'

I shake his hand, gather my stuff, and exit the grey maze of the job centre. I never want to set foot in here again.

Outside, I slump down on the kerb. I can't even get a job at the job centre. What am I going to do? I can't stay still and I can't move forward. I take out my phone and type 'graduate jobs' into the search engine. I scroll through pages and pages of jobs that a) require skills I don't have, or b) require a supplementary income I don't have. I key in simply 'jobs' and find that this makes little difference. Waitressing, bar work, retail salesperson, hotel receptionist: everyone wants experience.

When I look up, I spot Trackie Man number 632 standing across the road, licking an ice cream and staring at me through the Poundland window. I scratch my scalp and try to think of something, anything I can do…

I try Burley one more time. This is an emergency. It rings out again and again, and just as I'm about to hang up, he answers. 'Hello? Hello?'

'Dr Burley! Oh, thank God!'

'Poppy! Are you okay? Excuse the bad line, I'm on the train. How are you?'

'Great! I mean, great now that I've caught you, but other than that… really not great. Not great AT ALL.'

He sighs. 'I am so sorry, Poppy. There were never any guarantees, remember, but still, it all seems very improper; such a wonderful record, such a high score, a great student and a delightful person. So I wanted you to know that you've been in my thoughts, and however bleak things may seem, I have every confidence that it will all work out for you. Just keep your options open.'

'I do appreciate that, Dr Burley. I've been doing nothing BUT thinking about my options, in fact.'

'Well good for you. Can't keep a good girl down, as they say! That's the spirit, Poppy. Now do stay in touch – you've got my number – and I wish you all the very best with your future plans…' The rattle of a passing train breaks up our connection.

'No! Wait! Don't go! I have to see you! Dr Burley, please! I can't just let it all go, not like this! There might still be another way. Margot is retiring soon, right? I could be your assistant. I could work for free… well, nearly for free… for a small wage and accommodation.'

No dignity, but I can't help it. Without Burley, I am truly at sea, with very limited water-treading skills and a strong current of reality gaining momentum beneath me. If he doesn't sweep me back to shore now, I'll have drifted too far. I'll be out of sight and then… then I believe I will simply give up hope, stop trying to fight the inevitability of the tide and give myself up to be mercilessly tossed between the crashing waves until fate decides how I drown and when I'll be washed up.

I swallow hard. 'I need your help, Doc. Please, please. I can't lie. I'm desperate. Help me?'

'Oh Poppy, I really don't know how I possibly can. Dr Winters' decision is final, and she is under no obligation to justify her selection.'

'Please, Doc, I need this. I don't know what else to do; I don't fit anywhere else. Banbridge was my world… *is* my world. Please, anything.'

Another deep sigh. 'Leave it with me, okay? I'll make some enquiries, do what I can. As it happens, I'm meeting Dr Winters at a conference, so I'll see if I can gain some insight informally. If anything useful turns up, I'll be in touch. But what's important, Poppy, is that you keep your head high, remember all you've achieved and believe in your own abilities; I've watched you face and overcome bigger obstacles than this in your life, and you can do it again.'

'Thanks Dr Burley, this means so much to me. Whatever you can manage, I'll be eternally grateful.'

'Well, it's the least I can do for you. Ah, you know what would be worthwhile…'

'Yes?' I gasp, desperate for a final lifebuoy, for the driftwood of hope.

'You should ask Gregory to make some enquiries on your behalf. He is quite the golden boy at the moment; certainly in a very influential position to help you along.'

'Yes, that is certainly worth remembering.'

And I'm not even joking. Because if Gregory is going to have any say over my future, I'd better start calculating how much change I'll have out of £73.10 after I buy myself a KFC family bucket and a crystal ball.

I wipe my hands down my thighs and blow out my cheeks. What is going on? Not even a week ago, I was planning to spend the rest of my professional life less than five metres from Dr Burley's desk. I thought we were partners, a team; I thought we were friends. Sure, I know we were officially student and tutor, but surely, after more than ten years working closely with someone, with such pressure, such intensity, something more grows? A stronger bond? A deeper connection? I thought we were academic soulmates; that Dr Burley got me. He understood my thinking, and used to nod excitedly and tug at his beard when I made a particularly satisfying breakthrough. He was my mentor, my hero. But maybe I was wrong. Maybe I was just another student who would inevitably drift in and out of his care, soon to be replaced by a younger, fresher, brighter protégé just as hungry to achieve, just as grateful to be acknowledged.

'Out of sight, out of mind.' That was what my dad used to say after he split from his band. Once you've served your purpose and your time has passed, you're done.

Like Christmas decorations in January.

Like last year's *X Factor* winner.

Like an overqualified, underemployed postgraduate crouched on the pavement outside the job centre with a painful sense of rejection, betrayal and hopelessness.

I pick myself up off the kerb, zip up my coat and start making my way through the crisp autumn air towards the high street

Everything will be fine. This is just temporary. This too will pass.

Right?

CHAPTER FOUR

It's three o'clock now, so I've got an hour to pick up some shopping and be back home by the time my mum gets in from work. As an apprentice psychic, I can already foretell that this will be a fairly painful conversation, involving lots of *How did it go? And then what happened? And then what did he say? And then what did you say? Were you fidgeting? Are you sure? Well, you're fidgeting now. If you don't realise that you fidget, then you probably weren't aware that you were fidgeting right in his face. Fidgeting is not something a potential employer wants to see, is it?'*

Then she'll sigh and say, *Never mind, I'm sure it will all be fine* as she rubs her eyes and scratches her nose, which are universally accepted body-language cues that mean *Nothing will be fine AT ALL.* And then she'll give me 'the face'; lowered chin and pinched smile.

It's not a nice face.

It's a mix of jaded sympathy and rising aggravation, a distinct and unconscious facial expression that is tempered with a little martyrdom and a lot of disappointment. The mere thought of it has been an enormously motivating image in my life. It's her little way of saying *I could love you more, but at the end of the day, you are your father's daughter.*

If my mum wrote a book on parenting, it'd be called *Failure Within Failure Within Failure: a Russian doll approach to very conditional love.*

I do know why I feel like this; it was uncovered by a therapist I did a placement with when I had to undergo a few psychotherapy sessions as part of a compulsory module to 'identify with the client experience', so it was my turn to get on the couch. I talked, the therapist listened. When I didn't talk, she asked questions. When I clammed up, got angry, cried and broke down, she congratulated me and said that we were 'getting places'. Thankfully, I also got a ruptured appendicitis at this point and received a medical exemption, having covered the minimum amount of hours to pass the module. She kindly sent me a report, however, recommending that further sessions could really help me, but I found the whole thing very difficult so I scanned through it and put in a folder somewhere, never to be reread. Ultimately I know that the cause of the enormous guilt I feel at failing my mum is the fact that I am my dad's daughter – a constant link to and reminder of him – and this makes me feel very bad.

Of course, the therapist told me that it is irrational to feel this way; that nobody chooses who they are born to and there is absolutely no benefit to anyone in me carrying this burden around. And I understand that perfectly, in an academic, theoretical way, but truthfully, I can't say I feel it any less. Especially when I fuck up royally, like moving back home with no job at twenty-nine years of age. Which means Mum is still the one stepping in to pick up the pieces of a one-time love affair nearly three decades ago. She must totally regret ever setting eyes on Ray Bloom, and the destructive domino effect he has had on so much of her life.

I feel guilty that she couldn't have walked away and severed ties altogether; a clean break, a fresh start. And although she's made a go of it and has a fantastic life with Frank, I always feel that she could have been even happier a) without having a child in tow and b) without this child growing up to frequently reflect the man she walked out on. My mum has this lasting attachment to him through me.

Is this an exaggeration? A paranoid projection? Is it even possible for me to tell what the truth is or what is just an occupational hazard of being a psychologist? I guess listening to psychologists talk psychology day in, day out for a decade is enough to drive you mad.

I can't break through the crowd of shoppers in front of me, so I swerve in to Sainsbury's Local. I go straight to the wine section, then coffee, then bananas and pizza. This is a diet I know I can live on. Morning: drink, peel and eat. Rest of time: drink, peel and heat.

I take my basket and join the queue that snakes through the aisles of magazines and hand sanitisers. I throw some of these into my basket too; the perfect care package for my next appointment at the job centre. Oh God, I'm planning my next trip there! What if this is what my life is going to be like now permanently, and I'm deluding myself if I think I'm ever getting out? Heat spreads up my neck and I feel sick. I swallow and try to steady myself by holding on to a promotional biscuit shelf.

'Poppy?' I hear my name. Clearly hear it. But I dare not turn around. It can't be real. Nobody knows me in here. It's a trick of the mind. An aural hallucination. A distinct preliminary sign of madness. Holy shit, I've read about this in depth but never experienced it first-hand… never thought I ever would.

I hear it again. Louder this time, with a slight inflection. 'Poppy! Poppy Bloom!' The voice is getting closer, coming from behind me. I press my earphones deeper into my ears. I need to get out of here. Just as I am looking for a place to drop my basket and leg it home I feel a tap on my shoulder.

'Poppy 'Bonecrusher' Bloom? I knew it was you!'

I turn around.

Oh thank you, Lord, this is a real person and NOT a stress-induced aural hallucination. A real person who is standing in front of me! False alarm. I have not lost my mind. I let go of the shelf and give my heart a chance to recover to a normal rhythm while I study the tanned, ponytailed, muscular, glossy goddess of a woman who stands before me, smiling at me from ear to ear. She looks like she's been beamed in from the fitness channel. An apparition. A vision. I mentally scan across different sections of my acquaintance. Banbridge? Brixton? Netflix?

'Leanne Jones!' I say at last. I recognise her by the dimples; I've had massive dimple envy since primary school.

'Yes! How have you been? It's been so long! God, it's good to see you.' She throws her arms around me and squeezes really tight. My arms are pinned by my sides, so I do a weird nose-nuzzle thing to reciprocate affection. *Leanne Jones*. She still smells like vanilla and coconut. I close my eyes and breathe her in.

'I can't believe it's you. I haven't seen you since we left school! What's that, like over ten years ago? More? That's crazy! You haven't changed one bit!'

I relax a little. Leanne *has* changed, A LOT, from the tomboy I remember. She used to have cropped auburn hair and lived in tracksuits and football kit. We were inseparable in primary school but then got placed in different sets at secondary. I was filtered off with the advanced-studies kids, whereas Leanne got to stay mainstream.

I really wanted to stay mainstream.

Big classes, loads of different people and teachers, and fun. That didn't happen in advanced studies. We took extra classes before and after school; for fun we played chess, and at break times we tested each other.

But she sounds the same, and I'd recognise her smile anywhere. I give her a massive squeeze back. I can't believe how happy I am to see her. This is the single best thing that could've happened. We had so many great times together, playing out until dark, sitting on the kerb and sharing trays of mixed fried rice from the Chinese. We even started our own little business, running errands for elderly, immobile, busy or lazy people in our area. All Leanne's idea, the budding entrepreneur. We picked up dry-cleaning, prescriptions; we fed cats, posted letters, shopped for milk, bread, beer, cigarettes; you name it, we'd do it. We charged two quid a trip, and once we'd made enough, we took ourselves off on the train to Thorpe Park. It was amazing.

I take a deep breath and hold her shoulders with both hands. 'How has it been so long? It's been too long!'

'I know! I've thought of you so many times! Every time I go to Thorpe Park, actually!'

I smile at the thought. I haven't been there since.

'So how have you been? What have you been up to?' she asks.

'I'm okay,' I tell her. 'Just graduated. I got my PhD yesterday, in fact, so just picking up some bits and bobs. How about you? You look amazing – so strong.' There are dips and ridges in her arms like a bodybuilder. I take her all in: carved neckline, tight little waist, long lean legs. Leanne Jones is HOT. 'You're like a goddess. In Spandex.'

She rolls her eyes and shakes off the compliment. 'Oh Poppy, you really haven't changed a bit. You always know the right thing to say.' She hugs me again. 'It really is so great to see you.'

Once I got siphoned off with the other advanced-studies kids, Leanne and I saw less and less of each other. By second year, I'd made a new best friend called Crystal Pang, the only other girl in the class. We had the same IQ, but Crystal was a brilliant pianist as well, and she spoke fluent Cantonese. I can't play an instrument at all, nor can I speak any other languages.

As a result, Leanne hung around more and more with her twin brother Tom, who was easily the most popular, funniest, fittest, most drop-dead-gorgeous boy in the school. The Jones twins ran our school. Well, the best bits of it.

'So tell me about you, Leanne!' I say. 'What are you up to these days? Whatever it is, it suits you.'

'Well, Tom and I own a gym together, so that's fun. And I live in Dulwich, married to Leon Wright – you remember him?'

Oh my God. Leanne and I used to call Leon Wright 'Prawn', because he had a fantastic body but a horrible head. She married him? I remember seeing them walking to school together, but I never for one second thought they'd end up *married*.

I nod, smiling. 'Oh wow, of course I remember!'

'We have four kids now – two boys, two girls.'

Four kids? I try not to show my sheer… confusion. Leanne is a mother! When did all this happen? Where did she find the time? Four kids is a big deal. Four smaller people attached to you 24/7. For years and years. How would you even… I can't begin to imagine.

Leanne is a mother, a wife and a business owner. But she looks so *normal*. No, not normal; *better* than normal. I check myself. What was I expecting someone who has accomplished so much to look like? Jaded? Strung out, frumpy and fed up? Leanne is the same age as I am, but compared to me, her life has moved on in leaps and bounds. It's like she's had multiple lifetimes compared to mine. And what have I got to show for my time? Framed qualifications gathering dust in a shamefully messy bedroom.

'How about you? Married? Kids?' she asks.

I shake my head to both. 'Child-free and boyfriend-free at the moment, just temporarily, until I get set up,' I tell her. I feel like I've just woken up from a coma. I'm not saying I want kids; I don't even think I want a husband. But I do think I need to jump-start my life.

She nods appreciatively. 'God, I'm jealous, what I would do to be child- and husband-free for even one day! If you've got some time, we'll have to hang out, catch up. You remember Tom, right, my twin?'

'Yes, of course. How is he?'

She blows out her cheeks. 'Tom is Tom, no change. Still exactly the same as ever. He's great, he loves the gym; he does the business side of things. He's always looking for something new, wanting to move on to the next big thing. He gets bored quickly, can't stand still. Don't think he'll ever settle down, to be honest. Knows everything except what he actually wants, you know?'

I nod along. *Tom is Tom.* A lifetime later and I still flush at the thought of him. I used to sit by the study-room window and watch him play football with his friends. Tom was BEAUTIFUL, that's what Tom was. There was something about him that just made people flock to him. Maybe it was the way he smiled at them, or clapped them on the back when they missed a shot, or ran to defend the smallest player on the pitch. Everyone loved Tom. And I wasn't immune. Tom Jones was the reason I joined the swimming club. I just wanted to get closer to him. Hear him. Watch him. Think about him…

Leanne takes out a card and hands it to me. It's deep purple, with lots of swirls, and lists an array of phone numbers, websites and social media addresses.

'Take this, it has all my numbers on it. I run the women's fitness classes.'

I look down at the card in my hand: *Gymbox.*

'We're just behind the station, under the arches. Come down any time and I'll sort you out with free membership, taster sessions – whatever you're interested in. I'm always there, and so is Tom.'

'Wow, Leanne, I can't believe you've got your own business as well as a husband and kids.'

She shrugs. 'Most of the time I love it, but sometimes it takes over. That's life, though, so I'm not complaining. You'll come down and join?'

'Absolutely,' I lie as I realise that this queue is not moving despite the big red sign promising express service. I haven't been in a gym… ever. I love to mess around with a ball and I like to swim, but I would have no idea what to do with weights or machines except make a complete tit of myself by pulling the push one or sitting on something you should stand on. I have my own approach to weight management called 'just buy bigger knickers and then make sure all photos are headshots'. Tried and tested. A hundred per cent research-approved.

She squints at me and then begins to nod, as if she's just had a light-bulb moment. She tilts her head to the side and starts swiping through her phone.

'So I guess this also means that you're back in the game, ready for some kick-ass netball! We have the best team this year – absolute dynamite! I mean it. If we take this seriously enough, we could make the Superleague FINALS!'

I widen my eyes. I enjoy netball but I haven't played properly in years; there was just no time between lectures and exams.

'That's so nice of you to think of me, but I'm not going to be around here much longer – I'm probably going to be back in Banbridge really soon, so it'd be wrong of me to commit. I just have a few things to sort out and that'll be me out of here again, back at the university, lecturing or researching.'

Leanne stands with her legs shoulder width apart and roots herself to the ground. Her eye contact is intense.

'Poppy, listen to me. Remember the finals against Wandsworth? You scored in the last minute and broke Crystal's fingers?'

Shocked, I glance behind me to make sure nobody overheard. 'That was a complete accident, Leanne! I never meant to do that, especially to Crystal.!'

Leanne raises her eyebrows and sucks her teeth. 'Crystal deserved it; she was a complete bully! She looked down on everyone, thought she was so superior, terrorised the younger kids. And then you came on court; just flew up from nowhere like a phoenix rising. It was amazing! Breathtaking! No joke, that was one of the best games of my life. Promise me you'll play for us!'

I shrug nervously. It was one of the worst games of *my* life. Crystal's parents withdrew her from school, and my parents were called to say that I'd been involved in a serious incident. This was enough to allow Dad to get his own way and send me to an all-girls boarding school for A Levels. Mum fought him tooth and nail, but he said it was all the evidence he needed that inner-city comprehensive schooling was no place for his daughter, and no place for a child of my ability. I told him I didn't want to go, that I'd miss my friends. He said I could just make new ones. Turns out that's easier said than done.

Leanne starts tapping furiously on her phone. But I don't know where to look. The prickle of tears feels very, very close to the surface and I don't want her to know what a pathetic mess I am right now.

'Time to make plans. I'll call Tom and tell him we're going out to celebrate your graduation and your homecoming. We'll have a few drinks, catch up on everything. Just the three of us. It will be so great.' She raises the phone to her ear.

I'm starting to remember Leanne's single-mindedness. She's bossy. Once she's got an idea in her head, she bulldozes everything else out of the way.

'Hi, Tom, it's me. You will not believe who I am with right now!' She's smiling like she's going through a wind tunnel. 'Poppy! Poppy Bloom! Yeah? No. Not her. Yes, swimming. No, not that one either, that girl had a birthmark. No, Poppy was the one that broke that bitchy girl's fingers and then her parents went crazy and said her piano career was ruined and they pulled her out of school and sent her away to live with her grandparents in Hong Kong. How can you not remember that?'

This is mortifying. Tom Jones was my every waking thought throughout my formative years, and he has no idea who I am? Does that mean that I imagined all his sweet side-smiles in the canteen? That I didn't catch him looking at me when I mounted the diving block? That my entire recollection of events from my schooldays is nothing more than a subjective, heavily filtered and thoroughly flawed version that means nothing to anyone else but me?

Tom Jones does not know who I am.

Not that I want him to remember the Crystal thing. That was horrific and hand-on-heart a complete accident. I got overexcited; I lost control. I never, ever meant to hurt her. My first heartbreaking lesson in how to lose friends and injure people.

I pretend to slit my throat with my finger. Oh my God. This is utterly humiliating. Tom Jones thinks that I want to catch up with him like long-lost friends and he can't even remember me – if he ever knew who I was in the first place that is. Please, Leanne, can you just cut this conversation NOW!

'Poppy BLOOM! She was really smart and used to come round our house when we were at primary school. Mum was really fond of her because she had such lovely manners… I know it's a long time ago, but that's not really the point, is it? The point is that she's here now and then she'll be off doing something brainy and important again soon, so let's catch up, all right? Show her around and grab a bite to eat.'

She stops to listen. 'Okay, today is Thursday, I'm free but can't do tomorrow, the kids have appointments all day, and all next week is out as the accountant is in for three days. The next window I've got is six weeks' time. So it's got to be tonight.' Her voice is getting more hushed but more forceful. 'You're right, Tom, I *don't* care. Here's Poppy, speak to her yourself.'

She thrusts the phone into my hand and crosses her arms so I can't throw it back at her.

'Uh, hi?'

Tom sighs on the other end of the line. 'Hi, Poppy, I'm really sorry about this. As you can tell, Leanne is basically mental. I know this is probably the last thing you feel like doing, and I don't suppose you have the faintest memory of me from school either, but you know my sister, she won't let up. Kim Jong Leanne has decided that we are going out, so that's obviously what's going to happen.'

His voice is breathless and he's speaking a million miles an hour.

'Are you okay? You sound like someone's chasing you?' I say.

'I'm out for a run. I've had a shit day. I'm not great company at the moment, to be honest.'

'Oh well, snap! I've just been to the job centre.'

'No way! I thought the bank was bad, but the job centre, that sounds…'

'Utterly deflating?' I offer.

He laughs. 'Yes. Utterly deflating. That's a good way of putting it. Exactly.' Tom Jones is laughing at something I said. 'So maybe a drink isn't such a bad idea after *an utterly deflating* day, right?'

Part of me wants to say, whoa, hold up, I can't possibly agree to doing something tonight. It hasn't been arranged. It is frightfully short notice. I haven't psyched myself up properly, I don't know where we are going or what's on the menu or what I should wear… but then it hits me. I have nowhere else to be. I have nothing on tonight or any night until Burley gets back to me, except watching Mum and Frank shout wrong answers at quiz show presenters. And resisting the urge to social-media-stalk Gregory and Harriet.

'Yeah, okay. A drink would be great,' I say.

'Right, tell Leanne that I'll meet you both outside the Ritzy at eight, and we'll go from there.'

I hand the phone back to Leanne. She is smiling now. If anything, it looks like a smile of relief.

'Cashier number two, please,' calls the automated voice.

'You go first, Leanne,' I say. 'I know you must be crazy busy.'

'Ah, thanks so much.' She dashes ahead to the cashier in front of us and turns to face me while packing her bags. 'Poppy, you know you haven't changed at all.'

'Really?'

She nods keenly. 'Not even one little bit!' She waves and makes for the door. 'We'll see you later, can't wait.'

I start my journey home feeling a little lighter than I did when I set out this morning.

Today has been weird.

Harriet and Gregory are still sticky with each other's perspiration. A forensic orgy of mutual fluids. I am still the discarded, expired stock of the Banbridge elite. Nobody has called to say that there has been a dreadful mistake. Alternative offers from competing universities have not materialised. I am not a fellow. I am number 633. I have no job, and only shockingly depressing prospects to mull over.

I walk past the railway arches by Leanne's gym, past the park, the church, the charity shops, and soon I've got the footpath to myself again. I've got space to think.

I am going out for a drink with an old friend. A friend whose smile makes me happy. A friend who I've missed more than I realised. Not to mention her gorgeous blonde-haired, dimple-cheeked brother, who laughed at something I said even though he couldn't remember me from the shy, mousy army of admirers he must have encountered all through his school life.

I take the bends in the road and find that at the top of our street someone has put a large wooden wardrobe out on the kerb to be collected or recycled. I catch sight of myself in its scratched and darkened mirror. I'm not shocked or surprised at my reflection – it's exactly as I expect. I've never really looked any different. I'm fine. Average. Plain. A stock image of a long-haired student. On a deluxe colour chart I'd blend well into the light beige to medium tan. No wonder Tom doesn't remember me. I'm just myself; nearly thirty, tea-coloured with shades of biscuit.

Hold up… nearly thirty?

As in three-decades-old thirty? As in age 30–39, a brand-new age bracket in survey-based data gathering?

I demand a recount.

Thirty is the age where you are expected to know what you are doing. If I heard on the news that a thirty-year-old woman had been arrested for murder/drug smuggling/kidnapping, I'd think she was old enough to know better. No benign judge is going to rub her back and make excuses for her to the jury.'

Thirty? Me? Really?

Yep. In three months' time I will be thirty years old. I set my shopping bags down and look at myself from every angle in the mirror. In the grand tradition of denial when one approaches a milestone age, I feel I should say that I've never felt so alive or comfortable in my own skin, but the truth is that I'm exhausted.

Poppy, you know you haven't changed at all. Not even one little bit. I know Leanne meant this as a compliment. And I appreciate that most people would be delighted to be told that they haven't changed. But this is niggling at me. More than a niggle, actually; it's bothering me big time.

Its closer to fifteen years since I last saw Leanne and I haven't changed? Not one bit? I look the same, I act the same, I wear the same clothes, I go to the same places, I haven't moved into a new role as mother or girlfriend or wife or businesswoman. I'm still pretty much exactly who I was before. And that's not normal. It's static.

If you're not growing, you are decaying. That's nature in its full-blown brutality. I take a step closer to the mirror, pull out my topknot, shake down my hair and look again. Yep, she's right. I haven't changed one bit, and that's the bit I need to change.

Pronto.

CHAPTER FIVE

Mum is home. I can smell frying mince and onions as I open the gate, skip up the steps and turn the key in the front door.

'Poppy! Come in here. Tell me about today.'

I kick off my shoes in the hallway and join her in the kitchen.

'Were you able to sort yourself out with something at the job centre?'

'Yes, loads of very, very exciting stuff. Never realised that psychology was going to be so versatile! So yeah, watch this space. Not too closely straight away, but definitely watch this space.'

Mum seems to be channelling a lot of restless energy into the wooden spoon she's using to stir the meat.

'Does that mean you've got an actual start date? Is there an actual job with actual money or not?' Fuckery. Thought she'd just be content with glib good news.

'Not as yet. However, the guy at the job centre really knew his stuff, a total professional – he said just to hang tight, stay positive and I'll be in my dream job in no time.'

Mum continues at the frying pan with frequent stabbing actions. I swoop in with my salvaging titbit.

'And another piece of good news is that you won't have to worry about dinner for me tonight as I'm going out with some old school friends!'

She puts down her wooden spoon and turns towards me. It's the first eye contact she has made since I've entered the house. 'Go on…'

'Twins Leanne and Tom, we were close at school? I'm meeting up with them at eight o'clock.'

Mum starts to stir the mince again, but this time in a thoughtful, almost tender way.

'And is Leanne a single girl like you?'

'No, she's married with kids, but Tom is single, I think. They own a gym.'

She's smiling now. 'Ah, Tom.' She rolls his name around her mouth. 'I like Toms. If I'd had a boy I would have called him Tom. I can't say I've ever met a bad Tom. You know, I already have a good feeling about Tom. Well done, Poppy. See, didn't we say to surround yourself with people! Roberta will be well chuffed when I tell her that you followed her advice. Why don't you get them to pick you up here instead? That way we could meet them both, have a G and T together. I'd love to meet Tom. Owns a gym, you say? Must be a strong lad. Must look after himself.'

'I haven't even met him myself yet, not for years and years.'

Mum's on one now. 'I know your generation does things differently – leaves things a hell of a lot later. I was married, divorced and remarried by your age, but if it means you then move fast when you eventually do make up your mind... well, far be it from me to interfere. I think it's wonderful.' She opens her arms to me and wraps me in a cuddle, rocking us from side to side.

'Oh, a wedding, Poppy, wouldn't that be wonderful? We could have a marquee, or even go abroad. I love Spain, always have. And then maybe a baby... or two, especially if there are twins on his side, right?'

I let her envelop me in her embrace, indulging her in her reverie, breathing in the homely familiarity of her scent. I'm happy for the subject matter to be anything other than my current loser status. She pulls away and kisses my forehead, tucking my hair behind my ears.

'I'm not being selfish here, you know. It's for you I want all these things. All my friends have grown-up kids the same age as you, some even younger. But they are truly grown up – they've got careers and spouses and kids and mortgages and people carriers.'

I nearly find myself apologising. Just singing out a 'sorry' to placate her. But then I think, no. I've not done anything wrong. I've not hurt anyone. It's not like I've been sitting around doing nothing. I've worked my arse off, and true, it's not panned out the way I thought it would, but that doesn't mean I'm a write-off. I'm not apologising for not being someone else.

'Oh, I see,' I say, nodding, as if I've finally caught up with what she's really trying to tell me. 'What's a people carrier?'

She sighs and her arms drop to her sides. 'It's a car.'

'But every car is a people carrier – what a ridiculous and pointless thing to say. Is this something your friends do while they're comparing interest rates and how many times their kids can get pregnant? Make up new names for everyday items? Bet they have hours of fun: *Oh, can you pass me that concave metal eating instrument? Ah, this spoon here? Yes, precisely.*'

Her back is turned and she's at the hob again. She used to laugh when I mimicked her friends in my squeaky Frank Spencer voice. But right now she is not laughing one bit.

I start to unpack my shopping bags. 'So, about tonight... I've been thinking about trying out a bit of a new look. How would you feel about doing my hair? I fancy a change.' I walk over to the hob and take the wooden spoon from her and start stirring the mince myself.

Mum looks at me, eyebrows knitted together. 'A wash and blow-dry, you mean?'

'No, I mean a complete makeover – cut, colour, restyle.'

Her glasses slide to the end of her nose and she shifts her weight on to her back leg, like she can't quite take the force of what she is hearing.

'You mean it? You'll let me do your hair? Or do you mean you want me to book you in with one of the other girls at the salon? Annikka has just started, very on trend. I could ask her to fit you in.'

'Well, I was kind of hoping you could do it.'

Mum's hand lifts to her chin and she squints at me, shaking her head. 'So you're saying you are ready for a *change*?'

'Yes! Definitely! That's exactly what I want. I want to change. I want a new look, something fresh and fun and modern and memorable and—'

'Whoa, whoa, whoa. Sweetheart, all those things sound absolutely thrilling, but this is a haircut we're talking about. I'll try my best, but I don't want you to get your hopes up. We get this in the salon all the time. Someone gets dumped; answer: new hair. Someone gets fired; answer: new hair. A good hairdresser can go some way to helping in a crisis, but I'm not a miracle worker, love.'

'I know, don't worry. I think a change in how I look will help me look at myself differently, and then maybe I can make more changes… bit by bit.'

'You're sure?'

'I'm sure.'

'You trust me?'

'I trust you.'

Mum's face breaks into a huge smile and she shakes her head, lifting her eyes to the heavens as if her prayers have finally been answered.

'So, when are you thinking of making this big change?'

'Right now, if possible? I want something different for tonight, you know, something a bit more sophisticated, less studenty, today being *the first day of the rest of my life* and all that.'

She turns off the hob, grabs the wooden spoon from my hand and throws it into the sink. Pushing her glasses back up her nose, she runs her fingers through my long brown hair as if inspecting strands on a loom.

'Okay, scraggy split ends will have to go. The colour could do with something to bring it out more; we could go lighter, or darker? Bit of both? Of course gentlemen prefer blondes, so you may want to think on that.'

She flicks my side parting forward into my face, then folds my hair over my forehead for a faux-fringe effect. She scrunches her nose disapprovingly and narrows one eye. Then she scrapes it all back from my face, smoothing down any stray hairs and gathering it back into a tight ballerina bun. Nose scrunch again, along with lip curl, so this mustn't be working either. She then takes the tips of my hair and leans into me, holding them against my jawline, and she's so close that I can almost read the tiny cursive of her thoughts. Her face opens up, her lips part and her eyes widen. She steps backwards, holds an L-shaped hand up towards my face and starts to nod.

'Yes, yes, yes! I've got it now! Sit over there by the sink. I know exactly what I'm going to do with you.'

I sit at the kitchen sink, a starchy brown towel around my shoulders and a hideous whirring feeling in my stomach. She prepares her pots of dye, her brushes, spatulas, foils, brushes, scissors, hairdryer, curlers and straighteners, and plugs a very dangerous-looking hand-held device into the wall to charge. When she turns it on, it starts to buzz.

It is an electric razor.

I start to panic – what have I done here? I have pulled the grenade pin and now there's no going back. One thing you don't do with Mum is backtrack. Once the wheels are set in motion, you just have to hold your nerve or else she will make you regret it. So, this is it now. This is the last time I will look the way I do, for better or for worse.

Mum hands me a chilled bottle of cava and two glasses. 'Open that. It's high time we celebrated; with all that's been going on, we've hardly stopped to catch our breath.'

I fill our flutes of bubbly right to the top. Mum stands beside me in her black hairdressing apron, plastic gloves on, scissors in the holster at her waist, a wild look in her eyes.

'To new beginnings,' she toasts, and we clink our glasses together, keeping eye contact as we both swig back massive mouthfuls. Mum then wipes her mouth with the back of her hand, rolls up her sleeves and gives her shoulders a little pump to loosen them.

'So what happened with the other boy you were seeing? Jeffery?'

'Gregory. Not that it matters. It's over.'

Mum drains her glass and starts to comb my hair. 'And was that your choice? To finish it?' She tugs lightly, starting with the knots at the end.

I shake my head. 'Not exactly.'

'Well, never you mind, all the more reason for a ravishing new look. It was bound to finish. I'm just relieved it happened sooner rather than later; no use these things lingering on.'

I suddenly feel very defensive. It's bad enough everyone thinking I was punching above my weight with him, never mind my own mother adding to the chorus of critics.

'How could you know that, Mum? You never even met him!' I spin around in my seat. She stops combing and holds the brush high in the air.

'I didn't need to meet him to know that he was wrong for you. I could just tell.'

'Oh really? And how does that work then?'

'Because I always knew when he was around. When I'd ring you, I'd always be able to tell if he was in the room or somewhere in the background because your voice would go all quiet and small. Whether he meant to or not, he made you nervous and self-conscious and... well, let's say *not yourself.*'

I shuffle up in my seat. I think she may be on to something.

'How was I "not myself"?'

'You sounded different; you became all tight and whispery, like the air was being sucked out of you. It used to upset me. All those years trying to build up your confidence so you could take on the world, and then you get so far and fold yourself up again. So I know it's never nice to have someone call things off, but in this case Poppy, I'm relieved.' She strokes my hair gently and gathers it at the nape of my neck.

She's knocked me for six with this. 'I thought you'd be disappointed. I thought you'd like that he was so smart and charming and successful.'

'Ha! I fell for your father because he was smart and charming and successful and look where that got me!'

I grab at my knees. I hate this conversation. Usually I bite my lip and try to distract myself – think of a book I'm reading or an essay I'm working on – but this time, before I even realise it, the words have escaped my lips. 'I'm sorry, Mum. I am so, so sorry.'

'For what?' Mum moves around to the front of my chair and places her hands on mine. 'Poppy, talk to me. Tell me whatever it is. What's wrong?'

'What's wrong is that you fell for Dad and he was a complete shit, and then rather than just leave and start again, you couldn't because… you had me.'

Mum's eyebrows furrow in confusion. 'I'm not following.'

'That's what I'm sorry about. Sorry that you couldn't just start over with no baggage and have a proper family with someone who loves you, and not be constantly tied to your ex-husband.'

Mum's hand drifts to her eyes and she pinches the bridge of her nose. Then she sits on the lino floor in front of me and wraps her arms around my legs, resting her head in my lap. After a moment, she lifts her head to meet my gaze.

'Poppy, I need you to listen to me when I say this. I mean really, *really* listen. This is important.'

I nod my head and hold my glass to my lips to stop them quivering.

'Ray Bloom is not a bad man. He is just not good with people. He's *shocking* with people. And the drink, the drugs and the other women didn't help much either.' Mum grabs my glass from my hand and takes a swig. 'We were good together for a while, but we wanted different things, we stopped bringing out the magic in each other. Things got dark between us. Except for one glimmer of light, one spark of love and hope and warmth that lit something in both of us that we never knew was even there. A love that was – that *is* – bigger and brighter and more powerful than either of us realised we were capable of experiencing. And that is you, Poppy. He gave me you. So never, ever forget that having you was the most important and phenomenal thing that ever happened to me. To us both.'

I swallow a gigantic lump in my throat, grab the cava and top up her glass. 'Weren't you scared, leaving him, venturing out on your own?'

Mum tilts her head at me and smiles. 'People couldn't believe it when I actually did it. Actually packed my bags and left him. It was all over the newspapers; it made the six o'clock news. Why would a hairdresser with a small baby walk out on the drummer from the most famous band in the world? I didn't want his money. I just wanted to live my own life. I wanted to make my own choices and be independent. Always so overprotective, your dad. Wanted to control everyone, keep us away from anything he thought might hurt us. It came from a good place, I suppose, but I knew it wasn't right. Yes, I could have stayed in his gilded cage, tucked away in a mansion somewhere with servants and nannies and whatnot, but I hated the idea of it. Hated the idea of not living my own life the way I knew I needed to. He saw the world differently, as a dark and dangerous place; part of his artistic genius, I suppose.'

Her voices softens a little and she moves up on her haunches.

'The thing that people don't understand about being an artistic genius is that you're not like everybody else; you can do something the average Joe can't do. And that might sound like a gift, but to my mind, it isn't.' She stands, walks around to the back of my chair and resumes combing. 'Genius can be a curse. I dare say it was a curse for your father.'

'What do you mean?' I ask.

'As much as I couldn't always understand your father, Poppy, mostly I pitied him. Pitied him because his genius isolated him from the regular world and regular relationships. He saw the world a different way. He experienced things in a different way.'

'Like music?' I ask.

'Like everything. I'll give you an example. We were on holiday in Spain just after you were born. Lovely beach, lovely food, big jug of sangria – it was great. We're sitting on the balcony watching the sunset and I'm really enjoying it; I'm admiring the pretty colours, the relaxation. Ray? You think he can sit there and enjoy it? No way. Of course he can't. He starts picking up the cutlery and banging out a rhythm against the table. I say, "Put the knives down, Ray, we're on holiday. Why can't you just relax and enjoy the peace?" But he can't relax, he can't be at peace – that's his problem. He starts talking all this deep and meaningful nonsense watching the sun go down on the horizon – how powerless we are against nature, how we are conditioned to see things to suit ourselves because we don't like the truth… He was on one then. I knew something was rattling him inside and that I wouldn't hear the end of it, so I got up from my chair and told him I was going bed. I couldn't bear all this heavy, end-of-the-world stuff. I snuggled in beside you and smelt your lovely soft baby skin and he took himself off down the beach. Spent all night by himself, drumming knives and sticks on the rocks.'

There's a quiver in my mum's hand. I don't know if it's upset or anger. I reach up and take it regardless.

She sighs. 'But you know what?'

'What?' I ask.

'Next morning, he was fine. Better than fine. He was relaxed. It was like he needed to get it out of his system. He wrote the whole of *Solar Power* that night. Great album. Great sales. Artistic genius, see? Your father couldn't help but choose his music and his career over his relationships. And in my opinion he made the wrong choice, because at the end of the day, it's your relationships that keep you happy, keep you sane, keep you going. But that was Ray's choice. If I had the choice, I'd not choose to be a genius. I'd choose to be average, to be normal. To be happy with a nice meal and a glass of sangria at sunset, surrounded by loving friends and family. But I guess we all have to make our own choices, find a balance, right?'

'So how do you put all that behind you and move on?'

'Well, you need to decide what's good that's come of it. Then take that good and cherish it, be grateful for it. Give it all your love and attention. And put all the rest in a folder marked "Shit Bits" and file it away somewhere it won't bother you any more. Simple, but not easy, if you get me.'

My folder is looking fairly fat at the moment.

'Right, keep your head still. And I don't want to hear a word out of you until I say "job done", do you hear that? Let's give Tom something to get excited about.'

I start to nod, but she's already yanked my hair back and is clipping the top layer up.

I try to focus on tonight. Yes, okay, I admit I was slightly obsessed by Tom when I was a teenager, but that was a long, long time ago. When I was about fifteen. So a lifetime ago. He could be a completely different person now. He's bound to be. And I'm not looking for love anyway. I don't even know if I've ever been in love. I've had a few one-night stands and short-term flings, but Gregory was the biggest relationship I've been in…

Mum is painting something on to my hair that is very cold and so smelly it feels as though I've inhaled chlorine.

'Mum, do you remember—' I begin, but she grabs me by both shoulders.

'Poppy, we've agreed – not a word until I finish, all right? It's not just academics that need to concentrate on what they're doing, you know.'

Fair enough. I mumble a sorry and let the rhythmic sound of her brushstrokes on my harassed hair wash over me.

My thoughts return to Gregory. He is the first thing I've got to file in the Shit Bits folder. We were together a year, but were we in love? Honestly, I just haven't got a clue. My suspicion is that if I feel that way, then probably not. I have to admit, what Mum said makes sense. I did always feel terribly on guard around him; I definitely wanted to please him, to impress him. I was proud to be his girlfriend; I knew plenty of others deemed him boyfriend-worthy material, so who was I to contest that? But is that love? Even though Gregory wasn't perfect, it was really nice having someone to call on, to message, to enter a room with, to stand beside, to kiss. It was so nice to hand over all the business of having a social life to him. For the year we were together, I never had to worry about what I was doing on a Saturday night or on New Year's Eve or my birthday or Valentine's Day. And that took a lot of pressure and mundane logistics out of my hands. I did love *that*. The trappings and convenience of a relationship. But maybe I didn't love *him*.

Perhaps when I return to Banbridge I'll try to broaden out my circle a bit. Mix with people from different sectors, go to places a little off the beaten track where I can meet a more diverse crowd. And then perhaps I'll find someone who will be the yin to my yang. Maybe someone like Tom, but who actually remembers me. That way, I can carry on my work within the university walls all day, but the rest of the time will be totally different. The best of both worlds. A better balance.

Sitting here is relaxing and my eyes are getting heavy. I could definitely sleep now, just an hour of shut-eye to freshen me up before tonight. No sooner have I closed my eyes and started to forget about tonight, about Gregory, about my hair... than I hear the rattling of the front door lock.

'Ange, its only me, everything okay?'

'In the kitchen, Frank. We're getting Poppy ready to go out with some old friends tonight. It's with a TOM – he's single. Sounds good, don't you think?'

Frank shuffles into the kitchen, his face smeared in grease, his dark blue overalls reeking of oil from the flower van.

'Sounds lovely, Poppy, you enjoy yourself.' He starts to root around in his jacket pocket. 'Here you are, treat yourself.' He places a fifty-pound note on the kitchen counter. 'I can't think of what you youngsters like, so spend it on whatever you fancy – cocktails or shots or God knows what else. Whatever it is, just promise me you'll enjoy it.'

I can't get up from my seat to shove it back into his pocket, so I try to protest from my chair – 'Frank, no, you don't have to, honestly, that's too much' – but he's already got a forkful of the mince and onions in his mouth and he's waving me off.

'Ange, I'm going up for a bath. If I put the radio on down here, will you listen out for today's clue and scribble it down for me?'

'No problem, love.' Mum winks at him. 'You have a good soak, and by the time you come down, we'll be all cleaned up down here. Poppy will be off having a few drinks and we'll have our tea then watch a bit of telly.'

Frank pulls his aching body up the stairs and Mum turns on the small transistor radio, twisting the dial to 105 FM. Then she leans over and kisses me on the forehead.

'I know you had it all worked out, sweetheart. I know you had dreams of where you were going to live and how you wanted things to be. But being back home isn't the end of the world, is it? Surrounded by people who love the very bones of you. So it didn't work out in Banbridge. Big shizzle. It's only one place; there are plenty more, so who needs it? I know you better than you know yourself, Poppy Bloom, and I know that good things come to those who are kind and thoughtful and who work hard and try their best. So don't you fret about today or tomorrow or the next day. You are exactly where you're supposed to be, and I for one couldn't be more pleased. Okay?'

I nod my agreement. It is good to be home, although there is a funny tingle on my scalp, like my head's been scrubbed raw with a Brillo pad. I slug back my drink and settle into the chair.

'Now, I need to ring Roberta about how long to leave the colour so I get the tone just right. You listen out for this clue Frank's on about. They only announce it once a week on a Thursday and he's obsessed." She hands me a pen and paper. 'It's for a competition called "You Do the Maps". Ten weeks, ten clues and the winner gets ten grand.'

'No problem,' I say, taking the pen and paper in my lap, ready to scribble down the clue as soon as it's aired. They're playing 'Unchained Melody', which is a ridiculously long song, and it's making me sleepy. So I'm just going to listen with my eyes closed, and as soon as I hear the DJ speak, I'll grab the pen and paper and write down the clue. It's no problem *at all*. And the least I can do for Frank considering he just gave me fifty pounds. I'll just close my eyes until the end of this song…

CHAPTER SIX

'What's the clue then, love?'

'Hmm?' I open one eye to see Frank standing in front of me in a fluffy white bathrobe, looking like a bald polar bear. He leans in to read the piece of paper on my lap.

'What's that?' I ask, reorientating myself.

'The clue? Pass it over and I'll get my thinking cap on. I've got every single one worked out so far, so I'm in with a great chance for the ten grand prize.'

Mum brushes in beside him, and pats him lightly on the bum.

'Not just a pretty face, me,' he says. 'I love getting stuck in to a puzzle. Find it quite therapeutic, solving puzzles. I've been looking forward to it all day, truth be told. Actually, don't tell me yet; wait till I get my glasses, sort myself with a beer and put my feet up. Then I'll be in the zone to tackle it.'

I glance up at the clock. It's six o'clock. I've been asleep nearly an hour. I look down at the piece of paper, which is blank.

Shit, shit, shit!

I am livid with myself. How could I have drifted off? I've not got the clue! Oh, this is a disaster. How could I do this to Frank! I just love him; he always sticks up for me, always softens Mum up when she's angry with me. He never asks me to do anything and the one little favour he does ask I've completely messed up. Please let this not be happening. Frank is rubbing his eyes and circling the middle of the kitchen trying to locate his glasses.

My mother drags me over to the sink and rinses the last of the foul-smelling dye out. She then ushers me back over to the table where she begins hacking off great lengths with an over-zealousness that makes the blood drain from my face. If this hair thing is a total horrific disaster, I'm just going to change my name and pretend my whole awful life is happening to somebody else. I try to ignore the snip-snip of the scissors by my ears but fail abysmally. It's only been a few minutes and already my head feels so much lighter, probably because fifty per cent of my hair is now in furry little mounds all over the kitchen floor.

'What was last week's clue?' I ask Frank.

He's rooting in the cutlery drawer, still looking for his glasses. '"Crispy coated salt water" – Battersea. Get it?'

Ooh, a word puzzle. I love those. I used to do them for fun in between lessons. I could do word puzzles all day. 'Give me another one,' I say.

'Right, before that, it was "murky pond".'

'Blackpool?' I suggest.

Frank claps his hands together. 'You got it! I'll give you a hard one, Poppy, came out a few weeks back. I couldn't get it, asked the fruit sellers down Electric Avenue, the tube drivers, the girls behind the counter at Starbucks. Not one of us could get it. Nearly kicked ourselves when it was called out. A-ha, here they are!' Yes, right in there with the forks.

'What was it, then?' I ask.

'"Writing tools next to insects".' He hooks his glasses behind his ears and shakes his head. 'You'll never get it.'

'Let me think about it for a minute…' *Writing tools… Rulers? Pencils? Pens? Next to insects… Bugs? Roaches? Bees? Ants?* 'Okay, got it! Penzance,' I say.

Frank is looking at me open-mouthed. 'That's right. You're spot on… Just like that, you got it.'

'Give me another one,' I say. If I keep this up, he might forget about tonight's clue, or at least forget about it until I leave here to meet Tom and Leanne.

'"Female member of religious order cannot stop consuming"?'

'Nuneaton.' These are quite fun.

He's scratching his head. '"Monarch's girl"?'

'King's Lynn.'

'"Where ethnic music meets hard rock"?'

'Folkestone.'

Frank is smiling from ear to ear. He sticks out his hand to shake mine. 'Poppy, you are officially invited to join Team Frank. If we win this competition, I will give you half the money. Now how does that sound as an offer?'

I put my hand in his. 'Deal,' I say, and he looks pleased as Punch.

'So now I'm ready as I'll ever be. What's today's clue?'

I open my mouth to explain, but he shoves his hand up in front of me.

'And make an old man happy, Poppy – don't tell me the answer. I know you're a clever clogs, and I'm proud of you, you know that. But I love the chase, so just tell me the clue but not the answer.'

He's sitting in front of me, elbows on his knees, eyes closed like he's waiting to be anointed. I just can't tell him I have no clue.

'"Depressed dogs".'

His head tilts to the side, his tongue runs over his top lip.

'"Depressed dogs", you say? Are you sure?'

'Yes,' I lie. 'I am a hundred per cent sure. And I think I know the answer, too...'

His eyes spring open and he stands bolt upright. 'No, that's fine, I just want the clue, no answers.' He grabs his beer and shuffles out of the kitchen into the lounge. 'Have a good night,' he calls out to me, and that's it. I'm off the hook for now. While he's mulling over this made-up clue, I'll pop down to Electric Avenue and ask the fruit sellers for the real one. Tomorrow I'll just tell Frank that I misheard it but I know the correct version now so no harm done. Phew. Depressed dogs? Where on earth did that come from? Sometimes I think the psyche is one hot mess that should be left well alone.

Mum takes a hairdryer with a very elaborate nozzle and begins blow-drying separate sections of my hair. She's already plugged in a wand, tongs and a set of hot rollers. The kitchen counter is covered in serums, heat protectors, leave-in conditioners and, of course, cans upon cans of hairspray. My 'wash and go' days are well and truly over.

'Okay, now I'm going to let you into my thinking before we do the big reveal,' she says. 'You wanted sophisticated – you got it. You wanted more grown up – you got it. You wanted change – well, you certainly got that. The key thing with this look is that it is high-maintenance, and that is exactly what you need. If you don't get up in the morning to wash and style this baby, it's going to look like a rat's nest.' Yes, exactly what you want to hear from your hairdresser. 'But once it's done, even in your raggedy T-shirt and jeans, you'll look gorgeous, real old-school glamour. And you're going to be turning some heads, Poppy, so get used of it.'

She fans through my fringe with her fingers, sprays an ozone-destroying amount of hairspray at every angle and swings me around to the mirror.

HOLY SHIT. I am thoroughly not myself.

I am blonde.

The blondest shade of blonde I have ever seen!

I touch my face. I touch my hair. What's left of it. I lean in for a closer look, smoothing the long, tapered fringe down the right side of my face. It doesn't look like me, but I know it is, it has to be… I can see myself doing these things, but it does not feel normal.

'I had to take a lot off, to clear all that bulk – it was detracting from you.' Mum traces a finger down my cheekbone. 'You have a beautiful face, Poppy, look at that skin, those eyes.' She stands back with a hand on her hip. 'Dare I say you look a lot like I did at your age!'

I run my fingers over my neck and shake my swingy layers from side to side. They glisten with health and shine, the icy Scandinavian blonde making my skin appear more tanned and my eyes pop light blue.

How did she do this? Maybe Mum's ex-con crew look more like supermodels these days. Gun-toting, money-laundering, bad-ass hit women with smooth, glossy waves and indefatigable volume. I want to meet these women who have to make clean breaks and reinvent themselves again and again and again. Once everything settles, I'm going to take a trip to Mum's salon and pick up some tips.

I look to my mum's face in the background of the mirror.

'I love it. I absolutely LOVE it! Honestly, Mum, how did you even know this would work?'

There is a tear in her eye. I can feel a little tear in my own.

She fans herself with a tea towel. 'Job done. Nothing more rewarding than making people feel good about themselves. Best feeling in the world,' she says before she flops down on the chair and takes the remainder of the cava by the neck. 'Hardest bloody job I've ever done, though. Getting that colour just so… Anyway, it was worth it. You look stunning, sweetheart. Now go on upstairs and get yourself ready. It's Thursday night; as good as the weekend! Go and enjoy yourself!'

I've got twenty minutes to put on my face, slip into a simple black skater dress and slick some siren-red lipstick on. I'm ready for Leanne and for Tom, and I daresay, I'm ready for whatever else is thrown at me.

As long as it's good stuff. I'm definitely ready for some good stuff.

CHAPTER SEVEN

I am standing across from the Ritzy cinema. Couples drinking mulled wine and air-kissing friends are huddled together under outdoor heaters. This is our meeting point. The place I'll catch up with Leanne and Tom after nearly fifteen years of separate but parallel life paths. I wait on my tiptoes at the kerb. The pedestrian light is green but I won't venture over by myself until Leanne arrives. *Obviously*. I shudder at the idea of standing around like a random loner in full view of the Friday-night revellers. And what if Leanne is delayed? I'd have to shuffle around on the spot and pretend to talk on my phone. No thanks. I'll wait here, out of the way of the human traffic but with a perfect spy view of the Ritzy, shielded by the transient commuter mob.

Swingy-blonde-bob me. Red-lipstick-and-LBD me. Looking around Brixton, it's quite dazzling to take in the array of hair and fashion and body size and skin colour and tattoos and facial piercings. And the thing is, they all look so different, and extraordinary, amazingly artistic and individual in their own ways. Brixton has often been declared the melting pot within the melting pot that is multicultural London. But wow, this is really spectacular. The colours and patterns of the fabrics, the angles and cut of the clothes, the eye-popping make-up and jewellery make me feel like I'm watching a human gallery; a celebration of our species expressed in the most colourful and rich and eccentric way. And you know the best bit? It's unapologetic. It's unashamed. Everyone looks upbeat and unscripted because clearly they feel that way. They feel it from the inside out and they are not afraid to show it.

My phone rings. 'Hello?'

'Hi. It's Leanne. Where are you?'

'Just at the lights. I'll be there in ten seconds.' I glance over to the Ritzy, but still I can't see Leanne. I hope she hasn't been waiting ages for me to arrive.

'I'm so sorry, Poppy, but Leon's working late, the babysitter's not shown up and the owner of the pub next to the gym has just given me an earful about the alarm going off again, so I'm going to have to bail on you. I'm so, so sorry.'

'Not a problem! Don't worry at all, Leanne. We will definitely catch up again.'

'How much longer are you around for?' she asks me.

'Not sure really. I can pop into the gym sometime and we'll sort something out, okay?'

Ah well, it was good while it lasted. The thought of going out and having a laugh and showing off my new hair and gazing at Tom Jones with unclean thoughts was a nice idea. A great idea, even, but alas, not to be. So I guess it's back home for me to pack my 'Shit Bits' folder with a few more latent disappointments and unrealised dreams.

I hear a child's voice yelling in the background. 'That sounds like a really busy day you're having, Leanne. Are you okay? Can I do anything for you?' I offer.

'Cheers, but it'll be all right. Normal for this house.'

'Well, if you think of anything… I can come over and give you a hand if you like.'

'Ha! Thanks so much, Poppy, but honestly, I wouldn't wish that on my worst enemy. I'll save it for Leon when he gets home! But now that you mention it, there is something that would really help me out.'

'Yes, of course, anything at all.'

'Great. Can you go to the gym and tell Tom to charge up his phone and stop messing me about, and that the security alarm manual is in the bottom of the filing cabinet. He'll know what I mean.'

'Sure, no problem. Will do. See you soon, Leanne, and take care of yourself.'

As I hang up, I can hear at least three crying voices shrieking, 'Muuuummmm!' I didn't quite appreciate how much she had on her plate. My problems are minuscule in comparison. I've got no kids to feed or big bills to pay or employees to support. How does she keep going? I used to look up to Dr Winters and all her achievements and accolades, but really, I'm overcome with admiration for Leanne. I've probably focused too much on measuring success in terms of intellectual achievement through exams and grades and honours and awards. I've been applauded and celebrated and hailed by all sorts and I've enjoyed it, been proud of it, but... look at everything Leanne is doing, keeping so many things afloat, putting others before herself, taking charge and staying strong without a hint of recognition, without anyone giving her a medal or a title or a scholarship. And by the sound of it, this isn't a one-off event but an act of endurance, of stamina, of consistent effort and grit. Bloody hell, Leanne, I've got to hand it to you. You are SOME woman.

The pedestrian light turns from amber to red. As disappointed as I was to go home, it is a little bit terrifying to think I've now got to go and deliver Leanne's message to Tom ALL BY MYSELF!

But what choice do I have? Leanne can't come, and she can't reach Tom, and I promised I'd help. So what if he doesn't remember me, or if he remembers me as his sister's geeky little friend or one of the utterly indistinguishable small-voiced, downward-looking masses? Either way, it doesn't matter. It's not about me or who I am now or who I was then. I promised Leanne I'd help her, and that's what I'm going to do.

The light stays red. I take some deep breaths and shake out my swingy new hair, ready to put one foot in front of the other, walk right up to Tom Jones and do what I've got to do.

Gulp.

Despite the red light, I see a lull in the traffic and dash across the road towards the arches. I've broken into a sprint in an effort to get it over as quickly and painlessly as possible, but halfway there, I pause, stop and steady myself. I think of Leanne and my mother and the girls at the salon, how they meet stuff head on, and I decide that today, I'm going to do that too. Even if I'm just pretending, even if it's not quite right, I'm going to try it out. What I'm not going to be is the mousy-voiced girl who avoids eye contact and hides in books and puzzles. I slow down. I take a slow, sure step and a slow, deep breath and my heart takes a slow, measured beat.

Poppy, can you handle this? Just watch me 'cos I'm ALL OVER this.

I turn the corner, certain that I'm in the right place. I can hear the alarm blaring from here, and sure enough, there's a sign outside in graffiti lettering reading *Gymbox*. Two men are standing just outside the doorway. From this distance I can't tell if one of them is Tom; anyway, after all this time, he may be totally unrecognisable. Nearly fifteen years! He might be utterly changed.

But God, let's hope not.

The taller one lifts his sunglasses, breaks into a smile and pats the other man on the arm. Now there is no doubt in my mind. There he is; that's Tom Jones. Thoroughly unchanged. Same tousled blonde hair, dark green eyes and, of course, those dimples. But he looks bigger, broader, stronger, even next to the other guy, who has a tight crew cut and a puffed-out superhero chest.

The shorter man slices a finger across his neck, then slides his phone out of his back pocket. Tom nods sadly and turns his head towards the gym, his hand cupping his ear, before taking a long sidestep over to help a frazzled mother lift a buggy over the kerb. As I get closer, I can hear what the short man is saying.

'I'm sick of it, Tom. This alarm of yours is costing me business!' He points over to the pub on the corner. 'All my after-work drinkers have got up and left; who the hell wants to come and have a quiet pint with this racket in their ear? I'm done playin' Mr Nice Guy. If you don't sort it out, I'll sort it out for you, and believe me, you won't like it one bit.'

Tom keeps a light smile on his face, his eyebrows knitted together earnestly. 'I get it, George. I know where you're coming from and I'm sorry. I really, really am. This'll be the last time, I promise. Leanne's sending the engineer around right as we speak.'

'Oh yeah, ring her then.'

'I can't, my phone is out of juice.'

The angry publican shakes his head. 'Basics, Tom, you need to get yourself together. Make yourself a list, write stuff down. Maybe if you wrote down the bloody code, we wouldn't be in this mess in the first place.'

'It'll get sorted, I promise,' says Tom, crossing and then uncrossing his arms.

'Tom?' I wave as I try to interject.

He turns to me, a glimmer of hope in his eyes. 'Yeah?'

'Leanne sent me down to meet you,' I tell him, and try a muted wave to the publican as well.

Tom claps his hands together. 'Ah, see, George! I told you we'd sort it! The help has arrived! We'll have this fixed in no time, mate.'

The publican looks him up and down and then shrugs. 'Ten minutes, Tom, I mean it this time. If it's still blaring, I'm picking up the phone and reporting you to the coppers. I will shut you down, don't think I won't.' He clenches his fist and the muscles flex in his neck.

'I'm going to have it sorted, I promise. Ten minutes and everything will be just fine.'

I hope he's right. This guy looks like he might not be able to wait ten minutes.

'Let's get going.' Tom turns on his heel, places his hand on my elbow and guides me in through the rotating doors of the gym. 'Perfect timing. Thank God you're here. George was ready to beat the crap out of me. We need to get this fixed, and fast.'

The gym is empty, and it's no wonder. The shrill pitch and volume of the alarm is deafening. We walk by reception, through the weights area and into a little glass-panelled office with one desk, one chair, a bright pink filing cabinet and a flashing metal box in the top left corner of the room. I stand in the doorway as Tom points and shouts over the din.

'There it is, please work your magic.'

I tilt my head to the side and draw my brows together. 'What do you mean?' I ask.

'Fix it! Make it stop! As you've probably gathered, I'm under a bit of pressure. I've got eight minutes before George flips and calls the cops and then I'll be forced to use everyone's wages to pay the emergency callout guy and Leanne will string me up by my balls, so when you're ready...'

I raise my hands, palms open, and shrug my apology. 'But I can't fix it. I just know where the manual is. That's why I'm here.'

Tom tilts his weight onto one foot and rubs his neck. 'But you said Leanne sent you.'

'No. Well, yes. I'm Leanne's friend. *Poppy?* She sent me to tell you to turn on your phone and that the manual is in the bottom drawer of the filing cabinet.'

'Poppy, yeah, Leanne said we were at school together...' Tom runs his palms down his face and tightens his lips. 'I see. Well... shit.' He looks at his watch. 'Right, we now have six minutes. This bloody manual better have the passcode written inside.'

He hunches down on his knees and starts searching through the drawer. He pulls out the manual, leafs through the first and last pages, glances over the front and back cover and shakes his head.

'Nope. No code. No surprise. I knew I didn't write it down anywhere, I just thought I'd be able to remember it. Friggin' hell, a few numbers – you'd think that'd be easy, right?'

He throws the book at me. It is easily as thick as an old-fashioned phone book. I catch it with both hands.

'So there you go. Maybe you can work out how to disable it.'

Hmm… Disabling alarm systems isn't my typical night out party trick. But I can see the despair in his eyes. I need to try. If it's a manual, then it's pretty much designed to help normal people in exactly this type of emergency situation work out what to do. I swallow hard. Yes, just go to the index, find the instructions on disabling and it will stop. How hard can it be?

I open it up. The pages are tissue-paper thin. The font is teensy. I squint closer to the unfamiliar lettering… The manual is written *in Korean*.

'I don't think this is going to be much help,' I tell him.

Tom runs his fingers through his hair and shakes his head. 'No point looking at me. I'm dyslexic… I hate to write and I hate to read, so a big monster book like that is a complete head-fuck for me.'

He slumps on to the chair. Deflated. The screaming alarm pierces the air and overwhelms the tiny space. We sit in hopeless silence, the noise becoming oppressive and menacing.

Tom looks up at the flashing box. 'I don't know what else I can do. I've already tried everything. I know you're no engineer, but can't you just look at it? There's nothing to lose at this point.'

'I really don't have a clue about this,' I begin, but I see him sinking in front of me.

'Leanne is going to go absolutely berserk.' He breathes into his cupped hands.

I need to try. As Tom says, there's nothing to lose, so I don't have to worry about making matters worse or failing or messing things up. I can tell by his tone that we're already at rock bottom. So the very least I can do is show willing.

'Okay,' I say, and he jumps to his feet, a slight spark in his beautiful olive-green eyes. He looks to the revolving office chair, then to the box high up on the wall, and then to me. 'You won't make it standing on that chair, though. Wrong height, and it's too unstable.'

Okay, so I guess that's the end of that short-lived plan. Unless I can solve this telepathically or he's got a pair of stilts handy, there isn't a chance of me reaching that box.

He flashes me a look 'I know. We can still do this.'

'Really?'

'Yep.' Tom offers me his hand. 'Stand on the desk and then hook your legs over my shoulders. That way you'll be eye level.'

'Are you serious?'

'Yes. Of course I'm serious. How else can we do it?' he asks, a bemused smile playing on his lips.

'But I'm wearing a skirt!'

'So?' he says, his face unflinching.

'I don't really know you… like, not enough to put my, you know… beside your, um, head.' I can't even get the words out; they jam in my throat. I drop my eyes to the floor, my cheeks burning at the thought of the closeness, the intimacy. An hour ago I was nervous about shaking his hand after so many years, never mind clutching his head between my legs. Oh dear God.

He nods and then thrusts his hand out in front of him. 'Hi Poppy, nice to see you again.'

'Um… you too,' I tell him, shaking his outstretched hand, glad of the distraction. A bit of formality is a welcome distancing gesture. Civilised, chivalrous, manageable.

He bows with mock drama, and then glances up to the clock. 'So now that we are properly reacquainted, we've got three minutes left. So please, Poppy, for me, for Leanne, for George and my potentially broken and bruised body, for the party of a hundred and the band booked to play in the pub… please, climb on board.'

I open my mouth to say that I'm too heavy and that I think this is too much, too soon, but before the words can even leave my lips, Tom looks me directly in the eye and gently places his hand on my cheek. 'I won't drop you,' he says, and I nod and don't look away and I know that all my resolutions have dissolved into fine particles of dust.

I scamper up on to the table, and once I am standing, he crouches in front of me. I slide my thighs over his shoulders, tightening them around either side of his head. Then I hook my feet under his arms to steady myself. And I feel steady. He is rock solid underneath me. I guess there might be something to this going-to-the-gym business after all. He spins around with me in position and smoothly walks over to the flashing box as if I was light as a feather.

'Two minutes. Come on, Poppy. Give it your best shot.'

Oh, I really want to… I really, really want to, for him and for Leanne and for myself, but I'm not hopeful. I have never figured out a passcode on an alarm system before in my life. Fair enough, at school I was the chief codebreaker in the Mensa society, and we often had to decipher encryptions or work out complex sequences, but again, like everything in my life to date, this all just existed on paper as an exercise of the mind, a fun little challenge to do when you were bored. And I did get bored sitting upstairs in the advanced studies classroom, peering out onto the football pitch to gaze dreamily at Tom Jones…

I glance down and see his blonde wavy tendrils a fingertip's distance away from my belly button. I'm suddenly overcome with the reality of it. I'm alone in a back office with a gorgeous but strange man… Well, not exactly a strange man. A man I hopelessly crushed on as a schoolgirl. And now here I am perched on his shoulders. I feel dizzy at the thought of it. At the sensation of it; the warmth of him against my bare skin, his smell, like salty caramel.

'One minute thirty seconds,' says Tom from underneath my skirt. I clench, and then realise that the way I'm sitting, he's going to feel that clench. Probably right at the back of his neck. *This is no position for secret clenching.* I clench again involuntarily. Oh my God. Is this the best or the worst day of my life ever?

'Any luck? How does it look up there?'

Okay, Poppy, concentrate. Slap all impure thoughts about being wrapped around Tom Jones's beautiful head out of the way and try your damnedest to work this out.

'Well, the display shows that there are four digits required,' I call down.

'Yeah, I know. I've already tried everything I thought would work: 1234, then 0000, then mine and Leanne's birth year, but no luck.'

'Did you ever know the passcode?'

'Yeah, once upon a time… I just can't remember it. I've racked my brains, but I'm totally blank on what it could be.'

'Sure. I understand. If you could think back, do you remember if there were any double digits?

'Umm, let me think…' I hear Tom muttering to himself.

'Close your eyes and picture yourself at the keypad, and pay attention to where your finger is going. Is it top left? Top right? Over to the centre? Just try to visualise it in your mind. Use your finger if necessary.'

I examine the box while Tom concentrates. There are no clues anywhere – no sticker with a reminder, no numbers etched into the polished metal box. This is looking hopeless. I expect that fuming George the publican is watching the passing of every second, eagerly awaiting his time to pounce and make the threatened call. And at this rate, it looks like he'll be speaking to the police and lodging his complaint very soon indeed.

'Poppy, I think I remember! I can see it! I remember pressing the same number twice in a row on the keypad… actually, yes, I can picture myself doing it…'

'Amazing! What was it?'

'Aggh!' I hear him swallow hard. 'I just can't think… I'm sorry, it's my brain: letters and numbers just don't stick.'

'No, that's fine, that's good. The number of four-digit combinations is relatively easy to calculate.'

'Really?'

'Yeah… so you have ten choices for the first digit, then ten for the second, so that's ten times ten – a hundred choices for the first two digits; then you have ten choices for the third digit, so that's a thousand choices for the first three digits.' I'm speaking out loud, as much for myself as for Tom.

'I have no idea what you are talking about.'

'Well, it means there are ten thousand possible combinations…'

'Okay, great, get started. Try them all out.'

Tom doesn't get it. It's technically impossible for us to do that within the time we have available without a team of trained administrators and a methodical strategy to ensure no repetition.

'I can't. I'll need to write them all down, work out a system. We can't just randomly type in numbers; we won't be able to record what's not worked, and we haven't got time even with two of us' I explain.

He is silent for a moment. Then he shouts so loudly it makes me jump. 'Five! Right smack in the middle of the keypad! I pressed five twice! I can see it clear as day! The first two digits are five and five… a hundred per cent no doubt in my mind.'

'Okay, that's good, but it still means there are a hundred choices left for the last two,' I explain.

'Well, we've got a minute left. Start punching numbers in… Just try.'

'A hundred combinations in sixty seconds? We'll never do it.'

'What have we got to lose? Any system, any order you like, but just get on it, give it a try.'

'Okay,' I sigh. I admire Tom's optimism and fearlessness, but let's face facts: our chances of finding the combination are very, very slim. And within the time scale, highly improbable. But I do it; I listen to Tom and try to breathe in his optimism and I start to punch in the numbers.

5501

5502

5503

5504

Nothing. Surprise, surprise. If anything, the blaring siren seems to be getting even louder, screaming in my ears and making my head throb.

'Don't stop now, Poppy. Keep going,' Tom encourages.

5505

5506

5507

5508

5509

'How much time left?' I ask.

'Ten seconds.' I can hear in his voice that he's still hopeful, still believes we can do it.

I sigh deeply. 'But Tom, ten seconds and ninety more combinations…

'Don't stop now, Poppy.'

5510

5511

5512

5513

I'm beginning to lose hope. Tom might not even be right about the double fives. For all we know, we could be totally off.

5514

And then it stops.

The urgent red light stops flashing. The screeching of the alarm cuts to a halt. Perfect silence gushes forth from every angle.

I sit still on Tom's shoulders and wait for something to happen: for the box to blow up or the police to rush in or the power to cut, but nothing happens. Just beautiful, peaceful, silent nothing.

'You did it, Poppy! You did it!'

Tom's hands slide into the back of my knees and he starts to victory-dance in the middle of the office. I can't stop laughing. I can't believe this. I can't believe that we worked it out. I can't believe that we are here, like this, celebrating together. I slip my hands into his hair and hold on to the sides of his head as we bounce around the office, like I'm holding on to the saddle at a rodeo.

'Let me down, you nutcase!' I hear myself laughing, but his hands glide up to my waist and he bounces us left and right as if we're part of an imaginary conga line, out through the weights area, out through the front doors, into the busy Brixton side street and straight into George's pub, where he lifts me from his shoulders and plops me on the bar counter.

'That was incredible,' he says as our eyes meet.

'That *was* incredible,' I agree.

George appears behind the bar and flutters a hand by his heart. 'Whoa, you were cutting it very fine there, Tom: a second later and I'd have been talking to the Chief Constable. Anyway, all's well that ends well. You stopping for a drink?'

Tom turns to me with a glint of mischief in his eyes. 'Poppy, my beautiful saviour, would you do me the great honour of allowing me to buy you a drink?'

My beautiful saviour. Did he just call me that? Tom Jones thinks I'm beautiful? A surge of heat rushes from my chest to my neck. I need to compose myself. Take a minute before I start to gush and crumble and flake with sheer happiness and overwhelming surprise.

'I'd love that. Large vodka and Coke, please,' I tell him, and excuse myself to go to the loo.

Just so I can sit for a moment. Even if it is on a toilet. Just so I can think. Just so I can press my burning, flushed cheeks up against the cold white tiles and bring my temperature and my heart rate and my wildly inappropriate thoughts about Tom Jones right back down to earth.

I don't know what lies ahead, and I don't know if we have even the slightest chance of success – we're a highly improbable combination, an uncommon pair – but, just like our seemingly elusive passcode, no matter what the odds, it's always worth a try.

I stand up, smooth down my skirt and pat my cheeks. I'm going out there to have a drink with Tom Jones. Just the two of us. God, he is still divine. Divine and dimply and dashing and delicious. My stomach flipping, I breathe deeply, straighten my back and check myself in the mirror. Note to self: from now on, I, Poppy Bloom, promise not to be swayed or disheartened by the statistical probability of success. Instead, I'm going to give new things a try and I'm not going to give up until my heart, rather than my head, tells me to.

CHAPTER EIGHT

'Thanks for helping me out, especially because Leanne had to bail. You could've easily just delivered her message and legged it, so I really appreciate it.'

'It's no problem, really.'

'Are you hungry?' Tom asks me.

'Always,' I answer.

'Are you fussy?'

I shake my head. 'Not at all. I'm easy.'

Tom nods approvingly, and we drain our drinks and set off side by side along the pavement. To anyone passing, we look like two friends out for a normal evening. Two friends looking forward to some good food, some cold drinks and some laughs thrown in. I sneak a sideways glance at him as we cross the road. His features are still boyish under a thin veil of stubble, but of course he's all grown up. And he is mesmerising. My hand still tingles from his touch.

We walk through the Brixton Village food arcade, which used to be where people came to buy bags of chicken claws and ox tongues before it was transformed, Yuppified, gentrified and glorified as *the* foodie hub of south London. The inner arcade is lined with mismatched vintage chairs for the champagne bars and artisan charcuterie and cheese caves. Japanese cafés jostle alongside authentic Spanish, Mexican, Caribbean, Italian and Thai street-food stalls. Not an ox tongue in sight.

'Oh wow, this place has changed,' I say.

'You better believe it. I've been here all my life and I still can't keep up. How long since you were here last?'

'About ten years.'

He starts laughing and stops in his tracks. 'Where have you been all this time?'

'Oh, studying…'

'Just studying? For over ten years?'

'Um, pretty much.'

He shrugs in a live-and-let-live kind of way. 'Right, well in that case, we've got to get you up to speed. Follow me'

He leads me to a gourmet burger place on the corner called Dirty Dicks. I notice that they left out the apostrophe they need to show possession. Surely they mean Dirty Dick's? I want to point it out to them. I lie. I want to grab a felt-tip marker and stencil it in myself.

'The three-stack bacon burger with onion rings and slaw is immense. Half a cow in a bap,' Tom tells me.

'I see.' Everyone in this place looks like a trucker. There's food everywhere. Fine dining this ain't. Bread in their beards, cheese being sucked off their big hairy fingers; one old biker is even licking barbecue sauce off his forearm. I don't think they made a mistake, actually. I think they knew exactly what they were doing when they called it Dirty Dicks. *Build it and they will come.*

'This is… *was* my best friend Gav's favourite place. He moved to Australia. Haven't been here since he left.'

'I think it's great. Let's do it,' I tell him. Because after all, it's worth a try.

We wait by the door to be seated, and eventually the red-faced hipster owner shakes his beardy head at us: full and there's a waiting list. No apology.

Unfazed, we go to the Italian; also full. I peer inside; there's not even a tiny space on the long communal wooden bench for us to squeeze into. And then the same again from the rosebud-lipped waitress at the Colombian and the smiley gold-toothed jerk-chicken guy too. I spot that Mr Sushi has an empty table and nod towards it.

'That looks good – you okay with Japanese?' I ask.

I notice Tom take a deep breath and rub his eyes. 'Yeah, I guess.'

'What's wrong? They've got a free seat by the window. We can just have something quick,' I say.

He sighs and looks up and down the arcade. My stomach rumbles loudly; I feel hollow. I need to eat something in the next ten minutes or I'll get despondent. Or full of rage – it could go either way.

He shakes his head, a shy frown playing on his lips. 'It's not the food. It's this place. I used to come here with my ex, Tammy.' He pulls a reluctant face and scratches his neck.

I can tell he is still raw. This is about moving away, moving on, creating distance between what was and what is. So who is this Tammy who has left such a deep impression on him? Why is she his ex? Clearly he must have ended it with her. Who would possibly end things with him? But if he ended it, then why is he still so affected? I puzzle a moment. And then it hits me: she must be DEAD! Oh, poor Tom! He is grieving! He is grieving and I've just steered him towards a high-trigger emotional site and now he could experience a full-on emotional avalanche.

I grab him by the forearm. 'Oh Tom, I'm really sorry. This was clearly a bad idea… a good idea, but too soon… a good idea at a bad time, is what I mean. Why don't we head home, eh? Call it a night?' Another rumble from my stomach. A cluster of other people have spotted our table.

Tom looks at my hand resting on his jacket sleeve and then at me. Then he claps his hands together. 'Nah. Let's go in. I'm starving. And I need a beer. Tammy's off living her own life now, so why shouldn't I? It's been a long day, we should definitely be having a nice ice-cold beer by now.'

I agree with him. Wholeheartedly. And I breathe a massive sigh of relief that Tammy is in fact STILL ALIVE.

Tom swings open the door in front of us just before the other group make their move. Teamwork. Mr Sushi happily waves us to the table by the window, and we order two beers and a mixed platter to share. As we sip our drinks, we watch all the other would-be diners bounce from crammed restaurant to crammed restaurant. Crowds of people start flooding through the door only to be refused and redirected outside. Tom smacks his hands down on the table.

'So, you've been away for more than a decade, and now you're back and you're… married?'

I shake my head.

'In a relationship?'

I shake it again.

'It's complicated?'

'Warmer.'

'Well, I'm all ears. Tell me everything. And start from the beginning.'

It's like he's unlocked something. Because once I start, I just can't seem to stop. He doesn't interrupt me or compare my situation to his own or ask me intrusive questions or tell me what I should've done or what I should do next. He just listens. Really listens. And I do tell him everything.

I tell him all about my dad and my studies and Banbridge and Harriet and Gregory and moving back home and not having a job and feeling a complete failure and at a total loss about what I should do next. And he listens to every word I say, and the funny thing is, the *way* he listens makes me listen to myself. Stuff pours out of my mouth that I've never really said aloud to anyone before; that I never even knew was there. I never realised that what hurt me more than losing the fellowship was feeling so betrayed by the people I thought cared about me. But I also understand that they are not the only ones who care. I have Mum and Frank and Leanne, and even my dad in his own messed-up way.

Mr Sushi starts to sweep the floor underneath the neighbouring tables and we realise that we are the last ones in the restaurant. The kitchen staff zip up their hoodies and wave their goodbyes and we realise that we're probably the last ones in the entire arcade.

'I'm sorry. I've talked your ear off,' I say. 'We'd better go.'

We thank Mr Sushi and step out of Brixton Village into the yellow glow of the street lamps.

'Thanks for tonight. I enjoyed it,' Tom says, bracing himself against the wind.

'Really, you enjoyed it? You might need to pick up some Nurofen on the way home; your head must be ringing after this evening.'

'No need for Nurofen at all. In fact, I feel better than I have done in ages.'

He shuffles on the spot and for a second I'm actually afraid that he is going to lean in and kiss me. Really. I think Tom Jones is about to kiss me and I'm *afraid*. God, my teenage self would smack me across the back of the head right now.

I'm watching him. His eyes have drifted down towards my lips. It's not in my imagination, I'm certain of it. He has this half-smile and his lips are slightly parted and he's breathing through his nose and I can read the big bold lettering of his thoughts… He's thinking about it, but no, I can't. I'm not ready.

I thrust my hand forward. 'I enjoyed it too,' I tell him.

Which is the truth. The honest-to-God truth. I've had a great time.

But kissing him. I need to prepare for that. As in *mentally* prepare for that. I've dreamt of kissing him, and I admit to even practising on the back of my hand when I was younger, but it's different now, *I'm* different, we're older, I need to… I need more time. I slip my hand into his and he curls his warm, strong fingers around mine. But he doesn't let go straight away. And neither do I. We linger like this a beat too long, our hands locked together against the fading light, two virtual strangers in the middle of a swarming street waiting for the other to let go.

It's me who steps back first. I'm overwhelmed, my hand hot and sweaty from the intensity, the contact. 'I'd better go now,' I say.

We wave our goodbyes and I watch Tom walk towards the gym. Then I take five steps backwards before I turn and let the full breadth of my smile spread across my face.

All the fruit sellers have packed up for the night and Starbucks is closed, but I need to get this clue for Frank before I go home. I stop at the newspaper vendor outside the tube station.

'Excuse me, any chance you heard the clue for today? "You Do the Maps" on 105 FM?'

He pulls his chin into his neck, like I've just asked him to lift the lid on a matter of national secrecy. 'It doesn't work like that, love, that's not how you play the game. You really think I'm just going to help you out when I've done all the graft, and watch you scoop the ten grand from under my nose?'

'Sorry, but I just missed it tonight because—'

'If you want to know the clue, you'll have to listen in to the morning show with Jake Jackson and see if he repeats it for you – some days he does, but some days he doesn't.'

I buy a paper and thank him for his help, however hard-won, and the next thing I know, I'm back at home. Frank is in the living room, his face barely visible in the flicker of television light. He's tucking into a bowl of crisps, laughing heartily at the top ten funniest pet moments. My mum is stretched out asleep across his lap. The empty cava bottle is on the coffee table beside her feet.

'You're home early. How'd it go?' asks Frank.

'Great, thanks.' I touch my hand and think of Tom. 'Amazingly great.'

Frank shuffles up in his seat and gently lifts my mum's snoring head onto a cushion. I pull a blanket over her. I pause for a moment and let the realisation of how lucky I am wash over me.

'Thank you, Frank.'

'For what, love?' he asks, confused.

'For everything.'

He chuckles, probably thinking I'm a bit tipsy and getting overly sentimental. But I want him to know how much he means to me. How much he's given to my mum and how he shows me every day what small, ordinary love looks like. And this small, ordinary love is the truest sort of all, made up of unprompted acts of kindness and incidental smiles and hugs and winks and kisses.

I kiss him goodnight and set my alarm for 6.30, because I have a small and ordinary act of love that I need to accomplish tomorrow. I need to be wide awake for the morning radio programme so that I can get Frank's clue.

So, Jake Jackson, if you can tune in and pick up my vibe, please, please, please, feel the love and repeat the clue tomorrow, because I can't afford to miss it again, no matter what.

CHAPTER NINE

I hear the cold, whistling wind rattle against my bedroom window, so I do as I do every morning and pull the duvet over my head. One thing I've discovered about myself is that I always wake up about four minutes before the alarm goes off. And these four minutes are the only time I feel like I'm truly living in the moment, savouring every second, not remembering the unconscious past, effectively shutting down thoughts of the future. I love these gorgeous pre-alarm minutes; I want to stay in them forever.

But then the alarm actually does go off and I press snooze and the protective seal is broken. That's when the thought goons start to surface: *Why am I still here? Am I ever going to have enough money to move out? Should I go to the gym? Why is everything so heavy at the gym? Does Tom like me? Why did Gregory dump me? Tom only likes me because he doesn't really know me… but what if he's different? What if this is different? What if…* My brain is on rotation.

These snooze moments are fraught. I know I should get up, but I don't want to. I know I'm getting closer to the stage where it's best to move, to seize the day, to make waves. But I'll just stay here in the snuggly warmth one more minute and think about Tom… imagine, just imagine that… Tom and me… and then BEEEP! BEEEP! the bastardy alarm goes again. Already? A whole three minutes of snooze time gone already? I give the clock the evil eye and then slap it on its annoying flashing head.

Fine. Have it your way. I'm getting up.

I check out my new hairdo in the mirror. Good God. Mum wasn't wrong about the rat's nest analogy. Except this rat's nest looks as if it's been soaked in peroxide and scorched dry by a blowtorch. This must be similar to what Britney saw in the mirror that time, and it triggered such an existential breakdown that she had to shave it all off.

I step into the shower. The water is freezing cold, but I thrust myself underneath the shower head anyway. Slowly it warms to tepid. I scrub my face and let the water run down my body. For a warm, fluid moment, the world is beautiful again, bursting with possibility, and nothing hurts. I think about Tom touching my hand, nudging me at the table, smiling at me with his cheeky half-smile. But then the pipes make a clanging sound and the water glugs to a halt before the shower head suddenly sprays out absolutely boiling-hot water with ferocious pressure. I jump out, half scalded. If this morning has taught me anything, it's that timing is everything: don't hold out, don't be greedy, take what you need and go. I look to my hand. Be grateful for the tingle.

As I dress, I pinch some soft skin on my tummy and think about going to the gym. Two birds with one stone there, and I get to support Leanne's business. Plus I might actually enjoy it. I've certainly got the time. As yet, I still have no job. I'll check my emails this morning and see if Markus has come up with anything suitable. I'm not holding out much hope, though.

I *am* holding out hope that Dr Burley will call me back and say that he has charmed his devoted secretary Margot into taking early retirement so that he can slip me seamlessly into her position. I can return to Banbridge quickly and efficiently and stay there until I'm ancient. Perfect.

But today I might give the gym a go. Maybe I'll even bump into Tom.

Downstairs, I twist the dial on Frank's battered transistor radio. As my parents don't come into any contact with technology via their jobs, they haven't really boarded the spacecraft of the digital era. 105 FM is already tuned in and *The Jake Jackson Morning Show* will begin at seven o'clock. I start the coffee machine. 'Today is the first day of the rest of my life,' I sing to myself, and today it feels like it could be.

'Good morning, Britain!'

I turn up the radio. I haven't heard this guy before. He sounds youngish, maybe late thirties? There's laughter in his voice, like we've just caught him in the middle of something really witty or really rude. 'It's Friday! And wow, have we got a jam-packed line-up for you this morning, so stay tuned, people, this is a show you simply cannot afford to miss.'

He's right there. I can't afford to let Frank down. I need this clue as a gesture of thanks, to show how aware I am of how well he takes care of Mum and me.

'And we'll throw in a little cryptic clue that may help you on your way to winning a really great ten thousand pounds! Only here on 105 FM – your station, your way.'

He's going to do it! Jake Jackson is going to give out the clue a second time. He must've heard my prayer. I press my palm to my heart. Everything is looking up. Everything is starting to co-operate. Thank God.

I settle down with my fresh dark-roast coffee, pen and paper at the ready, and listen in as Jake introduces his first guest of the morning, renowned agony aunt, the 'straight-up, no-nonsense' Hilary Clive.

Ugh. I curl my lip at the little transistor. This woman is vile, constantly courting controversy with hateful and divisive comments. I've seen her on chat shows calling women fat, making fun of children's names and insisting that poverty is a lifestyle choice for the lazy. I can't understand why she is allowed on air, cannot understand why such cruel and hurtful comments are casually pumped into the ears of the nation.

I really don't want to listen to her ruffle feathers for no good reason beyond her own vain self-advancement. But what can I do? I can't turn her off or else I'll miss Frank's clue.

'Hilary will be here for the next hour or so to help with any problems or issues you may be facing of an emotional or personal nature. She's a self-professed relationship expert, with over twenty-five years of experience in dealing with the highs and lows between lovers, friends and families. So get in touch; our resident agony aunt is live and kicking here this morning to take your calls.'

I bite my lip. *One hour.* One hour of listening before I can turn this rubbish off. At least I'm alone, that's one small mercy. Imagine if anyone caught me listening to this trash. Imagine Dr Winters arrived unexpectedly to say that she'd made a horrible mistake and wanted me back, only to find me sitting here listening to the lowest form of populist media imaginable. Oh, the shame of it. I shiver with paranoia and pull my mum's net curtains across, just in case anyone of note is prowling around and might expose my dirty little listening secret. I remind myself that once I've scribbled down the clue, I'll be free of the aural torture that is Hilary Clive once and for all. I'll let whatever crap she spouts roll off me, water off a duck's back. No getting angry or riled or upset. I'm having a nice morning and I'm not about to let a snide old witch like her spoil it for me.

I hear her voice cackle across the airways. 'Good morning, Jake, lovely as always to be here. I understand that sometimes it can be difficult to share our intimate concerns with people close to us; we need a neutral pair of ears and an objective response. So feel free to reach out this morning, articulate your feelings, and we will try our best to ensure that you have some truthful, professional advice so that you are in better shape after your call than before.'

Better shape? Yeah, right, complete emotional carnage more like.

Jake chimes in. 'So, London, Hilary is live in the studio and available to take on whatever you want to throw at her. You can email us, call us, get in touch on Facebook or Twitter – whatever is easiest for you. We look forward to hearing from you. But before that, what better way to start the day than with a bit of… *uh oh, uh oh, uh oh, oh no no…* I know it's not very manly, or current, or acceptable in any measure, but you gotta love it. It's "Crazy in Love" by Queen Bey herself. Let's turn it up, people!'

I do exactly as he says. Turn my favourite song from my favourite singer right up to full volume. Good move, Jake! A bit of Beyoncé always takes the edge off. The music, the cryptic clues and Jake himself are all really good; perfectly listenable. So why on earth do they want to be within spitting distance of Hilary Clive, never mind give her such a prime slot? Ratings, I guess. What is it they say? Even bad publicity is good publicity. And Hilary certainly knows how to cause a stir. She has carved out a niche as everyone's favourite media villain, and even though I get that it's show-business, she still makes my blood boil.

I knock back the last dregs of my first cup of coffee and pour my second. Extra strong.

'We have loads of queries coming through via email, so let's get stuck in. The first is from Melissa, thirty-four years old from Lewisham, who says, "Hi, Jake and Hilary. Two weeks after the love of my life and partner of ten years proposed, I found out he had been repeatedly unfaithful. Up to this point I thought things were great. Then I started to get anonymous emails claiming my boyfriend was a cheater. He denied there was any truth to it, but I started digging and discovered he was lying. He broke down and told me he suspected they were being sent by a girl he had been sleeping with on and off for quite a while. I'm just so crushed. I was genuinely blindsided, but I still can't imagine my life without him. I'm really struggling with what to do next. I feel like he is serious about trying to fix this. I know that I still love him and I do think that I would be capable of forgiving him. I just worry that people who do these horrible things never really change and that maybe by staying with him I'm letting myself down. I'm not ready to leave him and move on, but am I crazy for wanting to try?" Ouch,' Jake concludes, mirroring my own sentiments exactly.

I place my coffee cup down on the table. I hadn't realised how much my hand was shaking. Gregory dumped me and ran into Harriet's arms. And that still hurts. It hurts that he doesn't want to be with me any more. That she forgot about me and dismissed my feelings so quickly. But this letter. This is hell. Because Melissa loves her boyfriend and wants him back. I realise that I don't want Gregory back. I don't know if I even want Harriet back. None of this is easy. None of this is clear-cut. None of us knows what the best thing to do is. I hear you, Melissa!

I listen to Jake as he clears his throat. 'Thanks for getting in touch and being so open and honest, Melissa. I'll pass this on to our in-house professional – my heart goes out to you, though.'

Hear, hear! I take the radio down from the shelf and put it on the table beside me. I'm intrigued to hear what Hilary's going to tell her. Stay or go? Return or cut free? How do we know when to turn back to what was, and when to move on to what will be? I need to hear the answer almost as much as Melissa does.

I hear Hilary breathe loudly through her nose. 'Well. You've got yourself into a right mess here, Melissa. You're crazy for wanting to try, and to be truthful, I don't know why you bothered writing at all, as it's clear that you have already made up your mind to take him back. Perhaps you're the reason for him doing this in the first place. He may never even have looked at another woman if he really thought you would ever leave him. And he's been proved right, hasn't he? Even after everything, here you are entertaining the idea of a happy-ever-after. Never in my twenty-five years have I seen a leopard change its spots, and that goes for your cheating fiancé and you as a spineless facilitator.'

I spit my coffee back into my cup. Have I actually just HEARD that? Oh my God, Hilary Clive. I knew you could be a heartless witch, but this is another level entirely; this is beyond decent! Talk about kicking someone when they're down! Poor Melissa. She wrote in for help and what has she got to show for it? A humiliating public whipping on air! Blamed for someone else's actions!

I am tempted to turn this toxic dragon off. Her poisonous claptrap is airing all over London. I know my mum listens with her girls in the salon in Holloway. I toy with the transistor, so close to just switching it off, but I need this bloody clue.

As soon as Jake coughs it up, I'm tuning out. For ever. One hundred per cent, this will be my first and last morning associated with this station.

'Whoa, Hilary, that sounds very harsh, and with all due respect, very unfair.' Jake's voice cuts in across her, snappy and urgent. It is clear that she has offended him too. 'After all, it's not Melissa that's done the cheating. Let's hear from our listeners; they're usually a compassionate lot. Caller on line one. Hi, Peggy, you're live on air.'

Come on, Peggy, give it to her! Tell Hilary where to go! Demand she packs her bags, threaten to protest or boycott, whatever, but let her know she's not speaking for the masses. Make sure she understands that she is completely alone with her venomous opinions.

'I don't usually agree with Hilary on this show, but today I think she's actually speaking sense.'

I slam my hand down on the table. What are you talking about, Peggy? Don't you fuel this! Think about Melissa! What do you think she needs to hear right now?

Peggy sounds like she's been smoking twenty Benson & Hedges a day since the end of the Second World War. 'I took back a cheating husband and it was the worst mistake of my life. They're hard-wired to do it; no amount of therapy or threats will change them. That girl needs to drop him now. And grow herself a brain in the meantime.'

I can't bear this. Since when did everyone decide that being cruel and judgemental and speaking your mind without any regard for other people's feelings was the best way to live? I sincerely hope that no kids are listening in to this, because if they think Hilary is a role model, the next generation is stuffed.

'Caller two, Daryl on the line. Have you got any CONSTRUCTIVE advice for Melissa?' Jake asks.

Come on, Daryl, we need you. As a member of the listening public, we need an ambassador, a hero, somebody to say that this isn't what we want to hear!

'I think the poor girl is being very wise in her approach here – she is treating the cheating like an addiction, and that's exactly what it is.' Daryl has a very gentle speaking voice, like he's reading the shipping forecast. 'We are taught to hate the sin but love the sinner, and that is what Melissa is trying to do – separate the bad actions from the individual. If her fiancé can cure himself of his cheating, then they have a real chance. I wish you well, Melissa.'

Okay, that's better. That's more like it. A bit of humanity, at least.

'Oh please, spare us the sermon.' Hilary is back on the mic. 'Peggy gets it; she knows what it's like to throw good time after bad. The only thing I can think of that could explain such an idiotic position, Daryl, is that you are a serial cheater yourself: separating the deed from the doer, a victim rather than a victor – we're not having it. It just doesn't wash. So before you call in here again encouraging people to throw their lives down the pan for laughable attempts at morality, remember, I'm on to you and I'm well aware that the devil can cite scripture for his purpose.'

My head falls into my hands. This woman is evil.

'So, as you can tell if you've been tuned in, we have had some rather savage exchanges already on the show today. Let's hope our next email holds something a little less explosive; fingers crossed we get a good old-fashioned blind-date dilemma or a nice mother-in-law issue – anything along these lines would see me right and might keep Hilary's blood pressure at an acceptable level, am I right there, Hilary?'

I can hear Hilary guffawing in the background.

No wonder this woman is so divisive. I've heard people describe her as Marmite; love or hate, but no room for any middle ground or grey area. I can firmly say that I hate her. She and her ilk draw their listenership from those who already feel angry and isolated and betrayed, but rather than help them, these people are prodding and provoking them further, throwing salt on their wounds, encouraging them to lash out and be spiteful, causing even more misery and division.

'As time is always of the essence here on the morning show,' Jake continues, resignation mingled with frustration in his voice, 'I'll move on swiftly to our second emailer: Joan, a retired nurse from Stockwell. "Dear Jake and Hilary," she writes, "I am so very worried about my twenty-nine-year-old daughter. She is a boomerang baby, as they call it, flew the nest for a few years but is now back at home and working in a dead-end job collecting glasses at the local pub. Sometimes she appears depressed about the whole set-up, throwing tantrums, blaming the government or rocketing house prices or a lack of graduate-level jobs, but other times she seems to revel in her predicament, spending beyond her means on clothes, make-up, parties, festivals and even holidays. My husband and I never went on holiday until our fifties and always played it safe with money. She is always on her phone. We can't understand our daughter's lackadaisical attitude to her own future. I don't want to hurt her or lose her or withdraw our support, but she's always been a late bloomer and I think now is the time she needs to be given a firm but fair push. It feels like she's in a game of musical chairs and very soon everybody else will grab their place but she will be left standing. I am interested in any advice or guidance you can provide.'"

Um… Strumming my pain with her fingers? Singing my life with her words? You are killing me softly here, Joan from Stockwell.

It's as if my own mother wrote this one. Although at least Joan's daughter has a job. That's what Mum would be thinking to herself. And is going on holidays. And did she say festivals and parties too? You know, just hook me up. I'm a few steps behind here.

Jake's voice continues over the airwaves. 'A very thoughtful letter there from a concerned mum,' he says. 'What kind of advice could you offer Joan in her situation? She does say that she doesn't want to hurt or lose her daughter, just encourage her to make some steps that will help with her future. But what do I know? Over to the professional; what do you think, Hilary?'

I hear Hilary sigh heavily into her microphone. This is not going to be good. Sorry, Jake; I can already tell that your subtle request for positive, professional guidance is never going to bear fruit. Joan, I hope your blood pressure can take whatever she's about to serve up to you.

'You get what you raise. You reap what you sow. Joan, your daughter didn't become a spoilt, unmotivated princess by herself. You have effectively disabled her. And it's all very well you having your light-bulb moment, but it's too little, too late. You are a casualty of believing that thirty is the new twenty, and frankly, as a trained nurse you should know better. Just because she's still wearing Converse and eating straight from the fridge…'

A bolt of fear shoots through me. What dark powers do you have, Hilary Clive? No word of a lie, the words emanate from the radio at the exact moment that I am standing inside the fridge door scooping Philadelphia into my mouth with my finger. I turn to my right to see my oldest pair of Converse drying upside down on the radiator courtesy of my mum, who thought they could do with freshening up.

She's not finished yet. Oh Joan, I bet you wish you'd never asked. I know I wish you'd never asked.

'Yes, people settle down later than they used to, but that is no excuse to waste a decade faffing around pretending to be a teenager with a bit more freedom. This is a real problem, Joan, and not just for you; I see it everywhere. Sadly, it is only the beginning of more problems for you and your daughter and all of society. The real consequences will become apparent over the next five to ten years. Mark my words, the worst is yet to come.'

Oh my GOD. Jake, DO something! You can't let her say this stuff! I clasp my hands around my ears. I can't listen. This is my life she's talking about.

Jake butts in. 'Hilary, surely we're not saying that the poor kid's life is ruined? She's only twenty-nine, for goodness' sake.'

Exactly. I loosen my hands. That's exactly right. Who panics at twenty-nine? It's ridiculous. Tell her, Jake. Then put on some Beyoncé and give me the clue and I can get on with my life and we need never cross paths again.

There is a sneer in Hilary's voice this time. 'Jake Jackson, you are as bad as the rest. All you media types referring to twenty-somethings as "kids" and "boomerang babies" and such; it's wrong. They are not kids or babies. You are letting them believe they have all the time in the world and that resting on your laurels in terms of career and family is living your life to the full because the only thing you place value on is fun. And this notion of fun is rubbish – worse than rubbish, it is benign sabotage.'

'Come on now, Hilary, you can't seriously—' I can tell that Jake is trying to cut her off more forcefully, but he's too polite, too professional. Hilary bulldozes on through.

'This is not my opinion. These are the facts. We know that eighty per cent of life's defining moments take place by the age of thirty-five. That means that eight out of ten of the decisions and experiences and life-changing events that make existence worthwhile will happen by your mid-thirties. So sitting around stuck to your phone all day only to collect glasses by night doesn't exactly set you up for a great adulthood or a stable society, now does it?'

I hear Jake sigh. I'm sighing too. He has not successfully killed this and he's the only one in a position to. Play some music, Jake, go to an ad break. Get her in a headlock. I press my palms into my eyes. It's audio car crash; I want to stop listening but I can't quite bring myself to do so.

'We also know that female fertility peaks at age twenty-eight, and that things get tricky after age thirty-five...'

Stop. Stop. STOP! I have got to make this stop! If I had internet connection, I'd email in right this second, but that's out of the question in this bandwidth dead zone, so I have no choice but to consider plan B, which will mean dealing with her head-to-head; real time and direct.

I pick up the transistor and rush into the hallway to the portable landline phone, punching in the studio number. It rings and rings and rings and an automated voice tells me that my call is very valuable, so much so that I am going to be put into a caller queue right away. A ukulele version of Take That's 'Patience' is piped down the line.

Jake is trying to take charge but he's just not cutting it. 'Okay, Hilary, is there anything constructive you think you can offer Joan in terms of how she can improve the situation – POSITIVE things that she can do to help her daughter?'

It's okay, Jake, just keep her talking. I'm coming. I'm in the queue.

'Well, I know you like to be the bearer of good news and maintain the status quo by spouting platitudes, but I can't do that. In Joan's case, there's no good news. The best she can hope for is to serve as a warning to other parents who are babying their adult offspring, resulting in perpetual dependence, financial instability and lifelong unfulfilment. It's a sad but self-inflicted case of closing the stable door after the horse has bolted.'

'*Your call is next in the queue,*' the automated voice tells me. Hurry up, queue, DO NOT end the segment just as I am about to give her a piece of my mind.

'Hilary, you've caused quite a stir on social media. Texts and tweets are flooding in.'

Oh, big surprise.

'We know you're straight-talking, but even by your standards this seems very harsh and damning advice this morning.'

'I disagree. I am here to help; I am here to tell people what they need to hear not what they think they want to hear. I am proud of talking straight. Indeed, I'll go so far as to say that if Joan had done a bit of straight talking with her daughter a few years back, she wouldn't be in the sorry predicament that she finds herself in today.'

'*Your call is next in the queue. Please bear with us while we try to connect you...*'

Right, Hilary, self-professed relationships expert, I'm nearly there. I'm next in the queue and I'm in fighting form. Don't you dare stop me now.

CHAPTER TEN

'Hello?'

'Hi, my name's Astral, associate producer here at 105 FM. Are you good to go on in sixty seconds?'

'Yes, great, okay.' I clear my throat.

'Three, two, one…' The phone line makes a clicking noise.

'Welcome back, listeners, we have a caller on line four. You are live on air, caller. What's your name, and where are you calling from this morning?' It's Jake Jackson. In my phone.

I'm LIVE on air. Oh God, I didn't really think this through properly. I can't hang up, but I can't let Hilary continue as she is.

'Caller, are you there?'

'Time-waster,' I hear Hilary say.

'Uh, yes. Yes! I am here. My name is Poppy and I'm a first-time listener to the show. I tuned in this morning to get the clue for "You Do the Maps", but quite frankly, I am appalled at the vitriol Hilary is peddling as advice. I'd like to pick up on a couple of points, starting with Joan's letter about her late-blooming daughter…'

'Sounds like you've got some opposition, Hilary,' says Jake.

'Let me get this straight, Poppy. You've called in with a problem and your problem is me? Let's hear it then,' says Hilary.

'Exactly. I'm calling because I fail to see how anyone has put you in a position to help anyone, never mind the public. Your responses this morning have been unprofessional, insensitive and uninformed.'

'Really,' Hilary says, sounding as if she's stifling a yawn. 'How so?'

'Misleading in terms of psychological evidence, for a start. People will be sitting at home this morning, listening to the radio, and if any of them are over thirty-five, they'll probably feel that all their best moments are behind them. Yet extensive research proves otherwise.'

'So, Poppy, you reject the idea that the decisions we make in our twenties and thirties profoundly influence our lives?' she asks.

'I believe that the decisions we make at *every* stage profoundly influence the lives of the people we are and the lives of the people we are to become. And sometimes we're not thrilled with the decisions we make, especially if we are too time-pressured to make them properly. Why, for example, do people pay good money to get tattoos removed or covered up when teenagers are paying good money to get them in the first place? Why are middle-aged people divorcing partners that younger people are rushing to marry? Because we have a fundamentally flawed perception about the power of time and the way it changes what we may think we want.'

Silence. I continue.

'So, you may be thinking, when is this magical point in life where the pace of change suddenly goes from a crawl to a gallop? Which is the defining decade? The answer is not always twenty to thirty; the answer is *now*, wherever you happen to be. And Hilary – and this is what I take issue with – the idea that twenty to thirty is more pivotal in terms of permanent happiness than any other time in life is *damaging*. It is a dangerous illusion that our personal history comes to an end at this age and that unless we force ourselves to jump forward scrambling for the next monkey bars of family, money and career, we will fall into the void. This is wrong.'

I pause for comeback. But there is nothing. Do I hear some shuffling papers? Not sure. I carry on.

'Hilary, you have told Joan that doing things younger means doing them better, that it's already too late for her daughter. This feeds into the toxic idea that everything younger is fresher, superior and more original, and that everything older is stale, jaded and washed up. Again, evidence does not concur. Let's take Picasso and Cézanne as examples – two world-famous, celebrated artists with two very different back-stories. Picasso was deemed a prodigy, famous in very early life. A painting of his done in his twenties is worth four times as much as any he completed in his sixties. For Cézanne, a so-called "late bloomer", the opposite is true. The paintings he created in his sixties are valued at more than fifteen times higher than those painted in his twenties.'

'What on earth is your point, caller?' asks Hilary.

'My point is that Cézanne, like many late bloomers, recognised that he was on a journey, an adventure of possibility, open to what might surface, not stuck with fixed ideas about how life should be and by when and with whom.'

'This is all very well, Poppy, but Joan did say that her daughter was on her phone all day and then partying by night. I don't think Cézanne spent his time so frivolously, do you?'

'Hilary, if she's on her phone it's probably because she's trawling job sites. Career planning. If she's going to parties, she's open to meeting someone. Relationship planning. Joan's daughter is doing things in her own way, at her own pace, not rushing into something that isn't right for her. This process requires trial and error; it takes time to get things right.'

I hear Jake's voice. 'Poppy, this is inspired stuff! You've really got me thinking here. I like it. I like this angle. And I agree with the time pressure thing. I'm only speaking from personal experience, but I know that any time I have had to work to a stopwatch or a deadline, I've panicked and messed up.'

'Totally! And that's well evidenced in studies, too: time pressure paralysis. The more time pressure a person perceives has been put upon them, the worse their performance and the more ill judged their decisions. Therefore our obsession with achieving marriage and career goals by thirty or whatever may be the very thing standing in the way of us getting these things.'

'Okay, Poppy, we've got floods of callers, texts and social media messages coming in. Are you happy to stay on the line?' asks Jake.

'Yeah, no problem.'

Floods of callers? Oh my God. People can hear me. People are responding. A short bark of laughter escapes my throat. I'm amazed and surprised and… well, delighted all at once.

'Right, message from Sherelle in Shepherd's Bush. "Thank God for this caller! I'm thirty-three and single so was very depressed after Hilary's comments this morning but feeling much better now – gonna take out my crayons seeing as I'm such a Cézanne! Keep her on, she knows what she's talking about."'

'Wow, thanks, Sherelle. That really means an awful lot to me. Thanks so much for emailing in.'

'Another one here,' says Jake. 'Isabella from Camden. "Who is this caller? She needs her own show. As I was listening to her I kept nodding my head – she's right, we are too obsessed with age and racing through life without stopping to think about what we really want. I never married or had kids and I am delighted with my lot in life – I'm doing it my way!"'

'Ha ha! You go for it, Isabella! What you're doing sounds awesome, real inspiration there. I wish you every success!' I call down the phone.

My skin is tingling. My voice has taken on a different energy, like I've unlocked something that has been stiff and closed for too long. I balance the receiver in the crook of my neck and go back to the fridge to slug some orange juice directly from the carton. Hilary wouldn't approve, of course. But Sherelle would. And Isabella, and all the rest of us who want to live the way we want to and make our own mistakes and our own discoveries in our own sweet time.

'Wow, Poppy, the phones are hopping, the messages are pouring in – you've struck a chord. It might be worth mentioning that Hilary has had something crop up and has actually left the studio, so she won't be available for comment. However, we do still have Poppy on the line. So can I ask you a little bit about yourself? Where are you from? What do you do? Fill us in.'

'Well, I'm twenty-nine, from Brixton, just graduated as a psychologist, currently living at home and looking for a job, so I guess Joan's letter struck a chord with me too.'

'Okay, a trained psychologist, now things are starting to make sense. And you're looking for work, did you say?'

'Yep, I've been to the job centre but there's nothing really suitable at the moment, so here I am, hanging around my mum's kitchen, trying to get the clue that might win me ten grand! So come on, Jake Jackson, I've been waiting all morning!'

'Fair enough, you've earned it. Yesterday's clue for "You Do the Maps" is…' He's cut to an ad. What is going on here?

I hear a click on the phone. 'Hi, Poppy, this is Jake – private line, we're not on air.'

'O-kay?'

'We have an internship programme here at the station. I can't guarantee that it would lead anywhere and I don't know anything about pay and conditions and all that malarkey, but one thing I can say is I think you would be a fantastic asset to the show.'

'Um, really?' My cheeks throb with surprise and embarrassment. Maybe he's joking? It's been a long time since anybody thought I was a fantastic asset to anything.

'Yes. Really,' he tells me firmly.

'Well, that's a lovely thing to hear, Jake, and I've got to admit that I am absolutely buzzing right now.' I blow out my cheeks and hold my jumping stomach. 'That was an amazing feeling. I'm quite overwhelmed by it all.'

'Excellent. So you'll join us? Come to the South Bank Studio, I'll tell reception to expect you.'

No, this is moving too quickly. I can't commit. I'm not going to be around for very long. What if Dr Burley gets back to me and I'm stuck up a transmission tower. No. This isn't for me. Well, not right now, anyway.

'But I haven't got any training or experience in media. I really haven't a clue about it.'

'All the more reason to come and learn on the job,' says Jake. 'Poppy, you're a natural.'

I feel pressure mounting in my chest. That was just one time. Just a fluke. The stabbing memory of losing the fellowship returns: getting my hopes up, but then everything vanishing from under my feet. No, I've been here before. Not worth the heartache.

'I'm not a natural, believe me. I'm just a listener with a bee in my bonnet. I'm not usually so outspoken; it's just that Hilary really wound me up,' I explain.

'Yes, but that's exactly why it was so good. You said what we were feeling. You cared enough to pick up the phone. You had the language and the skills and the confidence to help people, to sort the truth from the lies, and you didn't hold back. Nice to see that from the good guys for a change, eh?'

I run my fingers through my hair. This is crazy. I came down here to make a coffee and listen to the radio, and now I'm being offered a chance to come work with them.

A flash of Harriet snickering at the idea pops into my head.

I definitely don't want to tell Jake that my professors, my peers, even my dad would laugh me out of town if they heard that this was what my very expensive, highly selective first-class education had resulted in – a pop psychology slot on a morning radio show, squeezed in somewhere between the traffic report and the horoscope reader; an agony aunt. Nope. It is certainly not my thing.

'Poppy, you clearly know what you're talking about and you're not hell-bent on kicking people when they're down, so you're already halfway there. Media experience is something you can gain along the way. Learn on the job.'

Learn on the job. South Bank Studio. Floods of callers. I rub my hand up and down my arm. I've got goose bumps. Hand on heart, that was one of the best experiences of my life. The exchange, the urgency, the unpredictability. The callers flooding in with virtual high-fives. It was immediate and intense and so, so exciting. I lick my lips. Is this really happening? Could I actually do this?

'You'd be in a position to help lots of listeners with their issues. I've got to go now, but why don't you come in after the show today? I'll be here until midday. Have a look around. I'll buy you lunch. What do you say?'

'How about you give me the clue now, and you've got a deal.' I can hear by the way Jake is breathing that he is smiling into the phone.

'Great! Really great. You are exactly what we need around here, Poppy, someone fresh and smart and kind. All the rest will follow. So here's your clue…'

I scribble it down and thank him one last time as I hang up the phone.

Poppy Bloom, radio intern. Who'd have guessed? I get a fit of giggles. I can't stop laughing. Laughing at the way this morning has unfolded. How everything has unfolded. I grip my cheeks. How did this happen? I feel light and giddy and bursting with hope. And I know it's not specifically about the radio or about meeting Leanne again or Tom or any of the other singular things that have happened over the last few days.

It's the fact that they've happened of their own accord, as natural consequences of other events. Both my hands fly to my breastbone and I exhale deeply. Even though I never predicted or orchestrated it, stuff still happened. Good stuff. Wonderful stuff. And because of these wonderful happenings, I've realised something important: that mercifully, not every detail of my life is under my control. And it's glorious.

CHAPTER ELEVEN

I stare at my phone.

Everything had been going swimmingly, almost the perfect morning. But now there's this. It's been ringing now for three minutes non-stop. I know who it is. My ex-dad. Or real dad. Or biological father. Or compulsive gambler. Or drug-addled has-been rock drumming legend Mr Ray Bloom. Whatever you want to call him, he is now calling me. I let it ring some more. And then it stops. Thank God.

I will have to face up to this conversation soon, but not right this very minute. I push my empty coffee cup to the middle of the table, press my hands against the arms of the kitchen chair and lever myself up. I'll just leave it till after the weekend and call him on Monday morning. It's a universal rule of interactive human behaviour. *Leave it till after the weekend* was probably carved into one of the stone tablets that Moses most regrets leaving out in squaring off the commandments to a snappy ten. See, Moses, you shouldn't have rushed that rule-picking business.

The landline starts to ring. O-kay. He wants to talk. I'm going to have to take this. If he rings the landline, it means he is seriously pissed off and is even prepared to run the risk of having my mum answer the phone. This makes matters exponentially worse as then she turns on me and says that I should answer my mobile when my father rings me, that there is absolutely no need for him to have to contact me through her/she is not my personal secretary/she can really do without this type of bullshit after a hard day at work, etc.

It's ringing out and it's not going away. If I don't take this call right now, he could get in his car and drive over here. That's happened twice before; really not good. I pick up the receiver.

'Hello?'

'Finally, Poppy. What do I have to do to get hold of you these days? I've called, sent messages, left voicemails. What the hell is going on?' my father asks. He sounds even more puffed than normal.

'Sorry, it's been kind of crazy. It should all settle down now, though. How are you?' I never ask this. It will arouse suspicion.

'Fine. I'm fine. I'm a lot better now that I've pinned you down. Obviously I didn't see you at the graduation, but…' a heavy sigh, 'let's not get into that now.' He coughs a very wheezy cough to clear his throat. It doesn't work. His voice still sounds raspy and hoarse, like it's wrapped with barbed wire.

Uh-oh. I sit on the bottom stair in my mum's hallway. I'm glad this isn't face to face. My father is going to go even more insane than I did.

'They didn't offer me the fellowship.'

'What?'

'They didn't offer it to me. So despite me getting the highest marks in the class, the final decision was made by Dr Winters and she turned me down. She chose Gregory and Harriet instead.'

'I don't understand this; on what basis could she possibly turn you down?' He swallows the words in a breathy way, like he's trying to talk whilst being punched in the stomach.

'She didn't like my thesis, she doesn't like me, she doesn't think I'm mature enough for the role, lacking experience…'

More coughing. 'Harriet's father is a politician, that's why they chose her. Probably fixed it so that they'll secure extra funding or building permission or some other scam along those lines.' Here he goes with the conspiracy theories. Always someone else's fault, always a big national plot working against the little guy.

'Dad, I'm sorry. I've got to go. But don't worry too much, okay? Something may still come up. I've contacted my professor, Dr Burley, and asked him to see if there are any other vacancies. I'm going to get back there; I'm sure I'll be back in no time at all.' I try to close down the conversation, but no chance.

'… thousands of pounds we have paid in fees. *Tens* of thousands of pounds. I remortgaged my house. I traded in my car so you could do your PhD. And let me see if I have this straight? She turns you down because she doesn't like you?' He tears himself away from the receiver and I can hear the huge, laboured gulps of air he is trying to take in to calm himself down, but I can still feel the heat of his wrath from the phone line. I wrap my arms around my knees.

He gets back on the line. 'This is OUTRAGEOUS! Poppy, do you hear me? We can't just stand by and let this happen; what an absolute shower of chinless, inbred, Tory-parroting ass-clowns. We need to get a lawyer on to this. Sue the shit out of them. We can't let them get away with it.'

'Okay, I'll send them an email on Monday.'

'An email? That's a fairly toothless response to someone who just decided to ruin your entire career and flush tens of thousands of pounds of hard-earned cash down the pan.'

I wait. He's getting more and more worked up. It's best that I go quiet at this stage, as anything I say will just fan the flames.

'Poppy, you were going to change the world, remember? You were going to help people all over the place. This is important; you were going to help people get their lives back. What happens to your thesis now? Jesus… I need a drink of water.' The choking sound in his throat is back. 'Give me a second.' I hear a coughing convulsion in the distance.

My ex-dad is basically a slave to compulsive behaviours; drink, drugs, gambling, women – he has no check, no filter, he keeps going to the point of self-destruction. It's amazing he's still alive, to be honest. He's lost everything over and over and over. The losses chip away at him, but never enough to make him stop, and it's cost him his family and his band. He's lauded as one of the greatest living drummers and songwriters of this century; not much use, though, when your hands shake so much you can't hold a teaspoon.

He hasn't come back to the phone yet, so I rest my head in the palms of my hands. I can picture him now; I know exactly what he's doing. He'll have broken into a cold sweat; his cheeks will look waxy and grey. He'll have poured a glass of water to wash down his blood pressure tablets. He'll squeeze his eyes tight because his head is pounding, and then he'll go to the kitchen sink, run the tap and throw cold water onto his face. He'll undo his top button, pull his collar away from his neck and try to take deep breaths. It's a hot, tight, clamouring, soundless panic attack. I know this is what's happening because I've seen it lots of times; every time he loses big. And me not getting the fellowship is losing big.

'Dad?' I call into the phone.

I hear some shuffling around; the tap is on full pressure.

I wait some more. And some more. I sit on the stairs and pick at my bitten-down fingernails. Twenty minutes pass. He comes back on the line. I hear unfamiliar voices in the background.

'Dad?'

'Okay, Poppy. Carlos is here now. He's brought some young beardy guy with him. He's making a documentary or something about the band.'

'A journalist? Is that a good idea?' My mind flashes back to a damning *Rolling Stone* feature years before called 'Interviewing Ray Bloom; Never Meet Your Heroes'. The journalist reported just how appalling he was: one-word answers, nasty glaring looks alongside sulky silences, then torrents of abuse when they ran out of ice. Soon afterwards, he cancelled all his tour dates and fell out with the lead singer. This on top of losing everything he owned over a Las Vegas roulette table when I was just a baby meant he had to move, alone, to a little cottage on the Kent coast.

'A good idea? I doubt it. But I'm going to lie down now. Keep your phone on. I'll get us a lawyer.'

'Okay,' I say, and the line goes dead.

That actually went a touch better than expected. A small mercy that it happened over the phone and not face to face. So, he's massively disappointed. Do I feel guilty about it? Absolutely. But what's the point in wishing things were different when you know deep down that you are powerless to change them? I think I wanted to become a psychologist in the first place because I loved the idea that there was some way through apparent madness. That the landscape of the mind, however crazy and chaotic, could actually be navigated. Treasure could be retrieved. Building could commence. And I believed it in my first few years; I believed it so fully and wanted it so badly that it consumed me. I wanted to make Dad better. I thought it might be possible, if only I used the right tools and read the right books and showed him how important this was to me. Desperately, I tried to fix him, to solve him, to crack his code and make him well again.

But obviously that didn't work out quite as well as I'd hoped. In fact it didn't work at all, and sometimes I think it actually made things a whole lot worse. He didn't want my help, and that's what I couldn't accept, and so we lost our way. Perhaps I drove him to clam up by demanding answers and being obsessed with progress, too keen to talk rather than listen. And then there he was, wanting to be left alone, obsessed with the past, weary of life and resigned to failure. So maybe that runs in the family; this catastrophic sense of failure.

The only two things I wanted to do when I decided to become a psychologist was help my dad and become a professor. And after spending tens of thousands of pounds of my dad's money and ten crucial years of my own life, I've managed neither.

CHAPTER TWELVE

'Here she comes! The cryptic mastermind herself.' Jamaal jumps up off his three-legged stool and offers it to me. 'Grab a seat, girl, grab a seat. You need to take the weight off those feet so that your mind can work right.'

I give him a hug and he flashes me a broad, dazzling smile. Jamaal is Frank's best friend. He sells *The Big Issue* outside Brixton tube station and they've kept each other company for two decades, drinking very sweet black tea from a shared flask day in, day out, rain or shine. They couldn't look more different. On one side of the tube entrance there's Frank, who is built like an old-fashioned strongman at a vintage fairground, with his big shiny head, bright blue eyes and eyebrows knitted together like he's trying to solve a puzzle or remember something important. And on the other side is Jamaal, always hunched over, as though his belly aches from chronic laughter. His long, rope-like dreadlocks hang down either side of his face, framing his mischievous scrunched-up eyes. These two never seem to age, never seem to change, the pair of them preserved like iconic living statues, marking the point of passage for all those who pass in and out of Brixton underground, as constant and familiar and opposite as day and night.

I pat my crossover purse. 'Don't worry, Jamaal, I've got the clue and the answer right here.' I turn to Frank and kiss him on the cheek. 'I must've had some hair dye in my ears last night,' I tell him. 'I wasn't sure I'd heard it correctly, so I rang the station this morning and double-checked.'

'Just as well, we couldn't hear the radio this morning at all with this racket going on.' Frank tilts his head towards the road workers drilling and clanging a little further up the street. 'So what is it, Poppy? I was a little stumped by the one you gave me. "Depressed dogs"... Jamaal, didn't I say to you that I thought it was a mistake?'

Jamaal shrugs, then kisses his teeth and rubs his hands together, a teasing smile playing on his lips. 'He always say that, every day, and then he hear the answer and he say, "I knew it! Remember, Jamaal, I told you that would be the answer."'

Frank glances over at me, so I nod my loyal reassurance. 'Yes, well, the real clue is...'

Jamaal uses two rolled-up *Big Issue*s for a mini drum roll. 'I don't want no clue – the answer will do me just fine.'

Frank shakes his head. 'Hold up now, some of us like to work the ole grey matter, you know. Give us the clue first, Poppy, see how we get on.'

'"If north is starboard".'

Frank pouts out his bottom lip and raises his eyebrows. 'I'll take the answer now, please, sweetheart,' he says after a few seconds.

'Southport,' I announce, and Jamaal gives me a little round of applause. Frank thrusts his chin to the sky and clicks his fingers as if Southport had been on the tip of his tongue.

'Your ole grey matter is getting very grey and slow these days, Frank,' Jamaal teases, curling his arm around Frank's thick waist. 'But don't you worry about that, my friend. When you get older and slower and those knees finally cave in altogether, your ole pal Jamaal here will wheel you around Brixton town all day long. Because I got you, you get me?'

Frank slaps his hands away playfully. 'Get off, you big softie. It'll be you needing a wheelchair before me – I'm six months younger than you, remember.'

Jamaal throws his head back in laughter, his eyes creased into half-moons.

'See what nonsense I've got to put up with – twenty years of this, no wonder my poor brain has had it.'

A wave of dark-suited commuters suddenly spills forth from the underground stairwell, pouring out into the street right in front of us. Jamaal shakes a rolled-up magazine in the air. I step aside to avoid the flurry of people branching away from the crowd towards the flower stall.

'Mixed bouquet, please…'

'Twelve long-stemmed roses, mate.'

'Something for the house – non-allergenic.'

Frank whips up the flowers from his display, wrapping them in paper with one hand, handling notes and dispensing change with the other. It strikes me that after all my study, I don't really know how to do anything practical. I couldn't even run this flower stall if it came to it. What does that leave me with? *The Big Issue*? I look over to Jamaal; I can just about see the top of his Rasta beanie over the crowd. I flick the idea aside. This town's appetite for non-profit publications is just not big enough for the two of us.

'I'll take one, please,' says a voice that sounds familiar, warmly familiar, but I can't see past the crowds to locate who it belongs to.

A parting appears in the teeming throng, the traffic stalls at the lights, the pavement is clear for the first time in the mad midday rush. I stretch out my neck to catch a glimpse and my heart nearly explodes.

'Dr Burley!' I scream. I run to him and throw my arms around him, squeezing him really, really tight. 'What are you doing here?' I take him by the shoulders to make sure I'm not mistaken. This is really Dr Burley, here in Brixton, standing eyes wide right in front of me.

'I happened to be at a conference in Russell Square so I thought, why not come and find you?'

I grab him again and manage to pull him to me even more tightly. He wraps his arms around me too. Probably because he can tell that I've started to cry.

'It's okay. I know it's not been easy.'

I try to sort myself out by wiping the inside of my arm across my face. Jamaal hands me a tissue.

'Jamaal, Frank, this is Dr Burley. My tutor from Banbridge. He took care of me all through my studies.' I thread my arm through his.

Frank holds out his hand. 'Thanks so much for all you've done. It's a pleasure to meet you. Very good of you to come and see our Poppy.' He smiles and starts rustling around in his money belt. I hold up my hands to resist, but Dr Burley gets in there before I do.

'Actually I would love the chance to treat Poppy and catch up on all that's happened.' He turns to me. 'I only have an hour or so; are you free to grab a coffee?'

We set off arm in arm. We decide to walk through the park, grabbing two takeaway coffees and a packet of strawberry short-bread biscuits to share.

'So tell me everything,' I say. I love gossip, even if it's about me. I can't help myself, and Dr Burley knows. I've been bursting to hear what's been going on.

'Okay, then. But you've got to promise not to upset yourself, Poppy.'

'I promise,' I tell him, shoving a whole biscuit into my mouth and fixing my eyes on the distant horizon.

'After the graduation, I caught up with Dr Winters and asked her what on earth she was playing at. Everyone, I mean EVERYONE, was utterly shocked by her decision, and, well, it just didn't make any sense. Gregory is an excellent student and he has very impressive interpersonal skills, so in a way I understood that he was a well-rounded choice; he brings a lot to the table. But Harriet? This confused me. To my mind, she is a lovely girl, but fairly pedestrian in terms of innovation. So...'

I drop my eyes to my shoes. One foot in front of the other. Right, left, right, left. Even though I'm still technically furious with Harriet for jumping into bed with my ex-boyfriend, my instinct is to stand up for her, to tell Dr Burley that she has lots of strong points: she is particularly good at footnoting and retrieving accidentally deleted documents, and she is a great friend... well, she *was* a great friend to me.

'So?' I ask, wanting the next instalment but aware that it might not necessarily be good news.

Dr Burley veers left and takes the path towards the duck pond.

'So, I enquired a little further. I felt it my duty, as your tutor, to find and supply you with some answers after you'd been cast aside without explanation in that hurtful and confusing way.'

'What did she say?'

'Well... and believe me, it gives me no pleasure to relay this...' He rubs his hands down his thighs. 'Dr Winters felt that you didn't inspire confidence. She felt that as an ambassador for the faculty and the university on a world stage, you didn't have the *presence* necessary to make people sit up and take note.'

I stop. My feet won't move. 'Pardon?' I ask.

Dr Burley is now looking at his feet too. They have also stopped moving. '"Uninspiring" was the word she used.' He slips a boiled sweet out of his pocket and into his mouth. 'She feels that students who come to Banbridge from a non-academic background –students such as yourself, the first generation in a family to attend university, never mind Banbridge – are painfully self-conscious. That you ask yourself questions like "Do I really belong here? Do I deserve this place? How do I fit in? Do I want to fit in?" This added pressure may lead you to over-compensatory behaviours and a tremendous pressure to prove yourself. And this makes for an uninspiring ambassador, I'm afraid.'

I turn to him, part my lips to speak but then just shake my head. *Uninspiring.* Of all the things I've ever been called, I honestly think this is the worst, the most deflating, the most personal.

'I am so very sorry Poppy. I obviously don't agree one iota. You are and have always been a tremendous inspiration to me. Your work is staggering in its originality and its forward thinking, and always came from the right place.' He pats his chest, then looks furtively around the park and lowers his voice. 'Between us, I always thought that Dr Winters was a bit jealous of you,' he says. He drags a hand down his beard. 'But it is what it is. She is the boss and her decision is final.'

I shake my head. I cannot believe what I am hearing. So basically, my work is great, but what a terrible pity about my personality.

He steps away from me, leans backwards on one heel and pushes his hand deep into his pocket. 'I hope that goes some way to clarifying things. You have a clean slate now, free to move on to your next chapter.'

My chest tightens, so I try to breathe hard and deep. I want to scream and stomp and grab Burley by the shoulders and make him do something, anything, to put this right, to make it fair. I run my fingers through my hair, placing my hands on top of my head as if protecting myself from a meteor shower. I can't win – they've made up their minds. Anything I do or say now will only make matters worse. If I lose my cool with him, right now, here in broad daylight, it will only serve to strengthen this idea that I'm not as polished and composed as everyone else. If I cry, I'll look unstable. If I get angry, I'll look defensive. Allowing these emotions to leak uncontrollably all over the place… how common-as-muck of me. I swallow hard and tighten my grip on my coffee cup.

'Dr Burley, I'm going to have to go now. I want to thank you for everything you've done for me; thanks for fighting my corner and thanks for coming here.'

Burley softens his voice. 'What's done is done, Poppy, I want you to know that I wish you the best, and even though your plans haven't turned out exactly as you might have wished, I have every confidence that…'

'... they'll work out anyway,' I finish for him. I'm hearing this a lot lately.

'Exactly!'

I stare at my shoes again. He fishes his phone out of his briefcase. 'I'm going to get going. I'm presenting after lunch. I'll ring for a taxi to meet me at the park gates and bring me back to the conference venue. Can I offer you a lift anywhere?'

I shake my head and try to kick up some chewing gum that's melted into the gravel. I say goodbye to him and he skips off towards the park gates, alone.

So. That's it. *It is what it is.*

Well, at least I know where I stand now. Goodbye, Gregory and Harriet and gilded academia. Best of luck with the fellowships. Safe travels back to Banbridge, Dr Burley. Give my regards to Dr Winters and her theories. Hope you all enjoy the life that I worked my arse off for and that I once thought was destined for me.

I hear the 105 FM jingle blaring from a passing car: *bah-bah-bah-bombom!* It sounds like a Latino wind chime; fun and fresh, like there's a carnival just outside your window and gorgeous sequinned women are dancing with their hips and their eyes against fanned peacock feathers and waving you towards them with impossibly beautiful smiles. I like it. It's been stuck in my head all day. *Bah-bah-bah-bombom!*

I sling my bag across my chest and check my watch. It is much later than I realised. If I run along the old park trail and then through the gates to the bus stop, it's technically possible to get to the South Bank Studio in time to catch Jake Jackson and discuss the internship. And that's only a little late, right? That's not *drastically* late in the great scheme of things. I can happily forgo lunch. When I get there, I'll just blame the bus, the tube, the traffic, say I had an accident or that someone tried to mug me, that there was a security alert on the line so I had to walk, blah de blah de blah; all standard London stuff that nobody can bear to listen to or cares about.

I start to run. I can get there; I really want to get there. And not just in light of Dr Burley's news. I had fun this morning. And the callers didn't seem to think I was 'uninspiring'. I enjoyed offering my two cents' worth and hope it made a difference to someone, somewhere. One thing is for sure: I made more of an impact in an hour this morning than I did with my precious thesis. I felt I belonged on the radio. I felt comfortable and excited and like I had something to offer. And that felt great.

I dart along the gravel path that winds through the park. Every time my foot hits the ground, I know I am one step closer. I am going to get to the 105 FM studio. Jake Jackson, do not give up on me just yet! It feels like the wind is lifting me, like two little winged angels are carrying me through a Disney clearing; the birds are singing, the squirrels are squirrelling, the sun might just succeed in elbowing that big black cloud out of the way and send some much-needed rays down to shine upon us.

It's time to take a new direction, discover a new path. Eventually it might be something even better. That's exciting. I think it is, anyway. I know this isn't exactly the kind of news that my dad wants to hear – that I've cut my ties with Banbridge and I'm going for something totally different – but that's what it was all for, right? To find something meaningful. To do something that makes me happy.

It's off-piste for me. But I feel it's worth my best shot. What's the harm in trying?

Striding forward, one sure foot in front of the other, I race through the park, flushed with the fresh autumnal breeze. I feel weightless as I pass the benches, the buggies, the squatted dogs pooing on the manicured grass. Things are going to work out; I've got the world at my feet. As long as I'm hopeful and confident and keep moving forward, everything will be okay.

Although I feel a drop of rain, I keep pounding on, unfazed. I've got some new stuff coming through. I've got great parents and a roof over my head. I've got Leanne and Tom and I'm on my way to meet with Jake Jackson. And I don't care what the people at Banbridge think about me any more. I'm here and I'm open to whatever life throws at me.

But then, quite suddenly, dark clouds swell to fill the sky. As if someone has turned the dimmer switch, the air gets a little greyer, chillier; a bleak kind of shade descending. It blocks out the sun so completely that it feels as if the whole world has just been shoved into a forgotten drawer. Another drop, a fitful, spitting kind of wetness at first, until it starts to teem. I try to weave through the thousands of fat, unrelenting raindrops pelting down on top of me, but they just get thicker and faster and more forceful every second until a merciless wind-driven downpour forces me to slow down, to fall back into a walk and eventually surrender to a standstill altogether.

I slick my soaking wet hair away from my eyes; inky black 'waterproof' mascara comes away on my fingers. I stand by the park gates and watch the bus fail to stop at the empty bus shelter and realise that I am too late. Seconds too late to catch the bus, minutes too late to escape the rain, hours too late to catch Jake or the producer at the studio by the time I get there, and years too late to remedy being in this jobless, purposeless, sopping wet, panda-eyed life that I find myself in right now.

Even if another bus pulled up this instant and sliced through the inner-city traffic and sped past every stop along the way to drop me off directly outside the studio door, what would be the point? Who would even be there? It's Friday afternoon. It's already switch-off time for real, grown-up people who set alarms and keep bank statements and have IKEA store cards and all that stuff that makes my head feel tight. Grown-ups who are my age but who are not like me. They are real; they are doing things like it's supposed to happen.

I spot the bright amber light of an oncoming taxi in the distance. That could work. I could flag down this taxi right now and climb in out of the rain, and he could drop me at the studio so that I could salvage my only chance to live like a real person of my age, to get up in the morning with a purpose, to put my make-up on because I'm actually going to be seen by people, to eat Pret salads at my desk, to have conversations about new places to go and what's on sale in River Island. I wave my hand to hail the taxi. The driver has stopped at the lights and gives me an acknowledging nod and a wink. I run towards him, grabbing my crossover purse to stop it bouncing.

Ah.

A-ha.

I have no money.

I stop running, drop my hand to my side and shake my head at the driver. He shrugs and drives on. No Good Samaritan here offering free lifts to wet girls. Whatever. Fine. Suit yourself, why should you help me, right?

Fail, Poppy. Fail. Fail. Fail. Problem is, I only realised how much this was exactly what I needed, what I wanted, when it was too late. This is my fault. Nobody else's. I had the chance and I blew it.

I walk over to the bus stop on the other side of the street. The bus that will take me home. When did I fall so behind? When did everyone else get their TV-perfect lives together? Have they all been sneakily multitasking love and work and study and life generally while I've been doing my thesis and watching The Big Bang Theory on loop? I wrap my arms around my neck. Everyone else is just doing better than me… Harriet, Gregory, Leanne, all my mum's friends' kids. They've made stuff happen, they've got everything under control and they know where they are in life, and the more I think about it, the more frustrated and angry and sickened with myself I feel.

My so-called satin ballerina pumps start to disintegrate, the thin cardboard soles softening to a grey mush underfoot and breaking off in pieces on the pavement. What was I thinking?

I mean, really, what was I thinking about *anything*?

The bus pulls in to the kerb. I get on.

I scramble around in my purse for my Oyster card and it dawns on me that I will have to get off as I don't have a clue where it is. Not being able to board public transport is the epitome of adding insult to injury. The driver sighs, drums his fingers against the steering wheel and looks ahead blankly at the rain lashing against the windscreen. Flustered, I try emptying the entire contents of my purse into the tray, a total of twelve silver and copper coins, a stray tampon and a half-sucked Werther's. He looks through me with pale, unblinking eyes and tells me that he does not accept cash. I say some random stuff with a lisp, in a language I make up on the spot, just so that he might think I'm a foreign tourist and that I don't understand how London buses work. He shakes his head and ushers me on with a sharp upward chin gesture.

I climb the stairs and move towards my favourite seat – top deck, front right, so I can see the city streets sprawling out ahead of me. I spot a canoodling couple in the back seat, oblivious to my presence, oblivious to everything outside their merged love bubble. They are teenagers, but not gangly and pockmarked and greasy. These kids are beautiful, skin smooth and tanned, hair soft, shiny and tousled. The boy traces a finger over his girlfriend's Cupid's bow, causing her to smile and close her eyes like she's sinking into a dream.

I want to be cynical, to pull a face or tut or dismiss their young love as hormonal reflex or juvenile infatuation, but I can't. They are so sweet. Could it be that they are actually in love? Are they ready for something as powerful and delicate and enduring and difficult and ordinary as that? And if it isn't real love, is that because they are too young? Or conversely, is real love only possible for the young – is there a brief, unfiltered window where true love can blossom before it is cracked and clouded by expectation and competing dreams and unresolved injury? Does love need a window? What are the actual odds of two people's windows being open at the same time? And what about *my* window? Did I close it? Was it ever really open? Was I far too concerned with other people's windows, and as a result I shut it and sealed it tight? For ever?

I stare ahead, through the enormous bus window. Right now, beyond the rain, there is nothing to see.

A little old lady shuffles along the aisle and sidles in beside me. I budge up apologetically, despite the fact that she could choose any of the thirty vacant seats available and she's lugged a wheelie shopper up here to the top deck.

'My favourite seat.' She nods her thanks.

'Me too,' I answer, and she tilts her head at me, squinting in vague recognition.

'You look like somebody. Someone famous,' she says, and she starts rummaging in her trolley.

I sneak a peek inside and see that she has nothing in there except stacks of old cheap and glossy magazines. She pulls out a handful and flicks through them, finally settling on an outdated edition of *Closer*. Looks promising.

She licks a finger and begins turning pages. 'I know it's in this one. I can't place the name, but I'll find it for you. Someone famous but not talented.'

I'm quite intrigued now. *Famous but not talented.* Maybe I look like one of the royals? I continue to stare out of the window, thinking that I'll humour her since I'm nearly home.

'A-ha!' She folds the magazine open and shoves it under my nose. 'Told you I'd find it!'

I glance down at the headline: *Fallen Child Stars: From Riches to Rags!* There is a collage piece of five paparazzi shots; my new elderly friend points at the largest picture, in the centre of the page, showing a former child star, clearly startled by the camera, looking gaunt and lost and drug-addled as she takes out the bins.

When I try to look away, she pushes it closer and nods excitedly. 'I told you, didn't I? Spitting image!' I do not like my new geriatric magazine-hoarder bus buddy. She drops the magazine into my lap and starts rummaging again, this time inside the breast pocket of her coat.

Next thing, from somewhere in her deeply layered bosom, she slides out an iPhone and hunkers in beside me, smelling like soggy digestives and holding her phone at arm's length in front of us. 'Let me take a selfie.'

I excuse myself, get off the bus and walk the rest of the way home in the rain.

My mum calls me into the living room as soon I arrive. I tentatively put my head around the door. She is lounging on the couch in her slippers and gown, painting her nails. 'Good God, Poppy. Are you all right?'

I open my mouth to tell her about the worst day of my life, but I don't want to go through it all again. She holds out her arms and I let myself sink into them and unload all the sobs and tears and hiccups and sighs and wails that are hiding in every fold and crease of my body. And my mum absorbs them all. Every last one, as only mothers can.

And then she whispers into my ear. 'Don't forget that I know what you're made of, Poppy Bloom. I've not taken my eyes off you since the first moment you drew breath. You don't remember all the times you tripped over and pulled yourself up again; you don't remember all the hours you spent at that dining room table, your little tongue sticking out, learning your spellings, working out your times tables, translating God knows what. And I used to say to you, stop now, Poppy, you've done more than enough, off you go to bed. Do you remember?'

I nod my head, bent into the crook of her neck.

'And do you remember what you'd say?'

I shake my head. I can't remember; I just remember not wanting to leave it. Often I was only just getting started by bedtime.

'You'd say, don't stop me now! I'm close to the best bit!'

I stifle a laugh, a wet, snotty laugh.

'So don't you tell me, Poppy Bloom, that you are not made of tough stuff, okay? Any time you doubt yourself or you can't remember how much you have to offer this world, you just come back here, to this spot. Into your mother's arms. Because I know all about you and I'm not going anywhere. Promise?'

'I promise.'

'You need a good rest, Poppy. Tomorrow is another day.'

I press my palms into my eyes and walk towards the stairs. But just before I get there, I turn back to kiss my mum on the forehead and tell her something I haven't told her since I moved out ten years ago.

That I love her. Beyond any measure. And I'm so proud to be her daughter.

And then it's my turn to let her cry on my shoulder.

CHAPTER THIRTEEN

When I wake up, it's Saturday morning. Usually my favourite day of the week but after the rollercoaster day I had yesterday, I'm not feeling it. I can't be arsed to get out of bed. I can't muster the energy, or even the willpower required to muster the energy. My body aches, my face feels revolting. I can smell my own breath and it reminds me of cow dung. They won't be making any Yankee Candles inspired by my scent any time soon.

My mother has knocked a few times already, which must mean it's late morning. She hates late risers even more than she hates women who come into the salon asking for dry cuts or free fringe trims. At first there was some gentle tapping on the door with an almost caring voice asking, 'Anything I can get you, Poppy?' Then the last time it was a very firm rapping with a shrill and impatient 'Don't think this is the way it's going to be around here, do you hear me? If you're sick, go to the doctor. If you're well, get up. If you're lying there slobbing around in self-pity, move out.' I made some throaty coughing noises and ignored her until she huffed and puffed and went back downstairs.

I hear some kind of van thing pull up in the street below my bedroom window. Then a sliding door opens and a commanding female voice shouts, 'Give me five minutes, okay?'

Footsteps to the front door. Our doorbell rings. I shoot up. Who is this? What the hell could they want here?

I hear my mum, her voice sing-song 'Yes, lovely, brilliant, exactly, absolutely… of course she's available. She is *always* available these days. Upstairs, follow me.'

The front door closes.

Holy shit! What is this? They're coming up the stairs. I look in the mirror. I am an absolute ghoul. More steps, getting closer and padding their way in the direction of my bedroom. They are coming for me. I start slathering foundation on my face, slapping it on just to cover up, no time to blend. I glance in the mirror; I still look horrific, but now horrific in matt beige. I try to finger-brush the knots in my hair. They are on the landing, my mum and my mystery visitor. Their footsteps turn towards my door. I fling back the duvet, open the window and spray perfume in my mouth. I grab the robe from the back of the door and wrap myself up so I look clean… well, cleaner. The doorknob turns. I wipe my sweaty palms down my robe. The door swings open.

'Leanne?'

Leanne screws up her face like she has walked into a sour toxic fug. My hands fly to my neck. This is so embarrassing. I see her eyes trail around my room. Is it the sight? The smell? Which is worse, me or my bedroom?

'I was just sorting out—'

My mother cuts in. 'You were doing no such thing. Holing up feeling sorry for yourself, that was all. Well, Leanne is here now and she's going to sort you out.'

I watch Leanne survey the room, her eyes registering the blatant neglect, the outdated posters on the wall, the crowded vanity table, my wet clothes strewn in a heap on the floor. A horn honks outside. Leanne straightens up

'Superleague quarter-final. Today. Now. We need you.'

I nearly laugh. 'Ah, cheers for thinking of me, but there's really no way—'

'We need you so I'm afraid you don't have a choice on this one. I'm a player down – Tammy has decided to join the opposition; her nasty little way of sabotaging every little bit of what's important to us – so, Poppy, I'm not asking you, I'm telling you. Get your trainers on; we need to be on the road like twenty minutes ago.'

Outside, the horn honks again, but this time the driver holds their hand down on it, making one long, uninterrupted racket. I look to my mum, eye-urging her to step in and say something along the lines of 'Sorry, but Poppy's not really feeling up to playing today, why don't you call back another time?' But she just throws my trainers at me and smiles.

'Seize the day, Poppy.' Like she knows what's good for me and this is it.

I can see by Leanne's face that she is not messing around. 'I mean it, Poppy, you stall any longer and those girls down there will come up here and eat you alive. This is precious warm-up time we're losing.'

I take a look outside my window down to the street below, where a hot-purple minivan with *Gymbox Assassins* written on the side idles by the kerb. Five faces are pressed against the glass, gesturing for us to hurry the hell up and get a move on. Leanne comes up behind me.

'It's my team, I'm the captain; our gym sponsors all the kit, the works. We have built ourselves up from nothing and we are not going to lose today, so get your ass in gear before I carry you out of this stinking cave kicking and screaming.'

I slip my feet into my trainers. 'I'll be down in sixty seconds.'

It looks like the day is seizing me.

CHAPTER FOURTEEN

We get on the bus. Leanne introduces me as 'Bonecrusher Bloom', which is met with approval by all five girls – well, women, about my age – seated in rows, dressed in hot purple Spandex vests and shorts and straining towards the radio at the front whilst biting their thumbnails and stretching their necks.

'Defending champions South London Assassins will face Essex Vixens in the first of the Superleague quarter-finals today, live at the Copper Box Arena in London's Queen Elizabeth Olympic Park,' announces the sports reporter, the newly retired Sandra Skinner, the most fearsome netball captain the England national team has ever known. 'Vixens overcame the disappointment of their semi-final defeat with a 53–46 victory over Liverpool Firebirds a few weeks back. However, the Assassins bounced back from seven goals down to take victory over their northern rivals, Harrogate Hotshots. So there's a lot at stake for both teams. What we do know for sure is that somebody's going to be going home a loser.'

'So I guess we can expect the Vixens to be seeking redemption here today?' asks a second presenter. I recognise the voice: Jake Jackson.

'Absolutely, Jake, and as you well know, when it comes to netball, expect the unexpected. These women come here to play, and they play hard.'

Leanne turns down the dial and raises her palms upwards like a bad-ass evangelical Barbie. 'Okay, girls, you've heard it for yourselves: no prisoners today. It's going to be tough and that's no surprise. We've had a rocky season: injuries, absences and…' she clenches her fist, 'Tammy leaving us in such an abrupt manner certainly hasn't helped us much.'

The girls nod and snarl at each other. The curly-haired one opposite me smashes her fist into the headrest in front of her. Tammy's name is spat around the minibus like a voodoo curse.

Leanne clicks her fingers to regain order. 'But that is all behind us now. What's done is done and we got through it. And why did we get through it?' She points to the blue-eyed blonde in high pigtails sitting on the seat beside me. 'You tell us, Jess.'

The little blonde pushes a stray tendril behind her ear and clears her throat. 'Because we communicate, we understand each other and we listen to ourselves and our bodies.' She has a gentle, almost musical Aussie twang that makes me picture her with beads and braids in her sun-bleached hair, playing a ukulele and shelling prawns somewhere off the Gold Coast.

Leanne nods firmly. Someone whoops; I turn to see that it's the dark-skinned girl with the amazing spiral curls. The headrest in front of her has made a full recovery.

'Shanice, what else?' Leanne calls out to her.

'Discipline: we eat right, train right, sleep right and take no nonsense.'

Leanne nods, the evangelical Barbie loosening to the tune of her revved-up congregation.

More voices shout out. 'We did it because we are unbeatable!' Yeah! 'Because we are powerful!' Yeah! 'Because we are the one and only South London Gymbox Assassins!' Yeah! Yeah! Yeah!

I find myself overrun in a huge clatter of high-fives. Shanice has put me into a headlock, which I think is the Assassins' equivalent to a salutary peck on the cheek.

'So what are we here to do?' shouts Leanne.

'To win! We are here to prove ourselves! We are here to take control!' they holler back to her, to each other, to me.

Maybe it's the way Shanice's arm is wrapped around my neck, or maybe it's the youthful golden glow and sunshiney warmth of Jess's smile, or maybe it's the charged current of rousing energy that is coursing through our bodies collectively that makes me lose myself momentarily and I find myself joining in the raucous chorus.

'And have some fun! We are here to have fun!' I yell.

Slam. Mood splats to the ground. Energy out.

Shanice edges her arm away from my neck like I'm contaminated. Jess's lovely smile melts down her little face like a rained-out street mime. I dart my eyes from girl to girl; all of them look confused or disgusted. Except Shanice, who is sucking her teeth and gripping the headrest with both hands.

'What? What did I say?' I look to Leanne, my palms open in earnest.

Leanne leans towards me and clasps down on my shoulder. 'Poppy, let's get real here. Netball has never been and will never be about fun. Nothing worthwhile is ever about fun.' She juts her chin towards the broad-shouldered girl with the skinhead.

'Nikki, are you here to have fun?'

Nikki gives a cynical smile, shaking her head slowly.

'Tell Poppy why you are here then.'

'I'm frontline murder squad. If I wanted to have fun, I'd drink a bottle of Bacardi for breakfast. I see bad things. I'm here for perspective. To remember that every person I meet isn't an evil, raging, homicidal psychopathic bastard.'

I nod stiffly. I think I'm starting to understand.

'Laura, tell her, why are *you* here?'

Laura is the tallest woman I've ever seen; despite crouching, her head is still brushing the top of the minibus.

She shrugs. 'I work from home, I live alone. You guys are the only people I ever see face to face. Or who know what I look like. If I die tomorrow, no one would know until I missed netball training. That's the only way the world would know something had happened, because I would never, ever, ever miss netball training. That is why I am here.' She swallows hard and looks down at her hands. This is heavy.

'Jess. Tell us why you are here.'

'I miss my family and friends back home in Oz. I live in a grotty house share with ten people who won't look up from their phones to speak to me.' She sighs. 'Which is pretty bad, but mainly the reason I come to netball is because...' Laura gives her an encouraging nod. Jess blinks back and puffs out her chest. 'I need to come to netball because... I'm a primary school teacher. Five-year-olds, thirty of them, every single day. Thirty screaming voices calling your name... thirty dirty noses to wipe...'

Nikki winces at the thought and squeezes Jess's hand in support. 'It's all right, doll, we hear you. You're here now.'

'Shanice?'

'I've got anger. If I don't play, then I lose my shit.'

Leanne points a finger at herself. 'And why am I here? Because my husband lied about having a vasectomy... twice.'

Prawn. I knew he was never good enough for her! Leanne was – is – WAY out of his league. How dare he lie to her? How dare he try to trick her! The mood in the minibus thickens. I can tell I'm not alone in my outrage and disgust.

Nikki nods pensively. 'You'd have grounds, Leanne. I mean, in court, if you did, like, ever consider homicide as an option. Deceit is a credible motive. We've seen it before.'

'Thanks, Nikki, I'll keep that in mind, but,' she lifts a ball to her chest, 'what's done is done. So, girls, let's be crystal clear here: we are not here for fun. We are here because it is hard and challenging and difficult and we need strength to survive; we need to get strong, be strong and stay strong, and we know...' she takes a deep breath and slowly blinks her long eyelashes at the sky and then back to us, 'we KNOW that we are stronger together than we are apart.'

Nods, affirmations and wholehearted hugs are shared around like hushed amens at the end of Leanne's sermon. A very young, pale girl, possibly still even in her teens, who has stayed tight by Leanne's side this whole time finally breaks her silence.

'Why are *you* here?' she asks in a soft, delicate voice. Her eyes dip towards mine.

Who, me? Why is she asking me? Why *am* I here?

'Because Leanne kind of... made me,' I tell her. *Isn't that obvious by the way you drove up to my house totally unexpected and uninvited?*

I survey the circle of faces staring at me, waiting intently for more.

Why. Am. I. Here? It is a pretty profound question. What can I say?

I'm here because I have nowhere else to be, no one else knocking my door down and telling me they need me desperately and won't take no for an answer? I'm here because I haven't really got my act together yet in terms of life, love, career, money or even generic housekeeping and personal hygiene standards?

Why am I here? For someone who doesn't say much, this pale teen has certainly floored me.

'And maybe because I'm a decent goal shooter?' I say, hunching my shoulders to help cram my head down into my neck socket and thus disappear from sight turtle-style.

Leanne snorts, turns to the shy girl, hooks her arm and then points at me. 'I can tell you exactly why Poppy is here, Teagan. Picture this: you are in a really small, claustrophobic changing room in a very posh, exclusive kind of shop. It's hot, the room is airless and you feel clammy and sticky. Everything is too small or too tight and you get a dress stuck over your head, a very delicate, expensive dress that they've told you is your size, therefore it should fit, right? But you know it doesn't. It feels wrong. You like it but you know you won't be able to carry it off because it's just not you. So you feel panicky because you can't see or breathe and you can't wriggle out and you're afraid you'll rip it or ruin it and everyone will know and they'll all be hugely disappointed.'

Holy shit, Leanne, I know EXACTLY how this feels. It's not just Teagan nodding wide-eyed; we all are.

'Now imagine all of that, except that the changing room walls are actually made of mirrors. Hundreds of tiny ones as well as huge close-up, distorted, playhouse-type mirrors.'

A communal horrified gasp. Leanne continues.

'And that's not all: the floor and the ceiling are made of glass… like see-through windows onto the street, so everyone and anyone can look in and spy and comment and laugh and point and take your picture at any time.'

Trembling fingers have drifted to our mouths; Nikki looks like she is going to burst into tears.

Leanne lowers her voice to a whisper. 'Well, that's what it's like for Poppy living inside her own head ALL THE TIME.'

I am suddenly swamped by a fleshy mob of armpit bristle, bingo-wing skin and boob sweat. Strong, supportive arms wrap around each other's shoulders. We are a human tepee of strength and tears and hope and acknowledged failure. Well, okay, I can only claim the tears and the failure. And the majority of the boob sweat.

'How do you know that?' I ask her.

'You told me a long time ago. At a swimming gala,' she replies as she throws our purple bibs at us, kissing each one as it goes out.

'Laura – goal keeper; Shanice – goal defence; Nikki – wing defence; me– centre; Jess – wing attack; Teagan – goal attack; Poppy – goal shooter.'

The bus swerves into the car park. Leanne opens the window and catcalls a cluster of girls kitted out in black and green with a Gothic 'V' on their backs. 'Hey, Vixens!' She gives me a wink. 'We've got Bonecrusher Bloom here to mess you up!'

She holds up her open palm and all seven of us join in a huge clatter of high-fives. I have no idea what to expect, but I'm in, I'm part of this team, and there's no turning back now.

CHAPTER FIFTEEN

We win. Just by one goal, which Leanne reckons is uncomfortably close, but it is still a win and it feels amazing. I was a bit rusty – hardly surprising considering I've not played properly in years – and the first quarter wasn't my finest by any stretch, especially once I raised my arms to shoot the first goal only to realise that there was a small forest under my arms; I may have neglected to shave my pits for… oooh… maybe a few weeks?

In my defence, it is cold outside. Most people don't expose silky-sleek underarms in the middle of a British winter, do they? Also I was pounced on in my bedroom without any prior warning so hadn't time to exactly prep myself to Superleague personal grooming standards before the game. So upon discovery of this little furry faux pas, I tried shooting with my arms tight against my sides, but I just couldn't make that work. I know this because Leanne took me aside and gave me a fairly robust bollocking about getting over myself and putting the team first; about not waiting for others to provide me with chances or hoping that they would just come my way, but creating the opportunities I wanted and making them happen myself. And I listened and I nodded and I agreed and I promised I would do as she said and I did not argue with her or challenge her authority once. Probably because deep down, I knew she was right.

It's true that nobody cared about my hairy pits as much as they cared about seeing some great play, some sharp shooting and some tight teamwork. Leanne's words clicked with me and I got back on court utterly determined to give it my all. Within seconds, I started to see chances and opportunities materialising everywhere, right before my eyes, glimmering, shimmering chances popping up like gold coins on Super Mario.

And it was so fun, despite Leanne's anti-fun warnings. I'm not going to tell her that, obviously – I love her, but she is scary. By the final whistle, I had scored eleven goals and set five more up for Teagan. We were a double act on fire. So so *so* fun.

After the game, Shanice tells me that she thinks I'm brave and inspirational, which I am chuffed about until I find out it's due to the armpit hair. She thinks it's a powerful feminist statement and that we should all stop shaving as a team. 'Let it grow and put it on show,' she sings from her shower in the dressing room. She wants us to do this to send a message of solidarity to women everywhere. I tell her it's a brilliant idea and I'm going to bury my Bics tonight, but Leanne forbids it point blank. So 'let it grow and you are on the bench' is the bottom line.

But I wouldn't have said that to Shanice a year ago or a month ago or possibly even yesterday. Today, though, I feel like anything is possible. I feel like I can make things happen. I might not have even spoken to someone like Shanice or Nikki or Jess before today. These are people I would have liked to study, to read about, to discuss during a tutorial or diagnose for a theory paper, but they wouldn't have affected me beyond what I could take from them to use in my clinical research. I give Shanice a hug and thank her; she smiles back at me and I can tell that she doesn't think I'm weird. Alleluia and amen.

Leanne runs over to the media box to plug Gymbox for some free advertising and hand out some promotional goody bags and random purple paraphernalia: fridge magnets, car stickers, wristbands – she's got a sackload. I nip to the loo to freshen up, and just as I'm about to dry my hands, I hear a sniffle from the end cubicle. I wait a moment, but then I hear it again, except this time it's more than a sniffle; it sounds like someone is struggling to breathe.

'Are you okay in there?' I call out, my ear to the cubicle door.

The person inside is taking big gulps of air, but somehow it's not working; the gulps are desperate and fitful. I rap my knuckles against the cubicle door.

'Can you open the door for me? I just want to check you're okay.'

'Can't,' gasps the tight voice on the other side.

'I'm going to come and help you right this second. It's going to be absolutely fine. I'll be in there in no time at all, okay?'

I hear a strained 'yes'.

I climb onto the toilet seat in the cubicle next door but I'm not tall enough to see over the partition. I look to the ground. The door is about a foot above the floor. I lie down on my back and slide myself under. Even before I look up, I can tell by the electric-purple trainers that it's Teagan. She is leaning against the opposite wall, gripping it as if she is teetering on the ledge of a skyscraper.

She is shivering violently. I place my hand lightly on her back to steady her.

'Hey, lovely. You are going to be absolutely fine,' I tell her in my best calm voice. 'Breathe with me, okay, nice big deep breaths… that's lovely. And again…' Together we breathe deeply in and out, over and over.

My hand drifts to her shoulder and I guide her away from the wall so that now she is standing right in front of me and I can make eye contact with her. Tear-stained tracks meander down her cheeks. Her sweet chocolate-brown eyes are red-rimmed and wide with fear.

'You are doing so well, Teagan, just you stay with me.'

She's regaining control. With her breathing deeper and slower, I can see the tightness dissipating from her chest and shoulders.

'Now I want you to tell me three things you can see, okay? Any three things you like. Big, small, doesn't matter.'

She nods, and I can see her big dark eyes wandering around our tiny cubicle.

'Ceiling,' she says in one breath. If she can focus on something else to distract her from whatever terror has seized her, there's a good chance that her natural breathing pattern will kick in and her heart rate should return to normal. 'Door,' she says.

I nod and smile. 'Super, Teagan. Just one more for me now.'

'You. I can see you, Poppy,' she tells me, and there's a little smile in her eyes and playing about her lips.

'Great work. It's all going to be absolutely fine. Now, let's try two things you can touch.'

Teagan's hand drifts to my head and she starts to smooth down stray strands of my hair, patting them gently back into place.

'Hair; fantastic choice. One more thing you can touch for me.'

Her hand drifts back to her own chest and she strokes down the silky Lycra of her vest top.

'That is perfect, absolutely perfect. You keep stroking your vest for me, nice and slow, just like your breathing, okay?'

Teagan nods and closes her eyes, and I take my chance to quietly slide the bolt back and unlock the cubicle. The door swings open; Teagan opens her eyes and takes my hand to step out into the wide-open space of the changing room.

In a few moments she is at the sink, splashing water on her face and wiping under her eyes with toilet tissue.

'I'm so sorry, Poppy, I don't know what happened to me in there. You must think…' Her breathing quickens again and I see the returning panic in her eyes.

I place my hand on my own vest top and she takes her cue, mimicking me as I slowly stroke it, taking the time to feel the silky fabric brush our fingers, stroking it in time with our breathing.

'You are absolutely fine, my gorgeous girl. How about we get us out of here and grab you a drink?'

Once outside in the open air of the stadium and with a litre of water inside her, Teagan has snapped back to the striking, smiling teen I saw on the court. That's the bizarre thing with anxiety attacks – they come on fast and strong and they often disappear in much the same manner.

'Leanne's over by the media box,' I tell her. 'Let's head there to find the others and then we can go home. I'm starving.'

Teagan stops in her tracks and takes me by the arm.

'What's up?' I ask. 'Everything okay?'

She dips her eyes. 'It's just the media box – my dad will be there. Would you mind if… what happened back there, would it be okay if we kept it between us? He gets so worried about me.'

I hook her arm and pretend to seal my lips, lock them up and throw away the key.

Leanne has the microphone in her hand and is in full flow with Sandra Skinner. 'First quarter was tough – to be honest, I thought we were going to lose it based on our performance in that early part of the game,' she says.

'I'm with you there,' agrees Sandra, 'sloppy passing, terrible shooting. Your new goal shooter's attempts were quite frankly *pathetic* at times – no reach, poor angles. I thought to myself, where on earth did they get her from? And let's hope they have a return address! But somehow you did it. Something changed and South London Assassins got their formation, their flow – you made your chances and look what happened! An absolutely nail-biting ending to a fantastic game.' She raises Leanne's hand into the air.

The crowds in the stand rise with a thunderous cheer and Leanne throws bright purple fridge magnets at them, each emblazoned with her swirly Gymbox logo.

Sandra is whispering into the ear of a tall, good-looking man with very dark hair standing next to Teagan. Maybe that's her dad? He looks too young to have a teenage daughter, but then again, if he is mid-thirties and she's seventeen, I guess it's possible. He nods and smiles to Sandra and then types something into the media box computer. In an instant, Queen's 'Don't Stop Me Now' is booming from the stadium speakers and the crowds in the stands go totally insane. Sandra gives the man a thumbs-up and starts a victory lap with Leanne, throwing goody bags, wristbands, stickers and even more fridge magnets into the sea of grabbing hands.

Just as the song reaches its final chorus, Teagan calls me over to where she is standing with the rest of our teammates. The man thrusts a microphone into my hand and counts me down: 3, 2, 1…

'Judging by the reaction of the spectators, this stadium has Assassins fever!' he begins. 'What a fantastic game, absolutely thrilling second half. So, as the newest member of the team, what do you say? Assassins against Team Oxbridge in the Superleague final: can they do it?'

I am lost for words. His eyes are the same deep chocolate brown as Teagan's. And the way he is looking at me makes me feel like he's asked me something really important.

'I see I've stunned you into silence! And I understand – it's a big question, a question that no doubt will be on everybody's lips over the next few weeks as we wait to see the two strongest teams in British netball battle it out. One thing we do know is that it will be spectacular. So, I may try just one more time for an insider soundbite – Assassins as the Superleague winners, what are the chances?'

He smiles at me and I feel my cheeks flush with heat. I tear my eyes away from his so I can gather my thoughts and shake some words out of my mouth. And that's when I see it, the plastic security card around his neck, and on it his name: *Jake Jackson*.

I look to Teagan and she mouths, 'Absolutely fine.' I take a deep breath and raise my microphone to my mouth.

'Well, Jake, in netball, just as in life, you can't wait for opportunities. You've got to create your chances and make things happen.

Can Assassins make it happen?' I turn to Teagan and the rest of the team. 'Girls! Jake Jackson is asking if Assassins can make it happen? What do we want to tell him?' I hold the microphone in the air for them to answer.

'ASSASSINS ARE UNBEATABLE!' they scream back.

The crowd surges one final time, and a Mexican wave ripples through the stands. Shanice runs on to the court, hands clapping over her head, and starts thousands of people chanting: 'ASSA-SSINS ASSA-SSINS.'

I watch Jake cast a glance over to Teagan, who is clapping and chanting at the top of her lungs.

'Great game,' he says to me as he hands the microphone back to Sandra and pulls on his jacket. 'Good luck in the final.'

'Thanks,' I reply. I can hear Jess calling me from the court, shouting that we need to go. I watch Jake walk away from me and I have a sick kind of feeling that something is supposed to happen now and I know what it is and I know who needs to do it, but I also know that there is every likelihood that it won't happen. That I'll stand here, thinking, watching, stalling, and then my chance will be gone; it will just pop and disappear into oblivion.

I need to make this happen. Have some presence. Project confidence. Show him what I can do, who I can be. I run after him through the rows of plastic seating and catch him by the shoulder. He turns around, mildly startled.

I swallow hard, smooth my hair behind my ears and try to keep my focus as he fixes his dark eyes on me again.

'Really pleased to finally meet you, Jake Jackson.' I put my hand out in front of me and offer it to him. 'My name is Poppy Bloom. How do you feel about second chances?'

CHAPTER SIXTEEN

I lie in bed, my body now scrubbed, defuzzed, moisturised and beginning to succumb to that satisfying muscle ache that only comes from extreme physical exertion. A muscle ache that I haven't felt in a long, long time. Once I got home, I decided that it was time I cleared out the old to make room for the new. I tore down the posters from my wall, chucked all the crap from my shelves and bedside locker. I stripped my bed and put on fresh white cotton sheets. If anyone burst in through the door now, I think I'd be ready. But most importantly, I certainly wouldn't be ashamed. This room looks like it belongs to a young woman, not an overripe teenager. I put on some music, light a vanilla candle and watch the flame flit and flicker against the wall.

I think about what Leanne said on the minibus, about the glass-walled changing room. I'd totally forgotten about it until she mentioned the swimming gala. That brought it back.

I remember that we were both trying out for the school relay team. We'd lined up on the blocks. Fixed our hats and goggles and positioned ourselves, heads bowed, arms outstretched. Just as I bent my knees and arched my back to dive, I caught sight of my dad staggering into the poolside spectators' area, lit cigarette between his lips, long skanky black hair, tight leather trousers and his hallmark heeled boots. I was mortified.

The starting trigger was pulled and I launched myself into the pool with the force of a sub torpedo. I willed the water to be fathomless, enough to envelop and conceal me. I wanted to dive as deep as I could, and then deeper again, far from this place with its spectator rows and echoed shouting and down to the cold, dark, silent depths of the sea floor. But of course that oceanic expanse I so craved was in reality a twenty-five-metre community pool, and no sooner had I enclosed myself in water and escaped Dad's presence than it was time to come up again, to re-emerge and face the scrawny mess waiting for me at the poolside.

I broke the watery surface and felt grateful for the mask of my swimming hat and goggles. Not that it mattered much; he didn't need to see me to embarrass me. He was already doing that. I could hear him shouting, 'Kick harder! For God's sake, Poppy, this is a competition! You can do better than that! And breathe! Why don't you breathe?!'

I touched the white-tiled pool side. I'd come second; Leanne ahead of me by a hair's breadth. The rest of the swim team were lined up behind the blocks.

One of the male lifeguards climbed down from his station. 'Sir, there is no smoking allowed in the building.' His voice was high-pitched and self-conscious. I doubt dealing with drunk and confrontational ageing rockers was a core element of his training.

Dad waved his hand dismissively, which threw him slightly off balance. He reached into his jacket pocket and took out a bottle of beer. He won't be able to open it, I thought. That's good; he'll leave to get a bottle opener and then he won't bother coming back.

And that was what happened. He squinted upwards, swore loudly, turned on his heel and staggered out of the building.

I was absolutely mortified. I'd worked so hard at school to be exactly what the teachers wanted; I listened, I asked questions, I was never rude or troublesome. My plan was to keep my head down; if I didn't court trouble, it wouldn't court me. But then Dad showed up in full public view, drunk and dishevelled, shouting and staggering and yelling at me in front of my peers, in front of my teachers. In front of people I cared about and a future I was trying to build that was too fragile to support his mad, erratic outbursts.

Once I was certain that he was gone, I got out of the pool and went to the changing room with Leanne. I asked her to help me fasten my bra – partly because it was twisted up and partly because my hands were still trembling.

'Are you okay?' she asked. And that was when I told her about how I felt in my head; about the reflections and the distortions and the scrutiny. She went very quiet after that and I thought she didn't get it or hadn't listened or was a bit bored.

'What does your dad do?' she asked after a while.

'He was a musician,' I said. 'A drummer. Used to be. He doesn't do much any more, just some session work. He's on his own, so he gets wasted a lot.'

She shrugged and continued getting changed.

She never brought my dad up after that. And neither did anyone else; either because they didn't realise who he was or because Leanne scared them into silence. Either way, it was a huge relief. And I felt myself breathing again.

CHAPTER SEVENTEEN

On Monday morning, I find the studio in a converted Victorian warehouse nestled between the Tate Modern and Shakespeare's Globe, slap bang in the middle of the South Bank. It's so early it still feels like it's night-time, silent and dark with nothing but the clanging of bin men and a handful of revellers trying to flag down taxis. The security guard waves me through the big glass doors and directs me up to the fourth floor, to the 105 FM studio.

I stand by the huge ceiling-to-floor windows watching the first orange-hued rays of sunrise bleed across the sky and following the Thames as it winds gently through the city, neither blue nor brown but a glittering metallic grey, glistening as an occasional spear of light pierces the clouds and dances over its rippling surface. Breathtaking. It actually feels as if I am on top of the world.

I blink back a prickle of tearfulness. I feel like I'm on the cusp of something big, like I'm about to set sail to a new and foreign land, and I'm a mess of nerves and excitement. Or maybe I'm just super-tired. Despite my very best intentions, I didn't sleep a wink. My pained nocturnal activity consisted of turning my pillow over every five seconds, kicking my duvet about, counting sheep and visualising white sands and turquoise beaches in an effort to turn my mind off and sink into a peaceful slumber, but alas, it never happened.

Now I feel dog-tired. And hypersensitive, like all my feelings and nerve endings are prickly and razor sharp and just a tad too close to the surface of my skin. I have been known to get weepy and sensitive and irrational when sleep-deprived, even succumbing to the odd temper tantrum. *Keep it together, Poppy. Please, please do not mess up today.*

My phone beeps; a text from an unknown number. Who on earth could this be? And why would they be up at this crazy hour texting me?

'*Hi, Tom here. Got your number from Leanne, been thinking about you. Good luck with the new job. You'll smash it. T x*'

My heart swells in my chest and I text back my thanks. Tom. Thinking about me? Wishing me luck? Kiss at the end? As there is still nobody else here yet in the studio but me, I twirl around in one of the three swingy chairs lined up by the desk and survey my surroundings. There is a gigantic clock face fixed to the back wall of the studio. Above it hangs a glass panel with the lettering *ON AIR* illuminated in red. It will turn amber when on a ten-second countdown and then green when we are actually live broadcasting. The distressed red-brick wall showcases row upon row of framed autographed prints of guests who have visited over the decades. The most famous and celebrated singers, bands, sports stars, politicians, comedians and actors posing cordially by this desk, in this spot, this very studio. I'm drawn to the older sepia prints, which are flecked with age and sun damage, showing gel-coiffed, dickie-bowed presenters stiffly shaking hands with toothy crooners and beehived backing singers.

I squint forward to get a better look at a very familiar-looking photo in the top right-hand corner. Black Horn, from the late seventies. A long-haired, leather-clad group of three, the lead singer, Jonnie-O, snarling close up into the camera; Cowboy Carlos the guitarist clutching his instrument tight against his bony body like a low-slung sword; and my dad draped over the drum kit in a torn T-shirt, thumb and pinkie posed in his iconic devil-horn pose. It's weird seeing him so young, trying to look grizzled and hard with such soft, fresh features and bright eyes. *What happened to you, Ray? How did it all go so wrong?*

I swing around to the window again. I'm not thinking about him today. Too busy. Too excited. I clap my hands together. *Come on, today, I'm ready for you.*

At six o'clock on the dot, Jake Jackson pushes through the double doors in reverse. 'You're here! I knew you would be!' he says. His hands are full with two large takeaway coffees. He sets one in front of me. 'For you. Early starts are inhumane. This part never gets easier. But it'll pass, trust me.'

I breathe in the warm, rich scent. Colombian triple roast. My all-time favourite coffee blend. And it's extra-large, the kind of large that most people think is obscene and which contains at least four times the recommended daily allowance of caffeine. We sip in ceremonial silence until the caffeine trickles its way into our systems, the joyous hum of functionality kicks in and we start to light up.

'So what are you expecting?' Jake asks. His resemblance to his daughter is striking. They are the spitting image of each other, which relaxes me and makes me feel like I kind of know Jake already through Teagan.

'Um, some filing, I guess. I'm pretty good at general admin; I can take messages, answer emails, fetch coffees, snacks. I can… Just give me a minute.' I start groping around in my bag for my notebook. I find it, pull it out and flick through the coloured index tabs on the side.

'What's that you've got there?' he asks.

'Oh, just some notes I wrote up. I did a little research last night – how to succeed in radio, five key ways to thrive in broadcasting, how to be the perfect intern in eighty-six simple steps, that type of thing. This is really new to me, I've never even been inside a studio before, so…' I cough into my hand simply to stop involuntary words gushing from my mouth. Sure, this is just an internship, but there's a host of other graduates who would bite Jake Jackson's hand off, so the more I keep my cluelessness to myself, the better. 'I'm really grateful and excited to be here. Anything you want me to do, just shout. I'm a fast learner.'

He laughs and holds out his hand. 'May I?'

I pass him the notebook and he thumbs through my handwritten, dog-eared, multicoloured pages of notes, highlighted extracts and summarised key points. Actually, I'd started researching other fellowships and university posts outside of Banbridge last night but found myself googling radio FAQs at every opportunity. Maybe the prospect of this stint at FM105 is drawing me in more and more. Could it be that there is actually life and hope and a place for me outside of academia?

'Very impressive. You didn't do a little research; you did a *lot* of research.'

I shrug, delighted with being star student. 'I like to be prepared.'

'Sure, I understand.' He licks his lips and leans forward in his chair so that his elbows rest on his knees. He looks conflicted.

Oh my God, he's going to send me home! Say that it's all a big mistake and I should probably leave now before we waste any more time…

'How can I put this?' He taps his fingers on the notebook. 'I'm afraid all this research you did was a complete waste of your time.' He flicks to a random page and traces his finger across it. 'The majority of advice that you've got in here, things like "think of interesting questions to ask in advance, vary the tone of your voice and make encouraging noises to show that you're paying attention, repeat back what you just heard or summarise it" – I really want you to forget all that.' He closes my notebook. 'It's crap.'

He places my notebook in a drawer behind him and shuts it. I kind of squirm in my seat, not because I don't like what I'm hearing but… I really like having a notebook. I lace my hands together nervously. Today could be long; very, very long.

'Come here a sec, I want to show you something.' He swings around in his chair and walks over to the gallery wall at the back of the studio. I follow, pulling my fringe down over my right eye so that a thin veil of hair shields me against the looming presence of Dad's photo in the top corner.

Jake waves a hand across the gallery of photos. 'I make my living talking to people: I've been lucky enough to meet Olympians, billionaires, Nobel Prize winners and well-known people from every area. I talk to people I like. I talk to people I don't like, and sometimes I have to talk to people I disagree with deeply on a personal level.'

I survey all the different characters from different eras and disciplines with this in mind. It is impressive. I think of my dad being here back in the day. Before Jake's time of course but probably qualifying as one of the more tricky or obnoxious guests.

'And it can be challenging. But the reason I think I can do it is because it all boils down to the same basic concept: be interested in other people. Simple as that. There is no reason to research or theorise or try to prove that you are paying attention in a fake way if you are in fact paying attention for real.'

He points to a large photo in the centre of the wall. 'See that picture there? That's my grandfather.'

Holy shit, I recognise this person; he's super-famous, like best-friends-with-the-Queen famous. What's his name? Ooh, this is the kind of question you get in round one of *Who Wants to Be a Millionaire?* I should know it, don't tell me…

'Charlie Goldsmith!' I squeal. 'The journalist!'

Jake breaks into a smile. 'You know him, cool. Well, I was really close to him. I never really cared about his work or anything the whole time I was growing up, but when I turned twenty, my girlfriend at the time and I found ourselves expecting a baby –

quite a shock to us, even more so to our parents. I had to drop out of drama school, try and find a job, a place to live, learn to be a dad, how to feed, change, cope with sleeplessness… It was a steep learning curve. We had to grow up fast and at times it was hard.'

I study the photo. There's a fatherly, Churchillian air to this man's kind, lined face. He is sitting in a large leather chair, a pile of heavy books at his side and a resting dog at his feet.

'This picture was taken at that time; Charlie had just suffered a stroke and he needed some help. He offered me a job as his PA. It worked out like a dream. I got to bring my daughter Teagan to work with me, I got to spend time with my grandfather and learn all about his work in a way I never appreciated before. I look back and I think it may have been one of the happiest times of my life.'

'I know Teagan from netball, she's a great girl!' I tell him, remembering the stark contrast between the pale, shy girl I met on the bus, the warrior I saw on the court and then the panic-stricken, hyperventilating teen I found in the changing rooms afterwards. So much internal angst; so many dimensions to the one character.

'Ah, of course! You're an Assassin!' he says, recalling the connection.

I nod proudly.

'Yes, being part of that team has made the world of difference to Teagan. They let her be herself, you know? They've taken her into their bosom, and once you're in, well, like any tribe, they treat each other like family. Very loyal.' He sighs deeply. 'She wouldn't want you to know this, but she suffers terribly from anxiety. It's getting better, but it's still there. Very hard for a parent to know how to help. It breaks my heart to see her suffer. I just want to protect her.'

I think back to her panic attack and the way she wanted me to keep it a secret from her dad – she wanted to protect him too.

'If Teagan ever wants to talk, or text or email me, please let her know she's welcome. I'm really fond of her, and if I can help, I'd love to.'

'That's really kind, Poppy. I'll tell her.'

He smiles and studies the tiny lettering engraved on a brass plate at the bottom of the photo frame. *Forever in our hearts.* I have a vague recollection of a news story from a few years ago reporting how Charlie Goldsmith had died in his sleep, surrounded by family.

'You still miss him,' I observe.

'Every day. I learnt a lot from him. Charlie was a true people person, and if he couldn't make it to them, my job was to ensure that they came to him. We brought all sorts of people to the house, at all hours. I'd greet them, fetch them whatever they needed and show them into Charlie's room. Afterwards he'd say, "Do you know who that was?" I'd shake my head, and he'd say, "That was a man who forgave his wife's murderer", or "That was a girl who sailed around the world alone", or "That was the Prime Minister's mother."'

He wipes his face with his hand. 'The point I'm making is that I started to change my expectations. Everyone I met, whether in Charlie's house or not, I expected them to have something special, something unique or extraordinary about them. And I still do. And if you trust that people have that, and expect it, then it will happen and you'll never have to feign interest, because real people and their stories are the most interesting, most extraordinary experiences we can share.'

I think he may be right. Listening to him, I didn't need to insert an encouraging grunt or empathetic head waggle once. I just listened. The way I felt Tom listened to me the other night – with an open mind and full attention.

'Missing your notebook?'

And I realise I'm not missing it at all. Not one bit. I'm not referencing or researching or footnoting or paraphrasing. I don't feel like anyone is testing me or trying to catch me out or contradict me for the sake of argument. I used to be shy because I wasn't sure I'd be able to find the right words to describe what I wanted to say. That I'd be misunderstood. But the right words are there. And for the first time, I feel that I can find them. Express them. Hear them. Maybe they've been there all along but I didn't trust them. I presumed other people knew better.

'No, actually. I like this freestyling. It's liberating,' I admit.

'Good. And fun?'

'Very fun,' I answer.

He claps his hands together. 'Now we're getting somewhere… Let's get this show on the road.'

A girl with long wavy hair and a silver nose ring bursts through the double doors and blows us both a kiss. 'Good morning, cosmonauts!' she announces. She is the closest thing to magic I've ever seen. Her hair is literally other-worldly – a marbled blend of dark indigo, pale green and every other shade of galactic night sky you can imagine. How does she do that? Is brunette to aurora borealis a common colour change? I would pay to see my mum's face if she was asked for this at her salon. It is mesmerising.

Jake gives her a big wave. 'Astral, this is Poppy – remember, the one who sent Hilary packing on Friday's show?'

Astral, the galaxy girl, laughs out loud. 'Oh my God! You killed the wicked old witch! How can we ever repay you?' she says.

I actually feel like Dorothy, tripping over my tongue to explain that I didn't mean to, I'm really sorry.

Astral presses her palms together. 'We hated her.' Then she throws back her head with a mock-sinister laugh and dances a little victory jig. 'Ding-dong, the witch is dead! No more Hilary! Happy days! So I guess Carol, the other wicked old witch, will be lining up some airhead celebrities to take her spot?'

Jake shrugs. 'Let's just wait and see.'

He turns to me. 'Poppy, this is Astral, our producer. She runs the show. Any time she makes a face or gives any kind of hand gesture, it's best to just do what she wants or else she'll ask the universe to thwart your abundance or something to that effect; I'm not brave enough to ask.'

Astral gives me a massive wink. 'Right, so agenda for today: music is all lined up, as is the news; competitions, some more phone-ins and stuff to give away. But this is the biggie. Later on this week, we've got Khloe Fox in for an exclusive about her new tell-all autobiography.'

Jake twists his lips and draws his eyebrows together.

Astral fills him in. 'Khloe Fox is twenty years old and she's famous for having sex on TV – and that's it. That is the sum total of her contribution to the world.'

She turns to me. 'So, Poppy, I'll introduce you to the behind the scenes crew; they'll set you up with a log in and show you the ropes regarding social media, advertising, accounts all that stuff, and show you to the mail room. Then you'll be ready to access the show's email account and you can start weeding out our inbox. Sound okay?'

I nod fervently.

'Right, guys, nearly show time. Poppy, the next coffee run is at nine. Café Paul is in the market; he'll be expecting you.'

At 8.50, I make my way over to Café Paul, just a stone's throw from the studio. It is the most gorgeous little coffee shop you have ever seen. Gingham tablecloths, fresh flowers, quirky French jazz playing softly in the background, along with the most scrumptious smell of freshly baked bread. The patisserie counter is a work of art: a glassy mosaic of fruit slices and choux spheres.

'*Bonjour, mademoiselle! Ça va?*' calls out the smiling moustached waiter behind the counter.

'*Ça va bien! Très bien!* I tell him.

This place is heaven. Why have I never been here before? It's a short bus journey from my house and yet I never even knew it existed. I've spent so much time away from home that I've forgotten what amazing places exist on my own doorstep. From now on I'm going to rediscover my home city inch by inch, profiterole by profiterole, macaron by macaron… my favourites!

As I push back through the double doors with our coffees, I can hear Astral's voice booming from the glass-panelled sound box.

'I for one can actually feel that today is going to be amazing!' She glances up at the huge clock. 'On air again in two minutes, Jake. Be ready to rock.'

I can't believe how quickly the days pass. By Thursday, I am fully at home at the FM105 studio. I feel part of the crew, part of the family. I look out the window to take in the sunrise, a glorious golden symmetry breaks forth tinged with spectacular shades of pastel purple and pale pink stretching over the cityscape. I'm not religious so it's hard to know who to thank, but gratitude is definitely due. So I thank my lucky stars, wherever they may be. Astral calls to me. 'Poppy, you come this way.' We sweep out of the studio, away from the panorama of the skyline, and she directs me to a tiny windowless mail room at the end of the hall. 'Welcome to the mail room. You're best tucked up in here away from all the drama, to be honest. Carol King is on her way in, and she's in one of her moods.' She rolls her eyes.

'Who's Carol King?' I ask.

'The big boss of the radio section, so we've got to toe the line. She's a nightmare. She goes for style over substance at every opportunity – complete media vulture. If it attracts attention, good or bad, she jumps on it, regardless of anything else. Hence we have Khloe Fox in the studio today.' Astral mimics putting her fingers down her throat. 'So best leave you in here for now, okay? There are sackloads in here to clear. I'll leave it totally to your discretion. Shred or burn the lot if you like: your call. Have fun!' she hollers and disappears out of the door.

I look around. Not so bad. About twelve big black sacks, a shredder, a filing cabinet, a laptop and a portable heater. Almost my natural habitat. I rip open my first bag.

I don't notice the time passing until Astral pokes her head around the door. 'Wow, you've done well! Fast work, Poppy!'

I've sifted, sorted and shredded most of it already; since ninety-five per cent of it was old competition entries, fan mail, postal requests for shout-outs, press releases for celebrity tour dates and a handful of bizarre complaints regarding satanic music, it was pretty straightforward. And what right do I have to complain? It certainly beats tarot reading.

'Anything worth keeping?' she asks, not looking especially hopeful.

I shake my head and point to the last bag. 'I haven't opened that one yet, though, so who knows?'

'Ooh, that one could be interesting. Everything in there is addressed to Hilary.' She gives a dramatic shiver. 'Anyway, leave that for now. I doubt there's anything in there that needs your urgent attention. Khloe Fox is on her way in; could you meet her downstairs and escort her up, please? She's due on air in fifteen minutes.'

'Of course,' I say as I shred my last page and brace myself to meet my first celebrity.

Khloe Fox, nipped, tucked and sucked, is perched on the passenger seat of her car, splay-legged in a tiny miniskirt despite the freezing winter wind, facing a sea of paparazzi. I catch her eye and she nods blankly before dipping her chin coquettishly and widening her legs to the photographers a few inches more.

She tries to haul herself up by gripping the frame of the car door but slides back down again, her heavily made-up face and bloated lips making her expression impossible to read. She tries again, slides again and swears loudly. I muscle through the crowd, secure my hand under her elbow and give it a one, two, three lift. She is on her feet but she is unsteady, teetering on skyscraper stilettos.

'Where's the studio?' she asks.

I nod to the top storey. 'Up there,' I tell her.

'For fuck's sake,' she mumbles, and we start tottering our way to reception, her tiny skirt inching its way up her thighs with every step. It takes me twenty minutes to escort her upstairs, then she stops to reapply her make-up despite the fact that she is already running late and it's radio after all. Who is going to see her? But it's clear that Khloe Fox does not take orders from anyone, especially a lowly intern like me.

By the time we finally reach the studio, Astral is red-faced and flustered. She gives Jake an exasperated thumbs-up, and he nods and pulls the spongey microphone to his lips while Khloe Fox sits down and negotiates her headphones over her enormous rock-hard hair.

'Welcome back, London! Happy Monday to all and sundry, and if you've just joined us, wow, have we got a smashing line-up for you here today on the 105 FM morning show with yours truly, Jake Jackson. All the usual antics, with something a little bit different coming up for you too – an exclusive with reality TV star and self-confessed gold-digger Khloe Fox, live in the studio right now. Khloe, lovely to have you. How are you this morning?'

'Um… can I get a drink or something?' she says. 'I need a Diet Coke. Now.'

Astral flashes me a look and I scramble to the drinks machine. Jake fills the dead airtime with snippets from Khloe's file: her rise to fame, her future career plans. She remains silent until she has drained the last drop from her Coke, and then she appears to come to life.

'So, I understand you've been keeping very busy lately,' says Jake. 'Your autobiography is out, a new TV series, even a new single. Can you tell us a little bit about that?'

Sigh. Bu-rrrrrrp. BUURRRPPPPPP. She is burping LIVE ON AIR.

Astral press her palms into her face; Jake shuffles in his chair. Khloe Fox sits and belches into her mic and I decide it's best that I do what Astral said and hide in the back, out of drama's way.

In the mailroom, I tear open the final bin bag. Hilary's mail. It's clear how much she valued her listeners by the way she ignored every piece of mail addressed to her. I pick some out at random. The postmarks show them to date back more than three years. I think it's dreadful that she hasn't at least acknowledged those who asked her for help. I grab a handful and stuff them into my bag for later. I'll see what I can do. Maybe I can help even if Hilary won't. My heart twitches when I think of the care and courage it takes to pick up a pen and share your innermost struggles with somebody else. I can't shred anything in this bag. It would be wrong. Sacrilegious. So I start to file them in order of newest to oldest. Something needs to be done with them, and I'm now in a position to see that it is. Like an unfinished sentence or a lingering question, these people need a response.

Then I find a flimsy airmail envelope and open it to find a handwritten letter.

I brush the soft, tissue-thin paper between my fingers. The letter is written in old-fashioned blue fountain pen ink by a very light hand, the pressure virtually feather-light yet the characters perfectly formed, a smooth, quaint cursive with a slight quiver that could indicate an elderly hand or perhaps someone trembling with nerves. All the sentences in the body of the letter slant rather extremely to the left, which almost always means an introverted or reluctant character in terms of self-expression. A graphologist might claim that this is a classic marker of someone holding themselves back or fearful about pushing themselves forward in life. I could happily take myself off into a quiet corner somewhere and feed on the rich interpretative quality of this delicately penned letter right now.

I open out the folded paper to discover a tiny bouquet of dried lavender, delicate purple florets taped to the bottom corner. I raise it to my nose and fill my senses with the gentle scent of it; a sweet floral perfume mingled with fresh air and rich earth. It smells wonderful. What a darling little letter, and I haven't even read one word of it yet.

My heart jumps with fright as out of the blue Astral bursts into the mailroom. Is it a fire? Has somebody collapsed? I leap to my feet. 'What is it? What's wrong?'

'Find something, anything!' She points to the little stacks of letters I've made on the desk. She has an eye-popping, hysterical expression on her face. 'It's a car crash out there. Khloe Fox… Khloe Fox is just HORRENDOUS! Help me! Help us! Find something, something nice and normal and, well, miraculous. You have two minutes. Don't let me down, Poppy.'

I scan the room for a moment and then my eyes settle on the flimsy airmail letter. I think it's just the thing Astral is looking for. I hand it to her and she scans through it, then presses her palms together as if in prayer and mouths, 'Thank you thank you thank you.'

Back in the studio, she raps her knuckles against the glass partition that separates her and Jake. 'Right, we're going to go with this.' She glances at me. 'Poppy, in there beside Jake. Take Khloe Fox's seat. Jake, have a quick read-through and be ready when I signal you.'

What do you mean, sit in there beside Jake? I'm the intern. My place is way out the back. You asked me to FIND something; I didn't realise that meant becoming an emergency presenter.

Jake pushes the microphone away, takes off his earphones and tries to catch my eye. 'You okay? You're looking very pale.'

'I feel sick,' I say.

'Nonsense. You can do this, Poppy. Get that down you.' He pours a splash of his coffee into an empty cup and I take a massive gulp.

I seriously don't think I can do this LIVE, without preparation. Before, I was just a listener; I could hang up or go silent any time I wanted. Being a presenter means taking charge, being responsive. Handling shit as it emerges. And who knows what's going to emerge? I feel my internal organs convulse with fear and nerves and utter fucking horror at the idea that four million people are going to hear me blabber LIVE ON AIR across the capital. Four million people! I can't even quantify that, I can't imagine it. I've never seen four million anything – it's unfathomably huge. I take off my headphones. I'm not ready to do this. I want to go back to the mailroom.

Astral is dizzied by the flashing updates on her many screens. 'Poppy, we need you on air. Khloe Fox has caused uproar. We need to pull this back quickly, or we're all finished.'

Jake nods in my direction. 'No pressure, then.'

'I'm really sorry, Jake,' I say. 'I know I came to you and asked you for this chance, but actually, I don't think I can do it. It's just overwhelming. I can't make stuff up on the spot and casually dish out advice when I know that millions of people are listening.'

'Poppy, you're going to have to trust me here. I know it might seem scary, but you have nothing to worry about, I promise you. I wouldn't have asked you to do this if I didn't have absolute faith in you. That last caller on Friday – the one about the late-blooming daughter – that was perfect. I thought to myself when I heard you, if my daughter had a problem, what would I want for her?

I'd like her to be able to access a professional, to get some sound advice. But if she contacted the station, she'd have got Hilary.'

I look up at him, and he raises an eyebrow and shakes his head.

'No way. She was judgemental, she didn't listen and she made people feel like shit about themselves. I would like my daughter to call someone like you, Poppy. Someone who is real and relevant and positive and who can actually help. You have a chance today to help so many people; ordinary people, going about their everyday business, trying to do their best but in need of a little support, some encouragement, a nudge towards a decisive course of action. You can do that. You can give anybody feeling alone this morning access to free, professional support right from this studio. Right now.'

I'd love to think that this is true. It's what I've always wanted to do. It was what I was trying to achieve with my thesis. Is this the best way for me to do it? Is this exactly where I need to be?

Astral raps on the glass and holds ten fingers in the air. The panel above the clock turns amber.

'You can do this, Poppy,' Jake says. 'I know you can. I'll be right here. Take your cue from me. I won't drop you. Just trust me.'

I think of the last time I heard that: 'I won't drop you.' It was what Tom said to me just before I climbed on his shoulders. And you know what. He kept his word. He didn't drop me.

I look directly into Jake's eyes. I trust him too. 'Okay. We can do this. Let's do this.'

He dips his head to meet my eyes and places his hand on mine. 'Good luck.'

'Thanks,' I say as I fit my headphones and try to concentrate on the lights and the buttons and the levers and Astral's flashing fingers as the *ON AIR* sign changes to green and we go live across London's airwaves.

Astral taps the glass partition and counts me down from three. I hand Jake the letter, and he rustles the tissue-thin paper and raises a quizzical eyebrow at the decorative flower in the corner.

'Welcome back, folks. Hope your morning is going well so far… because of course, some things don't quite go as planned. That's live radio for you, live and unpredictable, as we've seen this morning.

'On a completely different note, we've got something just a little bit special for you… I'm holding in my hands a letter; yes, a real, proper, old-school, handwritten letter that one of our listeners took the trouble to write and stamp and post in a letter box; a rare effort in today's technological world. So, let's have it. It's from Benny, aka the Reclusive Gardener, who writes: "Dear Jake, I listen to your show every day without fail. I have done so for many years. I enjoy it immensely. However, I have never felt moved to write in before as Hilary's manner never sat well with me. But I'm in a terrible quandary and I need to seek some help. So much so that I am now sitting at my desk penning this letter, which I hope will find its way to you.

'"You see, I'm rather a hermit. I live alone in a lorry container, which I have refurbished to make my home. I am a gardener by trade, so I make a meagre living with odd jobs and maintenance work from the kind village folk, who accept me as I am despite my dullness and uninteresting ways. So where lies the problem? you may ask.

'"Well, I have hit a kink in terms of my routine and my emotions. A very well-to-do lady from the city, a retired florist, has relocated to the village. I was referred to her to carry out some weeding and plant beds of English lavender – her favourite. And what can I say? I am quite struck by her. She is a most charming, beautiful and warm-hearted soul and quite the socialite. To lose her friendship would leave me at sea; however, I understand that she could never accept me as I am presently. This social inadequacy of mine needs knocking on the head, ironing out, giving notice and showing the door. My wish is to become the man she deserves so that we may flourish and grow together. Is there anything that can be done for one such as me?"

'I have Poppy with me here. What do you think, Poppy?' says Jake.

I feel the adrenalin pumping in my ears. I take my cue and lean in to the microphone to begin my response. 'Yes…' I say. It comes out as a growl.

Sweet Jesus. I clear my throat and swallow hard. Then I try again.

'Yes, well, firstly, Benny… um, thank you so much for your very eloquent letter.' Jake gives me a wink and slides over a glass of water. I take a sip. And a deep breath. 'If you are half as charming as your turn of phrase, I understand entirely why the village folk and your lady friend care for you as they do. I am so glad that you wrote in, mainly because I think we can help you with some practical advice, but also because this is a huge issue. There are plenty of people at home or at work listening in this morning who have found themselves suffering from social anxiety at varying levels and as a result maybe withdrawing bit by bit from situations that make them feel nervous, uncomfortable, panicky or overwhelmed. To be honest, Benny, I've done this in my own life as well. In my own way, I tried to hide away from facing people or problems that I thought I couldn't handle. But you know, bit by bit I'm finding out that I can handle more than I ever thought I could. And it feels good. Really good.

'So let's see where we can make the most difference to you, Benny. You've described yourself as "reclusive" and "a hermit". I think there is a general assumption that somebody who lives in a remote or socially isolated way does so because they want to turn their back on society or be by themselves and away from other people. However, if you don't mind, Benny, I'm going to zone in on a few things I've spotted in your letter that tell me that actually this may not be the case with you.'

I'm studying the letter in my hand – so delicate, so heartfelt. I really hope Benny's listening somewhere out there. Jake turns towards me, listening intently, his index finger playing on his lips. I think it's going well. In fact I *know* it's going well. I can feel it.

'I believe that something else is going on here. Of course it was your choice to move into the lorry and create a distance between yourself and others; however, the way you describe yourself as "dull" and "uninteresting" and write that the village folk are "kind" to include you in any way tells me that you've created this distance not because you rejected your community but because you felt you were not worthy of being part of it. This is an easy trap to fall into, Benny. Believe me, I've done it myself. For a long time I labelled myself shy and quiet, until I started to realise that I'd outgrown that label. I wasn't that person any more. And my label was keeping me from things I wanted do, people I wanted to get closer to.'

I think of Tom. To think that I nearly went home rather than meet him by himself. I shudder at the thought.

Jake leans towards me. 'But if you believe that about yourself, Poppy, what can you do about it? How do you convince yourself otherwise?'

Astral is nodding in her booth. We are back on track.

'Great question, Jake. Really great question. We all have beliefs about ourselves that we can identify as core beliefs – they may have come from our childhood, our parents, our peer group. They can be entrenched very deeply and they can be positive or negative. For example, if I believe I'm rubbish at singing, then my musical skills will more than likely deteriorate because I'm not practising, so it becomes a self-fulfilling prophecy. But if I believe that I am a gifted singer, then I will have more confidence to sing, therefore I will sing more often and exercising my voice will lead to continued progress so…'

'So that becomes a self-fulfilling prophecy too,' finishes Jake

'Exactly! Once we acknowledge that core beliefs can work for us or against us, we are on the road to better things. So, Benny, in your case I think you have a negative core belief that you are dull and that if you approach or interact with people they will find you uninteresting. Because of this you have kept your voice and your ideas to yourself and you may be out of practice in the art of conversation. You need to get back in the game!'

'Poppy, do you think it would be fair to say that Benny might be being a bit hard on himself here; I mean, how does he know that he is dull or uninteresting? Might this only be his perception? For example, I could walk into his village pub right now and ask the drinkers in there, "What's Benny like?" And they might describe him as the life and soul of the party!'

'That is so true! So, so true. And when we hold personal beliefs about ourselves that are highly subjective, we have to make ourselves study the evidence carefully. So let's look at Benny's letter. He is clearly liked, even loved by his village peers, as they invite him to work for them and recommend him to others; and a brand-new beautiful woman has come to town and is very keen on him also. So I think Jake is onto something. Benny, we know you believe that you're dull; why you believe this or whose fault it is that this belief came about really doesn't matter now – it's gone, done, in the past. It is time to start afresh. I'm convinced that you actually want to connect, engage and get closer to people, particularly your new lady friend.'

Jake claps his hands together. 'A-ha! Now we're getting somewhere! I can see this; I can totally see how this makes sense. So now that we've got to the heart of the matter, what can Benny do to go about solving this "kink" as he puts it?'

I shuffle up in my seat. This is classic! I can definitely help Benny. One hundred per cent this is going to work. And his life will be transformed.

'Benny, I'm going to suggest a practical step that I want you to take. Nothing scary or dramatic; it's just to build your confidence and get you back into the swing of things. Over the next week,

I want you to ask your lady friend to help you buy a pot for her garden.'

Jake gives me a confused look. Astral juts out her top lip as if to say 'Wtf?'

'Trust me. She is a florist; she will delight in the task of shopping for something that will enhance the beauty of the flowers. You will delight in spending time with her and sharing your mutual interest in the natural world. An adventure awaits you, Benny, and I promise it will be joyous if you can just be brave enough to open up and take that first step.'

I know it sounds mad, but I can tell from Benny's handwriting and his language and the picture he paints of his life that this is the right course *for him.* Now I just hope he can find the courage to follow it through.

Astral motions a wrap-up through the glass and points to the wall clock. Four minutes to ten.

'Aw, guys, we're out of time!' says Jake. 'Where did that last twenty minutes go? I was totally immersed in Benny's world! Right, Benny mate, we are wishing you the best here, sending you all the good vibes, all the luck and all the love we can muster. Give Poppy's advice a go. And once you've followed through with it, get back in touch! Please send us an update. We want to know how this little love story between the reclusive gardener and the socialite florist blossoms! This last song is for you, Benny, and it's a classic; who couldn't use some Dionne Warwick to get them in the right frame of mind? Here we go with "What the World Needs Now"…'

Is that it? Is it over? Already? I was just getting started!

Jake throws off his headphones, Astral runs in through the double doors and both of them wrap their arms around me for a group hug. Astral grabs my shoulders. 'Our switchboards have gone ballistic! Social media has blown up! #Lovebenny is trending right this second. I told you I had a good feeling about this week!

What did I tell you! I am always right when I get that feeling! Welcome to the morning show, Dr Poppy Bloom – you're exactly what we need right now.'

Jake spins around on his chair. 'So you're ready to become our next big thing?'

'Yeah, why not. I'm ready for anything.'

As I walk home from work, I make a decision. I decide to practise what I preach. To take my own medicine. If I encourage someone do something I genuinely think will enhance their lives, then I need to be prepared to do it too. I can't tell Benny to step up and ask someone out if I can't muster the courage myself, can I?

So I'm going to find Tom and ask him out on a date. Now that I'm sticking around in Brixton and I've secured a job, there's really nothing left to stop me. So, Benny, I'm with you on this one. We're both going to have to brave it. Our future happiness depends on it!

I have a good feeling about this, Benny, like we're just getting to the best bit.

CHAPTER EIGHTEEN

The next morning, I show up for work at the same ungodly hour, but this time I'm bright-eyed and bushy-tailed and cannot wait to get stuck in. Astral whacks a contract down in front of me. It looks so good, I'm tempted to lick it on the dotted line. No hanging about; I start on Monday.

Omfg! I've got my dream job. And until last week, I never even knew it existed. *The next time I walk through these office doors it will be as Freelance Presenter and Guest Psychologist Dr Poppy Bloom.*

I sign it. I take a selfie with it.

Astral makes me a copy and I read it and read it and read it again on the bus journey home later that day.

I have a job. A job that pays money. A job that pays REALLY good money. And that I love so much it doesn't even feel like I'm working.

I call Markus to thank him for all his help and to let him know that I can now be taken off his register. I feel incredible. Strong and ready to take on anything.

My mum is absolutely thrilled. She loves the station. It's been playing in her salon for years and years, so she's my number one fan. Poor Frank wasn't as ecstatic when I had to break the news that we are now disqualified from 'You Do the Maps'.

'Sorry, Frank. Employees and relatives are not allowed to play. Just in case they cheat,' I say, and hand him a box of chocolates to ease the blow.

He shrugs. 'Never mind, small price to pay for a glitzy new job on the radio.' And then he takes the box up to the bath and eats it all by himself.

I go to bed for a nap. It's the only way I can manage to be bright and breezy with these early-morning starts and have a life as well. I set the alarm for 5 p.m. and then I'll head to netball training. I cannot wait to tell them about my new job.

When I get to netball, I find that the girls have already heard the news and are in discussion about this brave new direction that 105 FM is taking. Employing a listener and enlisting a real doctor who can assist with mental health rather than just aggravate and entertain. Apparently some people are saying it's a publicity stunt. A few even think it spells the end for 105 FM altogether. That it is a last-ditch attempt to revive flagging ratings.

Whatever it is, I've signed up to it. And I am so excited and so are all the girls.

'I'll tell everyone at work to tune in,' says Shanice. 'We've got you covered, okay?' I give her a massive hug and we all decide that we need to celebrate. So straight after training, we hit the town and I buy EVERYBODY drinks at a cocktail bar. Credit card all the way; as the barman says, doesn't matter now that I'm earning, that's what it's there for, right? Work to live, not live to work…

I need to scope out the Tom situation with Leanne. How would she take it if she found out that I was interested in her twin brother? Would it bother her deeply or would she even care? Would she encourage me to go for it or warn me off altogether? Maybe I have misread the whole thing and Tom is just a really friendly guy and I shouldn't get carried away?

'How's Tom doing?' I ask, trying to sound casual. She raises a quizzical eyebrow. Busted. She takes a deep breath and tilts her head.

'What's wrong?' I say.

'It's just that if you get together, it means you could break up. And if you break up, I will have to lose one of you. So basically, get with Tom by all means, but remember, unless you end up marrying each other, this whole thing could get very messy.' She drains her margarita and holds up her glass to the barman for another. 'I'm not against it. I just don't want to see anybody get hurt,' she adds.

I tell him to make it two margaritas. Actually, four. They take so long to make but are so quick to sink.

And then I tell Leanne that I'll be careful. That I'd never hurt him. Or her.

'Okay,' she says. We clink our glasses and make our way over to the dancefloor. It's Friday night after all and I feel on top of the world.

I try to convince everyone to stay out with me, but they've all got work and kids and early starts, and so I go to the off licence and buy three bottles of champagne. One for me, one for mum and one for Frank.

'Celebrating?' says the grinning server behind the counter.

'You bet!' I tell him. 'New job! First job! I'm earning, that's what it's there for, right? Work to live, not live to work…'

He promises to tune in to 105 FM tomorrow so I buy him a bottle of champagne as well. Just because it seems the right thing to do at the time.

I am finally ready to go to bed. I have let the adrenalin course through my system, and now I'm ready to lie down and succumb to an eight-hour coma. Frank is upstairs trying to figure out how to play Sudoku, and I clink the three empty bottles of champagne that my mother and I shared between us into the recycling bin. I push a cushion under my sleeping mother's head and pull the blanket over her.

I head to my bed, but before I go to sleep, I've got one last idea to make this the most amazing day in the history of my life… *NO, Poppy!* I try to warn myself. *There are no such things as good drunk ideas! Wait until the morning. Don't do it now! You're so going to regret this…*

All my coherent thoughts float out of my ear and burst like soapy bubbles. There was just so much heat, so much electricity in Tom's touch. His hand sent a bolt through me. And it's getting worse. I'm thinking about him all the time. I thought about him yesterday when I saw a couple kissing against a wall like teenagers. And again last night as I tried to get to sleep. It's becoming my default feel-good habit. Quite an addictive habit. I did it again this morning in the shower. As I stood under the water, I imagined him standing the same way, at the same time, in his own shower, at home or at the gym. Without clothes, running his lathered fingers through his hair and stretching out his strong tanned arms, soap bubbles sliding across his taut stomach…

I can't help it. I drunk-text Tom and then pass out.

CHAPTER NINETEEN

Okay, this is it. It is Monday. My first official show co-presenting with Jake. It's been rebranded and launched as *The Jake and Poppy Morning Show*, and I'm beyond excited.

When I woke up this morning, mum was already in the kitchen, fully dressed, with a full English breakfast on the table. 'Big day needs a big fry-up,' she said.

'Mum, it's crazy o'clock. Why are you up?'

'Couldn't sleep. Too excited.'

Yes. Excitement is a great euphemism for white-knuckle terror. I couldn't actually sleep much either. So I went to my stash of Hilary's unanswered letters and sat at my old school desk and penned answers to as many as I could until it was time to get ready for work. It was great. It helped me to get a handle on what kind of things are troubling people, and hopefully, when they get their reply, even if it's way past the time when they can implement the advice, they'll know someone at least read their letter. That someone actually gives a shit.

When I arrive at the studio, Jake and Astral have arranged for a massive platter of macarons from Café Paul to be delivered, along with balloons and banners to celebrate the launch of the new-look show. I pay attention to my breathing. I want this to be a massive hit just as much as they do.

I buckle in to my seat and brace myself for the morning ahead.

* * *

I don't understand what's gone wrong. Two hours and nothing. Nada, zilch.

'Wow, this morning sure is flying by – just a quick reminder that we have Dr Poppy here, live in the studio, ready, willing and waiting to take your calls and answer your emails or indeed your texts regarding any aspect of life that you need support with. Just an hour or so left to get those problems in to us at 105 FM.' Jake plugs my unwanted presence for the fortieth time. I doodle dead horses being flogged.

Nobody is calling in. Nobody is emailing. Not one of the four million 105 FM listening faithful wants to pick up the phone or tap out a message to me this morning. Not a single one. Anticlimactic doesn't even begin to describe the extent of my stomach-hollowing disappointment. I find it very difficult to believe that the whole of London has woken up happy and problem-free. What has gone so wrong? Why is this happening to me? To make matters worse, I've told EVERYBODY to listen in. And everybody I know has told everybody else they know that I'm on the radio this morning. LIVE. So there are millions of listeners out there; it's just that they are listening to me crash and burn. No, not even as dramatic or spectacular as that... they are listening to me flop and fizzle.

Perhaps something miraculous has occurred. Perhaps a Pied Piper of psychological malaise rode into town late last night and drove out all modern social spectres of interpersonal conflict, self-doubt and existential despair. I doubt it. More like a good ole classic case of rejection. They don't like me; perhaps Dr Winters was more perceptive than I gave her credit for. I lack charisma, the presence needed to draw people in. Yeah. I've heard that before. This was all a ridiculous idea, a ridiculous and highly mortifying idea.

We are into the last stage of the show and it looks like it's been a complete washout. Despite everyone thinking Hilary was such a monster, she was obviously much better at attracting listeners' attention than I am. Not one listener has made contact. That is shockingly bad. I have sent the ratings graph on Astral's screen spiralling downwards.

And yet Jake seems completely unfazed by the lack of response. He reckons it's just because this is a new segment; people take a while to warm up to changes to their established routine. 'It's nothing to be concerned about, Poppy. Give it time and the calls will come,' he tells me. He can see I'm upset even though I'm trying to stay upbeat. In between segments, I ask him to show me how to play sound effects and pre-recorded advertisements; we choose some songs together; we create some new clues for 'You Do the Maps'.

As we're eating the last of the macarons, Astral begins to rap frantically on the glass partition. She's flapping. 'Poppy, you have a problem!'

Yes, I think I know that, Astral. I'm a doctor with no patients. I'm a presenter with no audience. I'm as useless as a bicycle with no wheels. I know I've got a problem. What's weird is that she seems so freakin' happy about it!

She raises her hand to her ear in a phone gesture and then mouths, 'We've got a CALLER! A caller with a PROBLEM for YOU!'

I straighten up in my chair, take a sip of water and lean in to the microphone.

'Good morning, caller, this is Dr Poppy, tell me what's on your mind.'

There's a hiss and a click. *Caller one: Miss Demeanour from south London* shows up on my display board.

'Caller one, Miss Demeanour from south London, are you still on the line?'

'Hi, yes, I'm on the line and I've got a question for Dr Poppy. Are you there, Poppy?'

'Yes, I'm here.'

'ARE YOU THERE, POPPY? Can you speak nice and loud? I'm hard of hearing so you're going to have to speak up if you want me to hear you. Now tell me, ARE YOU THERE?'

Omg. It's Shanice. I'd recognise her sassy accent anywhere. She told me she'd have my back, and here she is. Rescuing me from obscurity. Oh Shanice, you diamond. I love you, girl.

I stretch my arms above my head, sit up straight and shout into the microphone, loud and clear, 'Yes, caller! I AM HERE!'

'Well, good. Because I need your help. I know this girl, she's fun, she's smart, she's strong, she's beautiful. But she doesn't know it. And I know you're going to say well, isn't that a good thing? Who wants to be around someone who is up themselves? But I mean, this girl, she REALLY doesn't know it. And my problem is that she's not the only one I know like that. I'm seeing these women everywhere, at work, among my friends and family. Why is it that these girls just don't believe in themselves?'

My heart swells in my chest. Shanice is making me think. Why don't girls believe in themselves? Why don't *I* believe in myself? How can I inspire anyone if I keep second-guessing my own abilities and believing in failure over success?

'Thanks, caller, thanks for picking up the phone this morning and thanks for asking such a great question. What can I say? Show me a woman who doesn't doubt herself and I'll show you a rare specimen. Whether it's our looks, our relationships or our performance at work, there's always something we wish we could change. There's always something we think we could do better, something we wish we had more of and something we wish we didn't have at all. My big arms. That bump in my nose. The muffin top I can no longer pack in to Spanx and that won't budge no matter how many sit-ups I do or how many carbs I give up.

'Show me a gorgeous woman with the perfect family and a great position at work and I can bet you her high salary that there's something about herself she wishes she could change. A study of the most influential women in the world has showed that all of them have one major thing in common. They all suffer, in one way or another, from an invisible symptom – lack of confidence.'

I swallow hard. I'm going in. This is important.

'And I know this to be true because I feel it myself. I was feeling it five minutes ago before you called in, Miss Demeanour. I thought I'd failed, that I was undeserving. That I wasn't up to scratch.'

Astral is nodding fervently behind the screen. She's feeling it too. I know I'm not on my own here.

'So are we born this way? Or did we learn it along the way? I believe it is learnt behaviour. And everything we learn, we can of course unlearn. So what can these women do for themselves? What can we do to grow in confidence? I would say do something that scares the crap out of you, and fail at it. And repeat. Repeat until you couldn't care less who's watching.'

'I like it, Dr Poppy. I like it because it makes sense to me. But don't you think there's something we can do to show women and girls everywhere that they've got our support?'

Ha! Shanice and her movements. She's a bona fide social activist. But what *can* we do? Something visual, impactful, but simple enough that people will want to do it, will want to take part.

I think of confident, strong women who support each other, who have supported me, and instantly the Assassins' purple kit comes to mind.

'Purple,' I say. 'Why don't we all wear purple on Friday? Come on, people of London, stick a purple jumper on, or use your favourite purple umbrella. Let's send the message out to our girls and women that it's okay for them to be themselves. That we've got their backs.'

Shanice whoops down the phone. 'Now you're talking! Great show, Dr Poppy – and you keep that voice nice and loud so that I can hear you!'

'Well thank you, Miss Demeanour. I sure will.'

Astral points to the clock: nearly time for the ten o'clock news. 'I just got one last thing I need to ask you. Just a quick one.'

'Very quickly, Miss Demeanour, fire away.'

'Friend of mine, Tom, he got a message late at night from this girl, but it's made him confused. He doesn't know if it was an accident or a joke or if it's serious… because he thought she was quite shy so he doesn't know how to play it now. What do you suggest, Dr Poppy?'

I flare red. 'I see. Maybe tell Tom that if he doesn't want anything more to happen, delete the message, pretend it never happened and move. But if he *does* want more—'

'Oh, I think he wants more!' giggles Shanice down the line.

'Well in that case, he should call her, text her, show up on her doorstep… anything, just let her know.'

The midday news cuts over us and I slump back in my chair, my stomach in shreds. 'Why do I feel like I've just come off a roller-coaster?' I ask Jake.

'Ha! That's live radio for you. Just when you think you know what's coming next, *bam!* it takes you on a completely new ride. Purple Day, eh? Well, that's one I didn't see coming. Go home and get some rest. I think we're going to have a pretty interesting time this week. Oh, and I've got a little something for you.'

Jake hands me a flimsy handwritten envelope. I recognise the careful penmanship instantly. Would I be right to guess that there is a slightly higher lift to the curves and sweeps of the letters? Are things looking up for Benny, or am I just imagining it? I open it up and begin to read.

Dear Poppy,
   It worked!
   I'm so pleased to be in a position to write you this letter, to give you this update. I'm indebted to you for your help.

I followed your advice and met with my lady friend at her cottage, and she asked me to join her for tea in the garden, which I promptly accepted. She chatted gaily about the lavender beds, the weather, the new kitten I had brought her the previous week – how she was settling in, the unusual colouring of her eyes and various aspects of feline psychology. All very pleasant indeed.

However, I was aware that I had a mission to complete and by passively basking in this wonderful lady's charm I was not quite pulling my weight. So I steeled myself, your encouragement and guidance ringing in my ears, and told myself, 'Come on, man! You can do it!' With that, I took a deep breath and came out with it!

I may have startled her; the suggestion to choose a pot together might have been a little unexpected. Unfortunately, she was in the middle of pouring a second cup of tea and she jumped in surprise, causing her to drop the teapot. It crashed to the ground and, being delicate fine bone china, shattered into pieces.

But who could have guessed that this would be so serendipitous! We both flew to the ground to pick up the scattered shards. I commented that it was a beautiful teapot and that it was a shame to discard it even though it was now broken. She thought for a moment, then smiled in her gracious way and said, 'I have had this tea set for over half my life. It was a gift from my daughter. I have sipped tea from it with my mother, my sisters, my friends. Its value is beyond its function to me. This old china has found its way deep into the creases of my heart. I can't discard something that's served me so well; it would feel disloyal.'

And then it struck me! There is more than one way to choose a pot!

I suggested that we use the shards of china as mosaic tiles and set them into a wet clay pot so that she can keep her beloved teapot and create a much-loved piece for her garden at the same time.

Poppy, the idea brought tears to her violet eyes. She clapped her hands together and thanked me and called me 'a treasure', and then she kissed me on the cheek. I said to her, 'We've only just begun,' and she laughed and laughed.

Today has been the most wonderful day. Thank you, Poppy, for attending to my letter, and thank you for sharing your gift for making lives such as mine shine with hope and promise.

Yours in gratitude,
Benny, aka the Smitten Gardener

My heart pounds in my chest. Oh Benny! We did it! We both did it! And I can tell you, you spurred me on as much as I did you! Marvellous. Blooming marvellous.

I skip up the steps of the tube station. At the top, facing into the crowd, stands Tom, the fading sunlight against his back. I catch his eye and take the slow final steps towards him. He hands me a bunch of Frank's flowers. 'Returning my call?' I ask, and then, before I even realise what I'm doing, I've wrapped my arms around his neck and my cheek is pressed up against his.

But we stay there a beat too long. I'm not sure how to go forward, but I'm certain that I don't want to step back. I want to stay. I want more. I want to be enveloped by him.

I feel him shift his weight ever so slightly forward and then take a deep breath that presses me closer to his chest. I do the same; like a silent dancer taking slow, deliberate steps, I mirror his every move. My hips slip closer to his. My skin feels fluid. He lowers his head just as I raise mine, and we are so close that I can feel the warmth of his breath on my lips. He brushes his mouth against mine. My fingers slide upwards, over his neck, across his jaw, to lightly hold both sides of his beautiful, beautiful face. And then it happens. I taste him and I realise that I have been starving. My heart rises in my swelled chest and my hands can't bring him close enough to me. I hold my breath. He kisses me again, fully, breathlessly, wildly. And the space between us explodes.

I have kissed men before, but it did not feel like this. I have looked into their eyes, but they did not burn me alive. Whether it lasts a few seconds or a few minutes, I don't know. All I know is that I have been waiting for this person since always. I have been waiting for Tom since always.

I can feel his eyes on mine. Then on my lips. And down towards my neck. He blinks and nods his head. I thread my fingers through his, and we take our first steps together.

CHAPTER TWENTY

As I wait for the bus to work on Friday morning, I take a moment to consider how lucky I am. I'm lucky that people have invested in me and lifted me when I was low. And now, look… I've got an amazing job and what looks like the beginnings of an amazing relationship, and I feel there's so much more to look forward to. So much more to come. And I don't want to keep this to myself. I don't want to stop now, at this level; I want to make as much of a noise as possible. I want the world to know how with the right support and a little bit of faith and a good dose of feel-the-fear-but-do-it-anyway, you can actually transform your life.

If only I could get that message out there. I know I can say it, but how do I know if anyone is really listening beyond the individuals themselves? How do I know, at grass-roots level, that we are in fact making some kind of wider positive change?

I board the bus, and something strikes me as unusual… cool but unusual. My Sikh bus driver is wearing a purple turban. I watch a gaggle of uniformed air stewardesses chattering at the back of the bus; all of them have purple ribbons in their hair. I look out the window, where a businessman is sporting a purple tie, a runner with her dog is wearing a purple fleece and leggings, and the display in the Body Shop window is completely purple – little bottles, pots and potions in every shade of purple, lavender to mulberry, with a poster in the middle reading: *The Body Shop supports 105 FM Wear it Purple Day. #girlpride Let's hear it for our girls!* I am overwhelmed by the moving purple landscape before me. It's like the city has been Photoshopped. There is purple EVERYWHERE.

I arrive at the doors of the studio. Even the security guards have purple gloves on. Tariq and Lee are here every morning, either side of the doorway, rain or shine. Tariq curls a lip at me and holds up his purple hand. 'Hey, where's your purple, Poppy? This was your idea, right?'

I smile, pull off my bobble hat and shake out my swingy purple hair that my mum dyed for me last night. They bend over laughing and take out their phones for a selfie: #girlpride #purpleday105 FM.

Astral rushes to me at the door of the studio. She is head to toe in a sequinned purple jumpsuit. 'Oh Poppy, we've got a REVOLUTION on our hands… come over here, wait till you see this.' She brings me into her office; every screen is showing the same image: Buckingham Palace, draped in purple bunting.

I look at her, paralysed with disbelief.

'Really?'

'Really. It doesn't get more real than this. The internet has gone INSANE!'

'Oh my God, what have I done? I thought it would just be… Well, I never really thought.'

Astral looks me in the eye. 'Sometimes it happens that way. The right person says the right thing at the right time. It's like they have an instinct, they can tell what the world needs to hear, what it needs to remember. And this, Poppy, this is one of those times. Sit down there, catch your breath, and pinch yourself back to reality while I go get you a coffee. What're you having?'

'Oh, a latte, please. And a purple macaron!'

I clench my fists and wriggle in my seat. How? What? When? I am having *such* a good time. No question, I'm having a ball.

CHAPTER TWENTY-ONE

Maybe it's this crisp wintry, fairy-tale weather, that snuggly, fire-crackling, cosy-pub time of year that makes me think that I'm in love. In love with my work and my boyfriend and my netball girls. We won the semi-final by the skin of our teeth, but none-theless, we are through to the Superleague final. Which is immense. It even looks like we may win. And we are IN FIGHTING FORM. Everything is going so well that sometimes I get a bolt of fear. Last night I dreamt that I was in a casino and I was winning. All around me I've got people telling me how wonderful I am and we're all drinking and laughing. I roll again, almost casually, but it lands on the wrong number and I lose the lot. The suited casino guy sweeps all my chips away from me, the crowd around me disperses and I'm left alone. With nothing. Hero to zero in the blink of an eye.

I open my bedroom window wide and breathe in the crisp, cool air. This weather is perfect. This weather could *make* people fall in love. This is the kind of weather where the world looks happy and peaceful and glorious, and people look rosy-cheeked and fresh-faced, and waiters smile at you, and strangers open doors for you, and you catch snatches of upbeat music as you wander from shop to bar to restaurant to pub hand in hand with your gorgeous boyfriend.

Tom and I have been together, practically inseparable, EVERY SINGLE DAY since the day he handed me the flowers on the steps of Brixton underground nearly a month ago. That qualifies as a serious relationship. Because of course we're not just talking days. No, siree. We are also talking nights. AND OH MY GOD. I do not feel for any friend, colleague or acquaintance the way I feel for him, feel around him, feel at the mere thought of him or mention of his name.

Yesterday, we bumped into a friend of Tom's while we were ice-skating and he introduced me as his girlfriend. Forget the ice sculptures. I was fit to melt. So he is officially now my boyfriend Tom Jones. I swirl it around in my mouth like something sweet and cool and exquisite. I say it aloud, trying it out like a new signature. Written in a new gel pen. A glittery new gel pen. *My boyfriend.* Does it sound too teeny-bopper? Too flippant?

I consider the word 'partner'. *My partner Tom Jones.*

It sounds like we're going to rob a bank or open a legal firm. Nah, I'm sticking with boyfriend. Tom Jones, the funniest, sexiest, yummiest man I have EVER been close to, is my boyfriend. And I am enraptured. I can't exactly narrow it down to one thing. He's funny. He's honest. He's kind. He surprises me. He listens to me. He's full of plans and projects and dreams and I feel utterly contented when we lie in silence reading magazines on a rug, or when he drags me out for a run through the park, or when I'm eating a big Dirty Dicks burger in front of him with a mess of mayo and mustard all over my face. I know I love him because he brings light into my life. He makes me feel like I'm enough. In the middle of the night he throws his arm around me and murmurs my name. In the morning he kisses me on my head despite my hair looking like it's starched and my eyes two black holes of unremoved eyeliner.

So yes... the weather. This weather is the perfect backdrop for us. It's weather you want to snuggle up inside, weather for a beautiful man to suggest that you stay in bed extra late at the weekends because its too chilly to get up, and then you have licence to stay put, with your head on your lover's chest and kiss him and stroke him and just basically adore him.

I am in love with everything. I sit in my room, filling my lungs with the homely smell of bubble and squeak that Frank is frying up for himself in the kitchen. I trace my finger over the name I etched into my desk fifteen years ago. It appears that I am in love with Tom Jones AGAIN. If I ever really stopped being in love with him, that is.

I hear Mum pounding up the stairs. Oops. This is a 'storm brewing' ascent.

Stomp, stomp. Mutters, 'Ridiculous.'

Stomp, stomp. Mutters, 'For God's sake.'

Stomp, stomp. Slaps hand down on the banister knob at the top of the stairs.

Big exasperated sigh. Sharp rap on my bedroom door.

Pop goes my love bubble.

I open the door to find her standing with a washing basket on her hip.

'I've got a question. How is it that I have become responsible for washing, drying and folding not one, not two, but seven netball kits every week?'

'We are a team,' I tell her. 'Everyone does their bit. Leanne already does so much, so I thought I'd volunteer to sort the kit out.'

'A-ha.' Mum points a long-nailed finger in the air. 'But YOU are not sorting it out, are you, Poppy? So, Missus Radio, you can talk the talk but you either can't or won't walk the walk.' She throws the washing basket down at my feet. 'If you said you'd sort the kit, then sort the kit. I have my own job to do and my own life to lead, thank you very much, without playing nursery nurse to a fully grown woman.'

I look down at the jumble of balled-up purple vests. Shit. They are filthy. She has just left them downstairs in the basket in a stinky, sweaty, mouldy mess since last Thursday's training. The least she could have done was wash them and then hand in her notice, or refuse to wash them straight away so I could sort something else out.

'Aw, Mum, come on! You can't be serious! I need these for this evening – I can't get them washed and dried in time now, can I? What am I supposed to tell the girls? What will Leanne think?'

She closes her eyes and shrugs her shoulder. 'Not my problem.' But I know she adores Leanne; there's no way she'd let her down. If Mum could daughter-upgrade, she'd definitely upgrade to a Leanne.

She huffs and then points down the stairs to the hall table, waggling her finger at the various envelopes spilling over onto the phone and propped up against the picture frames. 'And what about this pile of letters addressed to you? I've been asking you to sort through them for weeks now. But you just leave them to pile up and wait for someone else to step in and do the stuff that's too boring or too hard for you to manage yourself. Usually when you get a letter from the tax office or the bank it's because they have something important to tell you. But if you can't even be bothered to open the damn things, well, I'm certainly not going to do it for you.'

She gives me a cold, steely stare and sets her jaw. It's true. I've been so taken up with working through my sackful of Hilary's old letters that I've neglected all other forms of post; quite conveniently, I may add. There do seem to be a lot of bank statements and credit card notices amongst that lot.

'You better clean up your act, young lady. In and out all times of day and night, treating this house like a hotel…'

'You're right, Mum. I'm sorry, I've just been so busy lately, with work and Tom—'

She holds up her hands. 'I don't care what you're up to with Tom. That's your business. But you come in at all hours, not the slightest bit of consideration; you wake us up in the middle of the night, turning on all the lights, television blaring, making toast or cooking a pizza, and then what happens? You go off to bed expecting some little fairies to come and clear up after you.

But of course THEY DON'T and I'm the one who wakes up to a big mess in the morning – dirty cups in the sink, butter left out. You are an absolute nightmare, Poppy Bloom, and if you don't watch yourself, you'll be out on your ear. I mean it, out in the big bad world to find your own place to live.'

I straighten up. I can't resist her goading. I can't let her have the last word. That is the last thing I could ever let happen. If she wins an inch, it won't just lead to her taking a mile. She will draw in vast uncharted expanses of ground, claim and conquer it, stockpiling it until she is unassailable. It's crucial that I wrangle this inch from her.

'Funny you should say that. It's exactly what I'm going to do.'

Mum raises a sarcastic eyebrow. 'Oh really? Planning on venturing into the big bad world on your own, cooking and cleaning and paying your own bills? Have I just interrupted you in your house hunting? I'm ever so sorry.'

'In a way, yes, I was just about to confirm timings with my letting agent.'

Mum stretches out a hand to lean on the banister. 'What timings?'

'This evening. I'm viewing a property this evening,' I lie.

We stand facing each other in silence.

But it is a good idea. And something I could do. And the timing couldn't be more perfect. At the moment I'm staying at Tom's place for much of the time, and that's fine short-term while his flatmate Gav is away, but he may be back soon or he'll have to sub-let his room. So I'm going to go house hunting! I'm going to move out! I'm going to have my own place! I've got the money to do it; even though I'm only freelance, the show is going from strength to strength, so it looks like I've got a long and bright future with 105 FM.

Mum is shuffling on the spot, rubbing her eye to disguise the nervous twitch she's got going on. I nearly laugh out loud. I know she doesn't really want me to leave. She loves knowing my every movement and being in a position to critique and comment on every aspect of my life. But the possibility is starting to take shape in my mind – my own place, my own actual flat. Just for me. A rush bolts through me. This is PERFECT!

She taps her fingers on the banister knob and squints at me. 'This evening, you say?'

I nod.

'I thought you had netball this evening.'

'I do. I'm going to the viewing straight afterwards. Leanne is coming with me. She's a good negotiator.' More lies. Lying is so easy. People who say they can't lie are liars.

'How much is your budget?'

'Oh, you know. Reasonable. Modest. Average,' I say with the precision of an economist.

'And you've factored in utilities, furnishings, insurance, council tax, service charges, and contingency in the case of flood, burglary or electrical damage?'

'Yep.'

'And the landlord? They've carried out all the necessary safety checks? Has the boiler been tested, checked for faulty wiring? Pests, rodents, woodlice? What about carbon monoxide poisoning; does it have an alarm?'

'Sorted, all in hand.'

She takes a deep breath. She thought I would crack under her pressure. Mum, nil: me, one.

My phone rings in my pocket. 'That's probably the agent now, just confirming.'

She still looks a little sceptical. I take it out and glance at the caller ID. It's my ex-dad. I've missed loads of his calls the last few days and just ignored the texts. I've been so busy with work and Tom and netball and hangovers. I block the call and stuff my phone back into my pocket.

'And how are you going to pay for it?' she asks.

'Um, with my salary? I'm on good money, you know,' I try to reassure her. 'More than I ever expected. I can cover the rent.'

'But it's not a permanent contract, Poppy, that's what I'm afraid of. It could all go belly-up and you'll be stuck with this enormous expense. Why don't you just stay on here until they make things more secure, less risky?'

'Mum, I am almost thirty years old. Even if I wasn't with Tom or if I had a less-well-paid job, it would still be the right thing to do. It's time for me to move out and start to build my own life, separate from you and Frank and Dad.' I turn in the door to my room. 'All of this belongs to you. You should be so proud because you earned it, you worked for it, it's yours. And I need to do that too.'

She stares down at the basket of dirty kit. 'As long as you're sure.'

'I am,' I tell her. And I mean it.

'How soon do you think it will be?'

'As soon as possible.'

She rubs both eyes this time and a look of resignation descends on her face. Then she picks up the basket of dirty kit, sniffs a stray vest and pulls a face. 'So I suppose as this will be the last time, I'll make an exception. I'll leave it folded on the dining room table.'

'Thanks, Mum.'

'But sort out your letters before I burn them all. They're an eyesore.'

'I will. I promise.'

'And promise me, if you see any old washing machines, sofas or mattresses in the garden, you'll walk away.'

I nod reassuringly.

'Any snakes or ferrets or growling dogs,' she persists.

I wrap my arms around her shoulders and pull her tight. 'You don't have to worry. I'll choose somewhere perfect.'

And I mean it. I cannot wait to find my perfect new place.

CHAPTER TWENTY-TWO

'I'm going to get my own place,' I announce to Jess and Laura in the changing rooms before our training session.

Jess nods her head and sighs. 'Oh you are so, so lucky! I'd do anything to move out of my place. Believe me, house sharing is hell! It's fine when you're a student, because you want to stay up all hours and make a mess, but as an adult, it's horrendous. Oh just imagine, space, quiet… cleanliness!'

Laura shakes her head. 'It's not all it's cracked up to be. I've lived by myself now for three years and it can be very lonely, believe me. The evenings drag, every sound in the house makes you jump. I hate living by myself: too many rooms, too much void.'

I look to Laura. And then to Jess. And then back to Laura.

'Where do you live Jess?' I ask.

'Kennington.'

'And where do you live, Laura?'

'Camberwell.'

'Guys, you are practically neighbours! You could hang out! Jess, you could get your peace and cleanliness at Laura's house; and Laura, Jess can come and keep you company!'

Laura's face flushes red. 'Only if you wanted to, Jess. I wouldn't like to intrude on your plans.'

'Are you crazy! I would love to. I never knew we were so close. My geography of London is based on the tube map. Once I'm overground, I haven't a clue where anywhere is. Oh Laura, let's do it! I'll bring a bottle of some gorgeous Aussie white wine I've been keeping for a special occasion.'

For the first time, I see Laura's face break out into a huge smile.

'And I'll cook. I love to cook. I'll make my risotto. I haven't done that in ever such a long time,' she says.

Leanne pops her head around the corner. 'Enough gabbing, get on the court. We've got a game to play.'

As I warm up, running the laps of the indoor court, I think about how Jake said that the Assassins had changed Teagan's life. I feel that too. We look out for each other. We belong together somehow, despite our differences, and eccentricities and backgrounds. We fit. And we fit tight. Three times a week I come here to train with these girls. We get together rain or shine, knackered, broke, angry or covered in baby sick. We come straight from the office, straight from cooking dinner, straight from a fifteen-hour shift, straight from being fired or turned down for a bank loan. But we come. We gather here. Same place, same time, every other day. It's a commitment to the game, sure. But it's more of a commitment to each other. And when you invest so much in something, it's worth fighting for.

Two hours later, I'm at the letting agent's office, still in my netball gear, sweaty and red-faced. Leanne had childcare issues so couldn't come with me, but she did clap me on the back and wish me luck and invited everybody to my prospective housewarming.

'But not till after the final,' piped up Nikki, and the rest of the team nodded emphatically. We've got our date for the Superleague final against Team Oxbridge, two weeks Sunday. We're looking good for it: great rapport, tight passes, mean defence, two strong shooters. Well, one strong shooter, as Teagan's mother has pulled her from the team to ensure that she's not distracted from her scholarship application to a sports academy in the US. Izabel, the new cross-fit instructor from Leanne's gym will join Assassins to make up our numbers She used to be the number-one MMA fighter in her native Poland. I'm glad she's on our side.

As the reality of what I'm doing sinks in, I start to feel very excited. My own place. To do as I please. To invite people in and share my space with them. I love Leanne's idea of a housewarming party in my new flat, with my netball girls and Tom and Jake and the radio gang. There'll be music, drinks, fairy lights, nibbles. It won't be like a student party, with people mixing out-of-date drinks with forks in plastic cups, leading to dry-humping on the sofa and culminating in retching in the loo.

No, that's behind me now.

This will be a classy party, grown-up, elegant but without formality; simplicity with sophistication. Everyone will rave about the limoncello and the rhubarb gin and how amazing cucumber ribbons are. There will be laughter. There will be love. There will be Kettle Chips with home-made salsa picante so good it'll bring people together, nodding enthusiastically with mouths crammed with chips and dips.

The letting agent seems nice. He's about my age, wearing a blue designer suit that complements his gelled wavy hair and dark threaded eyebrows. His smile is curt, very busy, very businesslike. He hands me a wad of stapled property pages, complete with photos, inventories and floor plans, and we climb into the car.

'I'm going to be straight with you, Miss Bloom,' he tells me as he shifts gear and reverses out into the road. 'What you're saying you want and what your budget is saying you can afford are two completely different things.' He skids into traffic and talks to me through the wing mirror.

'Your current budget as is… well, it's really the low end of the market.'

Really? My budget is HUGE! Well, I thought it was huge…

'To be honest, if you were my sister or my friend, I'd advise against it. Not just from the aesthetic point of view, either; I think you know that bedsits and top-floor council flats are not pretty. But from a security point of view, a young woman living alone? There's no two ways about it: you're vulnerable. Do you watch *Crimewatch*?'

I shake my head. I watch *Gilmore Girls*.

He nods like it's no surprise. 'Was there much crime in your last area of residence?'

I shake my head. In my first year at Banbridge, someone tried to steal my bike from outside the pub but then returned it the next day with a 'sorry' note.

'Not really,' I tell him.

'In that case, I'd recommend something a little more secure.'

I shift up in my seat. 'Really? Is that what the stats and police figures actually say?'

He gives me a wry smile and puts his hand on his heart. 'Not in their interests to reveal that kind of thing; feminists would call it scaremongering. Media would eat them alive. But I'm telling you what I know from experience. Trust me.'

Is he telling the truth and looking out for me, or is he just a bullshitting sales weasel? I don't know. I just can't tell. I flick through the pages on my lap and remind myself to stay open-minded and objective, not get glassy-eyed with sales patter. I lift out the first property profile in the pile. A tall seventies tower block that looks more like a cheap filing cabinet than a place to call home. I flick through to the next one; it's on top of a kebab shop, which is simultaneously a pro and a con, so I investigate further. The second page shows the interior. And it's grim; VERY grim. Looks like a squatters' den, dirty blankets, cans and plastic bags strewn around. Disgusting. Not the right context for my salsa picante at all.

'So, before we waste any of your precious time – is this what you really want? For me to drag you around and show you these dives? Let you see for yourself how low the lower end of the scale actually is?'

I think he's playing me, trying to get me to spend more. I roll up the pages and wave them at him like a baton. 'Hold up a second. This can't be right. How does anyone live in London if this is what you get for hundreds of pounds' rent every single week?' I ask, like I'm Erin Brockovich blowing the lid on the whole rip-off rental operation.

'They share,' he answers baldly. 'All those properties you've got there are single-occupant. If you want a better but not necessarily bigger place, you'll have to compromise on space and privacy.' He opens the glove compartment and hands me a new wedge of property profiles.

I flick through and my heart sinks even more. One tiny bathroom to share between four people. Bedrooms the size of my mum's wardrobe. A kitchen that looks like it belongs in a caravan. And then there is the issue of living with strangers day to day. What if they are complete knobs? What if they are really messy or loud or work nights so I have to creep around all day? What if they eat smelly food like herring and keep it in the fridge *uncovered* beside all my food and then everything I eat and drink tastes like it's been infused with a dirty, vinegary, fishy smell? I nearly make myself gag. I open the window and let the breeze cool me down. Maybe Mum was right: I should stay on at home for a bit longer. Living with my parents can be annoying, but is living with a motley crew of strangers really a forward step?

I lay the brochures down on my lap.

I think about Mum and Frank. It's really not that bad at home. I'm safe and I've got my own room and there's always fresh milk and bread and toilet paper. Nobody eats anything smelly and we've got extensive Tupperware to ensure clean and compact storage of all perishables. Hmmmm… It's a lot to give up. Maybe I should knock this on the head now. It's hard to leave behind a nice family home only to pitch up somewhere smaller, smellier, more crowded and more expensive.

But then I think of Tom.

It's not just a space for me now, is it? It's a space for my new life. For dinner parties and Netflix and Pimm's in the garden and lazy broadsheet Sundays in bed. And an Italian coffee machine. And a cat. And a hammock. Somewhere I can call my own.

I turn to the agent. 'Okay then, what are my options? Tell me what I can do.'

He makes a swift turn off the main road. 'Well, there is a new development that's just come on the market. I literally saw it two minutes before you arrived at the office. Highly desirable location, spacious layout, comes fully furnished with all modern conveniences and finished to a very high standard throughout. Ideal pad for successful young professionals.'

I like the sound of that; a new label. I'm not an old student but a young professional.

We drive through the secure gates. There are manicured lawns on each side, some vintage wooden benches, a communal barbecue area. It looks like it may have been an old schoolhouse in a former life; charming and whitewashed, perfect fusion of old and new. A girl, *a woman*, about my age cycles up beside us and parks her bike. She's fit, tanned, smiling. She could be my neighbour. She could call around and we could chat and drink wine. When she has a party, she could invite me and I could make a whole new fleet of friends. We could go cycling together. I want this.

'Excuse me,' I say as she takes off her helmet.' Do you live here?'

'Yes,' she says with a slight accent: Swedish? Norwegian? 'Are you thinking of moving in?'

I nod.

'It's wonderful. Best place I've lived since arriving in London. Once I saw it, I thought to myself, I must have it, you know?'

'Yes, I can imagine. It's really lovely.'

She tilts her head at me. 'Do I know you?' she asks.

'I don't think so.'

She shakes her head as if trying to shake off a thought. 'No, ignore me. It's just the way you spoke, it was like I knew you. You must sound like a friend of mine or something.'

The agent's phone rings. 'Don't mind if I take this, do you?'

'Not at all,' I say. 'Take your time.'

'Dr Poppy! From the radio! You sound just like Dr Poppy,' she gasps. 'I knew you reminded me of someone!'

'Wow…' I say. 'Actually, I am Dr Poppy.'

She drops her water bottle and I bend down to pick it up. When I hand it back to her, she is beaming from ear to ear. 'I love your show. I love love love it. I've even told my friends from Sweden to listen to your podcasts online! I love *you*! I've never met a celebrity before!'

'Well, celebrity sounds a bit ambitious—'

She cuts me off in excitement. 'And remember Benny! Aw, I can't lie! I cried when he plucked up his courage. All for love!'

'That's amazing, thank you so much. I don't know what to say.'

People in Sweden are listening to the podcasts? That's insane! I never realised we had any listeners outside of the UK. Wait till I tell Astral. She'll be chuffed. I certainly am. I'm merely a lucky fluke who stumbled into this gifted position, much more by accident than design. I'm a hopeful impostor awaiting exposure; half expecting Scooby and the gang to rip off my mask at any time and send me back to the mailing room.

The estate agent comes back, the keys in his hand.

'Shall we?' he asks.

'Yes, nice meeting you…' I say, shaking the woman's hand.

'Ingrid. My name is Ingrid. And you should definitely move in here. In short, you will regret absolutely nothing.'

I thank her and we mount the stairs to view the one-bed show apartment overlooking the garden. The agent turns the key in the door and it feels like I have arrived in heaven. Everything is white and pale gold. The bay window is enormous, the view perfectly divided into blue sky and green grass.

'Every room is soundproofed, so you'll find it very conducive to peace and quiet. As you can see, there is security on the door; your safety is a priority. Seems a nice community amongst the other residents. It's ready to go, as it's the show flat. I imagine it'll be snapped up pretty quick.'

I've watched enough TV to know that only amateurs bite at the first property. So the next words out of my mouth are…

'I'll take it.'

In my mind's eye, Mum and David Dickinson throw their hands over their faces despairingly.

'Okay, well, that was quick! Congratulations,' says the grinning agent. 'Welcome to your new abode.' He nods happily and fetches his briefcase.

This feels SO right. This is where I'm going to wake up in the arms of my gorgeous dimpled man, wrapped in white Egyptian cotton sheets, basking in the mixed aromas of fresh coffee and manly musk. And there'll be croissants and pains au chocolat and the faint sound of a Chopin piano concerto playing softly in the background. Together we'll stand at this large bay window overlooking the grounds and the distant city skyline, like captains of our own destiny at the helm of a huge ocean liner, steering the wheel of our shared future together. Full steam ahead.

'I'll send you the contract and specifications and you can read over the details. There are some service charges, ground rent, communal extras and mandatory contributions, things like that.'

I wave my hands. You can stop the waffle now, agent-man, stop polluting the dream.

'There's no need. It's perfect,' I tell him. 'Where do I sign and how soon can I move in?'

I sign everything, about ten documents written in a teensy font that I start to read and then give up on as it makes no sense anyway; an archaic medieval language of waivers and penalties and forfeits. Once that's done, I write a cheque with so many zeros that I squidge my eyes shut as I sign it.

The agent hands me the keys. When he offers to shake my hand, I lunge forward and hug him tightly instead. He tries to wriggle away to protect his suit, but I just clasp him tighter.

And in short, I regret absolutely nothing.

CHAPTER TWENTY-THREE

Every morning, Jake reverses through the double doors carrying two huge coffees. Every morning we drink them together in ritualistic silence and we prepare to usher in the day. To my tremendous shock and surprise, everyone loves the show. Frank has bought a loudspeaker so that he – and everyone else on Electric Avenue – can hear Jake and me over the din of market life. My mum texts in hourly requests from the ex-con girls, ranging from ABBA to Eminem, with coded messages like '*Hope things stay good for you*' and '*Haven't seen much of you lately – where you hiding?*' We seem to be going from strength to strength.

Astral bursts through the doors with her graph and figures report. This morning is the best yet. So much so that she runs over to the open window, sticks her head out and bellows at the artists, mimers and musicians below, 'Its official! We are back! 105 FM is back on top! In your face, City FM, in your FAY-CE.' She needs to send out a press release and a shareholders' briefing, so we're in charge of ourselves this morning, but we're a team now, rock solid, with everything under control.

Jake explains to me that 105 FM had been in the top spot since people called radio the 'wireless'. Until this year, when rival station City FM started attracting listeners; marginal numbers at first, but more recently, stealing them away in tens of thousands every week. There were executive meetings, consultations, surveys, in-depth analysis; some key management staff were fired. 105 FM were forced to reassess what they were doing, what they were about and what was getting in the way of them being the top choice station for listeners across the capital.

'So what was it?' I ask.

Jake shuffles in his seat and strokes his chin pensively. 'It's a new age for radio. It's tougher, more competitive than it's ever been, so it's easy to lose the vision. We stopped listening to our listeners, as dumb as that sounds. Audiences these days have more choices than ever before – we are up against not only limitless fleets of digital stations from all over the world, but also audio books, podcasts, playlists… There was a point when I thought to myself: radio is dead. It's gone. There's no place for it any more. What can it offer someone over and above their own customised channel of self-selected, free, instant music, features and interviews?' He turns to me, an impassioned look on his face, beseeching me for an answer.

I don't know what to say. I love what I do but I'm far from an expert; more wing it and hope for the best. What do I know about audiences and broadcasting predictions? My job is just to listen and try to come up with the best response for the person on the other end of the line. It's as simple and uncomplicated as that. I bite my lip and offer a sympathetic smile.

'You're a listener, Poppy. That's how you called into the show in the first place. Why did you choose to listen to us rather than find something on your phone?'

I take a moment to think. I can't tell him it was because I fell asleep and missed Frank's clue. But I do know why Frank and Mum and all the other listening faithful tune in. 'Because it's… alive. Radio is real life – unexpected, unscripted, unedited. And that's something special. It's exciting that people don't know what guest you'll have next, or what song you're going to play, or whether there'll be a breaking news story that they could miss if they were stuck in the loop of listening to stuff that is pre-packaged and polished. It's fun and important to connect with others this way, hear their reactions, discover what's important to them, and you just can't call it; you never know what's going to happen next.'

Jake slaps his hand down on his knee. 'Exactly! The CEO, Carol King, she was doubtful, she told me that she was scrutinising the ratings carefully and that she wanted to see a ten per cent increase by the end of the month.'

I gasp. 'Ten per cent! That's harsh, that's like four hundred thousand people. How are you supposed to make that happen?'

'I didn't. *We* did.'

I'm confused. What's he telling me? What is it we did together exactly?

'I'm sorry,' he says. 'I'm rambling; the corporate side of things is dull and hard to grasp. Ignore me. I'm just a little overwhelmed myself.'

He opens the mini fridge and takes out a bottle of champagne, just as the crew flood in through the double doors with glasses and balloons and party poppers and streamers.

'Right, before Astral brings Carol over here, I've got some news to tell you. We received an email this morning. It's official: 105 FM is not only back on top, but we have exceeded our listenership for the first time in three years. We've been nominated for the People's Choice Award at the British Television and Radio Awards!' Jake stops to wipe his hand over his face. 'It's the highest accolade in the business because it's chosen by the public – it's a biggie. For me, it's the ultimate, because it means we are at the heart of what our listeners want; we're real people connecting with real people.'

He shakes the bottle of bubbly up and down.

'So all I really want to say is thank you. Let's get this party started!'

I am gobsmacked. I've watched the British Television and Radio Awards on TV ever since I was a little girl. It's one of those family things that everyone loves and looks forward to, where you are allowed to stay up late. It merits bowls of popcorn and fizzy drinks and going to bed without brushing your teeth. It's more than a programme or an awards ceremony; it's a national event! And Jake is spot on. What makes it special is that it brings all your favourite household names and faces together in one place: actors and sports commentators and soap stars and comedians and, of course, radio presenters.

Astral returns with a typically stony-faced Carol King at her side. Jake turns to the crew. 'Block your diaries, people – we're going to Edinburgh Castle!'

There is a confused murmur amongst the techies and researchers. Then a voice from the back shouts across, 'What, all of us?'

'You bet. We're a team. And this is a team effort.'

I glance around the room. This is going to be incredible. The energy! The excitement!

Astral widens her eyes and blows out her cheeks. I think this is the first she's heard of the arrangement. But she doesn't let it throw her, and goes into full project-manager mode. 'Right, let's get this straight, guys. Nobody, and I mean NOBODY, is allowed to get ill, injured or die until this awards ceremony is over with. Understand?'

We nod as an obedient, beaming collective.

'Poppy, start browsing some hot new British designers; we need to think about who you'll be wearing. We want to make a statement, show them that we're a hot ticket right now, ready to take on the world.'

She pauses to take a deep breath and closes her eyes. Then she screams at the top of her lungs, 'THIS IS OUR YEAR!'

And I believe it. I top up my champagne and take stock of what we have achieved in this tiny studio. It's been hectic, crazy, exhausting, nerve-racking, tear-wrenching, overwhelming and exhilarating all at once. It wakes me up in the middle of the night and drives me to write letters to complete strangers who have poured their hearts onto A4 paper, and causes me to collapse on the couch in the middle of the afternoon with no energy to even take off my shoes. But I love it. It's completely different to anything I ever dreamt I would be doing at this stage of my life, and I'm having a ball. So I can't help but wonder why I keep on having that casino dream…

CHAPTER TWENTY-FOUR

I roll over and he is beside me. The hazy late morning light streams through the bay window, gilding the golden blonde strands of his hair, which fan out on the Egyptian cotton pillow. I am the luckiest girl in the world. I want things to be like this forever. To stay exactly as they are now. Me and him, naked and side by side, bathed in light. He moves beside me. I slink in, manoeuvre myself even closer behind him. It's Sunday. We've got nowhere to be, no work, no netball, no meetings, no family stuff. Just us and an open run on the day.

Without warning, he stiffens as if startled, then jolts upwards to sit at the edge of the bed with his back to me.

I place my hand on his shoulder. 'Tom? Are you okay?'

He is rubbing his eyes, not quite yet awake, confused and disoriented.

'Tom? Are you all right?'

He nods, running his fingers through his hair. 'Yeah, God, that was vivid.' He turns to me. 'Just a bad dream.'

'You're as white as a ghost,' I tell him and trace my finger down his cheek.

'Night terror; it happens every time my mind is in overdrive. I dream that I've built a perfect house of cards and then people start opening and shutting doors all around me, letting great gusts of wind in that blow the house down, cards scattering everywhere. I scramble around to pick them up, but if I chase one, it means I lose another. And then I just stand still, unable to move. Because I can't decide. How do you decide which to chase and which to let go?' He rubs his neck and blinks in an effort to reorientate himself.

Issues around trust and control, I think to myself, then swiftly slap that thought out of my head. He's not a client, he's my boyfriend. He doesn't need a therapy session; he needs a sympathetic ear, some TLC. I tilt my head and stroke his chest.

Why is his mind in overdrive? He hasn't mentioned that anything is worrying him. Saying that, my own mind has been in overdrive since the awards were announced. It's been non-stop: interviews, magazines, photo shoots and promotional events. Maybe he's feeling this way because I've not been as attentive as I should be. Maybe I've been so caught up in everything that's going on with me, I haven't stopped to properly listen to what's going on with him.

'What do you think brought it on?' I ask him.

'This loan Leon convinced myself and Leanne to take out to buy new equipment is crippling us. I know he thought it was a good thing and all, but I really wish he'd just back off. He put so much pressure on us to snap it up, we got a crap rate and now that's rising and rising. Leanne's trying to sort it out by getting a new partner in so we can share the load; or get a sponsor, that's another option. That would really help. Anyway…' He wipes his face with his hands.

I drape my arms around him and kiss his ear. 'You'll figure it out, I know you will.'

He inhales deeply. 'Yes, well, I've got my hopes pinned on you guys winning the Superleague. That will be a massive help; we'll attract loads more clients and all the publicity means we can re-invest our advertising budget. So, bottom line, Assassins win, we all win.'

His phone beeps on the bedside locker. He squints at the screen with one eye. 'Ha! You won't believe this. It's from Gav.' He turns the little screen around to me, running his fingers through his hair. It's a photo of a giant burger loaded with onion rings, bacon, eggs and about four different type of cheese, with the caption '*My lunch #foodgasm*'.

'*Ha! Missing Dirty Dicks then?*' Tom texts back.

The phone beeps again. '*And there's more, mate.*' A second photo comes through. This time it's a beaming Gav standing on a beach with about twenty people running circuits. '*Personal training is a gold mine here, Tom. I'm full up. Four beach sessions a day. And then I surf. Paradise, man. Get yourself out here; best country in the world. I mean it, AMAZING. Fitness opportunities are off the scale. I could get you set up straight away, sponsor you a visa and you could be personal training on Bondi Beach this time next month.*'

I cast a sideways glance at Tom. He knits his eyebrows together. I know he misses Gav. He talks about him all the time. At one time he was thinking of emigrating to Oz too. I also know that he'd love to expand the gym, love to expand the business in general: nutrition, clothing, accessories and personal training. He has loads of ideas, loads of plans. I guess that's another reason I admire him so much. But Australia? That's too far away. He wouldn't go. He'd never leave Leanne and the gym and… me?

He raises his phone in front of us and I cuddle into his chest for a selfie. '*Cheers, Gav, but not on the cards. Got everything I need right here.*'

He squeezes my hand.

'Was that a hard choice?' I ask him.

'What?'

'Not moving to Australia with Gav?'

He swallows hard and runs his fingers through his hair. 'No. And yes.'

'Tell me.'

'I was the one who had the idea. I researched it, put the business plan together, just like I did for Gymbox.'

'What was it? A Gymbox down under?'

He shakes his head, animated and bright. 'No, it was different. Personal training to a new level. A full body-coaching programme tailored for the individual. And I know you're probably thinking it's been done before, but this was special. I created all the exercises from scratch, the nutritional plans, the playlists, the social media interaction. It looked amazing, and Australia was the perfect place to launch. Me and Gav were supposed to set it up together.'

'What happened?'

'Well, we had a few unforeseen expenses at the gym – broken machines, leaks, that kind of thing. Wiped us out financially. Leon got involved and ballsed us up further, so I couldn't leave Leanne. She's not just my business partner, she's my sister.'

I nod my understanding. 'I'm sorry, Tom.'

He shrugs. 'It's all right. It's all worked out okay. And now we're here.'

'So we are.'

And we dive back under the covers.

It's nearly midday by the time we're washed and dressed. I make coffee, because that's really all I've got. My inner domestic goddess hasn't exactly kicked in. Despite my best intentions, I've not yet managed to equip the apartment with the essentials. I've got all the cutesy soft furnishings and some drop-dead-gorgeous lingerie but keep forgetting things like milk. And bin bags. And washing-up liquid. And cutlery.

We drink our coffee black and try to decide what to do with the day – park or cinema or full English at a greasy spoon? My phone rings; it's Astral. Ringing on a Sunday morning? This must be important. I walk over to the bay window to take the call. From her tone, I can tell she's not in the best of moods.

'Hi, Poppy, please forgive me ringing you on a Sunday. It's just that there has been a fairly major misunderstanding…'

'Is everything all right, Astral? You sound a bit stressed?' I rest my hand on the window pane. She sounds hysterical.

'A BIT stressed! Yeah, that's an understatement and a half! It's the awards ceremony. Change of plan. Major change of plan.'

I pull the phone away from my ear and take a deep breath.

'They've decided against a live broadcast this year – there's a security issue – and in their wisdom, they're going to record on Saturday night and then televise for the public on Sunday.'

'Don't worry too much, Astral. I'm sure it'll be just as good. And they can edit anything out if we trip over or commit some other kind of gaffe, right? It'll work out just fine,' I tell her.

I hear her exhale heavily. 'It's just that it's my sister's wedding on that Saturday and I'm going to have to miss it now as we'll have to go to Edinburgh a day earlier than planned. Telling her is going be EXCRUCIATING. She has a terrible temper and a long memory – this is her third wedding for a reason – and I really wanted to be there. Anyway, these are the sacrifices we need to make, right? Okay, new and finalised details just in. Have you got a pen?'

I walk over to the calendar hanging in the kitchen and pick up a felt tip. Oh no. The realisation is just starting to sink in. We have to leave on the SATURDAY! This is a disaster.

'Give me those dates again,' I tell her, hoping I've got this wrong.

'Good, okay, our flight leaves London City Airport on Saturday the twenty-second of November at 14.30. As in next week… Got it?'

I get it all right. I'm staring at Saturday twenty-second November on my calendar. It is already circled in red felt tip. Anyone would think from the way it's marked that it was the most important and urgent date on the calendar. I guess because twenty-second November *is the day of the Superleague final.*

'Poppy, are you there? Read it back to me. We need to get this right once and for all.'

I look at Tom rooting through my cupboards, looking for something more nutritious than Coco Pops. This is a DISASTER. How am I supposed to choose between my netball girls and the station crew? How am I supposed to choose between the Superleague final and the awards show?

Don't make me choose, God dammit!

Leanne will go crazy if I don't show at the final. We've been training for months. She's never won it before and she feels this may be her last season playing at this level. So if she doesn't bring home the trophy this year, it's unlikely she ever will.

I feel sick.

Okay, I definitely need to be at the Superleague final. But where does that leave my job? What do I tell Astral and Jake? I can't simply not show up. I can't just casually email them with a 'sorry, can't make it, already something booked'. Astral would laugh in my face! She's missing her sister's wedding for this! And then I'd probably be summoned to Carol King's office to be ripped to shreds along with my contract. She already looks at me like I'm as welcome as a bad smell. Not attending the awards would give her exactly the kind of ammunition she needs to fire me. Or put me back in the mail room. And without my job, what am I? What have I got? Where else could I go? Back to Markus at the job centre? Back to borrowing money off Frank?

I look up at the calendar again. One day. Two cities. Might be an idea if the cities weren't Edinburgh and London. Opposite ends of the country. Even Concorde couldn't help me be at both.

I can't keep everyone happy, which means I'm going to have to let somebody down. The question is, who?

I bite down on my bottom lip as Astral talks me through the itinerary, the hotel arrangements, the staging, the speeches… Tom emerges from the bathroom. I watch him pull on his shorts and slip into his sweatshirt; he gestures that he's going for a run. I nod, and he kisses me on the cheek and flies out the door.

Astral is still talking at a million miles an hour.

'So,' I double-check with her, 'so we leave for Edinburgh on the Saturday?'

'Exactly.'

'The twenty-second of November – you are absolutely sure?'

'A thousand per cent. We are all going to be on red carpet on the twenty-second come hell or high water.'

Fuckety fuck.

This is my job at stake here. And this job is my future.

I stand in the bay window, shoving fistfuls of dry Coco Pops into my mouth, trying to think how I'm going to break it to Leanne and the Assassins that I won't be there to play in the Superleague final.

CHAPTER TWENTY-FIVE

Of course I'd rather email her, text her, leave a voicemail. Any kind of non-live, remote transaction is preferable to a face-to-face on why I won't be able to play in the final. But I can't do that to her. Anyway, she wouldn't let me; she'd show up at my door for sure. With an axe and a cast-iron alibi.

I'll have to visit her at the gym.

No excuses. No dilly-dallying. I put on my trainers, scrape back my hair and head to Gymbox to face the music. The godawful get-pumped, go-hard-or-go-home music.

Leanne is in the studio taking a Zumba class packed with rows of over-fifties dressed in jelly-baby colours swinging their hips and clapping their hands to what sounds like the Gloria Estefan Evangelical Church. It's only just started, so I decide to go on the treadmill until she's ready. I'm going to have to psyche myself up for this. Rehearse it in my mind…

I'll begin by saying sorry… No. She'll think it's something I can change. That it's under my control and I can actually do something about it.

I'll begin by explaining the dilemma to her… No. She'll keep interrupting me.

I'll begin by saying 'Okay, Leanne, I know you are going to hate me forever when I tell you this…'

Actually, I'm not going to rehearse this. Because the more I go over it, the more I feel the sting of guilt for having to say it to her in the first place.

I press the start button, add a few notches of incline and look up to the wall-size mural in front of me. It's a fitspiration shot of Leanne lifting a tremendous weight, with the words *Every step you take is a step closer to what you want and a step away from where you used to be.*

I press the button and take my first slow steps.

When her class finishes, Leanne sidles up to me. 'Hey, Pops, good to see you! Bit of extra training coming up to the final, that's what I like to see.' I go to press the off button but she beats me to it and ramps up the speed from seven to ten. 'You need to push yourself if you want results. What you're doing here is good but nowhere near your true capacity.'

'What? Leanne, this will kill me.'

'It only feels like you're dying; in fact you're getting stronger – weird, isn't it?' She switches it up one more notch to eleven. 'Now that's *meaningful*; expect to feel this.'

I can barely keep my breath.

'Good work, Poppy, go at this for ten more minutes and then a five-minute cool-down. I've got another class now, so I'll see you at training.'

She starts to walk away. I've got to tell her, but I don't think I can manage to turn this treadmill off and turn around and speak to her without running the very high risk of losing my footing and falling flat on my face.

'Leanne, I need to talk.' Words are hard to catch. 'About netball.' No air.

She stops and leans in. 'Always time to talk netball. What is it?'

'I can't. I can't make the final. Work. I have a work thing.' The sweat is pouring down my face, pooling into my eyelashes and stinging my eyes. 'So sorry,' I wheeze. 'So so sorry.'

Her face darkens and she slams her hand down on the emergency stop button.

I watch it like it's in slow motion. But then I feel it.

Bang! My legs give way and my face smacks the rubber conveyer belt underneath me. For a second, I'm actually glad to be lying flat, my body floppy and still. I groan face down on the belt.

'I can't believe you, Poppy! The girls trusted you. I told them to trust *me*, to give you a chance, to let you play. And for what? So you can bail on us when we need you most? The game is on Saturday. How the fuck am I supposed to find a replacement for you before then?'

'I know. That's why I wanted to tell you straight away! There was a mix-up. I just found out myself. If I had any choice at all…'

'You always have a choice.'

I try to blink my eyes open through the stingy beads of sweat. She is a blur, standing above me like a neon impressionist painting. And I know she's angry. I can feel her fury. It's making my skin prickle.

'Not this time, Leanne. I need to go to this awards ceremony. They expect it. Missing the game is a sacrifice I have to make. I'm sorry.' The words dribble out of my mouth but I can't get up yet. No bones, no breath, no energy.

'Fine. I get it.' She pinches the bridge of her nose and squeezes her eyes shut. Then she lifts her chin and takes a big breath. 'But I really, REALLY hope you don't drop Tom as quickly when a better offer comes along.'

And then she's gone.

CHAPTER TWENTY-SIX

The day has come. The day of the Superleague final that I won't be playing in.

The day of the British Television and Radio Awards in Edinburgh, broadcast live across the nation on digital and online channels.

And not only will I be in attendance, I'm a nominee. It'll be like Eurovision, our bonded 105 FM crew clenching teeth, crossing fingers and holding hands as we wait for the seasoned host to open the golden envelope and read out, 'And the winner is...' allowing a suspenseful pause, raising a playful eyebrow at the nervous titter from the back, which unleashes more nervous titters, and then releasing the final judgement in a glittery storm of golden confetti, '105 FM, *The Jake and Poppy Morning Show*! Congratulations!'

We will gasp and scream and hug and cheer and then Jake will take my hand, leading me through the maze of round tables, up the side steps to the stage. We'll swan over to the podium, accept our award and graciously thank all of our listeners for backing us, for giving us their support, for continuing to tune into 105 FM.

Oh what a night. What a night lies ahead. I place my hand on my stomach to settle it. In my current position, the last thing I need is a nervy bout of diarrhoea.

And by my current position, I mean that I am standing semi-naked in my mum's kitchen, wrapped neck to ankle in cellophane. Apparently, this is a very effective DIY inch-loss treatment, courtesy of HMP Holloway's beauty forum. My hair is stiffened into a bluish Marge Simpson peak with a silvering conditioning treatment. Tinfoil thimbles cover my nails, for some reason my mum explained, to do with gel polish and gravitational pull maybe? I don't know. I'm beyond quizzing her. This morning I'm her living doll, her grown-up living doll resigned to letting her have her way in poking and prodding and preening me as she pleases.

'So you've got your false eyelashes?' asks Mum. 'Make sure you have all your make-up in place and set before you do any gluing.'

Gluing my eyelids, like that's what nature intended.

'And then carefully use the slanted edge tweezers to apply.'

Sharp steel instrument to the eyeball: more sado-masochistic ex-con beauty tips. I need to review letting her do this to me. Or at least review the safety-consciousness of her sources.

'Poppy, I'm serious. If you don't apply them properly, it looks like you're drugged.' She *is* serious. I can tell by her pursed lips and heavy nose breathing. But it's not the brutal method of application she's worried about; just that I might look like I don't know my way around false eyelashes and hence bring shame on the family.

I feel excited, nervous and guilty. I can't help it. I know I've made the right choice; the grown-up, professional, responsible choice. But already, I can tell, it's come at a cost. I'm missing the final. I'm missing the girls. I'm missing the excitement and the nerves we would be sharing together today. It was a hard call, but I thought once the decision was made and I'd broken the news, it would get easier. Surprisingly, it hasn't. If anything, I feel worse with every passing hour.

I check my phone. I scroll through literally hundreds of new messages and notifications. '*Go for it, Poppy and Jake! From everyone at King's College Hospital… from Arsenal FC… from the Minister for Education… from all the salon girls keeping the show on the road while Angela does some celebrating!*' The reach and response is overwhelming. But I'm scanning for something in particular. And I can't find it. I sent Leanne a message for the team: '*Go Assassins! You can do it!*' But she hasn't responded. As far as I'm concerned, this is just a case of getting through a rough spot; in a few weeks' time, when it's all blown over, we'll pick up again where we left off. But I have a nasty niggling feeling that Leanne doesn't see it that way.

Tom has sent me a lovely good-luck-and-knock-'em-dead message. And a reminder that he's happy to receive drunk texts at any hour. He's trying to keep out of this the best he can; he's told both of us that he's not going to act as a go-between. When I tried to talk to him about it, he said, 'Leanne's my sister, you'll just have to work it out between the two of you.' I told him I was sorry and that I'd had to choose and I felt like shit about it. And he said, 'You're doing it again, Poppy, trying to tell me the stuff you should really be telling Leanne directly. It's not me you need speak to, it's Leanne.'

But I think Leanne will probably never speak to me again.

I raise my fingers to my temples. Such a nagging ache; I've had it for days.

I feel tears stacked in my throat. I fan my face and try not to cry, partly because I've had the eye-make-up warning, but mostly because if I do, I don't think I'll stop.

Mum's wrapped in the cellophane now too, and has a pillar-box-red dye in her hair. She's having a little get-together this evening; invited all the neighbours around to watch the awards show. She's made bunting and there'll be platters of sandwiches and Ritz crackers and a choice of drinks: beer for the men and white wine for the ladies. Anyone fussier than that can have orange squash or bring their own.

I so love that she's excited; that she's proud of me and wants to share it with her friends. I hear her on her phone again. She's been campaigning tirelessly since the online voting opened at the beginning of the week. 'Are you online yet, Jackie? Good girl. Now, I want you to click on the link I sent you. Won't work? Okay, then google British Television and Radio Awards. Yes, you've got it now? Good. Right, do you see a box that says VOTE NOW, People's Choice? Yes, it is yellow, that's right. Now hover over the box beside 105 FM, *The Jake and Poppy Morning Show*. Yes! And click! Good work, Jackie! Now get up off your chair and show everyone else in the centre how to do the same. We need all the votes we can get!'

I'm half an hour late leaving for the airport.

'You've got absolutely everything you need? You're a hundred per cent certain?' Mum asks as she hooks her arm around my neck and kisses me goodbye.

'Yes, everything! Now wish me luck and let me go.'

I climb into the back of the cab, the driver honks his horn and we pull out.

'Well if it's not Dr Poppy! What a pleasure!' he says through the mirror. 'What's the occasion? Going anywhere nice?'

'Edinburgh,' I tell him. 'For the British Television and Radio Awards.'

'Of course. Well, best of luck. You guys deserve it. I'd better put my foot down then, seeing as it's your big day.'

Yes, big day indeed. I turn to wave goodbye through the back window like I'm a lone bride setting off uncertainly on honeymoon all by myself.

CHAPTER TWENTY-SEVEN

Despite the cab driver's best efforts, we end up having to take quite a lengthy – and bumpy – diversion due to unplanned roadworks. We arrive at the airport a little later than expected, but I feel I'm pretty punctual all things considered.

When I walk into the VIP lounge, Jake is standing at the bar chatting intensely to Carol King, a glass of water in his hand. The first time I met Carol, she X-rayed me with a gaze that made me uncomfortable with its intensity. I remember watching her watching me – scanning, critiquing, evaluating, judging – and wondering what it was she saw in me. I asked Jake about it later, and he told me to just grin and ignore her; according to him, she only has time for celebs.

'Hey, you two!' I say, leaning in for a kiss. None comes, and I'm left hanging a moment, then Astral pops up behind me, grabbing my elbow and pulling me to the side. Her galaxy hair is twisted into rosebuds around her crown. I rub my eyes and blink twice; she's wearing a Black Horn T-shirt.

'Are you trying to give me a heart attack? You are over an hour late, Poppy! We're just about to head through to the gate.' Her eyes are flitting across my hair, my face, my everything.

Carol King glowers at me, pointing at her dainty silver watch. 'Cutting it very fine, Poppy. We'd like to keep things *professional* around here.'

Jake stands on tiptoes, waves one arm and shouts, 'Okay, everyone, time to make a move. Make sure you've got your boarding passes and all your belongings, you know the drill. We want this to run as smoothly as possible – no hiccups if we can help it.'

I take his abandoned glass of water from the bar, knock back the last slug a little too fast and hiccup loudly.

A peal of laughter and the tension melts from Astral's face. 'Okay, 105 FM, let's do this!' she squeals. The crew clap and high-five and we all crowd together into the lift to make our way through to the departure gates.

I end up in the line beside Carol King. 'So, are you excited?' I ask her, trying to make pleasant small talk as the queue inches its way to the boarding gate. She's on her phone, texting frantically, and looks up at me, slightly bemused.

'I beg your pardon?'

'Excited? About the awards?' It sounds a ridiculous question now that I've had to repeat it. Like an odd friend of your nan's asking if you like sweets or if you're looking forward to Christmas. She answers me with a tight 'yes', but it's in a distracted way, like she's already forgotten the question. Perhaps she's nervous. All of us react to stress differently – some of us kick and scream, some of us cry and wail and some of us need to withdraw from everyone so they can focus on one thing at a time. I place my hand lightly on her jacket sleeve, which should translate into some kind of primal code for 'it's okay, I understand'. But she flashes me a look, and not a good one: classic hint of aggravation there around the eyes; a single flared nostril.

Is she in a mood with me? I think she is. But why? What have I done? I've only been here five minutes, I haven't even had a drink yet. I've given up something really, really bloody important to me in order to be here. I decide to leave it. Everyone hates her anyway, whatever her problem is.

Astral turns around from the head of the queue, waves her phone in the air and shouts down to Jake, 'It's confirmed! It's her. A hundred per cent it's her.'

I see Jake rub the bridge of his nose and clench his fingers around his phone. He turns to me. 'I cannot believe this. This is INSANE.'

'What? What's insane?'

A ripple is moving through the crew. Hands flying to faces, grown men with beards squealing and bouncing up and down.

I turn to Carol. 'What is it? What's going on?'

She raises her eyes to me, and the faintest smile plays along her lips.

'Beyoncé.'

Umm…

'Beyoncé what, Carol?

'Beyoncé is going to play at the awards tonight.'

Omfg. This is incredible. I find that I am on my knees, heaving to breathe.

I overhear Carol explaining to Jake in the stratosphere above my head, 'Yes, it was a big secret to keep. If it leaked at all, she was going to pull out, that was the deal.'

Beyoncé and me in the same room, under the same roof, swaying to the same beat.

'Please have your boarding cards and passports ready for inspection,' announces the security guard. From my bended-knee position on the ground, I watch everyone pass me by – Carol, the sound guys, Astral in her Black Horn T-shirt – and I know what I'm going to do. It's not a choice. It's a no-brainer. I wouldn't even be here if it wasn't for Leanne whipping my arse into gear; I wouldn't have a radio show if Shanice hadn't called in as Miss Demeanour to kick off the calls. I watch my radio colleagues hand over their documents to the ground stewardess. I watch as she scans them routinely and everyone sails through, giddy, jumpy, elated. I feel the tension melt from my shoulders. I'm not walking away from what I really want. I'm actually about to walk towards it.

I watch as Jake passes through the gate and then turns back in my direction on the other side.

'Get a move on, Bloom! We've got a plane to catch!'

'I'm sorry, Jake, I can't come. You pick up the award for both of us, okay?'

He shakes his head at me in confusion. I give him a thumbs-up and signal for him to go. He shuffles on the spot, reluctant to leave without me.

Final call for boarding.

'I don't understand, Pops. What's going on?'

I find my feet. I stand straight and shout over the crowds. 'I'll explain later. Go catch that flight, Jake. Beyoncé's waiting!'

The ground stewardess picks up her clipboard and ushers Jake towards the aircraft. Bound for Edinburgh and red carpets and champagne and a night of glitzy, starry-eyed mayhem. Along with everybody else.

But I don't mind. I don't mind one bit. I sling my bag over my shoulder, sprint across the shiny airport floor, out through the rotating doors and straight into a cab.

'Olympic Stadium,' I tell the driver. 'Fast as you can manage.'

I grab my cheeks and shut my eyes. I did it! I can feel the adrenalin coursing through me. The taxi screeches out of the rank and we are on our way.

As we speed along the motorway, I know that this is truly the first time in my life I've done exactly as I want. Not what I should do, or what's expected, or what someone else wants me to do. I've done what my gut told me, even if it's irrational, even if it's unorthodox, even if it's career suicide. I don't care. I can deal with whatever comes next because I've got some good people around me. A team of really good people. And with that, I'm starting to believe I can handle anything.

I wipe my lipstick off with the inside of my arm and pull the pins out of my hair.

I've got a game to play.

CHAPTER TWENTY-EIGHT

'Welcome to Superleague Saturday! This is Sandra Skinner, broadcasting live from the Olympic Stadium in London. It's a clash of the highest order today, folks; the question on everybody's lips is whether South London Assassins have the team, the skills, the stamina to win this final. There've been rumours of trouble in the camp for the Assassins; issues around player commitment, team spirit and low morale that could have a devastating effect on their game. So is today the day they are finally in a position to clinch the title from reigning champions Team Oxbridge? Will the south London underdogs be able to turn the tide and seize a victory from the current titans of British netball? All remains to be seen, ladies and gentlemen, but one thing is for sure, there is no better way to spend a Saturday evening than watching the two best women's teams in the country go head to head in this year's Superleague final!'

I stand in the stadium car park listening to Sandra's voice boom through the massive speakers. She is certainly no passive pundit; she's the perfect commentator to appreciate the guts and the glory involved in getting to this point. The grand final of the Superleague, the biggest showdown of its kind in the northern hemisphere. There's a sell-out crowd; you know tickets are in high demand when the touts wait by the gate to offer fans triple the original ticket cost.

I walk the length of the car park searching for the purple Assassins minibus. When I find it, it's already empty, locked up with no kit or bags to be seen. I try to enter via the players' entrance, but a security guard turns me away.

'I need to get in – I'm the Assassins' goal shooter, Poppy Bloom.'

He checks his clipboard. I'm hoping that my name is still on the list from our last match, or that Leanne added me anyway, even as a substitute, holding out hope that I'd change my mind.

He shakes his head gravely. 'The teams have been warming up for the past hour; nobody reported any missing players.'

'Can't I go inside and double-check?'

He looks bemused, like I'm a delusional fan faking my way on court. Which I suppose I kind of am. If I want to get in there, I'm going to have to buy a ticket, even at the extortionate rate they're bound to be going for. I don't care about the price; my priority now is to get into that stadium and let the girls know I'm here and that I'm ready to rip the opposition apart.

Let's do this, Assassins!

I want to play, I want to score, I want to win, I want to high-five Nikki and get lifted off the ground by Shanice and be slapped so hard on the back by Leanne that it stings.

I *need* to get in there. *They* need me to get in there.

I approach a cluster of stubble-faced touts. 'Can I buy a ticket, please?' I ask, reconciled to the fact that I'll be eating cereal for the rest of the month to make up for this.

A synchronised shrug, then the middle one breaks the silence. 'No tickets, no tickets for love nor money.'

'But I really need to get in, I'm happy to pay; I'll pay whatever you're asking.'

He blows a smoke ring in my direction and scratches his neck. 'No tickets means no tickets. Can't spell it out any clearer, lady. You'd have to be media or royalty to get through those doors now.' He throws his cigarette butt down and grinds it into the gravel.

'Thank you very, very much!' I chirp as I reach into my bag for my lanyard and hook my 105 FM ID around my neck. I flash it at my old friend Mr Security and am promptly directed to the media box.

I find my way to the Assassins' dressing room by following the sound of Leanne's voice. Pep talk. I rest my ear against the door. I'll go in once she's finished; interrupting Leanne's team talk would be a very, very bad idea. They need to hear it. *I* need to hear it.

'I know you're worried,' she's saying. 'I know you're scared. I know you think we're going to walk out there and get battered to a pulp. And I can't guarantee that's not going to happen. They're tough. They're determined. They are here to defend their title. This is Team Oxbridge and they don't mess about.'

I raise myself on my tiptoes and peep through the small square panel window. I see them all, all my girls, Jess, Nikki, Shanice, Laura, Leanne, lined up on the bench, kitted out and ready to go. I spot a bona fide powerhouse of a woman with a platinum mohican and tattooed eyebrows who must be Teagan's replacement, Izabel. And what about me? Who will take my place? Maybe they weren't able to find anyone. Maybe they do need me to step in right this moment! Just as I'm pondering this thought, I feel someone walk up behind me. I spin around.

'Are you looking for something?' asks a tall, tracksuited girl, a wary look on her face.

She's caught me peering suspiciously into the girls' changing room, bouncing a little with excitement and basically looking like a pervert. I can see that she's a bit freaked. She's angling around for help. She looks familiar; she definitely reminds me of someone. Something about the shape of her nose and the way she holds herself with an easy confidence. But that might just be her age; she looks early twenties at the very most.

The dressing room door swings opens, nearly knocking me out. Leanne is standing right in front of me. Her face darkens.

'Yeah, this is exactly what we need right now. What the hell are you doing here?'

'I came to my senses. I'm so sorry for everything. I want to play.'

'Oh, you want to play now, do you?' Shanice steps forward to stand by Leanne's right shoulder. 'And what about your awards show? Isn't that where you're supposed to be? Was it cancelled? I don't get it. One minute you can't come; the next, here you are.' She raises her chin.

I watch Jess and Laura exchange disappointed looks. 'I know, and I'm sorry… I made the wrong choice. But I'm here now. They can do the awards show without me.'

Shanice folds her arms. 'So you decided to ditch the awards at the last minute and come play with us instead.'

'Come on, you need me. I'm here, use me – we can sort out all the other crap later.' I look at the team in front of me. Only six players. 'You're a player down. You need a goal shooter.'

The girl behind me taps me on the shoulder, then unzips her tracksuit top to reveal a hot-purple Assassins vest. 'I'm the goal shooter.'

Leanne raises her eyes to mine. 'Meet Emily Skinner. Daughter of former England captain Sandra Skinner. Amazing, isn't it? It's like fate brought her to us in our hour of need! Just back as a medical student from her gap-year overseas and shopping around for a team. I can't tell you how happy I was to be able to offer her a position. Twenty-two years old and queen of the long bomb. Shooting prowess second to none, silky shots from as far back as mid-court. Great jump, great flexibility, great timing.'

'Okay, so I guess you don't need me after all.'

Leanne shakes her head at the ceiling. She looks conflicted. I take a step to stand directly in front of her so that she has to meet my eyes. So she has to hear my words.

'Leanne, you were my best friend growing up. You made me realise how important having a best friend can be. So, it's my turn to be a best friend to you. Right now.'

I step into the middle of the circle so that I can see all the girls' faces, because what I have to say isn't just for Leanne; it's for all of them.

'You guys gave me a chance when I'd given up on myself. You welcomed me and played with me and invited me into your precious inner circle. You've taught me so, so much. Believe me, after a lifetime of teachers and lecturers, I thought I was done being taught, but you taught me how to speak out and how to stand tall and how important it is to stick by the things in your life that are most precious, because when life changes, as it inevitably will, it's those precious things and people that get you through.'

Jess is the first to step out of the circle and put her arms around me, followed by Laura and Nikki and Shanice, and finally Leanne blows out her cheeks and says, 'You are such a fuckwit.'

'I know.'

She points to Izabel. 'Give Poppy your bib, Izzy. We can call you up if we need a sub.'

Izzy salutes. 'Whatever you say, boss.'

She throws me her bib. Leanne slaps me on the back.

'Bonecrusher Bloom, glad you're back. Now come on, people, it's GAME TIME!'

CHAPTER TWENTY-NINE

I look up to the scoreboard. Team Oxbridge 0: Assassins 0.

We are billed as the underdogs, and we certainly qualify as such. Team Oxbridge have held this title for years. They are as close to a professional team as you will get at this level; their sponsorship secures them a coach and physio, their facilities are world-class, they can pick and choose the best and strongest young players in the country. Unlike us, who try to train between full-time jobs and family demands, out of a community gym and with just enough players to fill the court.

But actually, this doesn't daunt me. It makes me proud. With our meagre resources, we've qualified. We are here because we deserve to be. We have nothing to be ashamed of. And even if we don't win, we'll still be the Assassins. We will still be a team.

'Let's give this everything we've got,' urges Leanne before we break from our huddle and walk to our positions on the court. I take a deep breath and try to shut out the roaring crowds surrounding us in the arena and the clear, booming voice of the commentator echoing through the stadium.

'Will the south London underdogs be able to turn the tide and seize a victory from the current titans of British netball?'

Well, Sandra Skinner, we're certainly going to try…

I shake the voice out of my ears. I've got to focus. And breathe. I think of Leanne's words: 'Stay alert. Stay in tune with the rest of the girls.'

We're sixty minutes away from the final whistle and knowing whose name will be etched on the Superleague trophy. I tense every muscle in my body; I'm ready to play as hard as I've ever played before.

The whistle blows and the ball is fired up into the air. Game on. Within seconds, our new star player, Emily Skinner, nails the first goal. She's phenomenal. Long, lithe, powerful; if I wasn't her teammate, I'd pay to watch her play. She's surprised me. And I can tell she's surprised Team Oxbridge as well. They dart startled looks at each other and raise their stern chins in our faces. It looks like their feathers are ruffled, and I get the impression they thought we were going to be easy to beat. I catch Nikki's eye and she gives me a wink. She's a police officer; she knows the body language of the nervy, the rumbled, the bloodthirsty.

But I think we might just be in with a chance.

The crowd clearly think so too. Every single attack or defensive manoeuvre – at both ends – is met with a wall of screams from the stands.

At quarter time, Team Oxbridge lead 16–7.

'And that brings to a close a hectic opening quarter,' announces Sandra Skinner, 'which Team Oxbridge have bossed, to be honest. New player Emily Skinner is the Assassins' only hope; her shooting has been impeccable. But she can't do it on her own; the Assassins need to step up if they are going to be viable contenders. The dream is slipping further and further away from their grasp.'

Leanne gathers us all to the sidelines. She's walking with a slight limp, her face stricken with pain.

'Are you okay, Leanne? Are you hurt?'

She shakes her head at me and tries to smile. 'No, I'm fine. Get into the huddle.'

We cluster together and pour water down our throats.

'Right, we're doing well, but not well enough. Too conservative, too afraid to make waves. When we get the ball, we know what to do with it, but really we need to wrestle that ball out of their hands.' She raises her eyes to mine. 'C'mon, Bonecrusher, I know what you can do. Time to take back control.'

It takes us about twenty seconds, but then *boom!* Goal! Goal! And then two more goals and the Assassins are riding a small wave of momentum. By halfway through the second quarter, though, Team Oxbridge are leading 23–13.

'Well, after that initial wobble at the beginning of this quarter, Team Oxbridge have managed to settle and are back in their groove. However good Emily Skinner is looking for the Assassins, there's still a ten-goal deficit. I don't want to be a pessimist, but it is incredibly unlikely that the Assassins can make any dent in the game at this stage. It's less a question of whether they'll be beaten and more a question of how badly they'll be beaten. Not looking good for the Assassins…'

When the half-time whistle sounds, we're still looking at a ten-goal deficit. How can we ever recover from that? Even if we scored ten goals, we'd still only be level with them. And they're hardly going to sit back and let that happen. 'Livin' on a Prayer' blasts out over the tannoy during the break in play – presumably at the request of Team Oxbridge supporters who believe that they are indeed 'halfway there'.

Only thirty more minutes left. I run my fingers through my hair and try to catch Leanne's eye, but she's crouched over, holding ice against her left knee. If she keeps pounding down on that injury, she'll only do more damage. I open my mouth to speak, but then think better of trying to tell Leanne what to do.

The team are playing our little hearts out. We know what we need to do and we want to do it, but is everything going be too little, too late at this stage?

Halfway through the third quarter, Team Oxbridge are leading 36–28.

'The pressure is on the Assassins – they simply cannot afford to allow their level to drop, not one bit. If they do, then Team Oxbridge will be crowned Superleague champions.'

I survey the girls' faces. Even Emily is visibly puffed and seems restless with our current losing status. Shanice is crouched on the ground, tying and retying her shoelaces, not making eye contact with anyone. We're losing and don't we know it. We need a boost. We need some energy. But what can we do? What can *I* do?

Team Oxbridge will be crowned Superleague champions.

I'm trying to shut out Sandra Skinner's doom-laden commentary, but it's nigh-on impossible. The stadium's acoustics are simply overwhelming; you can hear the music reverberate under your feet. Ah. A-ha. I have an idea.

I rush over to the first row of seats, where I spot a little girl and her mother draped in Assassins colours. 'Could you do me a favour?' I ask breathlessly. And I send them to the media box with a song request, something that just may help us reach that fighting spirit we so need right now.

And the next time I feel the reverberations underfoot, I don't try and block out anything as 'Don't Stop Me Now' blasts out.

Jess launches forward, eclipsing the opposition and catching the ball with both hands.

And that's when we start to take charge.

Within two minutes we've pulled the deficit back to six, with Team Oxbridge leading 36–30.

'WOW! Never say never. The Assassins may yet have the last laugh here. Do we have a grandstand finish on our hands?'

As the soaring voice of Freddie Mercury breathes life back into our team, we are lifted by at least five thousand voices singing along from the stands at the top of their voices. I take it all in, breathe in the scent of perspiration mingled with floor wax, and I have no doubt in my mind that I made the right choice. This is exactly where I belong.

And I make a vow to myself that I will never let fear dictate my choices again. I am here, I feel electric, and I would have missed all this had I not followed my instincts, listened to my heart.

I look to the scoreboard. Three-quarter time: Team Oxbridge lead 41–39.

Every time Leanne goes near the ball, the crowd loses its collective mind. They might need a new roof on this stadium! The game is approaching squeaky-bum time, but Team Oxbridge have still got that two-goal cushion. And it won't matter if we lose by a little or a lot. We did not come here for a loss. So we keep on fighting. And we do not let up. Not. One. Little. Bit.

With Team Oxbridge leading 48–46 in the fourth quarter, Sandra Skinner's voice booms out around the court again.

'Emily Skinner has been impressive for the Assassins today, but marking Jan Collins is no easy feat… And just as I say that, Collins steamrollers into Skinner! Skinner raises a hand and smashes it into Collins' face! Oh goodness me, Collins is on the ground! She's in a bad way, blood on the court. Paramedics rush on. The umpire takes Skinner aside but she's not having it; she is showing the red card – Skinner is off! Ladies and gentlemen, what a turn of events. Skinner is walking away. She shrugs off her captain, who… Oh my goodness, Leanne Jones has crumpled to the ground. A sharp twist on her knee and she's writhing in agony – this is not looking good for Jones; seems her left knee has given way altogether. The paramedics are now attending to her. Think a pause is in order while we try to figure out what the hell is going on down there. Leanne Jones is limping off court; I've got to say this is a first. She's one tough player.'

I rush over to Leanne. 'Are you okay?' I ask, trying to keep the panic from my voice. She's pale; a worrying shade of grey. Her eyes are clenched tight. I've never seen her look like this before.

'You're captain now,' she gasps.

'But I—'

'Just do it, Poppy.' She glares at me, sharp, urgent, and then lets out a belly roar and slaps away the hand of the physio prodding her swollen knee.

I don't protest again. Leanne's cheeks are flushed now, a savage look in her eyes. Her chest pumps up and down as she sucks in fast breaths. She's like a wild animal; if I get in her way, she will lash out and claw me to pieces. She needs me to take over. It's not the time for questions.

We have three minutes of injury time. The team huddle together, a cluster of distressed red faces, sopping-wet hair and blotchy, bruised arms and thighs. Leanne tries to stand but topples back on to the bench. I take her by the elbow, supporting her lightly as she launches herself up again. She throws two pills down her throat and washes them back with a big glug of water.

'Izabel, you are on. Get your bib.' She's breathless, but it's not stopping her. 'Okay, we can do this. I mean it. It's not over, but you have to do exactly as I say.'

We close in our circle, arms around each other's shoulders.

'We'll have to mix it up now that we're a player down. We've got to change our play, mess with their heads; they think they know our weaknesses, so we've got to confuse them, make it hard for them to work out what the hell is going on. Throw your bibs in. All of them. NOW.'

We nod, even though none of us has a clue what she's on about. Mess with their heads? Throw our bibs in? I can feel that everyone else is as confused as me, but we do it anyway. In Leanne we trust. A heap of crumpled, dejected bibs lies at her feet.

'Versatility. Whatever position, whatever role you get, you will play it. Forget what you were, forget about your preference or your strengths. This is our team now, not the team we were or the team we'd like to be. THIS IS US NOW. Play with what you get and play it to the best of your ability.'

We each grab a new bib at random and slip it on. Everyone stares at each other in stunned silence, position reassignment proving as big a shift as if we'd changed our first names. Shanice is wing attack, which is terrible as her job is usually blocking and disturbing play. Now she will have to swap brute force for calm focus. Never going to happen. Laura is centre. Tall, shy Laura, who's best at protecting space, at keeping people out, will now have to charge around, involve herself with everyone, in every area, bringing the game to people. Whoa, Leanne, this is messing with my head, never mind the opposition's. I look down at my own bib. Goal attack. But I'm really playing two positions as we are a player down so that makes me goal shooter still as well. I'm going have to make things happen for the missing player. Everything we thought we knew has been dissolved.

'This is going to work,' Leanne says with a firm smile while taking us all in. 'If Team Oxbridge feel half as freaked out as you guys look, we're in with a chance.'

'Assassins are back,' announces Sandra Skinner. 'But back as what? They're a player down, injured Leanne Jones is on the bench with her left knee heavily strapped up, and every single player has taken up a new position! I don't quite know what's going on with this team today. It certainly is different.'

Different? Or at this stage of the game, just totally bonkers? I'm wondering if Leanne banged her head out there.

Shanice shoots me a look. 'This is never going to work.'

'Just give it a try,' I tell her. I rest my hand on her shoulder and try to meet her eyes. I know this feeling. I know it so well I could copyright it. I think of Tom and our passcode, and a smile rises to my lips. 'It's always worth a try. Just trust me.'

She searches my face, clearly wondering whether I'm confused or delirious. But then I see her expression relax. 'Okay, I suppose it's worth a try. Nothing left to lose, right?' She shrugs, and in that second I almost believe that Leanne's plan could work. Like a self-fulfilling prophecy, our only chance is in giving it every ounce of faith.

I clap my hands together and shout out to the other team, 'Buckle up, you are in for the roughest final minutes of a game you have ever seen.'

And with that, I see our girls bare their teeth.

* * *

'GOAL! Can you believe this! With less than a minute to go, the Assassins have drawn level. The crowd are on their feet! It's down to the wire; whoever scores next will be Superleague champions!'

One goal. If we score one goal, this game is ours.

Leanne screams at me from the sidelines. 'Phoenix rising! Do what you should've done!'

I nod. I know what she's telling me. After I broke Crystal's fingers, I told Leanne that what I should've done was go low. I should've played round her legs, where she wasn't expecting me to go.

I see the Team Oxbridge defence charging at me head on. I can do this myself; I know exactly what to do. I bounce-pass through Jan Collins' legs and back to myself, then leap high for the net. Almost in slow motion, the ball swooshes through the basket and bounces back onto the wooden court. But this time, nobody rushes to pick it up.

We're too busy rushing to pick each other up.

Because we are the Assassins. And we are unbeatable.

'South London Assassins win the Superleague final here at the Olympic Stadium by one goal! Cue wild celebrations on the court, on the sidelines and in the stands! A brilliant performance by every player and a deserved victory. Simple as that. A thrilling final.'

We are left to lap up the adulation of the crowd. There are whoops, screams, tears, hugs, handshakes, high-fives and noise, lots of noise. A baby makes an appearance, pompoms and flags are waved in the stands. The commentator places the microphone to Leanne's lips and asks for her thoughts.

Leanne rubs her hand down her face and pauses a moment. Her eyes well up and she grabs my hand. 'This is more than a game and we are more than a team... So many bloody emotions. Bloody hell.'

Bloody hell is right. We shake the opposition's hands before they slope off court, and try not to look ridiculously satisfied with ourselves. We douse ourselves with water and rub the tears around our sweaty faces as we leave the court so it doesn't look like we are crying.

But we *are* crying. Crying with relief, with love, with adrenalin, with victory.

Back in the dressing room, Leanne is howling in pain, pounding her fist on the bench as she reconciles herself to the fact that she's played her last game; her knee is totally ballsed up now. Jess and Laura are slumped against the dressing room walls, tears rolling down their cheeks from sheer exhaustion. Shanice is locked in the toilet cubicle, singing joyously to herself, the swell of tears evident in her gargling throat. Nikki sits beside me, her face buried in a towel. I put my arm around Emily's shoulders and we smile at each other. We look at our mottled hands and take long, deep breaths and allow ourselves the stillness, the silence, the sacred energy we share. We gave it everything we had out there. For a moment, there isn't anything else to do.

Until Izabel bursts in through the dressing room door, lugging a huge cool box of booze. She drops it to the ground with a crash, startling everyone.

'The game is over, girls. And WE ARE THE CHAM-PIONS!'

And at that, we all stand and raise our aching faces to the sky.

CHAPTER THIRTY

Oh my head. I have to go to the toilet, but I honestly don't think I can, my head hurts that badly. Every time I move, there is a scrapy, scratchy noise, like I'm wrapped up in a shell tracksuit. I realise that I am in fact in a tent. *Why am I in a tent?*

It's hard to breathe in here. The air is heavy and close and stale, like I'm sucking in my own bad breath over and over again.

And it's so bright.

And I feel so hot.

And my mouth is so dry.

And my tongue feels swollen and like it's covered in pigeon poo.

I raise my hand to my forehead – my head really hurts, tight and pounding. I very carefully raise one eyelid but then shut it again fast. No. Can't do it. Just… can't.

I hate tents. How am I here?

Something hits the fly sheet just by my arm. Someone outside is kicking a ball at me whilst I'm baking to death here in this sweaty little two-man oven.

A second ball. This one hits the pointy roof bit and knocks the pole sideways.

Why is someone attacking me with footballs?

I hear a groan. There's a body beside me. It mutters, 'Go away,' and shuffles deeper into its sleeping bag.

The ball is kicked a third time; this time it's a belter and within vicious short range, and it smashes against the back of my head, causing my teeth to rattle. Oh my poor, poor broken head.

I can hear the voices of very young boys going 'Whooaaa!' and then breaking up into fits of laughter. But seriously, that really hurt. I think my brain is bleeding now. I shout out, 'Leave us alone,' but my voice is split and squawky. There is a very brief silence and then an eruption of giggling outside. I prod the polyester-bundled body beside me. It doesn't move.

This is hangover hell. I'm dry. I'm tired. I'm somewhere I definitely shouldn't be. I'm going to have to move. I hate my life.

I try to hydrate myself by licking my cracked, furry tongue across my cracked, sticky lips. A useless and disgusting experience. My immediate needs are water and toilet. Secondary needs will inevitably involve an intensive wash, clawing at my face with shame and self-loathing and then eating anything warm and cheesy and wrapped in pastry from Greggs. Come on, Poppy, it's time to move; you need to get up off your fat ass or this situation runs the risk of getting a whole lot worse.

I run my fingers through my hair and a huge black spider falls onto my forearm. I scream and scream and thump the living shit out of whoever the hell is in that sleeping bag beside me.

'What? What do you... What is it? Just... what?' says a topless Tom, sitting bolt upright, eyes squinted, hair standing on end.

Tom? Oh, that's a nice surprise. But still, why am I in a tent with Tom?

'Spider! Get rid of it! I HATE spiders!' I point at the crushed black knot that I've shaken off onto the sleeping mat underneath us. Tom picks it up in his fingers. I convulse in disgust.

Need. To. Get. Out. NOW.

He rubs his eyes and brings the creature up to his face. I peep through my parted fingers; it's a weird-looking spider, with really dark thick legs... permed legs... way more than the standard eight as well. Tom sighs deeply, rolls his eyes and then flicks it back onto the ground.

'Noo! Get rid of it!' I scream. I scramble to the entrance, unzip the opening and dive out into the wet grass. Tom pokes his head out of the tent behind me, the spider in his fingers again.

'It's your fake eyelashes, you nutcase.'

Oh. I swing between 'Phew, it's not a spider then' and 'Cringe – how did I sink so low?'

But mostly phew.

I am on all fours in the grassy back garden of a large detached suburban family home. I look down at myself. I'm wearing a skin-tight black leotard. O-kay, I'm starting to remember now.

Izabel's booze chest in the changing room, piss-up on bus, piss-up at Leanne's, Leanne giving me a slutty makeover, putting my card behind the bar, dancing like a stripper, telling everyone how sorry I was and that I loved them, falling over, Leanne inviting us back to hers for more drink, Tom joining us. Oh, I remember now, *The Jake and Poppy Morning Show* won the People's Choice Award! So we had to toast that, naturally, with Prosecco and tequila, I think… Uggh, the taste in my mouth is disgusting.

And then… let me think. Oh, I can hardly remember. Then I think I told Tom I loved him and I think he said… I love you too? Then Leon came in and kicked us out to the tent because their kids were waking up… Ah. Kids.

There are five kids staring at me. Each of them holding a football. They are not laughing now; they look scared, a bit disturbed. Like they've just walked into an unflushed service station toilet and the evidence suggests that there are people among us who look human but are not; and this is the kind of mess they make when you catch them off guard.

I turn back to Tom. 'Did we?' It's all I can manage.

He shakes his head. 'No, couldn't work out your suit.'

I trace my hand down the million tiny fasteners that run from my boobs to my belly button. They held fast all right. Okay, that's one good thing. I'm still intact.

I slap his arm gently. 'No, silly, did we say… you know?'

'Say what?' He looks genuinely confused.

'Ah, nothing,' I say. 'Probably just drunken mush talk.'

He leans over and kisses me on the shoulder. 'Congrats, Ms Award-Winning Presenter.' He kisses me again. 'I'm very proud of you.'

'You are?'

'Yep. Not just for the award and the netball. But how you handled it all. I'm glad you and Leanne... you know. Top marks all round.' He lurches backwards. 'I feel awful. And I promised I'd help Leon fix his bloody bike.'

'Dad! Dad!' The children are shouting and pointing at me, and one of them is edging towards the house. I feel like I'm part of a Stephen King trailer.

'I'm going back to sleep. Give the kids money and tell them to go away.' Tom yawns and retreats back into the tent.

I hear a window open, a man's voice. 'It's nine o'clock on a Sunday morning – go and play! No Xbox until tonight. Now get your bikes and go!' That's Prawn's voice; Leanne's husband.

I need to get out of here and back home so I can clean myself up and be sick in my own toilet and hung-over in my own non-shouty space. I crawl away from the tent and out of the boys' view. Then I slide around by the garage and steal a pint of milk from the doorstep, glugging it back as I teeter in Leanne's stiletto heels down her street to the bus stop. I'll be fine. The worst is behind me. I'm safe – I'm in major pain but I'm not dying; it's just a hangover. Everything will be fine again, as soon as I'm in my lovely flat in my lovely PJs, and I'll sink into my lovely bed and sleep for the rest of the day.

There's nobody around at all. Everything seems eerily quiet, unusually peaceful. I flag down a taxi and give the driver directions to my apartment. My phone and all my money are stuffed into my bra, so I end up throwing three sweaty tenners at him and insisting he keeps the change. When I get to the communal door, I catch a glimpse of myself in the mirrored panel. I look like a Poundland Catwoman – tight black Lycra catsuit, spiky heels, hair backcombed to within an inch of its life, mascara smudged all over my face. Please let me not bump into Ingrid. This look would shatter any fragile illusion she might have that I am a hotshot who is professional at anything other than getting shitfaced.

Last night was fantastic, but I'm paying for it now. Even my hair hurts. It's clearly not a scaremongering myth that once you are staring down the barrel of thirty years old, hangovers hurt more, last longer and bring slightly more existential angst. I just need to lie down in a dark and silent room for, ooh, about ten hours and I should then feel marginally better.

I take off my bra. Better. I get into my PJs. Better again. It's my party and I'll slob if I want to. I've already decided that today is a write-off. I bring the duvet over to the couch and get stuck into a two-litre bottle of Fanta and two bags of kettle crisps – simultaneously, I might add. That's a hangover breakfast. This is now my girl cave and today there is only room for me.

My phone beeps. Ugh. I'm trying to be alone here, people.

It's a text from Mum, from last night. '*Isn't it a gorgeous venue? Like a castle!*'

It *is* a castle. That's what inspired the name 'Edinburgh Castle'. I'm spent. I'm going to bed. I don't want to know about everything I'm missed. I'm in recovery. Not able.

Another text from Mum: '*Yay! We knew you guys would win! Congratulations!!!*'

Another: '*Why you not on camera? Haven't seen you once. Eyelashes?*'

I also have three missed calls from Dad from just after midnight – God knows what I was doing then, singing Spice Girls karaoke most probably. Or was I telling Tom I loved him? Did that happen? If only I could remember… if only I'd stayed clear of the Jägerbombs… if only I'd drunk water…

There's a text message from Dad too. How bizarre – someone's made an emoji of him, unmistakably him, with his straggly black hair, middle finger up, tongue sticking out of a big satanic smile. And there's a link to a song: 'Baby, I Love You' by the Ramones.

I'll ring him later. It's been ages. Even ages by our low standards. I'll just get rid of this hangover and I'll call him tonight. Definitely.

My head feels light all of a sudden. A piercing cramp stabs at my stomach and I feel a seismic churn. I try to swallow, but it is no use – it's coming. A few dry retches, and then I heave a surge of curdled milk rippled with acid bile, which gushes all over my hands and my gorgeous cream carpet. I now see that colour-wise, Fanta was a really, really bad choice. I raise my head, a white beard of vomit dripping from my chin, only to see Ingrid peering in whilst unchaining her bike outside my window. I muster a wave. She pulls her sunglasses down and rides off. Thank God. Probably not exactly what she was expecting from her classy celebrity neighbour.

I shut my eyes really, really tight and concentrate on expelling this convulsive poison from my body. I manage to crawl to the bathroom and hang my head over the toilet. Once the puking subsides, I lie down in the bath, fully clothed but just relieved to be out of sight, to be alone, so I can be gross and immobile without apology or explanation for a little while. The past week has been hectic, physically and emotionally, and I feel like I need a break; just a little break with no alarms and no surprises.

My phone rings out from where I tossed it in an armchair... all the way back in the living room. I can't do it. Whatever it is, it'll have to wait.

I wake hours later, still in the bath. Freezing but feeling a damn sight better. I give myself a good ole scrub, change into fresh fluffy pyjamas.

I'm on my way back. Feeling good.

Feeling very, very good. So, Assassins won the Superleague. Our radio show won the People's Choice Award. Leanne and I are friends again. And maybe Tom loves me. That's pretty good going, I'd say. Almost as good as it gets.

I pick up my phone and check my missed calls. Mostly Mum, but two from an unknown number. And lots of texts, too.

Mum: '*Call me.*'

Mum: '*Emergency, call me.*'

Mum: '*Where are you? Call me.*'

Mum: '*This is urgent – I need to talk to you.*'

Mum: '*Your dad not well – SERIOUS. URGENT. CALL ME!*'

I call her immediately; she answers on the first ring.

'Where've you been? I've been trying to get hold of you all day!'

'Mum – tell me, what is it?'

There's a long pause.

'He's gone, Poppy. I'm sorry.'

'Gone? What do you mean, gone?'

'He died about an hour ago. Carlos rang from the hospital.'

She starts to explain things, but her words are garbled in my ear… interview, documentary, massive heart attack, ambulance, resuscitation… I can't string them together properly. I slide the phone away from me across the coffee table, my mother's voice tinny and incoherent in the distance, and I run to the bathroom to be sick all over again.

But this time it's different. It's not hangover sick. It's empty and angry and confused. It's almost like I can't physically digest this news, like my body's refusing to accept it, to let it in.

Where were you, Dad? Did you know? Were you frightened? Did you try and call me in your final moments? Is that why you sent me the song? Was it a message? I slump against the wall and stare at my phone, at my dad's missed call and his last message to me. What did you want to say, Dad? But there is only one answer and that is that I'll never know. Because I didn't take his call.

CHAPTER THIRTY-ONE

I arrange to meet Carlos and the journalist, Otis, at the hospital. Well, the hospital mortuary, to be exact. As Dad's only living next of kin, I'm going to have to identify the body.

Mum said she'd come if I wanted her to, to support me, though she's not religious and she's not into forgiveness so she feels it would be hypocritical to act like the mourning widow.

Or even a slightly compassionate acquaintance.

Her stance is more the scorned, retributive ex-wife, tag line: *That's what you get for being such a self-indulgent bastard.* Like death only happens to people who deserve it.

But actually, I get it to a degree. He wasn't easy. Definitely wasn't easy.

Tom makes me a cup of tea and we sit together at the kitchen table as I try to process the news. To work out if it is good news or bad news. And then try to face what that says about me.

If I think about him as Ray Bloom, the man who screwed up my mother's life, then it's good news, I guess. I love my mum and I hate that he treated her so badly, gave her no choice but to leave with a small baby and then carried on with the drink and the drugs and the other women like she was nothing.

But.

If I think about him as my father – as the man who read to me, perched on his knee at his drum kit; as the dad who was cut out of our lives overnight, who said that we deserted him, taking all the love with us and abandoning him to his demons; as the single most heartbreaking relationship I've ever known and that I will now never get the chance to put right – then it feels like it's very bad news. Very, very bad and sad news indeed.

I squeeze my eyes tight. Is it really over? Is this really how it ends? Will there never be a reconciliation, a… closure, a healing, a completion to this?

'Awkward, belligerent, stubborn, selfish.' I bang my teaspoon around the cup. 'Always criticising me and my mum. We never thought we were up to scratch, always felt we were such failures in his eyes.'

Tom looks up at me. 'So your mum tried to protect you?'

I raise my teaspoon in the air like it's a tiny silver staff. But then I stop a moment. I stop and think.

'Yeah, I think she was. He was an addict. Addicted to lots of things. He couldn't really help himself.' My voice softens a little and I take a slow mouthful of tea. 'As much as I couldn't stand my father, mostly, as I get older, I realise I pitied him.'

We raise our mugs and look to the ceiling.

'To Ray. You were your own worst enemy, but you were my father and so for that I say rest in peace. And genuinely, Ray, I hope you find it. I hope you find rest. And I hope you find peace.'

We observe a moment's silence.

And as much as I tried to think of him as my ex-dad in the same way my mum could call him her ex-husband, it's not the same, not so easy. There's all that ancestral blood and DNA and shared genetic bonds that tethers us, never mind the seeds of unconditional love that daughters clutch in the deepest cracks of their hearts, ever hopeful for the day when they will receive a little bit of light, a sprinkle of love to help them grow.

The next morning, the full force of Dad's death hits the world. Clips of songs, live sessions, interviews – some good and some utter cringe – are posted all over social media: #legend #nomoreheroes #daythemusicdied #endofanera. I watch the news: a flurry of journalists outside my mum's house in Brixton; Frank waving them off from the front-room window. There are floral tributes mounting up on the platform at King's Cross station, where the band famously played. The evening news is more indepth; Black Horn's music and the persona of Ray Bloom described as a reluctant, accidental zeitgeist successfully defining the restless and uncertain spirit of a period of history that none else quite knew how to express.

Tom and I take the train to Whitstable, the small seaside town in Kent that dad retreated to about ten years ago. He sold his house and moved into a little coastal cottage, with the idea that the fresh sea air and long, deserted beach would clear his mind and wash away his demons. But that didn't really work. When he did venture out of the cottage, it was into town, where he might play a short session with a young up-and-coming band and then hold court at the bar with free drinks and old-school tales of Black Horn.

I text Otis. '*We're in the taxi now, be there in five minutes; wearing jeans and red T-shirt*', I add bizarrely, just so he knows it's me and doesn't confuse me with the throngs of other estranged daughters lining up to identify one-time rock stars.

He spots us straight away and opens the door of the cab. I put out my hand to shake his, but he just wraps his arms around me and gives me a huge bear hug. 'I'm so sorry,' he says, but he's smiling widely. He rubs his hand down his face. 'Let me start again – today has melted my head.' He swallows and straightens his features.

'I'm really pleased to meet you. I'm Otis Clarke, *Legends of Rock* music journalist and Black Horn biographer. I've been with your dad almost every day over the past few months.' He raises his hand to his chest. 'Hand on heart, I'm not just saying this because it's you or because of today; it's been the most amazing and intense experience of my life. I kind of feel like I already know you – he talked about you non-stop. Could probably write your biography now, to be honest.' The corners of his mouth turn up again. 'Right, so that was why I was smiling; I don't want you to think I'm a heartless bastard, but I really am happy to finally meet you.' He hugs me again, more carefully this time, then steps back, eyes lowered. 'Though obviously I am really, really, really sorry to meet you in these sad, awful circumstances. I loved the man so I can only imagine what you're going through. I know you didn't always see eye to eye, but God, did he love you.'

I nod, a bit embarrassed. I'm used to the formula of 'Ray – bad father' not 'Poppy –bad daughter'.

I introduce him to Tom and we walk through the hospital corridors. I keep my eyes fixed to the floor and try to concentrate on the squeakiness of my trainers on the polished lino. We get to the mortuary door and I recognise Carlos's signature black cowboy hat straight away. Despite not having seen me since I was a little girl, he wraps his arms around me and then holds me at arm's length.

'Poppy, what a gorgeous creature you've grown into. You sure you're Ray Bloom's daughter?' He smiles a sad smile and bites his bottom lip. 'The magnificent bastard has left the building.'

Tom waits outside while Otis and Carlos come inside with me. They take my hand on either side and we agree to do this together. We make a bizarre trinity, standing in silence over the body of a man we all knew differently yet can all identify. Together we nod to the pathologist. Yes, we confirm that this is Ray Bloom. A man to love or loathe depending on him, depending on you.

It only seems right that we go for a drink afterwards. Yesterday's vow to never touch another drop dissolves as I order four pints of Carlsberg with whisky chasers. Today is no day to make promises that can't be kept. I knock back my whisky, then wince and slam the glass down on the counter.

The four of us settle into a booth in the corner. Carlos hands me a sealed plastic bag containing the belongings Dad had on him when he was admitted last night. I take out his battered leather wallet and open it. It is overflowing with betting stubs, cash, cards and a lone photo of me and him; I'm about two, sitting on his knee behind his drum kit. I show it to Carlos, who shrugs. 'Complex man. A dark and complex man. I guess all his secrets are gone with him now and we'll never know.' We sit in silence. Perhaps Mum was right not to come. I mean, he's not here to shed light on anything. God knows we tiptoed around him when he was alive. What did I expect? What could possibly change?

There is nothing around this table but death. Death and unanswered and unanswerable questions. My head hurts, my chest is heavy. I rub my neck to soften the stiff, cloying feeling that is creeping over me. I have a burning urge to get up from this stool and abandon all the shards of my father's life; to go out into the street and walk and walk and walk until I've left this place and every memory of him behind, until I am past all the little cottages and the looming coastal sky, until I am back out on the hard shoulder of the motorway, cars and lorries roaring past, walking and walking and walking until the soles of my shoes wear down to nothing, until I get back to my new life and my new flat and make a new resolution to pretend that Ray Bloom never existed.

Tom catches my eye, and I can tell that he picks up on the flash of urgency that must be written across my face. My breathing is tight. This is just too much.

'Are you all right?' he asks, placing a gentle hand on my thigh.

'I don't think so. I want to go now.'

He picks up my hand and plays with my fingers. 'What do you say we finish this drink, and then we can head back together? No problem at all.'

I nod. I can manage one drink. One drink to show my gratitude to Carlos and Otis for helping me, for being around. But that's all I can manage. Then we're definitely going.

Otis takes a swig of his pint. 'You know,' he tells me, 'by the end of the first month of interviewing, we thought we were going to have to cut the project; we couldn't get him to talk about anything other than you. How you were a genius, Banbridge graduate, psychologist, you were working on this amazing thesis that was going help people; not just in a superficial way, but in practical, life-changing ways. He said that's why he didn't mind being broke; he saw it as an investment. He'd put his money into his daughter and she was going to save the world – well, save the world's sanity.'

Really? This is news to me. I didn't even know he ever mentioned me to other people. I certainly didn't realise that he felt… well, proud.

'But then I brought this in to show him.' Otis opens up his laptop on the table and turns it towards me. It's a picture of a Black Horn album cover. Iconic black-and-white photo of Dad standing on the very edge of a railway platform, looking backwards into the tunnel. I was about a year old then. It was the year Mum left him. 'That's when he finally opened up to us. Started telling us stuff we'd never heard about before. That's when we knew we could justify carrying on, we finally started getting places.'

'What sort of stuff did he tell you?' asks Carlos.

'That this…' Otis indicates the album cover, 'was when everything started getting out of control. That the album – the words, the cover – was deeply autobiographical; he felt like he was always drawn to looking into the darkness, that he couldn't help it. That he thought he was going to be able to get through it, move past it, but it didn't work out that way. His wife left. Took his baby daughter away from him. He didn't cope. Couldn't cope. That was when his life broke down, and with nobody around, the darkness sucked him in.'

Oh my God. I've never heard all this before. I've never thought of it like this.

'Did he mention anything about Jonnie-O?' asks Carlos, tearing strips off his beer mat. Jonnie-O was the lead singer of Black Horn, who overdosed when he was just twenty-six, but I knew that he and Dad had fallen out before he died and hadn't spoken in ages.

Otis pauses and nods. 'Yeah, he did. Just once. He was very, very pissed. You could tell it still hurt. Still raw even after all these years.'

Hearing these two men speak about my father, I feel ashamed. I feel ashamed that I only ever considered how *I* was hurt. Didn't even think that he was hurt too. I only thought about him not being there for me. Not about me not being there for him. My father was an addict, he was alone and he was damaged. And even though I tried to help him, despite being his daughter, despite my training, despite how much I wanted him to get better, for us to be closer, it didn't work.

This is not something to solve or fix or figure out any more. My dad is gone now. And like my mother said, I'm going to have to take what I can from the good times we shared and try to learn from the shit bits. Whatever I could have done better, whatever he could have done better will have to be laid to rest now. Along with him and the ghosts of all we could have been.

Four more whiskies arrive on the table. I slug mine back and squeeze Tom's hand. Even though it's hard to hear, I'm glad we stayed. Maybe some of the unanswered questions are answerable after all.

Otis plugs in a tiny speaker to the side of the laptop. 'Listen to this. I recorded it the morning before he died; can you believe it? I asked him if he had any regrets – you know, generally.' He presses play, and my dad's disembodied voice grumbles through the speaker like a gravel-voiced ghost.

'Regrets? Every time you take a risk, you leave yourself wide open to regret. So of course I've got regrets, loads of them, because I've taken loads of risks. Some bad risks that I really regret; especially about the people I've hurt. But I've realised something, and that's if you want to live a life free of regret, there is an option open to you. It's called a lobotomy. And I think I've actually tried to lobotomise myself through drink and drugs and gambling and all the rest. But if you want to be fully functional and fully human and fully humane, I think you need to learn to live with regret. Who knows? Maybe I'll get there some day. I'd like to think I will.' The voice stops and there's a shuffle, a wheezy cough and a sigh. 'Here, have a listen to this; I'm not much of a talker. Forgive me.'

And then the music begins. It soars, a discordant symphony of slashing strings and crashing drums. There is something raw and powerful in the sound, its energy seizing the air, like it's causing the space between us to move, fluid and rhythmic as a current, thrusting us together then drawing us apart. Slowly Otis twists up the volume, then closes his eyes, his lashes fanning out to perfect crescents. The first low note of the lead vocalist, deep and slow, resonates from the walls, the floor, the ceiling. It swells in the space between us; the space we now share.

Carlos catches his breath, pressing his hand to his heart. 'I love this song,' he whispers, and begins to sing in perfect sync: '*Moon and stars; just holes in the blindfold of night. Across the eyes of those born of dust, and the eyes of those born of light…*'

We stay, wordless, cradling our warm, golden whiskies and listening to the original, uncorrupted, heartfelt, riotous music of Ray Bloom, our magnificent bastard, until the bell rings for closing time and the barman ushers us out into the cool night air. Then we stand at the door, Carlos in his cowboy hat, Otis with his beardy little face and me holding Tom's hand, with my throat full of tears, and we look up to the sky and sing the final chorus again in his honour. Together.

'*Moon and stars; just holes in the blindfold of night. Across the eyes of those born of dust, and the eyes of those born of light…*'

Somewhere in the dark and silent chambers of my heart I tell my father that although I don't understand everything, I forgive him.

And then I whisper to the darkness, 'Goodnight, Ray Bloom.'

CHAPTER THIRTY-TWO

Tom and I stay the week in Whitstable. Otis and his little crew have a rented house with a spare room they let us sleep in. Carlos deals with any press that arrive, speaking on my behalf, on behalf of the band, and answering questions about Ray as a drummer, as a writer, as a friend, as an addict. Tom and I clear Dad's cottage. It doesn't take very long. Everything of rock provenance we give to Carlos; the rest is binned – not even Oxfam-worthy. We scrub the place from top to bottom, music on in the background – Tom has a playlist for everything – and by the end I feel quite cleansed myself. The days follow a pattern, with me making coffee and French toast for the guys in the morning before they go down to the shed at the end of the garden, where they have set up an editing suite. I usually stay with them for a few hours each day; the process is fascinating.

'For us, the first point of call is to tell the truth,' Otis tells me. 'We may find interesting ways of getting there, but we always get there in the end. It's essential.' It seems really important to him that I know this. That he won't be distorting reality. He won't portray Dad in anything but an honest light, and whatever the audience makes of that is fine.

I start to understand Otis as a story-teller, cutting and capturing different shots or scenes or conversation snippets or moments of stillness to carve out a cohesive narrative. I love the way he listens to everyone, from the camera man to the sound guy, their core principle being 'never say no without trying'. I can feel he's really excited about the way it's coming along and believes that Dad's reflections will help people everywhere to understand the internal life of an addict, especially one who has essentially isolated the only people who could help him. I hope he's right. I genuinely wish him well with it and I've agreed to attend the premiere in London once it's ready. I've more than agreed; I've promised. And watching Otis and the boys at work this week has given me loads of ideas that can be easily transferred to radio, ways we can expand the show, develop our team, maybe reach out to more listeners using new digital technologies.

While we are all out the back in the editing shed, Tom is keeping us going, fuelling us with great food and banter. He is an amazing cook; every night we sit at a big family table with a delicious spread in front of us: lasagne, salad, baked potatoes and bottomless jugs of red wine. They are all so kind to me. We play charades, we listen to music, they try to beat me at Scrabble.

I ask Tom for commis chef jobs; he tells me not to be silly, to rest and enjoy the peace and quiet, to walk on the beach, but I insist, so he then tries to make up stuff to placate me; says I can chop vegetables or peel potatoes or cook rice if I really want to but not to feel that I have to. When I mention that I have a hankering for Coco Pops, he blows out his cheeks and throws me an apron. I catch it, smiling at the cheeky glint in his eye. 'Come on then, am I getting my own personalised nutrition lesson?'

'Yes. You need emergency intervention to get you off that chocolate crack you're on. Can't have you dying from sugar rot. Watch me now and write down this recipe.' Into a bowl he chucks a cupful of oats, a mashed banana, some cranberries and peanut butter. 'Mix that together, just roughly, no need to go over the top, and then form it into little balls.'

I do exactly as I'm told.

'Now, oven for ten minutes. They'll keep for a week in the fridge. So after I leave today, you'll have plenty to keep you going, okay?'

I nod my compliance. I don't know how I would have coped without Tom. After I called him about Dad, he dropped everything, flew to my side and has been here ever since.

'Promise me you will eat Tom's yummy balls every morning, and I guarantee, when I see you again next week, you'll feel like Superwoman.' He slurps his coffee and starts to gather his stuff for his journey back to London without me.

'What is it I need to do again?' I ask with a wry smile.

'Eat my balls. Every morning,' he tells me as I slide my arms around his hips and pull him close to me. He tips my chin towards his, and that's when he says it. No mistake, no fuzzy, fragmented, drunken mishmash of slurring sentimentality. Just us, bright as buttons, standing in this kitchen with nothing but the sound of the wind whistling through the windows and the gentle ticking of the clock.

'Poppy, I love you,' he says.

And everything else just falls away.

Because I am loved. And I feel it in every crease and fold of my being. And now that I know it, I'm never, ever letting go.

I wave Tom goodbye from the front door, which the heightened wind slams shut. I wish I was going with him. Otis and the boys will be leaving next week, and once I've fixed up some final paperwork with Carlos, I'll be on the train and back to the show. And I feel ready, I feel *excited* to get back to the studio, to go back to my lovely flat. I actually can't wait to see Jake and Astral and get stuck in.

I make my way to the kitchen and start up my ancient laptop. I take a bite of Tom's yummy balls. My nutritional intake improves forty-fold. As does my contentment, to be honest. So c'mon, Superwoman. I log into my work email for the first time in a week, since the netball final and Dad's death.

I wait for it to load, expecting there to be a couple of hundred unread mails: promos, agendas, schedule plans, playlists, meetings, policies to read, plans to check, billions of photos and video links to the awards, of course. I press reload; this thing is very slow. I imagine the hype, the energy that'll be all around the office next week. It'll be electric, absolutely phenomenal. I feel privileged to be a part of it, lucky to belong. I might call a meeting myself! Check me out! Who knows, I may even win over Carol King. May wrangle a Beyoncé interview now that I know she's so connected. Can you imagine? I'm giddy with the thought of it. So much potential, so much to look forward to.

The page loads, but something is still wrong. I stare at my inbox in confusion.

One email.

One email in my 105 FM inbox?

The connection isn't great here, so I reload again. But it still shows JUST ONE email marked unread. This can't be right. It was sent on Monday, the first working day after the awards show.

I open it.

Dear Dr Poppy Bloom,

This mail confirms that with immediate effect, we no longer require your services as freelance presenter at 105 FM.

This is due to a reshuffle in our programming and a new contract with a US media group that does not include freelancers in its terms and conditions.

I have been pleased with our prior relationship and it is my wish that we part on good terms. I wish you every success in your new ventures.

Please contact HR with any queries you may have regarding specific details regarding contract termination.

Best regards,

Carol King

Contract termination?

CONTRACT TERMINATION?!

I don't know what to do with myself. Panic rushes into my mouth, making it taste sour and tacky. I reread the email, just in case I've got this all wrong. Just in case they are EXTENDING my contract. But no, as I scan through, the words leap out at me: *with immediate effect… no longer require… termination.* Nowhere on the page does it say *extend* or *don't worry* or *of course you can show up here on Monday morning and get your coffee and joke around with Jake and make up the clues for You Do the Maps and be flooded with calls from listeners all over the capital.*

My hands fly to my face. How? How has this happened? Have they really sacked me for not attending the awards? I was expecting a harsh telling-off. But we won, for God's sake. Why cut a winning show? Why throw it all away when we're only just getting started? Why stop us now?

Heart pounding, I pick up my phone and punch in Jake's personal number. He doesn't know about my dad's death; I just told them I'd be off for a week for personal reasons.

'Hello?'

'Hi, Teagan. It's Poppy.'

'Poppy, wow! Congrats on the Superleague!'

'Oh yes, thanks.'

'And the awards! How amazing was that! I mean, Beyoncé, she was just PHENOMENAL, wasn't she?'

'Yes! She's phenomenal all right… Teagan, would it be okay if I had a word with your dad?'

'Of course, he's just walked into the room. I'll pass you over. Bye, Poppy!'

I hear the phone being handed across. 'Jake, it's me. I've just got a termination letter from Carol King! What's going on? Tell me there's been a mistake.'

'What? You got a letter? She didn't meet with you? I told her she had to see you; I made her promise that she would break this to you face to face. I know you're freelance and you weren't with us very long, but you made a big difference to us here; I felt you deserved that at least.'

Oh no, this means it's real. It's already accepted as a done deal. Jake is just upset about *how* it's been delivered to me, not the fact that it is happening.

'So it's true? It's not a mistake.'

'I'm so sorry, Poppy. Victims of our own success, it seems. Carol made a deal with a US media group that if we managed to win the People's Choice Award, they'd buy us up. So that's what happened. By the time we held the award in our hands, the deal had been signed.'

'I see. But why get rid of me? I was part of the show that won. Surely that counts for something? I put my heart and soul into that show. We made it what it was. Don't say it's over, Jake. Don't say we're finished.'

'Oh Poppy, believe me, I'm with you on that. That's why I've left the station, I quit over this. I fought Carol tooth and nail over it. But she believes it's our formula that's our real asset, not the presenters. Her plan is to roll out the same show but replace us with celebrities, well-known faces, bring in some heavy guns. She figures that if it can work with a regular person off the street, then it's going to be huge with a well-known, established personality.'

I swallow hard. I can't believe this.

'So what happens now? What are *you* going to do, Jake?'

'I'm going to take it easy. Spend some time with Teagan before she heads off to university. You know she got a scholarship?'

'That's fantastic, Jake. An amazing accomplishment.'

And I mean it. Even though my own heart is breaking, I'm so pleased for her. That's a big step from the petrified girl in the changing room toilets.

'Yeah, a few months ago, she could never have gone for something like this; she'd have panicked. But I don't know... recently she just seems to have got a handle on things. She's able to manage her anxiety a lot better these days: breathing techniques, focus, that sort of thing. She's a different girl and I have a feeling you played a significant part in that, Poppy, so I want to say thank you. From both of us.'

'My pleasure, Jake. It's what I do.'

Or at least what I did. What I should be doing. What I *need* to do.

'Yeah, it is. So, in a selfish way, this has come at a good time for me.'

A thoughtful silence. I hear Jake sigh into the phone.

'Poppy, you are a real talent. Best co-presenter I've ever had the pleasure of working with. I have every confidence...'

I know he means well, but this is just too familiar. I've been here before, let down at the last moment, turned away from the very thing I've bust my ass on. I know this script too well now: work hard at something and build all your plans, all your dreams, your entire life around it, and then *boom!* it's snatched away from under your nose.

I slump down in my chair. What now? What next? I can't keep doing this. I can't keep ploughing all my energy into evaporating dreams. I'm at a loss. I don't know what to do. I don't know what I *can* do.

'Something will come up for you, I know it will,' Jake tells me.

I make all the right sounds, I thank him over and over, and then I hang up.

I slam down the laptop lid and throw the cold dregs of my coffee down the sink. I lean on the edge of the sink and try to process what exactly this means for me now.

There is no more show. There is no more Jake and Dr Poppy. There is no more award shows or callers or listening figures or music or clues or Astral banging on the glass panel to tell us to 'Wrap up, people!' There is no more collapsing in giggles or snorting into the microphone or staying behind for hours after the show answering emails or ringing a distressed caller back to help them with whatever it is they're going through.

That's it. Terminated. Finito. Game over.

Back to square one. Back to being jobless and aimless and useless.

I rub my face with my hands. I baulk at the idea of calling Mum. This is what she warned me about. But I hand on heart never believed it would happen. I thought that because they liked me and I was doing a good job and the show was doing so well, I was safe, that I was somehow beyond axing.

I look to the calendar hanging on the kitchen cupboard door.

It is the last week of the month. I already know without needing to put myself through the torture of checking my bank statement that my latest pay cheque will barely cover my overdraft. Then there's the credit card balance that has been rolling over each month, with interest; it'll have to roll over again, with more interest. And my rent is due.

And I haven't got it. There is just no way there's anything left in the pot for rent. I haven't worked for the last week and now there's no more work, I've got no income. No funds coming in at all to stem the flow of my haemorrhaging expenses.

I slide down onto the ground. This is a mess. A real-life, what-the-hell-am-I-supposed-to-do-now mess. And I have absolutely no clue how I'm going to get myself out of it.

Well, I have a small clue.

But it's horrid. Almost unthinkably horrid. It involves raking up contacts that I thought I'd left behind.

I look to my phone. Do I have to do this? Do I have to make this call? Isn't there any other way?

I think of my mounting bills and I think of my mum and Leanne and all the sacrifices they make on a day-to-day basis. I

take a deep breath and remind myself that I need to take charge
of this. By myself.

I mean, what else can I do?

I take the last train to London. Carlos makes me promise to
keep in touch, says he has some bits and bobs that he knows
my dad wanted me to have. I take a window seat and brace
myself for the mess I'm returning to. I've deliberately not
checked my personal inbox this week in case there is a shirty
email from the letting agent or a subject line from the bank
screaming at me in capital letters. That needs to be sorted
asap or else I'll be turfed out of the flat with all my stuff and
lose my hefty deposit. If I let that happen, I'll have no choice
but to move back in with Mum, but this time it'll be even
worse than before, because on top of being homeless and un-
employed, I'll also have to bear the shame of being fired and in
overwhelming debt. She won't be able to look at me without
scowling and tutting and comparing me to her friends' kids.
No, that way madness lies. Getting kicked out of the flat is
NOT an option.

We enter a tunnel and the wind rattles the glass in the frame
beside my head. I could ask Frank for a loan, just to tide me over
until I get back on my feet. I know he'd bail me out; I can hear
him saying, *No problem at all, Poppy, we all need a helping hand
sometimes.* But then I'd have to deal with Mum. She'd go crazy if
she found out I'd tapped him for funds. And what if I didn't get
a job immediately? It was pure luck that the 105FM job turned
out like it did. Nothing worthwhile ever came through from the
job centre or from the graduate recruitment sites; nothing in my
line anyway. So then I'd be in debt to Frank as well as the landlord
and the credit card companies.

No. I can't ask Frank for money.

Back to the horrid prospect of what I'm going to have to do next. I've tried everything else. I tried making it in the real world. I tried to move beyond what I knew and rise to new heights and learn new things and meet challenges head on and all that crap that people say you need to do in order to grow.

Well it *is* crap.

It doesn't work.

I'm worse off today than I was on my graduation day, sat in the back of my mum's car, rejected, dejected, but still with a modicum of hope that I could return to Banbridge one day with my reputation intact. I haven't got that hope now. So all that hard work, all that courage and patience and soul-searching and faith in everything was just an obscene waste of time and effort. A cruel and fruitless exercise in self-battery. And now I'm out of time.

I need to face it, I've passed my peak. Far from being a late bloomer, I fear that I've already bloomed and nothing of any worth is yet to come. My student days are as good as it's ever going to get for me. This is what I feared, and it turns out my fear was real. So this is my mess and I must sort it out, however much it hurts. Overnight, I've lost my *raison d'*être – again. And now I'm going to have to crawl back to Banbridge with a Tyrannosaurus-rex-size tail between my legs. And then what about keeping my flat here in London if I'm working out of the city? I won't be able to commute as it's too expensive, so I'll have to rent somewhere in Banbridge and give up my flat in London. If I can even get out of my contract. My head starts to throb. This is going to be hard, there's no easy fix here.

Before I can change my mind, I take out my phone and punch in Harriet's mobile number, the number I know by heart.

'Hi, Harriet.'

'Poppy? Wow, is it really you? That's… great, as in weird… I mean, a surprise. In a good way, obviously. Yeah, a surprise, because I haven't heard from you… it's been ages… How are you? Is everything okay? Is something wrong?'

'Yes, you could say that. Everything's kind of gone tits-up for me on the work front and I'm not exactly being inundated with job offers, so… I'm calling because I'm stuck and I need to ask for a favour. I need some work; I can mark exam papers, answer phones, sort files… I'll take whatever you've got.'

'Are you serious?'

'Deadly serious.'

'Things must be really bad then.'

'Yes, thank you, Harriet, they are; hence this rather awkward phone call. So is there work going or not?'

'Yes, absolutely! You are a life-saver, Poppy Bloom! I am completely snowed under; Dr Winters has been asked to advise Parliament on a proposal, her book sales have gone through the roof so her tour has been extended, the paperwork is just mounting and mounting and I physically can't keep on top of it, especially to her exacting standards. And then Gregory is home for a few days and I thought I wouldn't be able to spend any proper time with him… so yes, there is shedloads of work for you if you want it.'

It's not that I want it. It's that I need it. 'I'll take it,' I tell her.

She titters into the phone. 'This is just the best news I've had in weeks. Can you start, like, tomorrow?'

'Why not?'

I thank her and hang up, feeling like I should be happy. Or at least relieved.

And maybe I am. But I'm just not feeling it yet.

I meet Harriet at our old local, the Fox and Hound. I take a deep inhalation of the sweet mahogany scent of the wooden panelling and wave to our regular barman behind the counter. He gives me a polite wave back. I'm a bit surprised, to be honest. I've known him for years. Well, I thought I knew him. But it's clear that he has no real idea who I am. Just another punter. Just another student. And then it dawns on me. I don't really know him either. I don't even know his first name. I guess that means our exchanges have mainly been me drunkenly philosophising to him and holding court. Therefore not really exchanges. I cringe. How embarrassing. How self-important. How naive to think that the barman was listening to me beyond any sense of professional duty.

I survey the old-world furnishings, the open fire. I spent at least four nights a week in here during my time at Banbridge. I passionately defended Freud and Jung in that corner. I stood on that stool and recited 'Invictus'. I coaxed Harriet out of the toilet cubicle during a deadline meltdown. I look around at the new, fresh-faced students sitting in the seats we used to sit in. Discussing the topics we used to discuss. Navigating the do's and don'ts of university life, like we used to do in my time. And that's it. It's *their* time now. My time here has passed.

We take our customary seats by the bay window, where we can overlook the master's lodge with its red and white blooms spilling over hanging baskets. Harriet orders our usual tipple, a mojito, which arrives in a gigantic Mason jar with fresh stalks of herby pond life plonked in the middle.

'Bit early, Harriet, even for you,' I say as I swish the crushed ice around with the stirrer. Remembering all the reasons that have led me back here.

'I've got to head home later on; I've got a family thing on tonight, Gregory's parents' anniversary meal, and the last train I can take is at four p.m., so… drink up, girl!' She holds her glass towards mine. 'To us,' she toasts. 'Back together again.'

We clink our glasses and I take a very cold sip. Then *bang!* Sharp rum hit.

Harriet continues her toast. 'To us sticking together the moment we entered Banbridge.' We clink and sip again. *Bang!* This rum pulls no punches. Harriet's on a roll. 'To our first day, when you walked over to me and invited me to come with you to find some decent coffee; not even realising that I was paralysed with fear and had made up my mind to drop out, scamper home and hide in my room for eternity.'

Clink. Sip. Going down as easily as Capri Sun now. If I have to be here, I may as well be drunk.

'I couldn't have done it without you, Poppy.' A final hearty clink and we drain our glasses. Harriet squeezes my hand across the table and gives me a very earnest look.

I shake my head. 'That's not true, Harriet, of course you could have done it on your own. You got the fellowship, after all...'

I really didn't want to bring up the F word, but she dropped the G bomb, so what did she expect? I've got to control myself. I'm here because I'm on the scrapheap, and I can't afford to piss her off. Even though it was hard calling her, agonisingly hard, at least she agreed to see me. At least she didn't ignore me or hang up on me or feed me some line about not being able to help me because she wanted to keep me out of the picture. She answered the phone and she has come to my aid. So however I feel, however raw and upsetting and utterly humiliating it is being back here, begging for scraps of Dr Winters' admin work, at least Harriet has given me that chance. So I nod and I drink, I try to keep perspective and fend off all unhelpful attitudes.

Harriet nearly chokes on her refilled drink. 'Cognitive and Clinical Neuroscience?' she splutters. 'Ha! Not a chance in hell! Even you have to admit, I could *never* have passed that without you.'

Yep, she has a point there. She was ridiculously shit at it. No matter which way I tried to present it to her, she just couldn't grasp it. I spent weeks in the library with her just explaining the basics, with no joy. If anything, I think she regressed, more confused by the end than she had been in the beginning. As the deadline date drew nearer, it was obvious that she'd fail, and I couldn't let that happen, so I just wrote up the damn assignment for her. It kind of became a bit of a routine after that.

'Everyone finds that hard,' I lie.

'Not you. You never find anything hard.'

I wave my hand dismissively. 'That was just one module, no big deal.'

Now she's shaking her head at me. 'What about Advanced Statistics, then? All that SPPSS stuff, or was it PSSSPS... PSPS? Oh, I don't know – I still don't get it! And Psychopharmacology? Methods in Applied Behaviour Analysis? God, that was tough.'

I laugh to myself. That module was so straightforward. Heartbreakingly simple. Pure common sense. My mother could have got the gist of it in ten minutes without any prior knowledge or training whilst drinking her tenth gin and tonic and hanging out a wash. Utterly easy.

Harriet widens her eyes. 'Oh my God, I can't believe I nearly forgot Basis for Addiction and Compulsive Behaviour! You were like the guru. You knew more about that topic than the lecturers. Dr Winters couldn't even answer your questions. Nobody in our class would have passed that module if it wasn't for you.'

I smile my appreciation, but mostly I feel sad, because my dad was my first teacher in that topic. Hand on heart, it's no fun being an expert in that one.

'And it's not just me, Poppy. Lots of us turned to you and you helped us through. Everyone's been asking about you.'

'Really?' I say, relieved but a little defensive. 'But nobody rang me. I thought they'd forgotten about me, or just didn't care.'

'Not at all, believe me. Nobody forgot about you. You were the talk of the faculty.'

'Elaborate, please. I need to know this, Harriet.'

'Well, there were lots of stories, rumours, observations going around, as I'm sure you can imagine.'

I nose-dive into my cocktail. I can imagine very well; everyone huddled together, celebratory glass in hand, each offering their own professional diagnostic of the live specimen presenting features of hysteria, narcissism, developmental irrationality or some other psychobabble crap right in front of their eyes. God, my cheeks are burning. I can feel the nerve endings in my ears. I really made an almighty tit of myself leaving without saying anything, rushing out through the fire exit never to return. *More mojito. Let's quench this shame.*

'It was quite a spectacular twist by Dr Winters,' Harriet says, chin pressed to her chest.

I flutter my hand as if to fast-forward her. 'Yeah, okay, I know that. Get on to what people were actually *saying*.'

'Well, that you were... unhinged, you'd had a breakdown, that they always suspected you could be a bit flighty, that you drank too much to be an academic, that there's often a strong correlation between genius and personality disorders...'

I point my stirrer at her face. 'For God's sake, I do not have a personality disorder. Whoever said that should be struck off.' I bet it was Gregory; he loves sweeping generalisations, especially if they sound intriguing. And it means very little to him if they hold less weight than a sheet of toilet paper. I can picture him running his mouth off at the bar, offering his insider crumbs as my ex, peddling our shared history for a tequila slammer or ten. 'Can you believe someone would say that, Harriet? That's like me going to the dentist with a cavity and him saying that there's a strong correlation between tooth decay and people who like cats... it's just false; moronic, stupid, misguided, uninformed, ignorant, just so annoyingly wrong, wrong, wrong—'

'Anyway...' Harriet cuts across me, 'some people were saying that the way you just vanished proved that Dr Winters was an actual genius, because she recognised this potential for you to crumble so easily and deemed you unsuitable because of it, and you went and proved her point right there on the stage.'

I flash her a really dirty look. I am the proof that Dr Winters is a genius. I don't even want to breathe at the moment in case I inhale particles of that disgusting, toxic thought into my lungs. I scratch the inside of my arm. Harriet drains her glass. We've finished the pitcher. She looks at me and I can see from her face that she's expecting me to run away again, do another vanishing act.

But I'm not going to.

I'm not going feed Dr Winters' fan club any further by proving her theories at my own expense.

Harriet raises her hand to the barman to order another pitcher and then looks out of the window, tapping her fingers on the table. I know that she hates awkward silences. I let her stew in it. The radio is on in the background; I can hear the traffic report and it makes me think of FM105. Harriet's head is tilted in such a way that it looks like she's listening out for something really important in the distance, her eyes angled to the top left and her mouth in a perfect 'O'. She reminds me of someone playing the part of a Second World War codebreaker in a really terrible am-dram production. An advert for windscreen repair comes on. And then some kind of shrieking sound followed by a garbled female voice.

Khloe Fox.

Khloe Fox has got her own radio show.

Harriet is still pretending to listen intently to the radio, but it's just a collection of noises, like a human farmyard. Hard to feign interest for long. Her theatrical skills well and truly stretched, she shuffles about and twirls the stirrer in her fingers.

'There was a rumour you'd skipped the country!' she blurts out, like it's good news. She glances around nervously; no sign of our pitcher yet. She puffs out her chest. 'You always loved Rio, right? And New York? Maybe they think you've skipped off to New York?'

Great. I am to bask in the comfort that my ex-friends think I've had to emigrate to escape disgrace. Harriet's aimless hand finds her neck. I watch the person I used to consider my best friend in the world struggle for something to say to break the tension. Everything is wrong. As the truth hits me, I feel a cold, sinking kind of panic, an emptying realisation. I can't believe how badly I've played this. I can't believe how much of an idiot I am. For so long I thought this was where I belonged, where I wanted to stay forever, but as I look around now, it means… well, it means *nothing* to me.

A fresh pitcher of mojito appears in the space between us. Harriet starts to pour immediately. She licks her lips and does a little shuffle in her seat.

'So, your turn now; what have *you* been up to?' she asks.

I spread my fingers out on the table and take a deep breath, speed-scanning though the time since I last saw her. What *have* I been up to? I can't tell her about the radio show because she'll just ask why I'm not doing it anymore. If it was so successful then why on earth am I sat here looking for scraps of admin? I don't want to tell her about the netball girls – she won't understand. She'll snigger and think it's some kind of sad, lonely-women's club. She won't appreciate the energy or the camaraderie or the loyalty. And I don't want her to know about Tom. She'll try and gauge him by all the external measures of eligibility. What university did he go to? Oh, he didn't go? He left school after his GCSEs? He works where? A gym? Oh, I see. She'll look down her nose at him and I know I won't be able to make her understand. I realise that actually I don't want to tell her anything. How can I when I just don't trust her any more?

'I dyed my hair,' I say; safe bet, I figure. Give nothing away.

She nods emphatically. 'Yes! I noticed. It's so different. I had to do a double-take when I saw you.'

I note that she hasn't said she likes it.

'I never saw you as a blonde.'

Still not complimenting.

'Did your mum do it?'

Ouch. I nod and take a straw to suck big, syrupy, acidic streams of rum and lime into my veins.

'Listen, Poppy, I'm going to cut to the chase. How would you feel about coming back to Banbridge. Permanently. With me.'

I know I should feel delighted. I should be over the moon. Harriet to the rescue. Reinstated in Banbridge. It's what I wanted all along, right?

Maybe. But not now. I know in my bones that this is not what I want now.

Harriet leans across the table, cupping my hands in hers. 'As my assistant, but obviously not really an assistant; only in name.'

I nod my head slowly in disbelief. I thought being Winters' assistant was bad. Harriet's assistant? Harriet's dogsbody more like. The reality is dawning on me. Oh God. Is there any way I can vacate my own body and watch this horrible, horrible scene on playback?

Remember, I tell myself, everybody has to make sacrifices. Everybody has to do stuff they don't want to do in order to get by. And now it's my turn. I need to lower my expectations. I had my dream job. I had a great time. But I couldn't sustain it. This is my reality now. This is where I belong after all. *Handle it, Poppy. Just handle it.*

'Labels don't really matter, do they?' Harriet continues. '"Assistant" is just a title to get us past the red tape and all that – we'd actually be total equals.'

'Um, and how do you propose to solve the little matter of Dr Winters and her career-killing hatred for me?' I ask.

'Well, that's the thing – she's hardly ever here! What with the promotional tour for her book and a new collaboration with Yale University, plus she's going in big for this major research bid in

Japan, so she will literally be on the other side of the world for most of the year.'

Hmmm. Interesting. Maybe this *could* work after all.

'Besides, I've already spoken to her about that,' Harriet whispers with a wink.

'No way. You need to tell me. Tell me *now*.'

She takes a large brown package out of her bag and puts it down on the table in front of me. 'Your thesis,' she says.

I can't believe my eyes. It's huge! Huger than I remember.

'Go on, open it.' She slides the envelope towards me. I stare at it for a moment, and then carefully open it and draw out the contents.

It is bound. It is *leather*-bound. It is dark green – British racing green, to be exact. Good God, it's gorgeous. It's more striking than I ever envisaged when I chose the colour at the bookbinder's. And now the real article is here, in my hands, and it is breathtaking. I pick it up. The leather cover is soft, slightly padded, very cool to the touch; a little texturing, not too much. Apparently too much is considered vulgar amongst the bookbinding fraternity; 'May as well add glitter and feathers,' the short, bespectacled master binder told me with great solemnity. I run my fingers across the cover again. So here it is. The fruits of all my study, a three-year PhD without extension or recess. Bloody relentless at times.

But worth it all now that I'm holding it in my hands.

I raise it to the sunlight flooding through the bay window so that I can view it from every angle. Did I really write all this? It's a longer, more voluminous document than I remember. I trace my fingers over the embossed gold lettering on the front: *Reclassifying the Classics: A New Approach to Standardising Psychological Classifications to Create a World-Wide Practice.*

I wanted to change the world with this thesis. I wanted to make it so that people from all over the world, regardless of money, gender, status or education, could access high-quality care.

I wanted to enable psychologists from first-world countries to educate and agree terms with doctors in less developed countries so they could share knowledge and research for the benefit of all. I wanted everybody who felt alone or unsupported to have their voice heard. All it needed was for me to find a common language. And within this racing-green leather binding lies the language to make it all possible.

'You'd be able to work on this again,' Harriet says.

I shake my head. 'No I wouldn't. Dr Winter's already slammed it.'

Harriet jumps up in her seat. 'That's not the case, Poppy! I spoke with Dr Winters. I asked her if she would consider the possibility of you coming to work for me... *with me*... seeing as she's going be away so much.'

I can't help stroking the green leather cover. It has my name on it.

In gold.

'Obviously, because we've kind of created the post for you, it won't pay much at first, but that could always change as Dr Winters' schedule gets busier. She's always saying how much she needs an administrator; her filing system is off-the-chart meticulous, OCD on steroids... Anyway, forget that, because you won't need any money; you'll be able to live with me! My parents have bought me a three-bedroom terrace, just a dinky little thing with a really cute garden out the back, five minutes from Dr Winters' office. It's nothing special, but it could be just perfect for me and you. Think of it Poppy, the two of us together, house mates again.'

This is like a miracle. I could actually believe in a benevolent intervening God based on this THING that's happening to me right here, right now. I am overwhelmed by Harriet's kindness. I am truly overwhelmed. It means I can stand on my own two feet and not be dependent on the reluctant charity of others because my life has crashed to a halt. It means I can hold my head up and hold down a respectable job and maybe, just maybe, build a future with the man I love...

Ah. Tom. What would this decision mean for me and Tom?

Well, the distance isn't ideal, but we could manage, I suppose. I could come home every weekend. But he'd be at work. And he wouldn't be able to come and visit and stay over because I'd effectively be Harriet's lodger. If we could just stick it out for a little while, maybe I could save up and get my own place again? Someday? Though on the money that Dr Winters would be paying me, that's highly unlikely. I've worked so hard to climb this ladder, only to slide back down again.

Maybe he could move to Banbridge?

I shake my head. If he passed up the chance to go to Australia so he could stick around for Leanne, he's hardly going to throw it all away to move here.

Oh Tom, what will this do to us?

I need to think about this some more. I'm feeling the weight of the decision. Who'd have thought I'd ever be reluctant to live in Banbridge because I have too much to lose at home?

'Poppy, what do you say? You've gone all quiet!'

'Wow, Harriet,' I stammer. 'I don't know what to say. I'm blown away. I just can't believe you've come to save me like this.' I take another drink to steady my whirring thoughts. 'So Dr Winters wants me here after all?' I ask.

'Well, I wouldn't exactly go as far as that. I won't lie to you, Poppy. She didn't *love* the idea straight away.' She focuses on pouring mojito right to the top of my glass before she meets my eyes. 'But after some persuasion on the phone last night, she came around. I told her how passionate you are, and how talented, and how well we work together and how important this is to you...'

'And she said yes?'

Harriet clenches her teeth. 'Yes! *Mostly* she said yes!'

I run my fingers through my hair. Oh my God, this is unreal. BLOODY HELL! What a U-turn! Perhaps Dr Winters has had some time to reflect after Burley's intervention. Maybe she's had a change of heart.

'There are some conditions, though. As you'd expect, right?' Harriet takes a sip of her drink.

'Like what?' I ask.

'Oh, just some clerical stuff to do with your thesis; she's put some notes in, edits and tweaks she'd like you to make.' Harriet curls two fingers of each hand to make quotation marks. '"Accepting these edits shows maturity, commitment and openness to change", or something like that. It's just a token of goodwill, I guess: she takes you on board, you agree to change a few things, and then everyone has reached a diplomatic compromise and you and me are back together in Banbridge just like old times!'

I'm nodding. Fine. I can do this. I can do this no problem. Change things around a bit to keep her happy. I'll show her that I am mature, committed, professional. We just got off to a poor start, and then she chose to spread malicious allegations about me that ruined my reputation, my career and my self-confidence... I rub my eyes. *Enough, Poppy. Enough.* I think of my mum, of Frank, of Tom. I think of how much this will mean to them as well as to me. It's time to put this childishness aside and step up.

My stomach lurches. This used to be my dream, and now it just fills me with dread. Over the past few months, I've come to realise that I was never meant to stay here. I'm not the same person now. I miss the world that I tried to shut out because it used to fill me with fear. I miss all the different people who came into my life. I miss playing netball till I'm a big ball of sweat. I miss listening to my mum filling me in on all the Holloway gossip. I miss the randomness and unpredictability of being fully alive and having to handle whatever comes at me. But this isn't about me and what I want. It's about making sacrifices and being responsible and mature. This is what my dad would want me to do.

'Okay, I'll do it. I'll make whatever changes she wants.' Why not? What difference does it make now?

Harriet yelps. 'Oh my God! I knew it, I knew you'd say yes! You will not regret this, Poppy. You and me are the A-Team. I could not do this fellowship without you; I *so* need you! This is going be AMAZING!'

I smooth my hand over my gorgeous, immaculate, gold-embossed, British racing green leather-bound thesis. I want to press my face against the cold, velvety paper inside, take in the scent of brand-new print, ink, glue, leather… but I know that will look weird, so I just stroke it some more. I'll do all the smelling in the privacy of my own home later on. It feels so good to hold it in my hands; my life's work, my best academic work ever is between these covers. I love you, thesis. We are together again and we could still change the world.

I wipe my hands on my thighs, blow any residual clamminess away and very carefully open the front cover and turn to the first page.

A sharp inhalation; my hand flies to my chest. I feel my stomach actually drop into my bowels.

'Wh-wh-what? What's happened? Harriet?' I can't catch my breath; it's too fast and too shallow. 'Harriet?' I find my voice. 'HARRIET?' That comes out properly loud. I am shrieking now. The bar staff have heard me. They look concerned. And so they should be. This is a fucking EMERGENCY.

There are red ink marks all over the first page. It looks like it has been stabbed. Repeatedly. Viciously. Psychotically. I turn to the next page, and the next, and then flick frantically through the rest of the book. Red, red, RED everywhere. Sometimes tiny flecks, other times huge long slashing gashes. This is a MASSACRE. I slide my hands under my poor bleeding book and slowly raise it to my chest, cradling it like a dying creature. I press my cheek against the corner of the binding.

'How could you do this?'

'It's just a few changes. You said you'd be okay with that. You said! Poppy, don't back out on me. I need you!'

This is not a few changes. These changes have MURDERED my work, mutilated it, chopped it up and scattered its vital organs all over the place. This is not my beautiful work any more. She's killed its spirit, its soul. These are just the scarred paper remains.

I gently put my thesis down on the table.

This is not a comeback. This is a back-down.

This is me ghost-writing for Harriet forever. This means me doing all the difficult academic work for her behind the scenes while she takes the credit in exchange for a leafy postcode and a respectable facade of success. This is me saying that Dr Winters is right and I am wrong. And that isn't the case. My work meant something.

It was good.

What am I saying? As long as I don't accept any of these changes, then my work remains intact, and that means it's still worth something; it means it's still good. And it *is* good. I'd actually forgotten how good. Dr Burley thought so too. And lots of others from academic circles all over the world. No, it isn't designed to keep psychological treatment as a luxury service that only the rich and educated can access, like Dr Winters wants. It's designed to help people, every sort of people. And yes, that means sharing your research for free. And yes, it means helping people who can't afford to pay you. And yes, it's an attempt to do the right thing, not the easy thing.

Actually, it is an 80,000-word description of what *The Jake and Poppy Morning Show* tried do.

I turn my thesis over so that it's face down on the table. I can't bear to see my name on the cover now that I know the horror inside. I slide it across the polished wood back to Harriet.

'I'm not staying. I can't.'

'But you can!' she protests.

'Well I don't want to.'

Her face darkens. 'Yes, well, if you're going, then just go. Go back to your tacky little radio show. You know, Gregory and I laughed, nearly choked with laughter, the first time we found your show online and listened. Dishing out advice like you knew what you were talking about! Telling some little old man who lives in a shoe how to get a love life. Ridiculous. Absolutely ridiculous. That's what you are, you know: a ridiculous pop-psychology *cartoon*. So please, just go, and don't bother calling again.'

'Goodbye, Harriet,' I say. I stand up and hold out my hand, but she just shakes her head and starts to rummage around in her bag, looking for her phone, I suspect.

'I mean, you know you're a joke, right? Be honest. Taking a job like that. Making an utter fool out of yourself. I thought to myself, please, somebody stop her! Doesn't she realise what she's doing?

And I wish she hadn't done that – asked me to be honest – because I've heard about enough. I'm not in the mood to have everything I cherish be ripped apart like it means nothing. After all, she *is* asking me. She's asking me, bold as brass: *Doesn't she realise what she's doing?*

I slam my hand down on the table. 'No, Harriet. The answer to your question is NO.'

I step towards her, my finger jabbing at every word, the force of its thrust making her step backwards towards the wall.

'No, I did not realise that I was pushing myself harder than I ever thought I could.' I take another step forward. She takes another one back. 'No, I did not realise that I was taking the time to listen to people who'd given up on being heard.' Another step; Harriet feels behind her blindly for a surface to support her. 'No, I did not realise that I was looking at myself and questioning myself and challenging everything I thought I knew by asking, is this what I want? Is this what I need? Is this going to make a positive difference to the world?'

I'm standing over her now, my face close to hers. I lower my voice to a whisper. 'And no, I did not realise that for all the language we learn and all the talking we do, what I really needed to say was sorry and goodbye and thank you and I love you to all the people who matter to me, who are *now* my world.'

I straighten up. Smooth my hair behind my ears and regain my composure. Harriet stays crouched against the wall, stiff with horror that I have dared to throw everything back in her face.

'So, Harriet, let me summarise it for you, once and for all, so there's no doubt about what I'm saying: I didn't realise what I was doing. But now I do.'

And then I turn on my heel and start to run. I run out of the pub and along the tree-lined avenue, past the redbrick dormitories and the bespectacled cyclists. I run past Ivy Court and the library and the chapel. I run past the manicured gardens and the low-trimmed hedges, and by the time I get to the station and take my seat, I barely have enough breath left to call Tom and tell him about my big, bright, bold idea. Which may be the biggest, brightest and boldest idea I've ever had.

CHAPTER THIRTY-THREE

'So like a talk show?' Tom asks me.

'Kind of…' I need to help him see. If I can't get Tom to see, then I won't be able to get any agent or producer to see either. I've burnt my bridges with the management at 105 FM, so there isn't any point writing to them. Carol King doesn't want me and she's taken Astral with her; Jake is gone. But I still have one media contact that I made along the way.

Otis.

He tells me to write a pitch for my idea and he'll see what he can do. No promises, no guarantees. But still, it's worth a try, so here I am, sitting at my kitchen counter with Tom, pen in hand, scraps of paper balled up on the ground as I try to explain my vision to him. In a way that makes as much sense to him as it does to me. But I'm not succeeding so far.

'Is it the kind of thing that's usually on the main channels at lunchtime?' he asks earnestly, holding my hands in his.

I swallow hard and start again. I need to make myself clearer. It's not enough that I know what I want; I've got to communicate it effectively. Try and help him to understand why it's so important to me.

'A bit like your radio show but on television instead?' he ventures again.

'No. More than that. Much more. What I have in mind is more than a daytime talk show, more than just entertainment. Much more than anything we've had before, anything we've even seen before. I want this show to help people; give them something to think about, something to support them in whatever they're going through. I want to talk to people who have hit rock bottom and managed to rise again. I want to hear about how people navigate their way through life; what makes them get up in the morning, what keeps them going. I want to showcase every sort of person: the ordinary, the famous, the struggling, the strong. This show will be their show, their stories and their voices. I want people to be more than simply entertained. I want them to be inspired, transformed. I want to get the top specialists on so that they can give solid support to ordinary people. I want them to tune in and laugh and cry and learn and feel like they are not alone.'

Tom slides the pen and paper in front of me. 'I think you've cracked your pitch. Go get 'em, Poppy.'

I desperately hope that one of the agencies or production companies will like the idea so that I'll at least get a response. But I prepare myself for the possibility that maybe no one will bite. There is a big chance that my time as a very public, accessible Dr Poppy is over. But this prospect, although it disappoints me, doesn't hold the power to make my world feel like it's imploding any more. Because I know I've got it in me to pull through, to get creative and work hard. I've got faith; as long as I'm doing those things, they'll lead me to exactly where I am supposed to be. Even if I can't see it at first.

Eight solid days I linger by the door each time the postman calls. Eight solid days of hearing the clatter of the letter box with no invitation to pitch landing on the doormat, no offer of a meeting. Nothing but takeaway menus and the odd bill. Mounting bills.

But today is the ninth day. And this time I am not breathing deeply and thinking about what the next unknown adventure will be and when it will decide to kick in.

No. Because today, on the ninth day, I am holding a letter in my trembling hand. I am slightly terrified of what is inside. It might be a rejection. And a rejection means that there may be more rejections; that my idea doesn't stand up. That there is no place for it in today's world. I look at the envelope. At least someone has gone to the trouble of replying to me. Even if it is a rejection, there may be some nuggets of wisdom, ideas to move forward with. But that doesn't completely assuage my fear that it might be a 'sorry but not for us' outright rejection, or a 'I don't think you should waste any more time on this' sympathetic rejection.

But I need to know either way. And indeed, not waste any more time. So frantically I tear it open and with a pounding heart slide out the letter inside, holding it up to the sunlight.

Dear Dr Bloom,
     You are invited to meet with Ms Fairchild at her London offices on Friday at midday to discuss your proposal.

It is not a rejection. IT IS NOT A REJECTION! Ms Fairchild, whoever she is, wants to meet me!

I run into the kitchen and quickly google her: *Dame Vivienne Fairchild is the award-winning chief executive of the biggest telecommunications network in Britain...*

'And I am meeting her tomorrow at midday,' I say out loud. Twice. And then again, for luck. And then one more time, just so I know I'm not dreaming.

I call Otis. 'I had no idea you were so well connected! I have a meeting with Vivienne Fairchild tomorrow,' I tell him, surprise rippling through my voice.

'Neither did I,' he admits. 'I gave your letter to her PA and next thing you've got a face-to-face appointment. That's unheard of... She's supposed to be a real dragon,' he confides. 'She rarely meets anybody these days, so this is one a hell of a chance. Best of luck, Poppy, we're all behind you.'

And I feel like they really are.

My old self would have fled to the bookshelf, taken out a pen and started writing notes. But I know that notes aren't much good to me now. I don't need them any more. I've learned to live by trusting my instincts and having faith in my own ideas.

I shut my eyes and press my hands to my chest to settle my thumping heart.

'You feeling okay?' Tom says, coming in to check on me.

I wave the letter at him. 'Yes. I am… well, I will be. Once I get my head around what's actually happening.'

'Once she hears your idea and how passionate you are, she'll jump all over it.'

'I don't know, Tom. It's going to be hard to win over someone so powerful. I mean, she might like the idea but want somebody else, or she might think, why take a chance on this?'

Tom cups my cheeks in his hands and lifts my face to meet his eyes.

'And that's where you're wrong, Poppy. This is why we do what we do. To take our chances, to take our place in the world. Why not you? Why not this? You can google a thousand famous writers who could put it way better than me, but my point is this: you don't have to wait for someone else to write that amazing show that touches on everything you care about. You don't have to wait for someone else to pitch your dream or nail your idea or capture your vision. *You* can do it, Poppy. I know you can. So don't stop now. Follow it through. Bring it to life. Get to the best bit.'

Oh God, I love this man. My stomach flips and I slap a big fat kiss on his lips.

He is right. He is right and he makes me want to follow through. Makes me want to keep going, keep trying. Get to the best bit.

So that's what I'm going to do. Whatever happens, I'm going in to Vivienne Fairchild's office tomorrow full of hope and confidence and I'm going to give it my very best shot. She won't be interested in how well I understand the ideas of experts and critics. She'll be interested in how well I understand my own ideas. And like every challenge, this is daunting in one way, but exciting in every other way.

But first things first. What am I going to *wear*?

Hours later, just as I think I've got it, that I can't go wrong with a simple black A-line dress, Mum knocks on the door and we go through everything again. And again.

'What do you think they're looking for?' she asks as we survey the landslide of office wear slung on my bed. She answers herself. 'I think they want professional but approachable, modern but timeless…'

And that makes me think.

Actually, they don't know what they're looking for. That's why they're looking in the first place. They're looking for something new, for something they can't quite define just yet. So there's no point in trying to fit the mould. The mould is redundant. Besides, I've given up trying to second-guess what other people want from me.

I go back to my wardrobe and spot a pale-blue shirt dress hanging in the corner. I've never worn it. It still has the tags on. I think it was the colour that caught my eye first, made me fall in love with it the moment I saw it draped in the shop window, despite the fact that I was feeling crap about myself; in the middle of exams, finding everything too hard and too long and too stressful. But as I stood and looked at myself in the mirror, the soft baby blue against my skin, it transported me to a time that hadn't yet happened, a time when I imagined I would be in full control of my life. A time when I would be making exciting plans and brimming with hope and optimism for the future.

I reach up for the pale blue dress and my mind is made up. I know what I'll be wearing at my meeting tomorrow. And it's exactly the impression I want to make, because it's truly the me I want to be.

I arrive at Vivienne Fairchild's offices in Marylebone. There is a village feel to this area; cosy old-world pubs snuggled up against intimate little bookshops, family-owned patisseries alongside high-end boutiques. Rich red window frames contrast with regal white stone buildings. So this is where Ms Fairchild has chosen to spend her days. I can't say I blame her; a beautiful yet understated corner of London.

I climb the steps of a tall red-brick Victorian town house and rap the huge brass knocker against the glossy black door. A soft breeze brushes my face, a delicious, caressing sensation that makes me aware of every single breath I take. And for a moment, I am struck with gratitude. I have so much; I am surrounded by love. Whatever happens, I'll keep moving forward, keep looking forward. Because I have so much to look forward to. And knowing this fills me with confidence, and dare I say it, joy.

The door is opened by a smiling secretary. I follow her upstairs to a large open-plan office with double windows overlooking the park. There is a light, floral scent in the air. It reminds me of something that I can't quite put my finger on. I stand at the threshold of Vivienne Fairchild's office.

'Shut the door behind you and have a seat,' she says as she swirls around in her chair to meet me face to face. Her long dark hair is tied back in a loose ballerina bun. Her white linen dress touches the floor, soft and flowing.

I sit down across the desk from her, smoothing my own dress over my knees. I take everything in. The room is astonishing in its bareness. It is almost like being inside a cloud. It is entirely white, every surface clear; everything seems so clean, so smooth. The only colour in the room bursts forth from a vase of lavender. It is so striking! Each little flower so dainty and elegant.

On the desk by Ms Fairchild's computer, I notice a mirrored photo frame. The black-and-white photo inside shows an elderly couple sitting proudly on a garden bench, beaming at the photographer as if caught unawares whilst laughing at the funniest joke ever told.

'So,' Ms Fairchild says as she settles behind her desk. Her focus settles on something above me, her startling grey eyes soft yet steely. 'I gather from your letter that this is the first time you have ever pitched to a television company?'

'That's right.'

'And what do you envisage as your next step?'

I sense that minimalism is her preferred medium, so I don't elaborate, I don't pad. I just tell it as it is; bare bones.

'I want to use my skills to make a difference in other people's lives.'

She gives me a slight nod and lowers her eyes to meet mine. 'Good.' This is the first time she has made direct eye contact, and it is piercing.

I sit in silence. *Good? That's all? What now?* Ms Fairchild is very hard to read. I'm trying to feel my way here as to what's going on. I look around the room, but of course there are no clues. Just wide-open spaces, vast blank canvases. And the lavender. I take a sip of water.

Ms Fairchild points to the couple in the photo frame. 'Do you know who they are?'

I shake my head. Is this a test? How would I know who they are? Maybe the owners of the TV company? The stars of a classic programme I've never watched? I'm out of my depth here for sure. But I'll stay, see what I can do. The worst that can happen is that she asks me to leave. I relax with this thought. It's not the end of the world if it doesn't work out.

She rises from her seat, walks around the desk and perches on the chair beside me, holding the picture frame lovingly in her lap. 'This was taken a few weeks ago. It is my mother. On her wedding day.' She is clearly moved by the image of her mother's laughing face. The boundless joy captured in a snapshot.

'That's so lovely,' I tell her. And it is. I remember my own mother's wedding day, when she married Frank and announced to the world that it was the happiest day of her life. And she was right. Who knew the happiness that lay ahead?

'If you wait a long time for love, it's a big deal when it happens,' Ms Fairchild continues, almost to herself.

'And so it should be,' I agree. I think of Tom. How his love has changed my life, my world.

She nods and taps her finger fondly on the faces in the frame. 'Love is worth celebrating, don't you think?'

'Yes, it certainly is,' I say, and I feel my heart twitch. It *is* worth it. It is a risk, but a worthwhile risk. And it dawns on me, for perhaps the very first time that that is what we are here to do. The realisation sends a rush of heat to my neck. How did it take me so long to understand? Gosh, for a smart girl I can be very slow…

She casts her eyes out of the window for a moment, lost in thought, and then looks back at me. 'I owe you a tremendous debt, Poppy. I'm not one for expressing emotion, but this is different.'

I sit up in my chair. Her tone has changed. It is softer, lighter than before. She's no dragon, that's for sure. I'm confused. I don't know what to make of Ms Fairchild.

'My mother married the most wonderful, kind-hearted, gentle man in the world and he has made her so, so happy.' She smiles at me and hands me the photo frame. 'His name is Benny; you may remember him.'

I study the faces in the photograph. Oh my God. Benny? Benny married Ms Fairchild's mother? I think back to his beautiful handwritten letter. Yes! He did say that his lady friend was well-to-do and from the city, a retired florist who loved… I glance over to the vase.

'She loved lavender!' I whisper, the realisation dawning on me. 'Really? Married?' I blush at the emotion in my voice. *Oh Benny, I am so, so happy for you!* My heart nearly explodes at the thought of him summoning up the courage to put pen to paper in the first place, to take that initial daunting step, and yet look! Look where his courage has led! Look at the brave new world that has opened up for him. And the ripple effect of this courage for his new wife. And for Ms Fairchild. And for me.

She breaks into a smile. 'Yes, Poppy. They are a wonderful couple. And so I've felt the benefit of your work first hand. It has transformed not only my mother's life but mine too.'

My hands fly to my face. I cannot believe it has come round like this, almost full circle. What a terrific revolution Benny and I have had! Both happy and in love and living our best lives. I swallow the tears rising in my throat.

Her eyes turn from grey to a glimmering silver 'When you love somebody, you want them to have everything they need. And now, as a result of your help, my mother has everything she needs. And that makes me so very happy.' She places her hand on mine. 'So, here is my proposal to you. Let me be the one who brings you and your show to the screens of millions of people. Every weekday, the nation will turn on their televisions and tune in to *The Dr Poppy Show*.'

Um, have I got this right? Is Ms Fairchild pitching to me?

'You have my word that it will be life-changing. And not just for you. But for as many people as we can reach.'

I hold out my hand and we shake on the spot.

'It's a deal.'

EPILOGUE

'Welcome, everyone, to *The Dr Poppy Show*!'

The live studio audience erupts.

I take a breath and raise my voice a pitch higher. Wow, they are already an excitable bunch. Wait till I tell them what we've got in store.

'Have we got a special show lined up for you today, folks. And not just because it's Friday! Not just because you are the most wonderful audience we could wish for! But we because today it is our BIRTHDAY! *The Dr Poppy Show* turns one today!'

The cheering and clapping and whooping raises the roof. Everyone is standing in their seats, streamers, balloons and confetti firing from cannons either end of the stage. It certainly is a full house today, and from my position on stage, I see all my netball girls, my mum and Frank and Tom laughing and joking around in the front row.

'So, you guys, before we start the party to celebrate our first phenomenal year, I've got some thanking to do.' I unhook my mic cable and move down into the audience. 'Firstly, huge thanks to every one of you who tunes in, writes in, calls in and shows up to our show day after day after day. We wanted this show to be *for* the people, *by* the people, and you *are* the people making it happen, so a big round of applause to you guys and please accept a glass of bubbly on us!' Trolleys laden with champagne bottles appear in the aisles, my mother beaming from ear to ear as she happily accepts a whole bottle to herself.

I wink and clap my thanks to the cameramen, the sound guys, the production team – everybody who has helped make this amazing breakthrough programme what it is. For the past year, the goose bumps have rarely had a day off. On the studio sofa I have laughed, cried and listened to the most extraordinary stories from ordinary lives. And what an education that has been. Vivienne Fairchild did exactly what she promised. She brought *The Dr Poppy Show* into the homes and hearts of millions. We are inundated with viewers, guests and calls; we have had to extend the show from one to two hours every weekday, and I've agreed to write a newspaper column to help give some insight into addiction and compulsive behaviours, which is, of course, an issue that will always be close to my heart. It has been the best year of my life. And I'm excited about all there is to come.

'And that's not all, you guys,' I call out. 'As it's our birthday, we wanted everybody to receive a little gift.'

The crowd start to ooh and aah, ripples of excitement coursing through the studio. The energy is electric.

'So if you would just have a little look under your seats, you should find a golden envelope. Open it up, because in there is our little present to you, courtesy of *The Dr Poppy Show*.'

I can't help but smile as I watch the audience excitedly feel around and find their envelopes stuffed with holiday vouchers and a host of other freebies. But it's Tom I keep my eyes on. I watch him as he slides his hand underneath his chair, draws out his golden envelope, tears it open and squints to read the two words I've written inside.

Marry me.

I see him bite his bottom lip. His hand travels to his eye as he blinks back a tear. And then he looks up at me and nods.

And somehow, despite the clamouring noise and high-spirited cacophony of this studio audience, I can hear him. I hear him loud and clear.

And my heart soars.

For all that we are. And all we are to become. And even all that's unknown in between. There is just no stopping us now.

LETTER FROM COLLEEN

Dear Reader,

We got there! Thank you so much for spending some time with Poppy and me. It's been a blast!

I would like to express my heartfelt gratitude to the many people who saw me through this *book*; to all those who provided support, talked things over, read, wrote, and offered amazing ideas and suggestions to truly make this story shine. Claire Bord, Kirsty Greenwood, Emily Ruston and Abigail Fenton have been my four guiding angels. A tsunami of gratitude to you all. What a privilege to work with such a talented and determined team of truly gifted women. The awe-inspiring team at Bookouture has truly changed my life. I can't thank them enough for their faith in me and all the kindness and support I've received along the way. I'm a very lucky girl.

Thank you also to my husband, who has been amazingly supportive. Thanks for listening to me and edging me forward. Thank you to my parents, Elizabeth and Lorcan, and my sister Shannon, who have never wavered in their belief in me and who encourage me all the time. And finally, thank you to my wonderful friends (you know who you are!), whom I love from the bottom of my heart, especially those on the other side of the sky, who we miss so deeply every day.

Just as Poppy found, life can throw curveballs. Mental health issues can touch anybody's life at any time. I'm absolutely sure that you know somebody who has needed support at some stage. Maybe you were the friend or the sibling or the partner who was there for them, and I bet that made all the difference.

Thank you for that.

A percentage of the sales from *Don't Stop Me Now* will be donated to supporting mental health charities for our young people. So by simply buying this book, you have helped again.

Thank you once more.

If you've come this far, then maybe you'd like to go a little bit further and post a review; a good one, please! As a reader, one of the things I like most is discovering new books and new writers, and the way I do that is through word of mouth. Someone tells me they love a book, I just have to go and check it out. So a Facebook share or a tweet or a recommendation or a book-club suggestion over a coffee or a glass of wine would be SO appreciated.

Please feel free to drop me a line. I'd love to hear from you whether you are a reader or an aspiring writer. The easiest way is through my Facebook page. That's where you'll also find information about my new books. There's always something in the pipeline. Whatever it is, hopefully it'll be tempting enough for you to pick up a copy, snuggle up on the couch and lose yourself for a few hours.

You can also sign up to my email list at the link below; that way, I can let you know when my next book will be released. And don't worry, your email address will never be shared, and you can unsubscribe at any time.

I really hope we hook up again.

Until next time,

Colleen x

www.bookouture.com/colleen-coleman/

 CollColemanAuth/

 CollColemanAuth

Made in United States
North Haven, CT
08 October 2021